sand roots

sand roots

by BEN DIXON MACNEILL

John F. Blair, *Publisher*
Winston-Salem
1963

Library of Congress catalog card number: 63-20784═════

sand roots

1

"CHIEF, SIR," THE YOUNG, DIFFIDENT SEAMAN SAID FROM THE doorway, "Ozycwicz says would you come to the radio room for a minute. Says there's somethin' screwy comin' in — somebody on a plane somewhere wants to talk to you. Says he won't talk to anybody else."

"So that makes it screwy, does it?" the massive man at the desk said without glancing up from the sheaf of papers, and the young seaman was sure that the panes in the window beyond the desk rattled under the impact of the massive voice.

"Yes, Sir — I mean, no, Sir," the young seaman stammered. His face became the color of his ruddy hair.

"And don't start Sirin' me. Didn't they teach you any better'n that where you went to get you some of that polish they call boot trainin'? What did you call that radio feller?"

"The operator, Sir — excuse me. His name's Ozycwicz. He just reported in last night. Come on the bus."

"Bring any first name with him?"

"Yes, Sir — excuse me — it's Frank, I think. And I think he wanted you to come right away."

When the massive man at the desk gave no sign of having heard him, or of any intent to heed the message he had brought, the young seaman hesitated a moment and then backed away from the door and went down the corridor toward the radio room. Chief Warrant Officer William Henry Ragland shifted his massive bulk and got lightly to his feet, towered above the flat top of the desk on which the Station's

3

morning reports were spread loosely. . . . Trouble about a war was that so much of its trifling detail had to be put down on paper. . . .

The Chief's disapproving eye searched the roster of names on one of the sheets of paper before him, and his forehead wrinkled. His huge fingers made a disorder in his thinning hair, and then a blunt forefinger moved down the roster of names, paused at the name of the new radio operator. His lips silently formed each letter as he spelled out the unaccustomed name. His voice reverberated throughout the Station.

"Scarborough!"

The young seaman reappeared at the door. Traces of a smile glimmered about the corners of his good-naturedly wide mouth. The Chief ignored him while he tugged open a drawer in the desk, fumbled for a cigarette, and then searched for a match. The seaman snapped a lighter into life and moved a step toward the towering figure, holding the lighter upward. The massive man waved it away.

"Don't like them damned things," he said.

Then his face relaxed. He had found a match, a long-stemmed sulphur match. He turned toward the young seaman, cigarette between the fingers of one hand and match poised in the other. Scarborough had resumed his place in the door-way and he waited, expectantly.

"Say this feller here is named Frank — that what this here initial stands for?"

"Yes, Sir — excuse me — I guess that's what it's for."

"Well, then, we're goin' to call him Frank. Damned if I can spend all my time untanglin' the knots I get in my tongue when I say a name like that. Where'd he come from?"

"I don't know, Chief, but there's lots of curious-soundin' names in the Service now."

Now the Chief leaned lightly against the desk, lifted his bare left foot until the heel rested just above the right knee. His right shoulder drooped a little and, reaching down, he brushed the match head lightly across the sole of his uplifted foot. The match flamed and the Chief lighted his cigarette. His eyes had not left the young seaman's face. The youth's lips were parted in a half-incredulous smile. He said "Gee" under his breath, and the sole of his own foot twinged when he remembered his own tentative experiments in the field of the Ragland legend.

Beyond the half-closed door at the end of the hall the voice of the radio operator mounted complainingly. "Hey, fellow, is the Skipper coming? This fellow sounds like brass and he's in a hurry."

Ragland's bulk filled the doorway within an inch of its height, but there was room to spare in its width. He was well above six feet; his chest swelled mightily, Ozycwicz saw, when he turned from the instrument panel to glance over his shoulder. Everything about him was massive: his head, his hands, his improbable bare feet, but they were so proportioned that not even his ears seemed over large.

A look of startled disbelief suffused the radio operator's face when he turned and saw the massive man standing there, his elbows spread, his flattened palms resting on his hips, looking down at him. The massive, placid face, the giant's bulk that filled the doorway — yes; but the feet, brown and naked and planted wide apart, the towering legs, bare halfway to the knee where casually rolled dungarees covered them — no! Three years in the Service had brought Ozycwicz face to face with many strange sights, but that such an uncouth apparition should command an important station ... the radio operator withdrew his gaze and his face reddened.

"Sir," he began in a muffled voice, "there's somebody on here that wants to speak to you directly. I think it's from a Twenty-nine somewhere west of here. Signals were thin at first, but they're clearer now. I think they're headed in this direction — if that's what it is."

The operator slid out of the chair, and the big man moved

lightly across the room and into the seat vacated by the slender young Pole. He picked up the earphones and put them on, then removed them to widen the spread. The operator hovered at his shoulder, reaching out toward the dials that studded the panel.

"He had our wave length," the operator said, "and I guess he's still on, Sir."

"That's all right, Frank," the Chief said mildly. He leaned forward, his elbows spread wide apart on the table. The operator and the young seaman stood back and Ozycwicz's glance sought Scarborough's eyes with anxious questioning. The young seaman nodded reassuringly.

"This is Ragland," the Chief said into the transmitter. He leaned back, glanced around at the operator and the young seaman. He thrust a forefinger under the rim of the receiver clamped against his left ear, lifting it a little away from his head.

Thoughtful of him, the operator observed silently; now we can hear both sides of it — if there is anything to hear.

"Hi, Chief! This is Danny." The voice came with surprising clearness.

"Danny? Danny-the-hell who?"

The operator cringed inwardly. Somebody somewhere would . . . . Ragland's broad face wrinkled in a wide grin when the voice came into the receiver again.

"Danny Gray, Chief. Has my voice changed or something since I left . . . down there?"

"Oh," the Chief's voice bellowed, and the operator hoped that the sheer volume of the next dozen or more words would make them indistinguishable in the wide wastes of the sky, which, by now, must have taken on a hue of deep purple. The big voice resumed with more prudently chosen words. "Sure — recognize you now. Where the hell are you?"

"Right now I'm about ninety miles west of you — I think the town off to the right is Kinston — and with this tail wind we're doing about five miles a minute."

"You still flyin' that damned thing, Danny — ain't you ever goin' to learn — "

"Aw, Chief — say, have you got a jeep or something handy there?"

"Sure I got a jeep handy — want me to come and get you?"

"No, Chief, but here's what I wish you would do for me: put somebody in that jeep right now and send him up home and bring Mama down to the Station. Bring Jerry, too, if they can round him up. Bring 'em down to the Station. I'm going to throttle back the engines and idle along at about one-eighty. Be there in half an hour. Tell Mama I just want to say hello to her and just look at her."

"Just a minute, Danny — you hold on and I'll talk to you some more."

Ragland turned to Scarborough, who was already poised just outside the door, and said, "Git!" The young seaman disappeared, and in a moment the jeep's tires ripped the loose shale of the driveway outside the window. The Chief returned to the microphone.

"Danny, that Scarborough boy's already gone after your mammy. Now see if you can talk some sort of sense. Where you been and where you headed for? You flyin' that damned thing all by yourself?"

"Heck, no, Chief; there's twelve of us aboard. We got into Los Angeles late yesterday afternoon and left there at one o'clock this morning. Have to be in Washington this afternoon at one o'clock, but we picked up such a good wind we have to loaf around awhile and kill time."

"What's your weather look like where you are now?"

"We're flying at fifteen thousand — visibility unlimited and a ten-mile northwest wind. It's shifted a little and dropped off. How is it with you?"

"Clear — wind southwest ten miles. . . . What's goin' on in Washington that you've got to get there in such a hell of a hurry? They ain't heard there was a war up there, have they?"

"Just orders," Daniel Gray said casually. "Some of the boys aboard here were running short of medals — or so they say."

"Wouldn't be meanin' yourself, would you, Danny?"

"You've been reading story books, Chief . . . say, let me have that operator of yours a minute before the jeep gets back, will you, Chief? Get him to report me."

Ragland removed the headset and passed it without a word to the operator, who identified himself and his station with rule-book smartness. And then . . . .

"This is Captain Daniel Gray. I'll be in your vicinity in a little while and after I'm on the course north will you report my position to Washington and say the time indicated in orders will be the time of arrival there? Make the usual report. Thanks, and let me have the Chief, will you?"

Ragland took the headset, adjusted it with a lifting forefinger.

"Danny, the tower reports a cloud of dust comin' and I'm of the belief that your mammy is right in the middle of it. But," he added, "she's safe enough. You know that Scarborough boy — no bigger'n a flea when you left here. He's drivin' your mammy. I've got him in the Station here now, and even if he did have to go off to what they call a boot-trainin' place where they learned him a lot of foolishness . . . well, I aim to make a surfman out of him if I have to tie knots in his neck — jeep's just turnin' in here now and your mammy's in it and — say, when have you seen that varmint — that Jerry? If nothin' don't happen to him, he's goin' to be the spit 'n' image of your daddy."

Brakes squealed beneath the windows, and the tires complained against the shale.

"Hear them brakes, Danny? Your mammy will be here in a minute. You can't land that damned contraption here, can you? Well, when are you comin' home, Danny? It's time you come on home here and joined the Coast Guard like — well, like all your people before you. You are Dan Gray's boy and don't you ever forget it — you hear me, Danny?"

William Henry Ragland's voice mounted into a roar that drowned the muted droning of four deep-throated engines that, by now, could be heard far out beyond the Lighthouse, beyond the Woods that covered the westward dunes. Outside the windows Jerry Gray, awkward, big with receding adolescence, stood with tilted head, his eyes and his ears strained toward the muffled beat of the engines. Polly Gray stood, quiet, placidly eager, in the doorway of the radio room.

2

EXULTATION BOOMED IN THE MAN'S BIG VOICE WHEN HE TURNED to the placid woman in the doorway. "He's home, Polly!" he exclaimed. "Your boy — Dan's boy — well, anyhow he's pokin' around in that little cloud yonder and you can hear him plain as day. He wants to talk to you, and you tell him it's time he got out of that contraption and got his feet back on the ground here where they belong. Never had any business in the Army nohow. You come here and sit down."

"Yes, Bill Henry," Polly Gray said. Her voice was uncertain, a little breathless, and her hands trembled when she reached for the headset Ragland held toward her.

"Just put these things over your head, Polly," he said mildly, "and you talk into this damned thing here. Just like you talk over a telephone — or did you ever talk on one of the things, Polly?"

"No, Bill Henry, I never did," Polly Gray said. "Never had any call to — not before. Don't let me sound foolish — I don't want Danny to be ashamed of me. Somebody might be hearing."

"Don't be a damned fool, Polly! You ain't raised any young'un that would be ashamed of you. Just talk like he is right here. Hold your thumb on this button when you're talkin' and take it off when you're listenin'. That's all there is to it."

Ragland took the microphone in his two big hands and said,

"Here's your mammy, Danny. Go ahead and talk to her." He passed the instrument to Polly Gray and stood back. The youthful voice came, clear, eager.

"Hi, Mama," Danny Gray said, "how are you?"

"Son —" Polly Gray's voice faltered into a lengthening silence.

"Sort of takes your breath away, doesn't it, Mama? Well, I had an hour on my hands, and I thought I'd just come by and look the old place over. First time I've ever really seen it from the air. I can see our house from here, and it looks like the first thing I'd better do when I get on the ground is to see if I can get a can of paint somewhere. How is everybody?"

"It does need paint, Danny — " Polly Gray began. Ragland interrupted with "Put your thumb on that button when you start to say somethin', Polly. Now — say it again."

"It does need paint, Danny," Polly Gray said again, "but there just hasn't been any paint and nobody to use it if there had been. You and Jerry can paint it."

"How is my little brother?"

"He isn't your little brother any more, Danny. If you are close enough to the Station, look out in front. That's Jerry, waving his arms at you, and he's as big as you are now. He . . . looks just like your father."

"Gee, I'm glad of that, Mama. I'm still sort of runty — guess I got stunted."

"When can you come home, Danny? It's been three years."

"I've — we've got this business in Washington today, and I don't know what's next until that's over with, but I've got a lot of leave coming to me and I'm going to ask for it as soon as I get straightened out. I've got to be on my way now, Mama — do you guess you could get Jerry in the house long enough just to say hello?"

"Fetch him," Ragland said briefly, and Scarborough slid from the room.

"Jerry will be here in a minute, Danny," Polly Gray said. Her voice was steady now, and confident. "Have you been well, Danny?"

"Never better in my life, Mama — maybe a little off my weight but some of your cooking would fix that in a week."

"It's been so long since we've heard from you, Danny."

"Well, maybe there were not too many of my letters, but I've been moving around a lot since I got back in the air in July."

"Everybody asks about you — Sally had just stopped by the house when Bill Henry sent for us."

"Oh," Danny Gray said, and afterward, when she tried to recapture these moments, wishing that she had thought to ask this or that question, Polly Gray was puzzled about the single monosyllable. It sounded so casual, so withdrawn. After a little silence he said for her to tell Sally hello for him. Then Jerry's eager voice was at her shoulder.

"Can I talk to him, Mom — when you're through? What did he say? When's he comin' home?"

"Good-bye for now, Danny," Polly Gray said. "Come on home as soon as you can — and here's Jerry."

Jerry's voice vacillated between the light tenor of adolescence and the thick baritone of maturity, and his big square hands were clumsy with the headphones. Ozycwicz, again in possession of something of his professional assurance, reached out and set them in place. He indicated with a gesture that the boy would do better if he sat down.

"Talk, boy," Ragland interposed tersely. "He ain't got all day to fool around here. He's got to go to Washington and it's a hell of a ways."

Jerry wrapped his bare legs around the legs of the chair.

"Gee, Danny," he said.

"Hi, Jerry," Danny replied. "How are you? Mama says you weigh a ton — and your voice sounds like a —"

"Heck, I don't weigh a whole ton, Danny," Jerry said, "but that pair of shoes you left home have done got too little for me. Say, Danny, is that a sure-enough Twenty-nine you're in? There's never been one of 'em down here before. All we ever see is PB's and stuff like that. Why can't you bring her down here close so's we can see her? Maybe we could see you, too, if you was to come close enough."

"Okay, Jerry, I'll come over in a minute. But what's the news down there? Mama forgot to tell me much. Got yourself a girl yet?"

"Heck, naw," Jerry said, "but I can handle a stern oar pretty good." The boy glanced uneasily at the Chief and then grinned. "Or anyhow Bill Henry don't cuss me about it as much as he used to. Maybe he's wore himself out. Say, Danny, have you got a name on your ship? What did you call her?"

"Sure, Jerry, she's got a name. I'll bring her down where you can read it."

"You didn't name her 'Sally' or anything like that, did you Danny?" The boy's voice darkened.

"No, Jerry." Danny's voice was drawling. "We didn't name her anything like that. But I'll tell you what: we are just west of King's Point now and flying at five thousand feet. You and Mama and the Chief get outdoors and I'll bring her around from the north, down past the Lighthouse and into the wind. I'll be about a hundred feet up when we come over and I'll throttle back. I'm in the pilot's seat on the left and I'll have the window open. Tell Mama and the Chief good-bye and you keep your nose clean until I get home. So long, now."

Into the earphones came a brief, conclusive click, and Jerry sat for a moment in a sort of haze. Then action galvanized him. He turned the chair over when he stood up and started toward the door. "Come on, Mom — you and Bill Henry. He's comin' over down low so we can see what he's named his ship and we can see him, too. Gosh! I wonder if it's the same one we read about in the paper. I wonder if it still shows where that —"

Jerry Gray was out of hearing, racing for the open courtyard before the Station. Ragland and Polly Gray followed, the Chief moving lightly on his bare feet. He shortened his normal stride to measure that of the woman beside him. Scarborough scuttled past them in the wake of the fleeting Jerry, and the radio operator, looking uncertainly at his instruments for a hesitant moment, followed.

Most of the Station's crew were already gathered in the courtyard, their eyes intent upon the westward sky. October lay bland and somnolent upon the earth, and the sea was placid, dappled with sunlight. Even along the Outer Diamonds only an occasional white-crested wave broke upon some hidden thing that rested in this place that three centuries of seafaring men had called the Graveyard. Today an unwonted quiet pervaded the sky and the sea and the earth, and the water was aquamarine.

For a quick moment sunlight caught the bright wing of the Twenty-nine as it moved downward in a narrowing arc beyond the Lighthouse, and its engines purred across the morning's stillness. Only Jerry broke the silence in the group with a wondering, awed "Gee!" Polly Gray's eyes followed the big plane as it circled, nose down. Its engines were throttled back until their throbbing was remote, muffled.

At the north limit of the wide arc in which it had been swinging, the big ship suddenly straightened out, and the roar of its engines came presently, full-throated. Jerry Gray shifted on his big feet, uneasily anxious, and glanced at the faces of the group around him. Polly Gray watched, her face serene, and Ragland, his massive features immobile, became grim when he sensed, with his seaman's instinct, what impulse had sent the big craft suddenly seaward.

Two miles north and eastward from the Lighthouse the big

ship's right wing dipped sharply in a turn, and the plane ne-
gotiated a complete circle before it leveled off with its nose
headed directly toward the Lighthouse and the Station. Polly
Gray's eyes met the Chief's in a brief, comprehending glance,
and her lips trembled.

"He has not forgotten, Bill Henry," she said softly.

"No," the big man said shortly and then, his voice softening, he added, "How could he? How could anybody who had
any blood in him — your blood and Dan Gray's blood — forget? And he's a damned good navigator — couldn't have gone
straighter to the place myself."

"Maybe he could see . . . from up there. They say you can
see deep down if you are high up above the water."

Again silence enveloped the group, and none save the radio
operator moved. Ozycwicz, with his lips close to Scarborough's
ear, whispered, "What's going on? What happened out there
to make Captain Gray circle the place like that?"

The young seaman regarded the operator in silence for a
moment and then he said, almost inaudibly, with an uneasy
glance toward Polly Gray, "That's where they got Danny's
father — the Germans. He was out there in the lifeboat with
some survivors he'd picked up. There were nine slugs in him
when they picked him up."

Oczywicz's eyes widened but he remained silent. By now
the big ship was coming upwind, passing just above the Lighthouse, its nose still slanted slightly down. It was incredibly
big. Off to the north a squadron of Navy Corsairs, their wings
black against the sky, moved in tight echelon, very like a flock
of inquisitve crows as they bore down upon a great eagle.

All color drained out of Polly Gray's face as she watched,
with immobile tensity, the great ship come nearer. Jerry's eyes
were eagerly alight, his face strained forward. His big fists were
clenched against the seams of his faded dungarees, and his
bare toes dug into the sparse grass that covered the courtyard.

Ragland stood, relaxed, his feet wide apart, but his eyes were narrowed in the intensity of his scrutiny of the big ship.

Polly Gray's eyes were riveted upon the open window at the left of the pilot's compartment. Now she could see him, the outline of his blond head, blurred by the hurtling speed of the ship and by a mist that gathered in her eyes. His face was turned slightly, and she was sure that she could see the blue of his eyes and the smile that curled his lips upward at the corners of his mouth. His hand came up in a quick gesture.

Jerry Gray's gaze was fixed a little forward the open window of the pilot's compartment, along the broad nose of the ship. His lips were parted as he spelled out the tall letters lined in black against the shining surface of the ship. His eyes widened and he felt something lay its weight upon his throat. He knew, without reading any more, what Danny had named this great ship which, so the papers had said . . . . Jerry Gray let out what he might have intended for a triumphant, mildly blasphemous whoop, but something was in his throat. . . .

Athwart the Station, with the left wing tip almost scraping the roof, the plane swept into a stupendous roar. For a little while the ship continued in level flight and then her nose came up sharply. The sunlight caught her wings squarely, and the ship shimmered with a blinding, borrowed incandescence. A mile away and a thousand feet up a wing tip dropped and the ship pivoted, turned, climbing. . . . The Corsairs, still very like a flock of crows, came down in the wake of the eagle, but none in the group before the Station, except the radio operator, was quite conscious of them. The Twenty-nine dwindled into the north, and in a moment distance engorged the beat of its engines.

It was Jerry who broke the spell of silence that held the group until the last pulse of the engines was muffled in the distance. Words tumbled out of him: soprano, tenor, baritone, and some that were compounded of them all. Big William

Henry Ragland smiled with grim indulgence. He took the nape of the boy's neck in a great hand and shook him, not ungently.

"Try it now, boy. What is it you are tryin' to get said?"

"Mom! Mom! Did you see what he named it? Did you?"

"Jerry, I — I —" Polly Gray hesitated, was silent in her confusion. "I was so busy trying to get to see Danny that —"

"Gee, Mom," the boy's voice swelled in a sort of incredulous wonder, "he named it for me and you — for me and you both. It was there as plain as anything — 'Polly and Jerry.' It couldn't be anybody but us. We've been off to war, sort of."

"Yes, son, I guess we have," Polly Gray said, "and now . . . now we're . . . ." Her voice faltered, broke. Her gray, wide-set eyes clouded, and her lips trembled. Her hands groped for her apron, gathered it in a convulsive knot. She lifted it to cover her face.

Jerry Gray looked uncomprehendingly at his mother. Ragland raked the group with a grim eye, and his colossal voice erupted in a monosyllable. "Git!" he roared, and there was no need for him to repeat it.

The group, without a backward glance, dissolved. The Chief laid a detaining hand on Jerry's shoulder and drew him away. Polly Gray's face was lost in the folds of her apron, and her shoulders moved convulsively. The boy held back, puzzled, troubled. His eyes sought the eyes of the towering Ragland.

"Gee, Bill Henry," the boy muttered, "did I say somethin' wrong? I never in all my life saw her cry."

"No, boy, you didn't do it. But whatever done it, I'm glad it's done. It's overdue. It's long overdue. You were a little runty feller then — three years ago. I saw your mammy when she stood on the beach yonder when what there was left of your daddy washed up. She didn't cry."

A strange and unaccustomed huskiness came into the big man's throat. He searched his hip pocket for a handkerchief and blew his nose explosively. He fumbled for a cigarette, and from another pocket he brought out a long-stemmed match. His left foot came up. . . . Jerry watched the performance with the same aspiring wonder that he had known the first time he could remember seeing Bill Henry light a match on the bottom of his foot. The big man inhaled deeply.

"No more did she cry the night when this beach was littered with dead men, half of them burned beyond where anybody could tell which was who. Your Uncle Tommy — guess you don't even remember him, he bein' a seafarin' man and never home since he was no bigger'n you. She raised him — almost.

"Women are strange critters, Jerry, and I ought to know — I been married to three of 'em — two good — and I'm still ignorant about 'em, and the better women are the less I can make 'em out. Your mammy yonder I just don't understand.

"There's some of 'em that cry to get things they want. I married one like that. But your mammy, she's not that kind. She's the other sort — and I had one like that, too — the first one. Cryin' does 'em good — if you can ever get 'em to do it. You are sort of young to know about these things, but if your daddy was here he'd let her cry awhile and then he'd ease up to her and put his arm around her shoulder and pat her. He was not a wordy man, so you don't have to say anything. She'll know."

Bill Henry dropped his cigarette in the thin grass and ground it out with his heel. When he spoke again his voice dropped. "You reckon you could manage to drive that jeep from here to your house? I'll send Scarborough over there after it." The boy's eyes lighted.

"Well," the big man continued, "it ain't exactly regulations, but hell, you go over there to your mammy, and as soon as I get in the house out of the way, you do what I told you your daddy would do. And then when she's sort of ready to go home, you put her in that jeep and take her, and if you scare her one little mite tryin' to show off, I'll take you apart joint by joint until there ain't one damned thing left of you but your ears, and I'll take them for a paddle and whale hell out of you!"

The Chief's voice rose with a spurious vehemence and then he added, "Git! And tell your mammy I'm damned tired of these Station rations. I'm comin' over there tonight and eat."

The big man strode off toward the Station entrance, and Jerry went, at first uncertainly and then with awkward manfulness, toward his mother.

3

WHEN THE BIG BOMBER LEVELED OFF A THOUSAND FEET ABOVE
the Point of the Cape and pointed its blunt nose northward,
Captain Gray turned to his copilot: "Take her, Scotty. Hold
her steady as she goes for twelve minutes and then pull up.
Two-seventy ought to hit Washington on the nose, but check
it. Keep the shore line on the left — I'd sort of like to just
look at some of this country."

The copilot took over. Steady as she goes . . . these nautical
terms of the Skipper's were mystifying, sometimes. He talked
like a sailor, especially on those infrequent occasions when his
mild blue eyes turned steely and his mouth lost its boyish
softness. Very privately, at such times, the crew called him
Long John, among themselves. It was the youthful waist gunner who had started it — probably read it in a book somewhere.
He was always reading. . . .

During the hour that began when the Skipper called the
operator up front and asked him if he could get the Coast
Guard Station on the radio, the crew had watched in speculative silence not unmixed with wonder. None except the operator knew what passed between the Skipper and the ground station beyond what they could guess when the operator said
briefly that the Captain was going to try to talk to his folks.

"I guess he knows what he's doing, but we're 'way off
course," the navigator commented resignedly to the crew
chief.

Most of the crew found places of vantage somewhere. "This

I got to see," the young waist gunner said. He peered out over the wide reach of the aquamarine sea. "First time I've ever seen this ocean. Got to see how it compares with the one we took away from Hirohito. I don't want to taste this one — just look at it. One taste of ocean is plenty for me. Remember the time, Pop?"

"You still talk too much," the crew chief said. "If the Captain wants to look at where he came from, we've got plenty of gas and plenty of time and if you was to fall out of here I guess we could manage somehow. There ain't any Japs on this side of this planet for you to bang-bang at."

"Okay, Pop, okay," the corporal said. "Not nary another word out of me until Mr. Truman asks me how I managed to win the war all by myself. Say, Pop, you reckon we'll see him, sure enough?"

"Don't know one damned thing about it except what's in the orders and they say to be there," the crew chief said. "Now will you shut up and look at the pretty scenery and it'll be okay by me if you jump right into the middle of the first nice fat woolly cloud we pass. There's always a cloud handy off there."

"You been here before, Pop?"

"Sure I been here. . . ." The crew chief's face clouded. He was suddenly silent, staring out past the slender shoulders of the young corporal. Far off, the blunt, predatory finger of Cape Hatteras thrust out into green, light-dappled water.

"You've been everywhere, ain't you, Pop?" the gunner observed. "But when was it you were here? I didn't know they'd even heard about the war 'way off here."

"It started here — almost," the crew chief said harshly. "They always start here. Back in eighteen it started here, and two days after Pearl the Germans showed up here again."

"And you were right here to meet 'em, eh, Pop?" the boy jeered.

"I was," the crew chief said soberly. "We had a few A-

Twenties back up the country here and — hell, ain't you ever read any history, you ignorant mongrel? I got to make the Skipper some coffee."

The young corporal got down from his perch and followed the crew chief to the little galley.

"How long you been with the Skipper, Pop? You come to the Pacific with him, didn't you?"

"Yeah," the crew chief said shortly. "I been with him ever since the Mediterranean. Saw him over there, and when they shifted him back to the States to check out on the heavies, he asked for me to come with him. Now get back where you belong and quit botherin' me."

After the copilot took over, Danny Gray relaxed against the cushions of his seat and closed his eyes. He was unaccountably tired. He knew that he ought to be awake, alert, savoring every last second of this moment that had crowded the dreaming of long months on the other side of the world, the moment that he would see home again. But right now he was too tired to look.

He could see it all, anyway, without looking, so long had he been seeing it in the warrior's dream of homecoming. It had been, of course, a boyish thing to want to do. He had wanted to come home in the "Polly & Jerry." He had wanted . . . oh, hell! maybe it was kid stuff, but it had happened just like he had wanted it to happen. Down there, he knew, there were some, maybe a good many, who thought — though not many would say it, ever — that he had run away from the war when it was blazing with grim fury right there in sight of home. . . .

Well, maybe he had run away. . . . "It just don't make no damned sense," Big Bill Henry had stormed. "You belong here — you belong to the Coast Guard. Your daddy belonged to it, and they've got him. Your granddaddy and your great-granddaddy, five generations of you. You don't have to go and hunt the war. Haven't they killed your daddy right here in sight of the house you were born in?"

This and much more he had heard from his father's friend. Polly Gray had said nothing. Those early weeks had been, for her, weeks of numbed, waiting silence. It was on the night of his eighteenth birthday that he had told her that he wanted to go away and join the Army. He wanted to fly. Offshore there had been another fearful explosion when dusk slanted across the tumbling water. After supper they had walked to the top of the dune to watch.

By night the water was livid with the light of the burning tanker. Far down the beach the mighty voice of Big Bill Henry roared above the thunder of the surf as he went about launching his boat through the surf; and, nearer by, the figures of men patrolling the beach were limned against the glare of the burning tanker.

"It looks like they're too much for us, son," his mother had said. "There will have to be some other way to stop them."

"There's nothing now but these Army bombers, Mama," he had replied soberly. He remembered it now, as clearly as when he had watched it happen, in midafternoon and in broad sunlight. The silhouette of the submarine was clear against the horizon, and the flash of its guns, trained on a fleeing freighter, was almost blinding. Offshore there were five separate columns of black, oily smoke, leaning lazily with the wind. . . .

Another roar, of another texture, cut across the staccato bursts at the muzzles of the submarine's guns, the roar of an aircraft's engines, coming out of the sun. There were seven of them, long-nosed, gaunt against the sky; and they screamed, defiant, vengeful, challenging. White splashes dotted the water around the submarine, and in a moment the raider seemed to leap out of the water and fall apart. Then came the dull roar of the raider in death that seemed to shake the Lighthouse itself. . . .

That was one less submarine, anyhow. His father had gone out in a fragile, unarmed wooden craft. That was when the crippled Hall boat had been forced to land at sea when a shell from a raider went through her wing. From the lookout at the Station they could see her, rising on the crest of a breaker and wallowing off into the trough. Somebody had to go, and in that sea — it was an oarsman's task. Three of the crew had been picked up and then . . . the submarine's searchlight had sought them out in the dark . . . and the tide had brought his father home. . . .

On the day after he was eighteen Danny Gray went northward along the Outer Banks and joined the Army for flight training.

Without opening his eyes to see, Danny Gray knew that if he reached out with his right hand, not more than six inches, his fingers would encounter the warm handle of a cup. There would be hot coffee in the cup, and along its far side and under its bottom would be the strong, thick fingers of his crew chief. It had been so . . . since Italy. When they were out of it he would lean back, like this, and shut his eyes; when he opened them there would be Master Sergeant Dragonnetti — with coffee.

In this company Dragonnetti — The Dragon — was an old man. He was thirty-two. He was lank and sinewy and hard and ugly and gentle. His voice was a very terrible voice . . . surely the equal, even, of the voice of William Henry Ragland, who could outroar any hurricane that ever ventured around the Cape. It was a part of the ship's legend that the Dragon maintained its engines largely by vocal intimidation. It was also a part of the legend that he could take a 4,000-horsepower engine apart with a bobby pin and that his thumb and forefinger were the equal of any wrench. He had been in the Army since he was seventeen.

Danny Gray adhered to formula: he reached out with his right hand without opening his eyes. The cup was there; Sergeant Dragonnetti was there. It was also a part of protocol that the cup be taken without spoken thanks. Gratitude in any of its manifestations was, where the Sergeant was concerned, highly objectionable. But it was permitted to look grateful, provided it was done with suitable dispatch. Danny Gray looked at Sergeant Dragonnetti gratefully and briefly and then he looked out the window. The engines purred contentedly at reduced speed, and for this Danny Gray was grateful also. The long ribbon, yellow and green-dotted, of the Outer Banks flowed past smoothly. Danny drank the coffee and when the cup was emptied he held it out without looking. The Dragon's hand would be there to take it. Like that joke about Queen Victoria and the chair, Danny thought. He grinned, secretly.

The Dragon was still there. He was looking out the window at the flowing ribbon of the Outer Banks. He said, "This is your home country, Captain?" Danny Gray nodded and the Sergeant said that it was a very interesting-looking country. Even if he had glanced at the Sergeant, Danny Gray might not have noted the look in his eyes — a look that was strangely misted.

"Yeah, Sergeant," Danny Gray went on presently, "it is a curious kind of country. You ever hear of a man by the name of Mitchell? He was in this Army."

"You mean General Billy Mitchell, Sir? If it hadn't been for him we probably wouldn't be riding along here now."

"That's the one, Sergeant. Well, do you see that level place yonder — just this side that line of houses over against the Sound? That village is Rodanthe on the maps, but they call the Station there Chicamicomico. After some Indian, I guess."

"Yes, Sir. There used to be a lot of Indians along here — I guess."

"Back yonder when my daddy was about the age of our gunner back there, or maybe a little older," Danny Gray went on, scarcely noting the Sergeant's observation about aborigines, "he joined up. He was stationed over there. General Mitchell brought all the bombers the country had and landed them there — all thirty of them. Then he started bombing a battle-ship.

"They had Daddy working in the kitchen then and he used to wait on the General. Used to tell me about it. Captain Johnnie was living then — that's Captain John Allen Midgett. He got the Congressional Medal in the other war — you wouldn't believe the ocean could catch fire, would you, Sergeant?"

"After what we've seen in the Pacific and the Mediterranean — well, I guess this ocean would burn, too — give it a good chance. That was the 'Mirlo.' "

"So you know about it, do you, Sergeant?"

"I — I've read about it, Sir."

"Well, it did burn — and I've seen it. Well, General Mitch-ell bombed the battleship and started an argument that got him kicked out. Everybody liked him down here. Daddy said he could outcuss a sailor when he got going. One day he gave my daddy a funny-looking sort of medal. Told him to tote it in his pocket for good luck. Saint Somebody, and it had German words on it. He had it with him when they got him back down the beach yonder."

"You mean your father was —"

"Yeah," Danny Gray said shortly.

A narrow inlet slid past the left wing tip. A tiny ferryboat was docking at the north side, and from it a cumbersome ve-hicle was waddling ashore. "See that bus coming off the ferry down there, Sergeant? That's the way the folks down there on the Banks get out from there. I came up on it the day I left to join the Army. There's a paved road up ahead ten miles but this is pretty rugged going — unless you fly."

"It is that," the Sergeant said.

Another lighthouse, less massive and not so tall as the Great Light on the Cape, slid past. Danny Gray set his chin in a cupped hand with his elbow on the window ledge and looked musingly across the narrowing Sound.

"Sergeant, alert the crew and tell them that in about three minutes we'll be over Wright Monument . . . they might want to know. That's where they flew the first airplane, and while I'm doing this damned Cook's tour, tell the radio boys that over to the left is a place called Roanoke Island. Two men named Marconi and Fessenden sent the first radio telephone message from there. They had some sort of curious notion that it wouldn't carry over land. The receiver was set up back yonder at the Cape. My granddaddy heard it."

The Dragon's voice thundered down the length of the fuselage; in a single sentence that condemned the ancestors of the entire crew as practitioners of strange sins and their descendants of worse things, he said that, although none of them in their untutored ignorance had ever heard of it, some people by the name of Wright had invented something called an airplane that flew like a bird and that they were coming to the place where these things came to pass, and the site, suitably marked with an unseemly effigy, was about to appear off the left wing tip. The crew scrambled into activity, and the Sergeant returned to his post beside the pilot.

Still grinning at the content of the Sergeant's eruptive admonishment, Danny turned to the copilot: "Scotty, there's a sort of tradition among flying people around here to dip their wings when they pass Kill Devil Hill. Might as well circle it and give the boys back there a look. We've got plenty of time and here's where we end up this sight-seeing tour anyhow."

"It's sort of funny, now that I think of it, Sergeant," Danny went on when the Hill had come into view. "The first time I ever saw a general was down there at the foot of that monument. They always have some sort of a celebration on December Seventeenth to commemorate the first flight, and that year there were these two generals. I was a little shaver about thirteen, I guess, and I hooked a ride up there on a Coast Guard truck. They were going to have a lot of airplanes, the paper said."

"Who were the Generals, Sir?"

"One of them was named Andrews and the other was The General, and I got my picture in the paper. I was standing there with my tonsils getting frostbitten or sunburned, I forget which. I was looking up at the airplanes and they took the picture. Not mine — I just happened to be in the way when they were taking the picture of the generals. It got in the paper and Daddy used to kid hell out of me about it. And Jerry, too."

"I guess you'll be seeing the General again today, Sir. Andrews got killed. I used to be in his outfit."

"Maybe," Danny Gray said. "Maybe he'll speak to me again, but if he does, I'll not get near the kick out of it I did that day down there."

"What did he say, Sir?"

"Aw, nothing. Guess he was tired of looking at my tonsils and thought maybe if he could get me to say something I'd shut my trap. He just said, 'Hi, sonny,' and then he told me maybe I'd be flying ships like that someday."

Sweeping around the pylon-crested hill in a wide turn, Lieutenant Scott gently nudged the throttles, and the roar of the four engines thickened. Danny Gray slid the window shut and fastened it. Kitty Hawk Bay was below and then the big bomber climbed above Albemarle Sound. Scott brought it around on the course indicated by the navigator.

"A lot of things seem to have happened in this country of yours, Sir," the Sergeant commented.

"Some fellow who has written a lot about it down here said we've had a sort of ringside seat at the making of a lot of history. I guess we have."

"I'd like to come and see it sometime — some more, I mean, Sir, when I could get out and walk around."

"You'd like it, Sergeant. Come down sometime after we're out of this and I'll stand you and Big Bill Henry Ragland a mile apart on the beach and sit halfway between and listen to the two of you carry on a casual conversation."

"I — I'd like to, sometime," the Sergeant said.

"Where is home to you, Sergeant? I don't believe I've ever heard you mention it."

"I — I — well, I guess you might say the Army's my home, Sir," the Sergeant said. His eyes avoided Danny's quick glance.

"Well, that's all the more reason for you to come down to see us. You'd like that country. I've got a clipping back there in my brief case that I've carried with me all through — let me out of this seat, Sergeant, before I get the cramps. I'll fetch it. The teacher read the thing to us when I was in high school. Take over here a minute, will you?"

Sergeant Dragonnetti slid into the pilot's seat and looked across at Scott. The copilot nodded, and the crew chief took over the controls in practiced hands. The ship continued to climb and the world flowed lazily past. Presently Danny came back and with a gesture indicated to the Sergeant to keep his seat. He handed him a yellowing bit of clipped paper.

"May sound sort of screwy, Sergeant, but I thought it was right good at the time. Maybe it is — maybe it isn't."

The Sergeant read: "... this land where yesterday is tomorrow and tomorrow is yesterday and today is compounded of them both ... this land where Time stands placidly still and is not vexed by anything that can ever happen because it has already happened ... and though it may, as it has already, turn the rest of the world into new and strange paths, it can not matter here because this is a land that lies under an enchantment — this first, this unchanging, this last frontier. ..."

The Sergeant read it through a second time and, puzzled, looked directly into the Captain's eyes. "I didn't know you might be like that, Sir ... like this. I'll come home with you — sometime."

Danny Gray nodded and took the paper and went back through the ship. The young corporal gunner, sitting on a pile of parachutes, scrambled to his feet.

"Soon be there now, won't we, Captain?" he said affably.

"Half an hour or so."

"Gee, it'll be good to be back. It's two years now, since — since I've seen any of my folks. Guess they won't know me, I've grown up so much."

"How old were you, really, when you joined up?"

The corporal reddened.

"Sixteen, Sir. You see —"

"Yes, I know — there are lots of them."

"But I just had to join when — when my brother — he was with Colonel Rogers. There were just two of us. Us boys, I mean. My daddy was in the other war."

This eager boy, Danny thought — why, he's scarcely any older than Jerry . . . and if it had not been for him probably none of them would be alive. As it was, there were slug holes in the ship's tail surfaces that still showed. And he thinks I'm — I reckon he calls me the Old Man when I'm not hearing and me only three years older than he is. Gosh, it's been a crazy war!

"You'll be home before you know it, Corporal," Danny said, and to himself he added, dammit, I almost called him 'son.' "You've been a good gunner and a good soldier, but you'll be hearing that, I reckon, before sundown. Hadn't you better borrow a razor from somebody before we get to Washington?"

"Gosh, Sir, do I need a shave?"

"Wouldn't hurt," Danny said, and went toward the radio room where the operator was signaling him.

"It's Washington, Sir — they want to know our position and time of arrival. Maybe you'd better speak to them, Sir."

"This is Captain Gray," Danny said, taking the microphone. "We are twenty minutes out and will be over the field at twelve hundred fifty."

"What uniforms have you?"

"Summer only. Each man has a fresh outfit."

"I suggest that you, your officers, and your men get your-selves presentable by the time you land here. Apparently there is to be something in the way of ceremony, more than we first thought. The apron is crawling with photographers. You have twenty minutes. Orders to tower are that you be given priority over all traffic when you come over. You land immediately. The General left the Pentagon five minutes ago, and there is a four-star admiral's aide having a litter of kittens at the gate. This is Captain Stevens, Captain Gray, and welcome home."

"Thanks, Captain, we'll be right along."

Danny Gray passed the instrument to the operator and looked him over briefly, nodded approval, and went forward to the pilot's cabin. He beckoned Sergeant Dragonnetti.

"Sergeant, in a moment of irresponsibility I told our young corporal to do something about his whiskers before we get in. He's probably taken me seriously. Go back there and lend a hand, will you — and see that everybody, including me, has his ears clean. I've just talked to the field."

"Right, Sir," the Sergeant said imperturbably. "Your collar is not buttoned, Sir."

The Dragon looked appraisingly at Lieutenant Scott, dis-approved with a glance an unbuttoned, turned-up cuff, and went toward the rear of the ship. This time he uttered no word, but his glance searched out minute imperfection. When the gunner's belt buckle showed tarnish he pointed an accusing finger and from a pocket drew forth a wisp of polishing cloth. He came to the young corporal, shirtless and ambushed be-hind a hedge of lather.

"Gimme that," he said shortly and took the razor. With six deft swipes he had the youngster cleanly shaved. He swabbed him with a towel and spun him around to peer at the flaps of his ears. "Get in that shirt and stick the tails of it in your britches."

With a last look around, the Sergeant went forward.

"They're all ready, Sir," he reported.

"Thanks, Sergeant. I've never landed here before — are there any tricks in it?"

"Not in landing, Sir, but — well, everything will be all right. You met the General when you were a little shaver, Sir. There's your signal."

4

"HEY, MOM!"

Jerry Gray lay sprawled, face down, on the grass in the shadow of the oleander that now, in October, was in the last ecstasy of its blooming. His bare feet reached out beyond the shadow, their soles turned upward to the warm sunlight. . . . Maybe that was the way Big Bill Henry got the soles of his feet so tough that he could strike matches on them. . . . The boy planted his elbows and raised his chin to rest in his cupped hands.

"Hey, Mom!" he called again.

Polly Gray answered him from the kitchen window.

"Mom, I forgot to tell you, but Bill Henry said tell you he might come to supper. Said he was tired of Station rations."

"Yes, Jerry, I thought he might come."

"Want me to get anything from the store? You know how he eats."

"I don't think of a thing right now, Jerry," Polly Gray said. Presently she emerged from the door of the kitchen ell of the house and came across the yard. Jerry glanced apprehensively at her when she approached him, but what he saw was reassuring. There was no slightest sign, now, that she had ever cried in her life. The sight of his mother's tears that morning had disturbed him deeply.

But now Polly Gray's face was serene and a soft light glowed in her placid eyes. They were like the sky after rain had washed it, after the wind had carried away the clouds, carried them far out to sea and dropped them. The feeling formed vaguely in the boy's mind. His mother had spoken no word when he was driving her home from the Station. She had seemed as if she might be a million miles away, as if she might have, somehow, climbed into that airplane with Danny and flown off with him. Jerry had felt unaccountably lonesome.

But by the time they got back to the house she had been back with him, somehow. When he stopped the jeep for her to get out in front of the house, she had remained in the seat for a little and then she had said, very quietly, that he was a good driver. Jerry had felt something inside him swell up, big, when she said that . . . the beginning of being a man, of feeling a man's pride. . . .

Polly Gray sat down in one of the homemade deck chairs. Dan had made them the summer before war had come, and the two boys had painted them. They were white and neat and, in Polly Gray's judgment, just as fine as any pictured in the mail order catalogue — her "wish book" Dan had always called it. Daniel Gray had modeled the chairs after pieces of one he had picked up on the beach, one that had, apparently, been swept overboard from some passing pleasure liner in rough weather off the Outer Diamonds.

Once, when they were planting the oleanders, she had wished for some chairs, and Daniel Gray had started making them from some boards that had been left over when they added the kitchen ell to the house. It was a neat, plain, stout house, set at the top of an open space that sloped gently to the road. The yard was flanked at each end by huge live oaks, Centuries of wind had twisted their limbs into grotesque shapes, but their leaves were perennially luxuriant, perennially green. Gray moss curtained the trunks of the trees.

Behind the house the ground lifted steeply in a hill studded with yoepon, whose wax-bright leaves glistened in the sun. So even was their growth and so dense that they seemed to be clipped like a hedge, like pictures Polly Gray had seen in seed catalogues that came every spring. She and Dan Gray had set out a hedgerow of cedars running from the road to the foot of the rise behind the house, and between the yard and the rutted sandy road they had planted a neat row of palmetto palms.

Beyond the road, down in front of the house, the ground fell away into a wide marsh, and beyond the marsh a pine-studded hill rolled away toward the ocean. The Lighthouse, with its candy-stripe spiral in black and white, lifted skyward beyond the crest of the hill. The intervening marsh was turning brown, now in October, but there were marsh mallows — the catalogues called them hibiscus — still blooming in a last surge of sap, red, white, and all the shades between. Brown foxtails crowded across the marsh.

Even before they were married Dan and Polly Gray had chosen this space of earth for the house they would build one day . . . when Dan had made his rating and could begin to save some money. It was a part of the lands that his great-great-grandfather had claimed when he, a castaway, came into Buxton Woods. Dan Gray liked the place because the great oaks and the yoepon-studded hill sheltered it from the winds that, in winter, roared down from the northeast.

Polly Gray liked it for that and for another reason: this level space of earth would make a nice yard. She had known that when she first walked that way on Sunday with Dan when he was not much older than Jerry was now. . . . Polly Gray winced inwardly at the thought. . . . What was then the fanciful dream of girlhood was now the reality that encircled her. But Dan Gray was buried beneath the hill back of the house. People said, when they came to look at her yard, that it was a miracle that she had been able to make anything grow in white sand.

There had been nothing miraculous about it, Polly Gray thought when she looked at her hands. Nothing miraculous, unless there was magic in all the loads of black muck she and Dan had brought up from the marsh, in all the loads of leaves and straw they had hauled from far ridges and worked into the earth here. Gravel from the beach had been brought for the walks that led down to the road, to the corner off to one side and back of the house where the vegetables grew . . . and to the other side where, shielded by fig bushes, Daniel Gray rested . . . out of reach of the sea. . . .

Almost anything would grow in the garden, and that was why Polly Gray did not send Jerry to the store now. Her pantry shelves were laden with all sorts of vegetables. There was a shelf with nothing on it except fig preserves, figs from the massive bushes at the other corner of the yard. And there was another shelf for jelly and marmalade from the scupper-nong grape vine whose trellis hid the little workshop where Daniel Gray had set up the small power plant. They had ordered the plant from the "wish book."

Daniel Gray was buried at the foot of the hill, in a little level space beyond the fig trees and the cedars. After Danny had gone she and Jerry had brought gravel from the beach to make a path to it and to secure the mound above the grave. It was here that Daniel Gray had wanted his grave to be made. There is no public burying ground in the Woods, no church-yard, nor are its people morbid about death nor afraid of the dead. Every family buries its dead nearby, where life has been lived.

Every day there were fresh flowers on Daniel Gray's grave. Polly Gray went, every morning, first to the beds that ranged the perimeter of the yard, where phlox and petunias and gaillardia, gladioli and geraniums and daisies, zinnias and marigolds and snapdragon grew. Sometimes she would cross the road to the marsh and bring, for the grave, things that grew there, things that Daniel Gray had, in life, always liked to see blooming.

Jerry Gray stirred lazily and rolled over on his back, stretching himself luxuriously. A forearm covered his eyes, shielding them against the bright afternoon sun. How like Dan he looks,

Polly Gray thought . . . big-framed . . . and that unruly fore-lock of blond hair . . . so utterly like Dan's was when she first began to be aware of him. . . .

"What you goin' to have for supper, Mom?" The boy's voice sounded sleepy, dreamily content.

"We could have fried chicken, I guess, but we have that big sea mullet that 'Lonzo brought us this morning." She considered for a moment before she continued. "It's going to be cool after sunset and we could have a fire. You know how Bill Henry likes a planked fish. This mullet must weigh all of five pounds. I'll clean it and you can get some oak wood to make a bed of coals in the fireplace. I guess we'd better get started at it."

Jerry sat up, his ankles crossed, his elbows on his knees. "That'll be swell, Mom. Couldn't we have a lemon pie? It's been a heck of a time since you made one."

"We can if you can find any lemons down at the store — it's been so long since they've had any. You can run down and see after you get the fire going. Not too big a fire, Jerry — just enough to get a good bed of coals."

There were lemons at the store, a whole dozen of them, and Jerry wheedled Mrs. Grady into allocating him four instead of two. The wheedling involved, mostly, a broad, awkward grin and a persuasive "Aw, come on, Miss Minnie, Mom's goin' to make me and Bill Henry — he's comin' to supper — a lemon pie and you know how he eats. It'll just take four lemons — unless you want to hear of me starvin' to death."

Mrs. Grady was disposed to bargain, saying that if Polly would save her a piece of pie she would come down after supper and eat it while his mother told her about her talking with Danny. Jerry protested that he couldn't make any promises, not with Bill Henry around, but for her to come on down and he'd try to save her a piece himself.

"You all must have got a kick out of talking to Danny — him being up there in the air like that," Mrs. Grady said with lively concern. "What all did he say and when's he coming home — I mean on the ground?"

"Didn't say much," Jerry replied with negligent pride, "but he did tell Mom that he had a lot of liberty comin' to him — he calls it leave, him bein' in the Army — and he was comin' as soon as he could."

"It's all of three years, ain't it, Jerry? We've sure missed him, all of us — Sally there in particular." Mrs. Grady's glance darted in the direction of the slender girl just entering the store.

Jerry turned toward the girl briefly and then away. His face, still alight with the disarming smile that had wheedled Mrs. Grady into parting with more than his quota of lemons, went darkly scowling.

"She ain't been lonesome none that I've heard of," he said dourly. "Thanks for lettin' us have the lemons — and you come on down after supper and Mom'll be mighty glad to see you." He stalked out of the store without another glance in the direction of the girl. Her face had gone suddenly pale.

Jerry laid the four lemons on the kitchen table. He was moodily silent and there were stormy lights in his eyes. His mother started to speak but thought better of it. She opened the paper bag.

"Oh — four lemons! That's wonderful, Jerry. We can have another pie tomorrow, or for Sunday."

"Better make two now," he said, still dour. "Miss Minnie, she wanted to dicker. She said she'd be down after supper and to save her a piece. She wants to know all about Danny."

"That's nice," Polly Gray said. "Who all did you see at the store?"

"Nobody much. That Sally Tillett, she was hangin' around — like usual."

Again Polly Gray's impulse was to speak, but again she thought better of it and said nothing. Jerry's increasingly apparent hostility to Sally Tillett was something she could not

quite fathom. Jerry moved over to the window, standing irresolute, looking at a circling osprey above the yoepon-studded hill
back of the house. Presently he turned away from the window.

"Anything you want me to do, Mom?"

"You can fix the table for us, Jerry. We'll eat in the dining
room. Bill Henry's just too big for this kitchen. Get out the
red-checked cloth and napkins. You can serve the fish from
the plank, so leave the plates be just now; I'll put them here
to warm. Remember, spoon and knife on the right with the
blade toward the plate, and fork — two forks, since there's
pie — on the left."

"Aw, what's the use bein' so particular, Mom?"

"When there's two ways to do a thing it's just as easy to do
it the right way, Jerry." Polly Gray smiled her gentle smile.
She managed never to sound as if she were preaching. "We
ought to have some flowers, too. There's still enough snapdragon to make a bouquet and you can bring them in while I
make the second pie."

Supper was eaten in that comfortable silence possible among
people who, by inheritance and by lifelong association, have
achieved a sort of communion that makes talk superfluous,
especially when there are other matters to absorb the attention of the senses. Of all the senses. The sea mullet, when
Jerry brought it from before the fireplace, was such a matter.
Big Bill Henry emitted a long, incredulous whistle when Jerry
set the plank at the head of the table. The boy cocked an eye
at the big man on Polly's right and grinned. "Just a minute
now, Bill Henry. Don't grab. This fish would burn your fingers." The big man grinned silently.

Planking a fish before an open fire was something that Polly
Gray had learned from her grandmother. Indeed, this plank,
dark with age and stained and mellowed by generations of
use, had been inherited. It had been in the family for more
generations than she knew. It was hickory, two inches thick,

twenty inches wide, and half again as long. The process of planking was simple enough. First the plank was set on edge before the bed of oak coals on the hearth and left until the wood was heated through.

Meanwhile the fish was prepared for the plank, first scaled and slit down the back and the backbone removed, leaving a flat, wide filet. By then the board would be hot enough to make the fish sizzle when it was placed, skin against board, and secured in place by a criss-crossed copper wire.

Even with so large a fish as the five-pound sea mullet, all the rancid oils and blood were drained out of the fish while it slowly turned a golden brown before the glowing coals. This had been an especially happy brown at the moment Jerry lifted the plank, loosened the copper wiring, and tossed it into the sink in the kitchen. Jerry cut it across the middle and quartered it, leaving a fourth piece for the big man's second helping.

There were beans from the garden and fluffy mashed potatoes, and Polly Gray had opened a jar of her precious watermelon rind pickles. There were crisp corn cakes, and there was steaming black coffee. Beside Bill Henry's plate stood a tall glass of white scuppernong wine. "Not yet for a year or so, Jerry," Polly Gray had said when Jerry teasingly asked her if there was no glass for him.

Until the Chief pushed back his plate, empty, there had been complete silence around the table. Now and then the guest emitted a gargantuan belch which was evidence not of bad manners but of profound contentment.

"There's never been a better piece of cookin' on these Banks since the first castaway landed on 'em, Polly," he said. "Damn fryin' a fish — this is the only way to cook 'em. Of course there ain't always a plank handy and then you have to fry 'em or boil 'em. . . . Didn't I get a glimpse of some sort of a pie out there, Polly?"

"A whole half of one for you," Jerry said. "You all sit still —

gimme your plates and I'll bring the pie."

More silence befell when Jerry set the pie before them — two plates each with a quarter of fluffy-topped perfection before the big man's place. When both his plates were clean Big Bill Henry leaned far back in his chair, balancing it on its rear legs with the balls of his feet touching the floor.

"Polly," he said solemnly, "you're a damned good cook — among other things."

Polly Gray did not answer him but her face glowed happily. Jerry spoke up with "Mom, you and Bill Henry go on in the house. I'll get rid of these dishes in no time after I feed my cat. You ain't seen him around, have you, Mom? Guess he's off courtin' somewhere, the dam' scut — excuse me, Mom."

"Boy," Bill Henry said, "if your mammy could get some cookin'-sense inside that thick skull of your'n I'd put you in the kitchen out yonder at the Station and chain you there." He pushed his chair back from the table. "Come on, Polly, let's get out and let him be of some use around here. Your daddy was a good cook, boy, when he first joined — and don't you forget that he was the damnedest man with an oar that's been on these Banks in my time, either. He was as good as me."

Jerry took his time with the dishes. First he cleaned the plank, taking it out under the eaves of the house where there was clean white sand and scrubbing it. He washed it off with boiling water and stood it up to dry. No soap ever touched the plank.

Dusk had chilled the air, and the warmth of the dying coals on the hearth was comforting to the bottoms of the boy's bare feet when he came in from the kitchen. Big Bill Henry was smoking in replete silence at one side of the hearth and Polly Gray was at the other side. Jerry put some small sticks on the embers and presently the room glowed with the crackling flame. The boy settled himself, cross-legged, on the deerskin rug before the hearth. He glanced at the ship's clock above the mantel.

"Gosh, I mighty near forgot — time for the news."

Jerry Gray turned the dials on the small radio on the table beside the chair where the big man sprawled. The broadcast came on, in the middle of a sentence. Somebody was speaking from Moscow.

"Guess with Danny back home, we don't need to bother with the news so much now, Mom," Jerry said.

"Let's listen, anyway, son," Polly Gray said. "We've got so used to it."

The broadcast continued. News these days, Jerry thought, with the war over with, was not so hot. . . . "And now we take you to Washington, our nation's capital — come in, Washington."

"This war-weary capital," the voice began, "was stirred out of its lethargy this afternoon, for a little while at any rate, by one of the most unusual ceremonies I have ever witnessed. There was no advance fanfare about it. Radio and newspaper men were not notified until a few minutes before it happened, but most of us managed to get out to the airport by the time the big battle-scarred Twenty-nine was over the field.

"Already there ahead of us were the Chief of the Army Air Forces and the Commandant of the U. S. Coast Guard and members of their staffs. The big bomber, piloted by Captain Daniel Gray, Jr., of Buxton, North Carolina, was given landing priority over everything in the air, and when it landed, one of the General's aides went aboard immediately, I suppose to make sure that there would be no confusion among members of the crew about the impending ceremonies. The bomber left Japan less than four days ago, flying directly here with only refueling stops."

Jerry's voice was shrill with excitement. "Mom, are you hearin' what that fellow says — it's about Danny!" Polly Gray laid a quiet hand on the boy's shoulder. The voice went on. . . .

"Presently the door of the big plane opened and Captain Gray appeared. He looked astonishingly young, even for an

Army that has become predominantly young. He looked more like a high school boy than a veteran bomber pilot whose battle career began shortly after the invasion of North Africa. The other members of the crew, all except one looking equally immature, came down the ladder and lined up in single file beside the ship.

"Perhaps there had been some sort of formal ceremony planned. There must have been — there always is. But ceremony went by the boards. The General must have seen that these boys were too bewildered to know what to do next, so he just went over and introduced himself to the youthful captain, and I heard him say, 'Captain Gray, let these boys relax and introduce me to them as you come to them. We'll skip the ceremonies for the present.' You can always count on the General to be human.

"Flash bulbs started popping all over the place. Then the General turned to his adjutant, or somebody, and told him to hand him the medals. The General pinned the Distinguished Service Cross with palms on the Captain's shirt and did the same thing for a young corporal gunner who shot down two Jap fighters on one raid over Tokyo. Every man in the crew got some sort of medal.

"But now comes the pay-off on this story. When the Army was through passing out medals the season of informality was past. The General stood back and the Commandant of the Coast Guard came forward with his four stars shining. He singled out young Captain Gray and this youngster stood rigidly while the Admiral addressed him. He said, as well as I can remember his words, that he was happy, on behalf of the President of the United States and on behalf of the U. S. Coast Guard, to inform Captain Gray of the award to his late father, Chief Boatswain's Mate Daniel Gray, of the Distinguished Service Cross in recognition of devoted service to his country, a service that had cost him his life.

"Chief Gray, I learned later, was killed by gunfire from a

German submarine off Cape Hatteras, North Carolina, early in 1942. Chief Gray had put out from the Coast Guard station at the Cape in an effort to rescue members of the crew of a Coast Guard patrol airplane that had been forced down. He rescued the crew, but returning to the shore at dusk Gray was killed by a fusillade from a lurking submarine. His son, then only eighteen, joined the Army Air Forces shortly afterward. The Admiral, when the formalities were over, warmly greeted the youthful bomber pilot and inquired after members of his family, many of whom are well known to him. . . . And that's all for now from Washington. . . ."

The Chief stirred in his chair, hauled himself to his feet. "Polly," he said unsteadily, "I got to go. I had about all I can take for one day and I reckon you have, too." He stood uncertainly before her, and his big hands fumbled downward toward the collar of the boy's shirt. His fingers closed and he hauled the boy upward.

"Good night, Jerry." His voice was strangely soft. "You come over to the Station in the mornin' when I'm doin' boat drill. It's time somebody started educatin' you some."

5

"WHEN WE COME OUT OF THERE," THE DRAGON SAID IN HIS MOST terrible voice, "I'm goin' to search you guys and if I find so much as one of the General's toothpicks on you I'm goin' to break your neck." The Dragon described their necks collectively with seven obscene and two blasphemous adjectives.

"Not nary a toothpick to remember him by, Pop?" The young corporal managed to sound plaintive.

"You got enough to remember him by already, you expurgated adolescent faker," the Dragon replied. "Give you a medal, didn't he, when what you deserved was a kick in the slats? Shook that filthy hand of yours, didn't he, when he could have busted you in the jaw? And now he's goin' to feed you. Off'n a plate, too, you what was raised out'n a garbage can. And, furthermore, one sip of coffee out'n your saucer and I'll bust it over your head, even if they take it out'n my pay."

"He didn't say anything about coffee, Pop. I heard him tell her it might be a good idea if she fixed a barrel of chocolate milks."

"Okay, okay — you unweaned and unwanted heifer. I missed one of them whiskers when I was barberin' you. I got them three that was on each side of your pock-marked face and clean missed that one on your chin. Hold still."

Sergeant Dragonnetti took the seventh whisker between the nails of his thumb and forefinger and yanked it out by the roots. With elaborate distaste he lowered the window and made all the motions of dropping the offensive thing into the Potomac River. He wiped his hands daintily with a handkerchief.

"Thanks, my good man," the corporal said, and after a moment he went on, "I still can't figure out how all this happened — how we come to be going to eat with him."

"It's all on account of the Captain, you mouthin' hunk of misfortune," the Dragon assured him. "I heard it all. After that Admiral got through, the General he come and asked the Captain if he would come to his house for — for dinner. The Captain, he looked surprised and he was right on the edge of sayin' he'd come when he looked around and saw the rest of us famished heroes. Maybe he remembered all the times we've been hither and yonder and maybe he thought he'd better stick with us.

"But the General, he's got sense. You don't have to draw a diagram and paint pictures on it for him to see a thing. The General, he saw the Captain didn't want to be separated from us and so he went and telephoned his house and asked if he could bring the whole pack of us home to supper. And that, you misbegotten get of a tumblebug, is how."

"Thanks, Pop. I just don't know what I'd do without your wise and pious counsel," the young corporal said. Presently he went on, ignoring the Dragon's grim rejoinder. "Things sure happen fast when a general starts talking, don't they, Pop? Here we were practically naked when we got here, and now look at us — brand new uniforms and everything. First time I ever knew you could get your pay that easy in this army. Gosh, we got everything, even down to the campaign ribbons and a regular bed to sleep in. Gee!"

"Now shut up, you mongrel street walker, we're almost there. I rode through this place once. You remember what I told you — you shake hands and you tell him and you tell her what your name is. You must have heard sometime or other

how people who live in houses act. Try to remember it and
don't be no disgrace to the Captain."

Little of the Dragon's coaching had been needed. Accompanied by one of the host's aides, Danny Gray had arrived at
the house a few minutes before the rest of the crew, and when
they trooped into the big living room he was there, with the
host and his wife. The General shook hands with each of
them, passed them on to Danny to be presented to the hostess.

Much as he had dreaded the ordeal, nothing, when it happened, had been so easy and natural as this meeting with the
hostess. Her hair was almost snow white but her face was
young and her figure lithely slender. She just makes you feel
like you've known her all your life, Danny thought . . . like
your mother, and at the same time like — why, I've seen the
ocean off the Cape just the color of her eyes sometimes. . . .

Almost before all of them had been presented, down to the
young corporal over whose youth she exclaimed wonderingly,
saying that he seemed even younger than her own son, a
white-coated butler came in with a tray. There were twelve
tall glasses of foamy chocolate milk, and the young corporal
exclaimed unbelievingly, "Oh, boy!" The hostess, smilingly
surveying the group, came to the Sergeant.

"Sergeant, there's something perhaps a little more invigor-
ating on the sideboard if you'd prefer it. Or any of the others.
Will you tell them for me, please?"

"Thank you kindly, Ma'am," the Sergeant replied, wishing
that he could kick himself destructively for sounding so inane.
"Thank you again, Ma'am, but — well, I guess we're all sort
of behind with our chocolate milks."

"Of course, Sergeant," she said. "You must be one of us old
regulars. How long have you been in the Air Corps? I still call
it that — can't quite get used to 'Forces.' "

"Yes, Ma'am, I am. I joined fifteen years ago when I was
seventeen. I've been in it ever since."

Afterward, when he thought about it, the Dragon was amazed at his own volubility, but he was comforted by her alert, informed interest. He named over the fields at which he had seen service, remembered officers under whom he had served. She knew all of them. He mentioned old regulars and, astonishingly, she knew them, too. She knew ships, also, their good points and their bad points.

Most of the men gravitated toward the hostess and she effortlessly included them all in the talk. The corporal, his upper lip smudged from his second — vanilla this time — worked his way into the group, standing beside the Sergeant. The Dragon, hissing vengefully under his breath, told him to wipe his mouth. The corporal ignored him and smiled disarmingly at the hostess.

"You know, Ma'am, my mom would look like you if I could get her to fix her hair like that."

"How nice you are, Corporal. You must have told me where you are from, but I'm a little confused by so many at one time. It's Ohio, isn't it?"

"Yes, Ma'am — a little place just outside Dayton." He added irrelevantly that he had seen Mr. Wright once. The General joined the group.

"Isn't it about time we had something a little more substantial than milk, Mother?" He smiled at her.

"Supper is just ready, I think," she replied. "It had to be chicken. I wanted steaks, but maybe you've heard of rationing out there. It's buffet and you boys can help yourselves to anything you see. I hope there's plenty."

After coffee had been brought in, the General, raising his voice to include all the group, said that he was not sure what was in the orders for them for the next day or two, but that he would recommend, first, a night in bed. Tomorrow they could go out and look at the town if they felt like it.

"There will be transportation for you if you want it or need it, and one of my people will be over in the morning to lay out the day with you." And then he added, "For the rest of the evening I think I'll take Captain Gray away from you — if he isn't too sleepy; I want to talk to him. Mother, will you ask George to have the cars sent around?"

When the group, standing ready for their good-byes, gathered before the host, the corporal approached the General, diffident and awkward. With an apprehensive glance in the direction of the Dragon, he took a carefully folded paper napkin from his pocket, one of those personalized bits of paper with the names of the hosts lettered in red.

"General, Sir," the corporal blurted, "would you mind autographing this for me? I want to take it home and prove to Mom I've been here."

"Sure, Corporal. . . . Mother, you come put your name on it, too."

"Gee, thanks, Sir. Thanks, Ma'am."

And then, to the corporal's amazement, the Dragon, his face impassive, extracted a similar napkin from his pocket and silently tendered it for signing.

"Anybody else?" the General asked. . . . "Mother, we're not out of these things, are we? Get George to bring in some more."

Presently they were gone, each with his autographed napkin. Danny Gray took out his wallet and folded his bit of paper carefully, with the lettering facing the snapshot of Polly and Jerry that he carried always in the left pocket of his shirt.

"So you are from Cape Hatteras," the General said from his chair across the hearth.

"Yes, Sir — or rather from Buxton. That's the village up in the Woods, away from the Cape."

"Yes, I know. Would it surprise you to know that I've been there?"

"Why, no, Sir. Maybe we don't surprise easily down there,

but I sure wish — when were you there, Sir?"

"Six years ago, the first time. And I was over that country in the spring of forty-two."

"Did you fly over it the first time, Sir?"

"First, yes, and then I drove down one day. It's an awful trip, isn't it? Or do you folks get used to it?"

"No, Sir, we — well, I guess we are used to it, but still it's a hard trip unless you get the tide right and drive the wash."

"Some of your Coast Guardsmen from Nags Head drove me down in a truck, and it was a hard trip. But what I started to say was that back in thirty-nine, after they got going with their war in Poland, I was sure we would eventually have to come in.

"History has to repeat itself, and I guess it always will as long as people make it. The human race isn't very original somehow. You were not born, then, but it was off Hatteras that the Germans hit us first back in the other war. I was sure that, when we got into this one, they'd hit us again in the same place. I just wanted to look at it.

"Altogether — and I'm not telling you anything you don't know already — there's been more fighting off Hatteras than any place this side the Atlantic Ocean. I've seen translations from the Spanish archives that tell of a fight off there more than four hundred years ago."

"Yes, Sir, I've fished with my daddy at an old wreck off the Point that old-timers say is a galleon."

"It's been so all down the years. There are people along your Outer Banks that have pirate blood in their veins. You may have yourself and I have a profound respect for it. They were venturesome people."

"I don't know if there's any of it in me — but I wouldn't be surprised," Danny laughed shyly. "But Big Bill Henry Ragland is descended from Blackbeard and he's proud of it."

"That big fellow at the Station down there? I remember him well. He was pretty skeptical about aircraft."

"Yes, Sir, I guess he is," Danny said. "He's one of the last of the great surfmen down there and — well, I'm afraid he'll never forgive me for — for not staying down there."

"They're great fellows, those old surfmen," the General replied. "Especially along that coast. They've had to be to survive. They were there back in sixty-two when the Union government almost collapsed at news of the loss of the 'Monitor.'"

"Yes, Sir," Danny interposed. "I've seen the hulk of it many a time when I've been fishing off there with my father. He used to say that sometime somebody would raise it."

"Maybe we should," the General went on. "I imagine if we could get at them we would find very nearly every type of vessel that has been in use for five centuries buried in the sand there. There are, I know, submarines of both the first and this last world war."

"Yes, Sir — I saw one of 'em blown out of the water. That's when I — I left down there and joined the Army."

"Why didn't you join the Coast Guard, Danny?"

Surprised at himself and wondering at the ease with which it was possible to talk about things that he had kept, prisoned, in the back of his consciousness, Danny Gray told the General how the Germans had come, bringing with them their own lightship to replace the vessel off Diamond Shoals, which they, rightly, supposed would be withdrawn at the first indication of attack, of how they had used it as a decoy for shipping.

"We heard one day that an Army bomber had sunk it for them," Danny remembered. "From the start it looked like everybody in the world had forgot us except that squadron of Twenties. Daddy said they were from up at Fort Bragg."

"They were based there," the General said. "We had been using them in maneuvers all that fall, and I thought it might be a good idea to hold them in that area until we could see what was going to happen. Anyhow, you saw what happened."

"Yes, Sir, I did. I had a sort of feeling that it was the same submarine that got my father. Anyhow, I hoped it was."

"I hope so," the General said. For a while they were both silent.

"And what now, Captain Gray?" the General asked presently.

"How do you mean, Sir?"

"I mean what are you going to do? You are young, you have as good a record as any pilot in the Forces. Are you going to stay with it or do you want to get out and go home? Now don't give me any quick answer. The chances are that you have had little time to think about it. But I'll tell you frankly that I'm gravely concerned about the Forces. The whole Army is falling apart. That's natural, and it's inevitable. We're not a warrior nation and we just don't like the military, as a people. But we are going to need an Army, especially an Air Force."

"I have thought about it, Sir, thought about it a lot. I like to fly an airplane, but I know there's a lot more to being an officer in the Air Force than just being able to fly. Especially in peacetime.

"You see, Sir, I was just halfway through my freshman year at State College when I quit and joined the Army. Mama and Daddy had always wanted me to go to college. I didn't know much about it and I guess I went because they wanted me to. I know I'm pretty ignorant, and that would make a lot of difference, in the long run, if I stayed in the service."

"Think you want to get out and go back to college, Danny?"

"I don't know the answer to that, Sir."

"I know the pull that country down there has on you people — I've seen it. Mother and the boy have spent many summers at the beach north of you, and I'd get down for week ends. Is there a girl in the picture somewhere?"

"No, Sir, not exactly. There hasn't been much time for girls, and there weren't very many around most places I've been the last couple of years."

"You didn't leave one back home, waiting for you?"

Danny blushed. "There was a girl I used to go with when I was in high school, but — well, she's still down there. I — she's there but I don't know that she's been waiting for me."

"You have a lot of accumulated leave coming to you, of course. Maybe it would be a good idea for you to take some of it, as much as you want. Go back home and see how things look, but I wish you would keep in mind the fact that I don't want to see the Air Forces fall apart."

"Yes, Sir, and thank you a lot. But I hate to break up my crew. What becomes of my ship?" Danny hesitated, shy, not quite comfortable. "You know I named it for my mother and my kid brother."

"I think they want the ship out in Dayton for something — probably to take it apart and see how she stood the beating they gave her. Like to fly her out there?"

"Yes, Sir, I would. Three — no, four — of the crew come from out there somewhere, and I could get them that near home. They have the same leave coming to them that I do, don't they, Sir?"

The General nodded. Somewhere in the house the telephone rang, long, strident, insistent. Danny had never lived in a house with a telephone and he was always uneasily conscious of one when it rang. . . . Along the Outer Banks the ringing of a telephone usually meant tidings that were, too often, not glad. . . . The house boy came in, looked inquiringly at the General.

"What is it?" the General said.

"It's long distance, Sir. From New York. Calling Captain Daniel Gray."

Danny started, his face revealing alarmed surprise.

"Me? How would anybody know I'm here?"

"I think there was some mention of your arrival on the radio, and the afternoon papers had pictures," the General said mildly. "Tracing you here would not have been too difficult."

"But who is it — who'd be calling me? I've never been in New York in my life."

"Find out who is calling Captain Gray," the General directed, and the house boy departed. Presently he was back.

"It's a Miss Hale, Sir — a Miss Judith Hale, and she says the matter is urgent, Sir. . . . This way, Sir."

6

DANNY GRAY GAZED REMOTELY OUT UPON THE WORLD FROM THE right blister of the lumbering PBY. In Washington the Coast Guard people had been very pleasant about it when, upon his return from Dayton, he had gone over to inquire if there was any chance of a ride as far as Norfolk. There was, they had told him, a Catalina leaving in an hour for the base on Pasquotank River. They would take him that far, if it would help any.

For no reason that he could have put into words, Danny Gray's fist, thrust deep in his trousers pocket, closed tightly around a small metal disc, curiously lettered and bearing a strange figure that looked like somebody out of the Old Testament . . . a figure that a legendary man had given to his father. By now the lettering was so worn that the words, even if he had known what they were, had become almost completely illegible.

It was not that Danny Gray was superstitious or that he had any active belief in the miraculous . . . or in saints. . . . Lots of fellows he had known in the past three years wore images of Saint Christopher on little chains around their necks; and he had seen men bloated in death on strange beaches with their little charm pieces about all that was left of what they had on them when they got hit.

It was not that Danny Gray was, consciously, superstitious, but this bit of metal in his left trousers pocket was something that had belonged to his father, something that his father had carried from the day the General had given it to him. He had carried it when he went to his death in the bight above the Point. His father had not been superstitious, either. Any active belief in saints was wholly alien to the simple Wesleyan faith that was a part of the heritage of all men of the Outer Banks.

When Polly Gray came upon the little disc after they had buried Daniel Gray at the foot of the hill back of the house, she had held it in her hands for a long while and then, without a word, had passed it to Danny. Without looking at it, he had put it in his pocket, the left pocket; his father had always carried it there . . . more to remember the General by, Danny thought, than from any belief in its efficacy. . . .

And, like his father, Danny Gray had carried it, never actively conscious of it nor wholly unaware of it, until that unforgettable morning when he was scheduled to make his first solo flight. Waiting his turn on the line, his fingers had encountered the thing deep down in his pocket. He had taken it out, then, and held it tight against his palm. It was something that bound him, that linked him, to his father . . . and to the air's legend. He had been intent upon it when he heard his name called out. . . .

He remembered, now, that his fingers had been red from gripping it when he prepared for his first bombing run over enemy territory, coming in low above the glittering blue of the Mediterranean . . . like the roaring, vengeful Twenty that had, that day, come sweeping down above the Cape and, in a moment, had seemed to lift that submarine out of the water and tear it apart. . . .

He had had his hand gripped around it, three nights ago, when he lifted the telephone receiver at the General's house.

But now a voice was speaking to him: "Say, ain't you Danny Gray from Buxton?"

Danny Gray had never, he was sure, seen the man's face before, but there was a familiar quality in the voice, the way its vowels rolled and some of its consonants blurred. "Elizabethan," people from the outside called it, and they seemed always to find something "wonderful" in its strange survival anywhere. . . .

"Somebody at Headquarters called up out here and said if you showed up lookin' a ride to fix it for you. Must be on account of your daddy. We could run you right on down there, if there was any way to get you to land after we got there."

"That's — that's too much bother, I'm afraid. If I can get to Manteo I'd — I'd kind of like to ride the bus. That's the way I came away from down there."

"Okay — we'll set you down at that Naval Air Station they got on Roanoke Island. How long since you been home, Captain?"

"Three years, just about. They let me off two days right after I finished primary."

"Long time," the voice said. "Got a bag or anything?"

After the take-off from Washington, the pilot, an enlisted man with Chief Aviation Pilot rating, motioned for his copilot to get down and let Danny have his seat. It was his first time in a Coast Guard workhorse patrol plane and, after the Twenty-nine, it seemed almost rudimentary. Danny took over the controls, flew it casually for fifteen minutes, and then indicated that he had had enough.

Danny's thoughts were not on flying. Home was ahead of him and it had been three years since he had been there. So much had happened, especially these last four or five days. The medal for his father, for one thing. He could scarcely wait to get home and give it to Polly Gray — and Jerry. Its leather case bulged against the pocket of his blouse. His own medal was in his bag.

His mother, and Jerry, would be awfully proud. Not, to be sure, that such things were any novelty in the family . . . in anybody's family down home, for that matter. Grandfather Gray had been voted a medal by the Congress for that rescue in 1907; and, before that, Great-grandfather — his name was

Daniel, too — had been to Washington where the Swedish minister had decorated him for saving the crew of a Swedish merchantman when it foundered on Diamond Shoals in 1887.

Great-grandfather Gray — Danny could just barely remember him — had made a great joke of his medal and come home with gusty tales of how he had probably disgraced his race forever by his — as he reported it — uncouth behavior in the presence of the King's minister. Great-grandfather Gray had insisted that Polly Gray use the thing as a teething-ring for Danny when he was little, but Danny Gray had not cut his teeth with the help of a strange medal.

Polly Gray was proud of the medals. After they had moved into the new house she insisted that Daniel Gray make a little case for them. He used a piece of mahogany he had picked up on the beach. For its cover he cut down a piece of clear glass that had covered a porthole of a wrecked schooner. Polly Gray lined the little case with a bit of white satin brought out from the sea chest which was her treasure house. That was where she kept the little silver pitcher.

It was not that Polly Gray wanted to show off these evidences of heroism. When the little case was finished she placed the medals against the white satin lining and Daniel Gray fastened down the glass cover. She put them away in her sea chest; it had been her great-grandfather Hawthorne's, and maybe his father's before him. Often, when he was little, Danny had heard from his mother the story of the storm that, in 1818, had brought the first Hawthorne to the Outer Banks, a castaway. The chest was all that he had saved from the ship.

Now there would be another medal for Polly Gray's sea chest — two more, Danny Gray reminded himself. . . . No, three, counting his air medal; four, counting his Purple Heart. He couldn't feel very comfortable about that . . . the wound, compared with injuries suffered by others of the crew, had seemed so trivial, no more than a scratch across the back of his head where the splinter of a shell had hit him. It didn't even show, now, when he combed his hair over it.

Danny Gray's homeward-faring thoughts raced ahead of the lumbering Catalina.... It couldn't be very long now. He glanced at his watch, checking the time they had been in the air, and then downward at the wind-ruffled upper reaches of the Pasquotank. Off to the left, in the distance, he could make out the row of great cream-colored dunes lining the upper reaches of the Outer Banks. Roanoke Island was a dim blur in the haze directly ahead. He got down from the copilot's seat, nodding to the pilot, and made his way astern.

A young seaman in battered dungarees got up from his lookout place in the blister and, by gesture, invited Danny to sit down in his place. He held the seat, one that automatically folded into the bulkhead when no weight was on it, while Danny lowered himself into it. The youth counted the ribbons on Danny's blouse, whistled to himself.

"What's that one there, Sir?" he asked, raising his voice above the rumble of the Catalina's engines. Danny told him, briefly, using the three-letter abbreviation, and the youth commented, "Don't see many of them around here." Danny smiled deprecatingly and turned to the bulging plexiglass blister.

In a minute now the Catalina, already slanting downward, the roar of its engines muted, would cross the Sound and below would be the Outer Banks — and home. Danny's fingers went down into his pocket, closed around the thin metal disc. Beyond the blurred wall of the blister the upper reaches of Kitty Hawk Woods spread out below, and Danny was conscious of a feeling of surprise that they looked so much like the Woods that stretched backward from the Point of the Cape.

Far out, and half hidden in the haze, a group of what looked like transports plodded northward toward Hampton Roads, trailing long flat plumes of white water behind them. Probably troop ships, Danny thought, with a lot of fellows like me, heading for home. He started to count them, but the Catalina's left wing tilted up sharply and the blister rolled with it until its lower ledge came up past the horizon. He stood up, the seat snapping up flush with the bulkhead. The young seaman said they were almost there now.

Almost there. . . . Roanoke Sound was under the wing now, and the village at the head of Shallowbag Bay, seeming somehow bigger than Danny remembered it when he had passed that way, three years ago, was spread out in the morning sunlight. The courthouse, the ragged waterfront with its small docks seeming to fall apart, the boatyard that had grown astonishingly. But that's not strange, Danny reflected. Everybody down here knows how to build boats . . . and the world had been suddenly in need of so many boats.

Coming down into the westerly wind, the lumbering patrol plane touched the runway lightly, rolled to a stop, and swung in toward the apron in front of the small hangar. Danny Gray told the young seaman standing ready with a ladder not to bother but just to toss him his bags when he got down. He went forward and thanked the pilot for the lift and, returning to the blister, dropped lightly over the side. The concrete apron was surprisingly hard.

Danny Gray had been thinking so intently about touching the earth of home again that he had the soft, yielding sand of the Outer Banks in his mind when he dropped down from the blister. Above him the young seaman was holding the first, the older, of his two bags. The other was brightly new. The youth waved a friendly hand and closed the blister. The Catalina's engines roared.

Lifting clear of the runway, the big ship's landing gear began to creep into its belly the instant the wheels were clear of the pavement, Danny noted admiringly. . . . "Get 'em out of the way when they're no more use to you. . . ." The ship climbed above Croatan Sound and dwindled into the northwest.

With distance widening between him and the ship that had

brought him this far on the way home, Danny Gray felt a surge of something that must have been homesickness, as if a tie had been severed, a tie that bound him to the sky. It had been three years, now, since he had gone anywhere except by air, since he had had any purpose, any actual existence apart from the air. And now the ship had gone, had left him standing there, alone, in the middle of acres of concrete.

The voice that brought Danny Gray back to his immediate surroundings was not a familiar voice, nor was it friendly. It was a voice that clipped off words as if it were a sharp knife, and it was slicing them impatiently. Danny turned from watching the dwindling Catalina to discover that the voice belonged to a sharp-faced young ensign whose duties for the moment, to judge by the service pistol in the holster strapped around his lean middle, must be Officer of the Day.

"Who was that fellow?" the young ensign demanded, "and what does he mean by taking off without checking in and checking out of here?" He managed to sound aggressive, and he added, "And who are you and do you have permission to land here?"

"I'm Danny — " Danny Gray started to explain and thought better of it. "I'm Captain Gray of the Army Air Forces," he said evenly. "I'm on my way home, and that Coast Guard plane gave me a lift, with the approval of the Commandant."

"Well, he hadn't filed any flight plan," the ensign said irritably. "And he didn't ask for permission to land here and he took off again without clearing."

Danny had recovered from his slight discomfiture. Not that he minded the poor lad's officiousness; he was accustomed to that. But somehow he had conditioned his thoughts for home, for friendly, soft voices and the familiar neighborliness that he knew . . . like that pilot on the Catalina.

"Definitely hostile, I should say, Mister," Danny commented, "but he seems to have gotten away with it — unless you send out a flock of your Corsairs and shoot him down.

He's on the way to the Air Base up the river yonder, and by now you might have to shoot him on the ground. Or you might hold me as a sort of hostage until he can be brought back here and dealt with properly. What would be the chances of seeing your commanding officer and wangling a ride downtown? I've got to catch a bus for Buxton."

"You come from Buxton?" There was now a tincture of mild disbelief in his voice as he surveyed Danny anew. Then his dour face lightened. "You're not the fellow I heard about on the radio? Your picture's in all the papers. Captain Gray, I'm Ensign Walters."

Ensign Walters stiffened and brought his hand to the visor of his cap in a precipitate salute. For a moment Danny eyed the rigid youth in faintly amused detachment, then casually returned the salute. He held out his hand.

"I'm glad to see you, Mr. Walters. And now what about a ride downtown? Think we could manage it without disturbing the Commandant? That is, if you think you don't have to jail me for this one-man invasion of your post here."

"Sure, send you right down. Take you myself but I'm tied up here with this OD job. How about lunch before you go? The Skipper would be glad to have you, I know." The Ensign raised his voice and two sailors came. "Put Captain Gray's bags aboard the Skipper's car, will you, men. This way, Sir, and I'll find the Skipper."

Danny avoided the Commandant's lunch with polite inventions about things that he must attend to before the bus took him on the last leg of his journey home. Actually there was nothing he had to attend to, no one that he needed or wanted to see. Actually, when he thought about it, there was not a soul in the town that he could remember, except very vaguely. There were a lot of kinfolks, he supposed, on both sides the family, but his acquaintance with them was tenuous and undemanding, and he was anxious to begin this last leg of his journey home.

7

THERE WAS NOBODY ABOARD THAT DANNY GRAY KNEW WHEN HE
entered the ungainly bus. It was new since he went away; or at
any rate it was different — there was nothing new-looking
about it. It had begun its existence as the chassis of a truck;
the body, awkward and high-roofed, had been added. Its
wheels were salt-rusted, and its fat, oversized tires were beginning to show wear.

Danny stood in the aisle, a bag in each hand. There was no
baggage rack. The bus was almost full, but not a face had any
line or feature that was familiar. The passengers, except for an
elderly woman and a little boy who must be, Danny thought,
a grandson, were in blue uniform, and above the right wrist of
each of them there was the white shield of the U. S. Coast
Guard.

That, at any rate, was familiar. Most of the passengers were
young. One of them had a very marked discoloration beneath
his left eye. He and the others had the wan, listless look of men
who had spent their leave time with an abandon that, now,
they must be regretting. They must be, Danny surmised, bound
for one or another of the shore stations along the Outer Banks
below Oregon Inlet. Things must be different down there now,
with all these strangers.

All of them looked speculatively at Danny when he entered
the bus, and one or two of them seemed startled at the sight of
an Army uniform. One of them, halfway down the aisle, with
a seat entirely to himself, started to move toward the window,

making room, and was about to invite Danny to share the seat with him when another voice intervened from outside the bus.

"There's room for your bags in the back," the voice said.

Here, at last, Danny thought, as he turned back toward the door, is a voice that sounds like a voice ought to sound . . . soft, blurred, friendly. But when he turned back to the door he felt anew the sense of disappointment, of frustration; he didn't know this one, either. The boy was young and blue-eyed, and he seemed woefully slender, immature, to be driving a bus.

Danny got down from the bus with his bags and went around to the back, where the boy was unlocking the baggage compartment. He lifted his bags into the place and watched while the driver slammed the door and secured it with a wrench. The boy turned and said, casually, "You're Danny Gray from Buxton, ain't you?"

"Yes — yes, I am," Danny stammered in surprise.

"I guess you've forgotten me since you've been away from here," the boy said. "I'm Stockton Midgett."

"Why, Stockton!" Danny exclaimed, holding out his hand. "Gosh, you've grown! How long have you been driving the bus?"

"Haven't grown much — just three years older, I reckon. Been drivin' since the Army took Anderson. Somebody had to drive."

"So Anderson's in the Army!"

"Yeah," the boy said. And then he added, "Your mama will sure be glad to see you — she's always on the porch when I pass there goin' down. Most of the time Jerry's out in the yard. He's a'most grown. Guess we'd better get goin' if we're goin' to make the three-o'clock ferry."

When they were back in the bus, the boy surveyed his passengers briefly. One or two of them started to take out their wallets, but he waved them aside. He said he'd collect when they were crossing the Inlet, and to the passenger across the aisle from the driver's seat he said, "How about movin' back

there so Danny can sit up here in front?" The passenger moved
and the boy slid under the wheel.

"How old are you now, Stockton?" Danny asked when the
bus backed out into the street.

"Sixteen," the boy said briefly. His arms seemed awfully
slender, Danny thought. He saw lithe muscles tense along his
forearm as he hauled the big steering wheel around. The bus
gained headway. The boy lighted a cigarette and settled himself against the cushions. He drove with casual, effortless ease.

At the end of the long causeway across Roanoke Sound,
where the paved highway swings northward in a wide, sweeping curve, the bus continued toward the beach. There was no
sound of clashing gears when the driver put it into second gear
to negotiate the deep-rutted trail lifting across the ridge of
sand. The engine complained but the lumbering bus went
steadily forward. "Never let her lose headway," Danny remembered — the cardinal rule for driving the sand of the Outer
Banks.

Among the passengers in the seats back of him Danny Gray
could sense a feeling of tense uneasiness, of apprehension.
That makes them strangers to this sort of traveling, he
thought. He could almost feel them holding their breath in
the long moment when the bus labored through the sand at
the crest of the low ridge. The boy drove placidly, one arm
casually along the rim of the steering wheel, the other along
the sill of the open window. The wind twisted the smoke from
the cigarette that drooped in the boy's fingers.

Danny could almost feel the exhaled breath of the passengers in the seats back of him when the bus came through the
sand and its wheels touched the smooth hardness of the open
beach. The tide, he saw with an accustomed glance, would be
dead low by the time they reached the Inlet. Seeming scarcely
to move his hands, the driver shifted into high gear and the
fat tires sang against the wet sand.

Now and then a thinning wave raced through its own foam

to snap at the tires of the bus. Sometimes the boy would avoid it by a quick turn of the wheel, and again he would let it snap. Then a thin spray veiled the windows for a moment. Never, Danny thought, had he seen the ocean quite so smooth, or quite this shade of blue — this color of blue, he corrected his thinking; people didn't think of shades of colors, but colors of color . . . down here.

Nowhere in all the sky was there any least dot of a cloud, and the wind itself was resting somewhere beyond the horizon. Save for the ripple of the surf in the ebbing tide, there was no movement in the water anywhere — except yonder, where a porpoise played tag with its mate. Offshore there were a half dozen fatback boats smudging the clean blue of the sky with the exhaust from their engines; and, nearer by, there was a purple patch, oily and slick, where a school of fatback were moving southward. Now and then light flashed when the sun caught a leaping bluefish or a small shark feeding on these oily pariahs of the sea.

Danny relaxed against the thin cushion of his seat and looked ahead of the rolling bus. The beach flowed evenly toward them and under them. On the right, low ridges of sand, studded now and then with sea oats beginning to turn brown, stood immobile in the windless sunlight. On the left, the ocean reached off to the horizon, placid and blue, mixed with the faint green of — of Judy's eyes, and, far out, with the gray blue — of Sally Tillett's eyes.

Lucky to catch the tide right, Danny thought. With the tide out and the beach smooth, twenty minutes would be enough to make the ferry nine miles down the beach. If they had had to drive the inside road, which was not much more than a trail, deep-rutted and sandy, it would have taken a good hour to make it, and below the Inlet it would have been worse. This way, Danny calculated . . . cross the Inlet by three-twenty, stops maybe at Rodanthe, at Salvo, Waves and Avon . . . ought to be home by five o'clock or anyhow by five-thirty.

The boy drove with casual concentration. Now and then he glanced out across the water, but never was he unaware of what was immediately ahead, measuring and appraising every foot of the beach ahead of him, at once alert and relaxed, his reflexes attuned to every changing texture of the sand. Once the bus slowed, for no reason that was apparent to any of the passengers except Danny. The boy slid it into second gear, and in a moment it was out of and beyond a soft spot in the beach.

Ahead loomed the silhouette of an automobile, standing still against the luminous haze above the sand. Beside it were two figures, both in blue enlisted men's uniforms. The rear wheels of the car were buried below their hubcaps in the soft, yielding sand. The bus slowed, passed a little way beyond the foundered car, stopped. The driver glanced over his shoulder but said nothing. He pulled the lever that opened the door. The passengers scrambled out and went back toward the car.

Danny Gray got down from the bus and the driver followed him. There were, of course, enough others to pick the half-buried car up by its fenders and carry it to firm beach but, Danny reminded himself, nobody ever sat still while anybody else was in difficulty. It was just not — procedure. You got out and pushed, whether you were actually needed or not. The car, old and decrepit, was evidently something that these fellows were bringing back from some adventure, and they were not used to driving the beach.

And so Danny leaned his weight against the back of the car in accordance with what is customary along the Outer Banks, and presently the vehicle wheezed and groaned its way out of the watery sand and lumbered off. Its driver waved his thanks and went on his way. Stockton Midgett, lighting another cigarette, said casually that the beach was always tricky along here when the tide was this low. They climbed back aboard and the bus got under way.

Cap'n Toby Tillett's shallow-draft "Barcelonia" — he had added the extra letter in the spelling of his ferry's name out of sheer exuberant generosity — was waiting, its landing ramp set in the white sand at the edge of the little mooring basin.

"Well, you made it in good time," he greeted Stockton Midgett cheerfully when the bus lumbered aboard the ferry. "Good drivin' beach today." The driver smiled and turned to face down the aisle. Danny Gray took a crisp (the Army always gave you brand-new money) bill from his wallet and held it toward the boy. The driver appeared not to have seen it and continued his way toward the end of the aisle, collecting fares, making change, without a word. He seemed to know where each passenger was going. He came back up the aisle and again Danny proffered his fare. Again the boy seemed not to have seen it.

"Here's my ticket money, Stockton," Danny said.

"Ain't chargin' you nothin' to bring you home," the boy said. He glanced, a little self-consciously, at Danny and turned to the open door of the bus.

Danny got down and, when he had lighted a cigarette, stood for a moment on the deck of the ferry, looking about him. Things were changed . . . and yet they were not changed at all. Here the currents had altered the contours of the shore a little, cut off a corner there and hauled it around to here. He glanced southward. Yonder, across the Inlet, was the familiar silhouette of the Station a mile below the ferry landing, and beyond it, stretching beneath a shining canopy of haze that hangs always above the beach when the sun is shining in a clear sky, the Outer Banks. . . . Yonder was home.

From the pilothouse Cap'n Toby Tillett surveyed the deck below him. Glancing up, Danny saw that here was something else that had not changed. Cap'n Toby's face was broad and smiling, shrewd and kindly, as he had always known it . . . as he had remembered it, he didn't know how many times, in the great loneliness that he had known above strange seas . . . in that other world he was coming back from. He called out, "Hi,

Cap'n Toby!" Cap'n Toby glanced down, and then he stared.

"God bless my soul!" he exclaimed.

Then the skipper of the ferry disappeared from sight. In a moment he came around the pilothouse, both hands extended. His voice shook a little.

"Danny Gray! I liked not to have known you — it's been a long time since you've rode across here with me, boy. How you been farin', Danny?"

Cap'n Toby turned to the bus driver with feigned accusation.

"Stockton, why didn't you tell me you had Dan Gray's boy on here?" He turned back to Danny. "It's time for us to go — you come on up in the pilothouse." He turned to Pam Gallup. "Come here, Pam, and see who we've got aboard." The mate, who seemed to Danny to look more than ever like one of the seven dwarfs in "Snow White," came and held out his hand, smiling wordlessly.

When he had backed the ferry out of the narrow slip and swung around into the devious channel, Cap'n Toby said, "I been hearin' about you and I been thinkin' about you a lot. I know your daddy would be mighty proud of you if —" He hesitated, fell silent. Danny leaned against the window ledge, looking out across the width of the Inlet.

"Thanks, Cap'n Toby," Danny said.

"Saw your picture in the paper the other night — wife showed it to me when I got home."

Danny smiled a little and returned to his contemplation of the shining width of the Inlet.

"Tide's low and I got to take the long way across," the ferryman said, "but we'll make it. May be a little late but you ought to be home before dark."

"It's good to be home," Danny said after a while.

"I guess you've seen a lot since the last time you rode across here with me."

"I even saw you the other day, Cap'n Toby," Danny said, "and it was a good sight to see, even if you didn't look up when I passed over."

"You must have been in that big one that passed here four or five days ago — were you flyin' it yourself, Danny?"

"Not when I passed here, Cap'n — I'd turned it over to the copilot so I'd have nothing to do but look. We had an hour to kill before we were due in Washington and I thought I'd come by and look at home."

"How long you goin' to be down, Danny?"

"I wish I knew, Cap'n. I've got ninety days' leave and I'll be here that long, anyhow. I've got a chance to stay in the Army, and in some ways I'd like it a lot. I like to fly. But I like it down here, too. I didn't know how much until I got away. I wonder if anybody ever gets over being homesick when he gets away from here?"

"The good ones don't, Danny. This country's in your blood. Why, I remember like it was yesterday when your daddy and mammy come across here with me, the first time. They'd just got married and they were on the way to Norfolk or somewhere. . . . You ain't as big as your daddy, Danny — not yet, anyhow. But you look like him."

"I guess Jerry got Daddy's size — from the glimpse of him I got the other day when I flew over down there."

Cap'n Toby's smile was pleased.

"Sure enough!" he exclaimed. "He don't seem to be much for travelin' around — don't remember that he's been across here with me since . . . . Maybe you don't remember it, Danny, but I left Pam here to run the ferry and I went down there the day they brought your daddy ashore. Jerry was a little feller. But that's been three years ago — more'n that.

"I went out there on the beach where they brung him ashore, Danny. It was not just curiosity. Your daddy was my friend — I knew him all my life. There was blood on the beach where they laid him down. Maybe I'm mixed up and sound like an old fool, but that ground down there ain't just ground and it can't never be . . . not to you. It's got your blood on it and you belong to it. . . . I talk too damned much, Danny."

"Not too much for me, Cap'n Toby. I did know you were there that day. I saw what you saw in the sand. I've never found any words for it, but I guess that's what has been pulling me back here. Partly, anyhow."

"You'll find it just like you left it, Danny. People come out from down there. I haul 'em across this Inlet and they go on up yonder and hit that paved road. It rides good to 'em, but they always come back, and the country down there don't change. There's some sort of a spell on it, I reckon — what was it that feller wrote in the paper? 'En —' "

" 'Enchantment,' Cap'n Toby? I didn't know you had read it."

"My wife read it to me. Yes, that's it. And whatever it is — well, Danny, I know your mammy and all the rest of 'em down there are goin' to be mighty proud to see you, but there ain't none of 'em any gladder'n I am."

By now the little ferry was nearing the south shore of the Inlet, and seemingly Cap'n Toby had forgotten that Danny Gray was even aboard the craft. He was intent upon his approach through the strong current of the outflowing tide. The ferry nudged the shore gently and Pam went forward to let down the landing ramp. Danny Gray unbuttoned the flap of the breast pocket of his blouse and turned it up until it hid the silver spread of his pilot's wings. He took out the flat leather case.

"Here's something I'm taking home to my mother, Cap'n Toby," Danny said. "I thought she'd be the first one to see it, but I know she would — and Daddy would, too — want you to see it."

Cap'n Toby looked at the cross, shining against the white lining of the case. Danny unfolded the citation that accompanied it.

"You read it to me, Danny — my wife does all my readin' and there's somethin' wrong with my eyes right now."

Danny read him the essential part of the citation. Stockton Midgett was backing the bus off the ferry, and the passengers were crowding toward it.

"He deserved it, Danny. And you got one like it, didn't you?"

"Yeah, sort of, Cap'n, but — but I didn't —"

"Well, you would have if your number had been up. Go on home to your mammy, now. And Danny," Cap'n Toby's voice was almost stern, "you'd not have been afraid any more than he was."

"I might not have been afraid, Cap'n Toby," Danny said, his tone half jocular, "but I was sure scared as hell the times it looked like it might be up."

Cap'n Toby's smile broadened across his kindly face.

"So long, Danny, and tell your mammy howdy for me. And bring that Jerry up here sometime and let me look at him."

Two passengers for the Station nearest the Inlet left the bus and climbed aboard the Station's jeep, leaving the bus free to swing out toward the beach instead of laboring through the sandy trail. The tide was at dead low water and the beach was as hard as any runway that Danny could remember. Set a Twenty-nine down here without any trouble — landed 'em in worse places than this, he mused. The tires sang against the sand and Danny watched the speedometer's hand climb around the dial: forty . . . fifty. . . . It wouldn't be long now.

Danny leaned forward in his seat, his forearms along the rail that ran from the door to the aisle. His cap was in the seat beside him, and the wind, rushing in through the open panel in the door, tumbled his bright hair over his eyes. Something, he hadn't quite known what, had come over him . . . back there on the ferry. All the tenseness had ebbed out of his muscles. . . . Maybe it was talking to Cap'n Toby.

Pea Island Station rushed at them and Danny was so intent watching for it that he missed the old, rusting hulk of a Yankee gunboat that had, for eighty years, been sort of a landmark and milepost along the beach. The bus stopped and a young Negro, smartly uniformed, came from the back of the vehicle. Danny, not recalling his name for the moment but knowing him, spoke to him. The boy smiled broadly.

"Good to see you back down this way, Danny — excuse me, Sir, I mean Captain Gray."

Danny grinned.

"It's still Danny Gray down here and I'm glad to see you, Marshall," he said. "That's a smart uniform you've got."

"Thank you, Sir — we try to keep 'em that way at our station."

The men in uniform on the seats behind him, Danny knew, stirred with curious interest and eyed him with renewed, amended speculation.

Off Chicamicomico the bus turned in from the beach, put off three passengers at the Station, and continued past it to the little weather-beaten store. The driver's mother waved from the door, and Danny, when he recognized her, knew that the years of the war had laid their weight upon her. She seemed older. He got down and went over to her.

"I'm Danny Gray from Buxton," he said.

"Why, you've grown up so, Danny," she said in pleased surprise. "It's been three years since you passed here, hasn't it?" Danny visited with her while Stockton refilled the radiator. The trip, so far, had made little demand upon the bus, but — well, you could never tell how it would be by the time you got to Hatteras.

There were no passengers for the next two villages that almost adjoin Rodanthe to the south. The bus swung back toward the beach again, and Danny leaned forward, noting that here, where the old wreck had lain for as long as he could remember, a storm had tossed it higher on the beach. . . . That hurricane last year, he surmised. . . . The burned-out hulk of the "Kohler" still lay embedded in the wash of the beach, and the bus had to slow and get into low gear for the climb to the top of the bank to pass it.

At Avon the old lady and the little boy got off. Ten miles, now. . . .

It had always been a sort of a game that his father had played with him, and with Jerry, when they drove down the beach — who would be the first to sight the Lighthouse. When Jerry had grown big enough to take part in their game, he had been awfully cocky about it, Danny remembered.

How far away the Light could be spotted depended a good deal on the sun. On a good day Danny had seen it from as far as seventeen miles, halfway between Rodanthe and Avon. Strange, Danny thought now, how the Light seemed to dominate the life of everybody who lived within range of it. On the other side of the world he had mentioned, sometimes, that he was born in the shadow of Hatteras Light, and somebody would speak up, somebody who had seen it from far out at sea, or had flown past it, or had seen pictures of it. . . . There was not a place anywhere in all Buxton Woods, no matter how dense the growth, from which the Light could not be seen.

Danny's eyes strained eagerly ahead now, through the waning light of the October sun. The bus was almost empty now and Stockton Midgett had, somehow, withdrawn into himself. Danny felt almost as if he were coming home utterly alone.

"There she is," the driver said suddenly.

There it was. . . . There was the Lighthouse and, almost within its shadow but hidden beyond the vaulting live oaks, beyond the dunes over which the yoepon spread its matted protection against the wind and the sea, there was home. Danny's fingers closed around the little disc that lay in his pocket, against his thigh. . . . In a moment, now, they would pass ... they would pass over the spot where they had laid his father when he ... when the tide brought him home. ...

Now the tide was flowing again. The little thin tongues of foaming water thrust along the sand were reaching up, and when the boy slowed the bus as he approached the turn through the ridge of sand, water splashed against its sides and Danny knew there was salt in the drop that flecked his cheek and dried there. The sea was changing from blue to deep purple — to the color of purple.

Although he had come this way, he supposed, a thousand times in his life, there was for Danny Gray an unending wonder at the change these few hundred feet always made. They divided the world into two parts. Along the Banks the narrow beach was treeless, barren except for here and there a clump of myrtle or of yoepon, and tough beach grass. The sand moved, tireless, with the wind, almost like the desert sands over which Danny had flown in Africa.

But when the bus, protesting its labor with loud groans, cut across the rutted ridge, floundering a little despite the expertness of its driver, the world changed with a suddenness that was a continuing miracle to Danny. He had never been so conscious of it as now, after three years ... three years that were, after all, one-seventh of all the years he had lived.

Nothing was changed. The yoepon-studded dunes stood off the wind and the sea, shutting out even the muffled rumbling of the surf that pounded endlessly beyond the Light, where the Cape thrust its blunt finger. Great live oaks, their limbs arched above the narrow road, reminded Danny of the battered arches of a cathedral he had seen somewhere in Italy. The waning light came down through the leaves, as it had come through the holes in the roof of that vast church. The tires of the bus were silent in the soft yielding sand, and its engine was almost idling, almost soundless.

A pair of wood duck, with a brief whirring of wings, rose up from the marsh and were momentarily limned against the glowing sky. Immemorial quiet brooded above the Woods and something of it flowed, like a flooding tide, through Danny's veins, through his muscles. His fingers relaxed around the little flat disc, and it lay, warm, against the palm of his hand.

For an instant Stockton Midgett held his left hand poised above the horn button in the center of the steering wheel as if he were about to break the stillness with a heralding blast. He thought better of it and let his hand fall loosely along his left thigh.

"Thought I'd let 'em know you were comin'," he said, "but I guess they know it anyhow. Your mother will be there on the front steps, and Jerry'll be halfway down to the road, just lookin'."

8

JERRY'S VOICE WAS AN ASSURED, ALMOST MAN-TIMBRED BARI-
tone when he called from the deck chair beside the oleander
that the bus was coming, but a moment later it slipped its
moorings and foundered in crosscurrents of excitement when
he undertook to add, "Gee, Mom, it's slowing down." He
scrambled to his feet and started toward the house.

Halfway to the front porch he fell sprawling, and by the
time he had gathered his arms and legs together and restored
some orderliness of purpose among them, Polly Gray was on
the front steps. She was wiping her hands, hastily, on her
apron. Jerry got up and stood beside her as the bus came
nearer, slowing down. It was moving so slow Jerry knew it was
going to stop.

"It's him, Mom, it's him! I can see him."

Jerry's voice was almost a whisper. He wanted to run, to
jump clear over the low hedge of palmetto palms, but somehow his big feet had taken root where they were, in the gravel
of the walk where nothing grew. He stared, transfixed and
motionless, as the bus drew to a halt before the gap in the
hedge, the gap where they had intended to put a gate, a gate
with clean whitewash on it. . . .

The bus stopped, its entrance door even with the gap in
the row of palmetto palms. The door opened and, without
waiting for his passenger, the driver slid out of his seat and
was on the ground. He did not glance toward the house as he

went to the back of the bus, opened the baggage compartment, and took out the two bags. He closed the door and came with the bags and set them down in the sand. With a brief "So long" to Danny he got back into the bus, closed the door without a sound, and was gone.

Danny Gray stood before his father's house and for a long moment life seemed somehow to stand still. All volition, all power of determination, had gone out of his legs, his arms, his voice even; only his eyes held on to reality. Up the walk, not more than ten paces away, were his mother, his brother; around them and beyond them were the yard, the familiar house; and he could not, in that moment, move toward them nor cry out to them.

Nor did Polly Gray or Jerry move toward him or cry out to him. They, like himself, were caught in this fleeting moment when life and time stood still about them. None of them could have ever measured, by a watch's time, the moment's length, nor could any of them have said with any sureness which of them moved first. Danny came up the walk, slowly, as one in a dream; and his mother and his brother came down toward him, walking a little apart from each other. A small warm smile lay, like a shadow, against the corner of Polly Gray's half-parted mouth.

Life came back into Danny's arms when he came within reach of his mother and his brother. An arm was around Polly Gray's shoulder and around Jerry's and their arms were around him. They stood there in the gathering twilight. Polly Gray's cheek lay against Danny's. She did not kiss him. Her arms reached across the shoulders of both her sons and drew them.

It was Jerry's voice, eager, urgent, that lifted the enchantment, brought them back to the world where Danny's ticking watch measured time, where the dusk gathered and a high-riding moon slid down the sky from its meridian, a world in which lighted lamps beckoned them toward the house and beyond, where kitchen smells enticed them. Jerry jerkily disengaged himself from the triple embrace that held them.

"Say, let's see that medal they give you, Danny — did you bring it home — and did you bring me one of them swords they gut theirselves with?"

Danny's smile was indulgent, big-brotherly, even though Jerry had grown astonishingly big. Their eyes, when they met, were on a level. Jerry was tall, but his gawky frame still needed a lot of filling out before he got his growth, Danny saw. His hands and feet were tremendous, and something ought to be done with that darkening fuzz that made the sides of his face look like they needed scrubbing.

"Yeah, I got some stuff," Danny said, "but it's out there in my bags. How about lending a hand with one of them, big boy?"

"Heck, I can tote both of 'em," Jerry said. "You and Mom go on in the house."

Jerry went down the walk at a trot and Polly Gray and Danny went toward the house. When she was at the top of the steps she turned to watch Jerry coming up the walk, his shoulders sagging only a little under the weight of the two bags. She held the door of the screened porch open while he sidled through, managing to bump each bag against the door post.

"Where you want me to put 'em, Mom?" Jerry inquired.

"Why — I just hadn't thought, Jerry."

Polly Gray looked from one to the other of her sons. Not until now had it come quite home to her that they were not any longer her two little boys, sharing the same room, the same bed. They were grown up now, and in all her anticipation of having Danny come home it had not once occurred to her that one bed might not be big enough for both. Polly Gray felt a sense of shocked dismay.

Jerry set the heavy bags down, waiting for his mother to speak. He sensed her irresolution, but Danny had missed it altogether, preoccupied with looking around this room that was

so familiar. Nothing had been changed, except for that photograph of himself in its frame on the table. Polly Gray's
troubled, uncertain glance went past Jerry to the half-opened
doors of the two bedrooms. The door of her own room opened
off the other end of the living room.

"Heck — he ain't company," Jerry said. "He's goin' to sleep
with me same as he's always done. He ain't so big."

"Well, you boys settle it between yourselves." Polly Gray's
smile was relieved. "I've got to get back to the kitchen — I can
smell the chicken almost ready to burn."

Jerry carried the bags to his room and Danny followed his
mother to the kitchen.

"What's for supper, Mama? Coming home or something
has made me hungry as a shark. Got me a cake?"

It was Jerry who answered. "Naw, ain't no cake — but we
got a lemon pie."

Polly Gray, anxious over her supper and not a little flustered
at the presence of two kitchen-filling, grown-up men, said,
"You boys run along and get ready — I'll have supper in just
a little. Danny, you'll want to wash up, won't you, and Jerry
— look at your hands! I declare, I don't believe you've washed
behind your ears this whole week!"

Jerry grinned his disarming grin.

"Come on, Danny," he said. "Want to take a shower? We
got a shower bath now — hot water'n everything. Bill Henry
gave it to me. One they were throwin' away out at the Station,
out of them barracks they built for all them fellers they
brought down here right after you left. He showed me some
about how to fix it, but I done most of it myself. Come on —
how about a shower?"

Danny shook his head but went with Jerry toward the bathroom, washed his hands, and stood by while Jerry scrubbed
his neck and poked at his ears.

"Mom's always after me about my neck — sometimes I

wish I'd been hatched without one," he said thickly through his soapy hands.

"Training for the House of David or something, Jerry?" Danny demanded, running a forefinger along Jerry's fuzzy cheek.

"Oh, them?" Jerry said blandly. "Guess I'll have to cut 'em off one of these nights — say, you got an extra razor, Danny, one I could have for my own? I sent off after one when I dam' near cut my dam' head off tryin' to use Daddy's old straight razor one time, but they wrote back and said they didn't have any right then. Looks like Mom's 'wish book's' just a list of things they don't have now."

"You can use mine until we can do better," Danny promised. Jerry's easy fluency with mild profanity was a little disconcerting . . . and not a little remindful of the Chief.

"Gee, that'll be swell," Jerry said with the air of one newly come upon a solution for one of life's major perplexities. "Say, what's that purplish ribbon for?"

"That? Oh, that's for a — just something they give you if you get scratched up."

"Purple Heart — you mean wounded, don't you?"

Danny nodded, trying to make it seem indifferent.

"Did it hurt much, Danny?"

"Just a scratch on the back of my head — no, I didn't even feel it."

"Lemme see it," Jerry urged, and Danny ducked his head forward, flinging the hair away from the scar. Jerry stood on tiptoe, exploring with his fingers. "Turn around a little so's I can see, Danny. Gee!"

Danny combed his hair back into place with a pocket comb and rolled down the sleeves of his shirt, buttoning the cuffs. He glanced at his blouse on the hook back of the door.

"Put it back on, Danny," Jerry said earnestly. "Just for supper, anyhow. Mom's never said anything, but I got a notion she'd like to have you all dressed up. Mom's funny, maybe. You didn't notice it because you ain't been here, but she's set the table herself and she's put a plate where Daddy used to sit. Ain't been no plate there since — since — hell, you know." Jerry's voice was rough.

"Okay, Jerry," Danny said. "How about holding it for me?"

Jerry held the blouse and Danny thrust his arms through the sleeves. Jerry surveyed him with veiled admiration and then looked at himself in the mirror.

"Goddammittohell — look at me!" he exclaimed. "I got to get out of here and put me on some clothes or Mom'll make me eat on the back steps — if she feeds me at all."

Jerry fled toward the bedroom, and when he appeared at the supper table his unruly blond hair was slicked down and he wore a clean shirt, gay with all sorts of fantastic animals. Danny Gray sat in his father's chair at the table.

"Will you say the grace, Danny?" Polly Gray's eyes were half smiling, half sad.

Danny felt an excruciating moment of self-consciousness, and he glanced unhappily at Jerry, at his mother. Jerry's face was stolidly immobile; his mother's tranquil, trustful, reassuring. Danny bowed his head, doubting whether he could remember how it went, how the simple grace that his father used to say was worded. Then it came back to him. . . .

Polly Gray had fried a chicken, and there was rice, fluffy and soft, not soggy, to take the brown gravy. There were red-ripe tomatoes and tender black-eyed peas, the last she would have this year from the garden beyond the fig trees. There were a few leaves of crisply green lettuce and the season's last snapdragons. The garden and the flower beds had been good this year, lasting until Danny was home.

"Who gets the other piece of pie, Mom?" Jerry demanded before he had swallowed the last mouthful of his initial share.

"Why, you and Danny can divide it, can't you?"

Jerry managed what he considered a suitably sacrificial sigh.

"Aw, he can have it all. I'm sort of full already. I'll fetch it."

Polly Gray smiled a pleased, secret smile. Here, she knew, was the ultimate expression of her youngest's awkward, inarticulate adoration of this brother who had come home. Jerry brought the plate and set it before his brother. He gathered up the plates and empty dishes and carried them, noisily but without breaking any, into the kitchen. He removed the coffee cups after asking Danny if he would have some more. When he finally came back and tumbled into his chair, the white cloth was clear except for Danny's pie plate and the bowl of snapdragons. He planted his elbows on the table, rested his chin in his cupped hands, and watched the pie disappear, down to the last crumb.

"What you got in your pocket, Danny?" Jerry demanded when Danny pushed his empty plate away and lighted a cigarette. "This pocket." Jerry tapped himself on the breast with a finger tip. "The one that's all bulged out."

Danny's fingers trembled a little as he started to unfasten the buttoned flap of the pocket and as he tugged at the slender case that fitted neatly inside. Jerry and Polly Gray watched him in silence, the boy's eyes widening when he saw the dull leather of the case. Danny laid the case on the table.

"It's yours, Mama — yours and Jerry's. I guess you heard about it."

Danny's thumb pressed the hidden latch and the case opened under his hand. The ceiling light fell upon the glowing cross when he withdrew the folded paper. He let it lie there a moment, halfway between Jerry and his mother, doubting whether to pass it to his mother first or to Jerry. This boy, he thought, is amazingly perceptive about things. Danny resolved his hesitation and picked up the case as he arose from the table.

"Come over here, Jerry," he said, "and you sit still, Mama."

Jerry got up slowly from the table and came around to stand at his mother's left shoulder, and from her right Danny leaned over and placed the open case between them. He unfolded the citation and laid it on the cloth.

In silence and utter stillness, each of them read the citation through. Jerry shifted his weight from one foot to the other. Polly Gray's hands, until now folded in her lap, came up, trembled as they reached toward the shining cross. The tips of her fingers almost touched it, but she drew back her hand and sat, silent. Jerry wondered, uneasily, if she were going to cry again.

Polly Gray did not cry. Her voice was steady when, after a while, she said softly, "We must take good care of it. It was good of them to — to think that way — about your father. We must take good care of it and — and live up to it."

She stood up, resting her hand on the back of the chair, but her eyes still brooded upon the shining thing in the white-lined case. She picked it up slowly and handed it to Jerry. He took it and, after a little, closed the cover of the case.

"You got one just like it, didn't you, Danny? Where is it?"

"Oh, mine looks just like it," Danny said, his voice not quite registering the casualness that he intended. He un-buttoned his blouse, took it off, and tossed it carelessly toward a chair beyond the door of the living room.

"We'll look at mine after we've washed these dishes, big boy," Danny went on, addressing Jerry. "Let's see if you are in good standing as a dishwasher. Mama, you go and get your-self pretty — somebody might come in and there's a smudge of flour under your ear. Come on, Jerry, let's get this done and I'll show you something I brought you all the way from yonder."

Jerry grinned and went toward the kitchen.

9

THEY WERE AN UNCOMMONLY LONG TIME WASHING THE DISHES,
it seemed to Polly Gray. From the living room, after she had
washed her hands and tidied her hair, she could hear them,
their voices — mostly Jerry's — coming blurred and softened
through the closed kitchen door. Now and then Jerry's exuberant, uneven laughter rocketed above the murmur of their
voices.

Polly Gray felt a twinge of fleeting loneliness, of being left
out of this comfortable partnership; and once an impulse
urged her toward the kitchen, to go out and join them, but
she put it out of her mind. She would not think of going to
the kitchen to see if they were leaving it as she would leave it,
each plate and cup in its proper place, all the knives, the forks,
the spoons in their separate compartments in the neat cupboard Daniel Gray had built.

That would not be Polly Gray's way; when she left Jerry —
or when she had left Danny — with a task, she let him feel
that it was his task, his responsibility. That was something
that she had learned from her father, a lesson that living with
Daniel Gray had confirmed: give a man a job to do and let
him — never make him — do it.

It never occurred to Polly Gray to think that there was anything unusual in the fact that her menfolks were, as they said,
handy around the house. They could cook or scrub, if it were
needed, if they wanted to do it, or if there was no other thing
in their man's world — the sea's world — that demanded them.

It was a part of their seafaring heritage. Behind them were centuries of ships and the sea, generations of service, of experience, in lonely stations or ships, each a little world in itself where floors had to be scrubbed, where kitchens had to be kept.

Polly Gray put away her momentary feeling of loneliness, busied herself around the room, straightening a chair here, putting away a rumpled newspaper. The door between the kitchen and dining room opened and she turned expectantly. The boys were still out of sight. She heard water running from the tap above the sink, gurgling in the drain. And then Jerry's voice again.

" 'Wash hands together, friends forever' the old sayin' goes, Captain," Jerry was saying. "What do you reckon your men would think if they was to see you a-washin' of dishes and a-washin' of your hands with a common person that don't even wear shoes? Gosh, Danny, you ought to have seen how stuck-up some of them young squirts that called theirselves ensigns were! Wouldn't hardly speak to anybody, and Bill Henry would mighty near puke when he had to look at 'em. Say, Danny, a captain is higher'n an ensign, ain't he? I mean a captain in the Army?"

"Yeah," Danny said briefly. "How about letting me have one end of that towel?"

"Sure, Captain — excuse me," Jerry said with mock humility. "It's all yours. Say, Danny, there's some of that second piece of Mom's pie on the end of your nose. Here, gimme that towel — now it's off. My, ain't that scandalous! A captain with fifteen medals leakin' pie at the nose!"

Polly Gray heard the sound of brief scuffling beyond the door, and then both her boys came toward her, the younger with an arm across the older's shoulder. A great contentment welled up from somewhere deep inside. Danny, quiet, strangely mature, in some surprising ways almost old; Jerry, ebullient, young — young like a kitten, Polly mused. Lately, since he had started to grow so astonishingly, he had been increasingly morose sometimes, withdrawn, aloofly meditative. But now his face was alight, impishly happy.

"I do believe he has missed Danny even more than I have," Polly murmured to herself. Jerry took his arm from around Danny's shoulder and gave him a little shove.

"You sit over there in Daddy's chair, Captain — you're the big man around this house now."

Danny sat down in his father's chair and Jerry went to the bedroom, reappearing a moment later with Danny's bags. He lugged them across the room and set them down, one on each side of Danny's chair. He stood back, his feet planted wide apart on the deerskin rug, his flattened palms against his hips with thumbs hooked in his belt.

"Now, Danny, let's see what you brung home from yonder."

"Spoken like the beachcomber you were born to be." Danny laughed and, leaning over, tugged at the fastenings of the older of the two bags. Jerry sat down, cross-legged, on the rug. He scrambled up and shoved his mother's chair over beside Danny's.

"Sit down, Mom," he directed her and then settled himself on the rug, his face turned upward toward Danny.

"Now you just hold your oar, pirate," Danny said. "Santa Claus will get around to you after a while if you are a good little boy."

Danny took a flat, paper-wrapped parcel from the bag and passed it to his mother.

"Here's a piece of cloth I got for you, Mama," he said simply. "I thought it might make you a right pretty dress."

Polly Gray slowly unwrapped the package, being careful with the string that bound it, and with the paper.

"I thought you'd look nice in it; I don't believe I've ever seen you with a silk dress, have I, Mama?"

"Oh, Danny," Polly Gray's voice came in a soft whisper. The shimmering sapphire cloth fell across her lap and her hands caressed its soft folds. She held it up against the light, held a fold of it across her breast.

"Danny! It's — it's just like — there was one time, before you were born — your father and I were in Norfolk and he wanted me to buy cloth enough for a dress. It was — just like this."

"Didn't you get it, Mom?" Jerry demanded, breaking the little silence that had fallen.

"No, Jerry," Polly Gray said slowly, remembering. "We bought the bed in your room, instead."

"You really like it, Mama?"

"Yes, Danny," Polly Gray answered softly.

"Here's some stuff you can wear with it, maybe," Danny continued. "I swapped cigarettes for it."

Polly Gray opened the fragile package and held the delicately carved bit of ivory in her hands.

"I'm not sure where it came from — must be Chinese. The Nips didn't seem to be so good with that sort of work."

Danny turned back to the bag.

"Most of the rest of this stuff is just a lot of junk that I picked up here and there," Danny went on. He took a longer parcel from the bag, displacing another, the observant Jerry noted, that was the same size and shape as the one that had the blue silk in it. "This, you blood-thirsty brigand," Danny said to Jerry, "is for you."

The short sturdy blade of the sword glittered as brightly as its jeweled handle. Jerry tried the edge of it with his thumb, whistled softly, and hefted the weight of it. He was strangely silent. Danny handed him another, somewhat longer, parcel.

"I traded that out of a fellow who had been through Guadalcanal," Danny said. Jerry unwrapped it and held the small rifle in his hands, sighting along the barrel. "I've got some ammunition for it somewhere around here," Danny went on a little doubtfully.

"And the rest of this stuff is mostly junk — flags, some of

their money that isn't any good, and stuff like that. You can have it, Jerry," Danny said. He dropped it in Jerry's lap and pushed the depleted bag away with his foot.

"Where're your medals, Danny?" Jerry demanded suddenly.

"Oh, they're here somewhere," Danny said, almost too carelessly. "They're in this box — Mama, you and Jerry can sort them out and put them somewhere out of the way."

Jerry laid aside the rifle and the other things that Danny had called junk and took the box in his hands. He opened it and took out the case that contained the cross and examined it minutely. He laid it on the rug beside him and turned back to the box, taking out each medal separately and studying it closely before laying it in its place on the rug. When he came to the Purple Heart he held it a longer time, looked up at his mother speculatively, and handed it to her.

"He's got a place on the back of his head, Mom — make him show it to you."

"It's just a little scratch," Danny protested.

"There's more ribbons on your coat than there is medals here," Jerry commented presently.

"Campaign ribbons," Danny said briefly.

"Gosh, you sure did get around for a poor Outer Banks boy," Jerry said. "What's in that other package you got there — the one you didn't open?"

"Oh, that?" Danny said, flushing a little. "That's just another piece of cloth like Mama's, only a different color."

"Who's it for? Who'd you bring it to?" Jerry persisted.

"Jerry!" Polly Gray interposed. "You ask too many questions."

Jerry continued to gaze directly into his brother's face. Danny averted his eyes.

"Sally Tillett?" Jerry's voice was dogged, insistent.

Without waiting for any answer Jerry swept the decorations back into their box, picked up the small rifle, the sword, and the other things from the floor. He turned on the light in his bedroom and Polly Gray and Danny could see him laying his trophies neatly on the blue counterpane of the bed. He looked at them, one by one, and then, picking up the ceremonial sword, turned off the light. He had the sword in his hand when he came back to the living room.

"Mom, I got to go up to the store a minute. Can I bring you anything?" He ignored Danny.

"Not a thing that I can think of, Jerry," Polly Gray replied. "You won't be gone long, will you?" Jerry mumbled a negative and went out through the front door.

"What on earth do you suppose is eating on him?" Danny demanded in some bewilderment when the door had closed behind Jerry. "Did I say something wrong, or isn't he satisfied with what I brought him?"

Polly Gray's silence, before she answered Danny's question, was thoughtful, troubled.

"There's nothing wrong, Danny — I'm sure of that. He's been something of a puzzle these last few months. He is moody, short-tempered sometimes, and then he is the sweetest, most thoughtful thing you could imagine. It's the period he's going through, and I try to be patient with him. He's so much like his father was when he was that age."

"But what did he mean about Sally?" Danny, still puzzled, questioned. "As a matter of fact, I did bring it for her. I don't know why I didn't open it."

"That's perfectly natural, Danny — there's no reason why you should. Jerry has been strange about Sally lately. He just seems to resent her without saying why. It could be, in this — this transition time that he's in the middle of he just can't abide the idea of sharing you with anybody. You know how he's worshiped you all of his life."

"I didn't know it, really, but I'm glad you're telling me. I guess he does have it pretty tough. I know he missed Daddy a lot, more than I did because I didn't stay. . . . But what do you suppose made him run off to the store like that?"

"I'm not sure," Polly Gray said, "but if I had to guess, it would be that he couldn't wait another minute to show off. I bet that he has swaggered into the store — you noticed that he took that sword? — and by now is telling a rapt audience of two or three people how you took that thing from somebody in bloody combat . . . and I'll bet we'll hear him whistling at the top of his lungs when he comes back."

"Does he run around with anybody? Has he got a girl?"

"Of course not," Polly Gray said. "He doesn't go around with anybody in particular — that is, of his own age. I think he would spend all of his time with Bill Henry if he had his way about it, and the major ambition of his life just now is to be able to strike a match on the bottom of his foot."

Danny smiled at his mother's words. "I thought," he said presently, "that I detected something of the Chief in Jerry's expanding vocabulary."

"Oh, you mean his cussing?" Polly Gray said placidly. "Yes, I've heard him, when he thought I wasn't within range, or when he wasn't thinking of me at all, but somehow I don't mind too much. There's always been something sort of pious in Bill Henry's swearing. Not," she added quickly, "that I approve of it. Not altogether, anyway. Bill Henry has been a steadying hand for Jerry. He takes him down to the Station for boat drill."

"Maybe it's a good thing that somebody is keeping the art of rowing a boat alive," Danny conceded. "There's a lot of emphasis, right now, on air. Does Jerry have any interest in airplanes?"

"Not in the least — except for yours. I think he just tolerates them. At heart he's a surfman, and I think he would rather pull the steering oar on a lifeboat than — than fly that ship of yours, Danny."

"Just born in him, I guess," Danny commented.

"I guess it is," Polly Gray went on. "Your father was like that, except for a little while when that General was down here. He used to say that they might sink a battleship with an airplane but they'd have to call on a man with an oar in his hand to pick up the survivors."

"I've seen it happen."

Danny fell into a musing silence. Contrary to Polly Gray's prediction, there was no whistling to proclaim and to herald Jerry's return from the store. Without any warning the door suddenly opened and the bulking figure of Chief William Henry Ragland stood there. Jerry was a little ahead of him, dragging at a mighty arm and with his free hand pointing at Danny with the ceremonial sword.

"There he is, Bill Henry — just like I told you," Jerry said, his voice ringing. His eyes were alight with pride and with a deep inner glow of realization. "There's the hero himself in person — didn't I tell you?"

The big man was curiously ill at ease.

"I knew he was home, Polly," he said, "but I didn't want to come bustin' in on you the first night. This varmint here —" he gestured in Jerry's direction — "why, he even threatened to jab me with that toy sword if I didn't stop by. . . . How are you, Danny?"

"We're glad you've come, Bill Henry," Polly Gray said. "Danny and me were just talking about you and wishing you would come."

"Hi, Chief," Danny said, holding out his hand. "It's sure good to see you."

"I'm glad you're back, boy — and I wish you'd never gone off from here. Goin' to stay with us now?"

"I — I just don't know yet, Chief."

"We sure do need you, Danny," the big man went on, his voice rumbling. "The whole Service needs to be careened and her bottom scraped. They took all our fellers and sent 'em off yonder somewhere to put their armies ashore and they sent me a lot of puny fellers that don't know an oar from a bed slat — why I got one critter over yonder at the Station that I don't dare sneeze but what he thinks I've called him."

Jerry chortled. "He means that radio operator — you talked to him the other day, Danny — name's — well, they just call him 'Sneeze' for short now."

"But you must sit down, Bill Henry — my gracious, where are all our manners?" Polly Gray put in.

"Naw, he ain't got time to sit," Jerry interposed. "And anyhow, I've done explained to him that Captain Gray is terrible tired and I got to put him to bed."

"I got to get back, sure enough," Bill Henry said. "I just come out here to get off some of that damned paper work in the mail and get me some cigarettes and run into this little feller here out playin' soldier with his little sword — you didn't actually gut a feller with that, did you, Danny? It just ain't big enough to do any harm with."

Danny shook his head smilingly. It wouldn't do to be too specific in denial of any legends that Jerry might have put into circulation, inventions that were needed to supplement the weapon's material deficiencies. . . . After all, it was not much of a sword.

"Git for home, Bill Henry," Jerry urged. "Me and Danny's got to go to bed so we can talk — like we used to when we were little."

Jerry's voice was softly drawling, disarming. Looking at him, Danny thought, "Lord, how that child can turn on the charm when he wants to! When he gets his growth he will be a terror among women — and men, too. . . . There's steel in his eyes."

The Chief departed, with sulphurous reminders to Jerry of the hour of tomorrow's boat drill. "You come over, too, Danny — do you no harm to watch it sometime. There was never a better boatman than your daddy — except me."

Jerry's procedure in undressing himself was a thing of efficiency and economy. With a single movement of his hand he unbuttoned his shirt all the way down the front and loosened his belt. He wriggled his shoulders and the shirt fell off; the faded blue dungarees collapsed around his ankles. He stepped out of the puddle of clothes, and with a single backward movement of his large foot the puddle disappeared under the bed. Jerry stood naked, except for his shorts.

Danny started to say something in the way of gentle remonstrance but thought better of it. After all, the garments would be there in the morning, and hanging them on a hook somewhere or spreading them over the back of a chair would not, he reflected, contribute anything material or important to the betterment of the universe or of the garments. Danny had always been neat and methodical — and Jerry was, too, about some things. Danny remembered with what meticulous precision Jerry had stacked the dishes in the cupboard when he dried them after supper.

"How you like these shorts, Danny? Ain't they the stuff, though?" Jerry's voice bubbled. "Mom thought they were scan'lous when they come. Ordered 'em out of the 'wish book' and she thought that green and yellow mixed was just not nice for a decent little white boy . . . they're too tight, though." Jerry flexed the muscles of his thighs, drew in the muscles of his lean belly.

"They look okay to me, Jerry — and anyhow you don't wear 'em where the neighbors can see how scandalous they are."

"Yeah, but Mom, she can't hang 'em out after she washes 'em without blushin' and she always hangs 'em where nobody can see 'em when they pass by here." Jerry smiled engagingly.

Danny undressed with exemplary neatness. He took off his trousers, folded them neatly with the crease, and placed them on a hanger. Then his shirt, his shoes. He spread his socks across the tops of the shoes and set them neatly under the side of the bed. He reached in his bag and brought out a pair of pajamas. Jerry, cross-legged on the bed, watched with tolerant speculation.

"Gosh, you sleep in them things, Danny? Ain't they sort of

sissy? Me, I sleep naked, mostly, or in these here shorts. Sometimes Mom comes in here and makes me put on them things.
Say! I got a set of 'em I just got to show you. Red ones. Mom
made 'em."

Jerry crossed the room to the bureau and took out a pair of
flaming nylon pajamas. He held them up with a look of
amused disdain.

"Where on God's good earth did you get the stuff to make
them out of, Jerry?"

"Parachute," Jerry said. "There was this ship droppin' some
stuff over the beach — practicin', or somethin' like that. I was
watchin' 'em and they went off and left this one. It had somethin' tied to it, but Bill Henry took it. Said it wasn't none of
my dam' business what it was, but he said I could have the
parachute. It was tore up. Mom made me these things — you
want to sleep in 'em?"

"No thanks, Jerry — a little too fancy for a man of my
simple tastes."

"They ain't never been slept in," Jerry said. "I did put 'em
on one night but they were too dam' hot — which side you
want to sleep on? Same old side?"

"Anywhere suits me, Jerry."

"Okay, you can have the outside — say, you ain't started to
snore while you been gone, have you, Danny? If you do I'll bop
hell out of you."

Jerry moved over to the side of the bed next to the wall and
stretched out his long legs. His arms were crossed above his
head. Danny lay down on the outer side of the bed and Jerry
reached for the cord fastened to the head of the bed. The ceiling light went out and with it the smaller hooded bulb at the
head of the bed, and the warm darkness covered them.

From the living room Polly Gray could hear their voices,
with now and then Jerry's eruptive laughter. She did not wonder what they could be talking about, and she no longer felt
left out of their lives. She thought, with a little twinge of re-

morse, how foolish she had been, after supper, to be thinking such things. She thought now how good it was to hear, again, laughter in the house . . . to hear Jerry's laughing that sounded so like another boy's laughter . . . long ago. She was scarcely aware that there were lengthening gaps of silence in the murmur of voices that flowed from beyond the door.

Danny stubbed out his cigarette in the ashtray beside the bed. Jerry turned over on his side, facing him in the dark.

"Sleepy, Danny?"

"No, not especially."

There was silence for a while.

"Say, Danny?"

"Yeah, Jerry." When Jerry did not say anything for a moment, Danny waited, then continued, "What's on your mind, Jerry?"

Jerry's voice was hesitant. "It's — it's all right about that package you had in your bag, Danny. The other one, I mean."

Danny did not say anything, but his arm came up, his fingers burrowing under Jerry's neck. The bending elbow caught Jerry's neck in a soft vise, squeezed, relaxed; and the hand lay on the boy's shoulder. Jerry's fingers closed over the muscles of the upper arm.

"Thanks, Jerry," Danny said.

The boy did not say anything for a little. After a while his voice, muffled against Danny's shoulder, came.

"Danny, you remember when we — when I was a little bit of a boy?"

"Yeah, Jerry."

"Remember how you used to put me to bed and make me say my prayers?"

"Yeah, Jerry."

"Reckon it sounds foolish as hell now, but remember how I used to kiss you good night? I reckon you are the only person I ever kissed in my life, Danny. Mom's never been much for kissin', has she?"

"Yeah, Jerry, I remember — and I don't know as there was ever anything foolish about it. I guess I thought about it a lot of times — out yonder."

Jerry's fingers relaxed their hold on Danny's upper arm and his hand moved across his chest, rested against Danny's throat.

"Night, Danny," Jerry murmured, and in a moment Danny felt the muscles in the arm across his chest, in the shoulder under his hand, go limp. Against his shoulder Jerry's breath came in the long pulsing rhythm of sleep.

Danny Gray lay for a long time, his hand resting on Jerry's warm shoulder, staring up into the warm soft night around him. Through the window came the pulsing beam of the Light, flicking its brief patch of light on the wall beyond the foot of the bed. It came in the unending silent beat of the Light's revolving above the Woods . . . as he had remembered it, as he had longed for the sight of it. . . . Far off, muffled by distance and the intervening dunes, the surf rumbled against the beach. . . . He gently withdrew his arm from around Jerry's shoulder and turned over on his side. Jerry's fingers were warm against his throat.

10

DEEP IN THE NIGHT DANNY CAME AWAKE. NOT JERKILY AND with every fibre of his body tense, as so often had happened, especially toward the end, when he had tried to sleep after a mission. It was as if sleep had ebbed away, like the tide when there is no wind, leaving him there, beached, dry, in full consciousness.

Nothing had disturbed him. Far off, muffled, muted, the rising tide's roar against the Cape reached him. It sounded like the cadenced thunder of an airplane's engines, like the "Polly & Jerry's" engines, far off and high above the earth, and for the moment Danny wondered if somebody were flying in the night. But then he knew the sound for what it was: the surf was beating itself to a froth against the Point.

Danny wondered what time it was and his hand went up to the cord at the head of the bed. He and Jerry had fixed it, a long time ago, right after they had got the small electric light plant for the house, so they could put out the light after they went to bed. It was Jerry's idea. His fingers closed around the cord but he did not pull it. The light might wake Jerry. What did it matter what time it was, anyway?

Reaching out, his hand found his cigarettes and a match on the table beside the bed; raising himself on an elbow and turning away from Jerry, he cupped the lighted match in his hands. He glanced at his watch in the glow of the cigarette; it was five minutes to three. Danny lay on his back. He parted his lips and let the smoke drift upward out of his mouth.

The Light made a square pattern on the wall beyond the foot of the bed, held for an instant, and was gone. Remembering, Danny counted off the seconds until it would come back. The Light flashed its brief pattern against the wall and was gone again. The same thing was happening, Danny knew, on the wall of every room, or almost every room, throughout the length of the Woods.

It was happening, too, though with a lessened intensity, in the houses of the village eight miles northward along the Outer Banks and in the houses of the village a dozen miles westward. It was happening, too, on the cabin walls of ships far out, beyond the reach of the Outer Diamonds. From the bridge of these ships men must be watching for the flash of the Great Light, and even aircraft, high and remote from the earth, were reassured in their reckonings. The patch of light came and went on the wall beyond the foot of the bed in a measured, rhythmic procession.

Above the sleeping village, above the Woods, the beaches that were ghostly dark, now that the moon was gone and the sun not yet stirring the eastern sky, the sweeping finger of the Great Light moved in unrelenting vigil. There was something hypnotic about the waxing and the waning of the Light across the wall. It was as if the Great Light actually breathed across the darkness, or as if its heart beat. . . . Maybe it is a part of the enchantment, Danny thought.

In the brief flashing of the Light, everything in the room was visible. The outline of objects was not sharp, but softly diffused, like a picture not quite in focus. Danny lifted his foot and held it in the path of the beam. It was something that he used to do when he was a boy . . . something that Jerry had watched with unending childish amusement — the grotesque distortions of his foot in the shadow against the wall.

Beside him Jerry slept. In the blurred reflection of the patch of light it seemed to Danny that the boy had not moved a single muscle since he went to sleep. He had not moved except to withdraw his arm from across Danny's breast and make the hand into a loose, relaxed fist and hold it against his chin. His breathing was almost soundless.

Danny put out his cigarette and lay with his arms crossed above his head. There was something that he wanted to think about, a lot of things.... Things like Sally ... like Judy — Judith ... and whether he was going to stay in the Army or come home. Like whether he was going back to school or coming back home to join up like his father, his grandfather, all of them as far back as there was anybody. Or maybe he ought to see if he could pass the examinations and go to the Academy.... Daddy had talked a lot about that when he was a lot younger....

"I wonder why I'm all the time thinking about when I was a lot younger," Danny murmured to himself. The Light came again ... and went. He was not so old — twenty-two next March — but so much had happened.... Of course he had always been old, compared with Jerry. He remembered — it surprised him how clearly — when Jerry was born. He was six-going-on-seven. There was no mystery about it. Daddy told him all about it. He said they'd have to look after Mama.

They looked after Mama. Things hadn't gone too well with her, somehow, and there were a lot of times, when Daddy was away, that he had looked after Jerry. Danny remembered, with a little rueful laugh, the first time he had changed Jerry's diaper. "What a godless mess I must have made of it," Danny said, almost audibly, "but it had to be done and Mama couldn't get up that day, and Daddy was at the Station, and Mrs. Drinkwater had to go home and look after her own family."

But, Danny remembered, Mama had not scolded him. She was patient and gentle with his awkwardness. Jerry hadn't minded at all. Even before he was three months old he had had that way of his now, that way of grinning at you. Before Mama had got her strength back — it seemed a long time to Danny — he could do pretty nearly everything that had to be done about the house, and Jerry would crow and gurgle contentedly.

Danny lighted another cigarette. He would put Jerry and his diapers out of his mind. He had other things to think about. The Light came, went; the Light was unrelenting, purposeful, looking into the room almost as if to see if all were well there ... looking into every room where the people of the Woods lay sleeping, watching above the sleeping village, the villages along the reaches of the Outer Banks, the sea and the ships that went, in immemorial dread, around the Outer Diamonds. ...

Beside him Jerry stirred in his sleep, drew a knee upward until it touched Danny's thigh. The boy turned and Danny felt him relax against the mattress and then the sole of his foot rested against the calf of Danny's leg. Danny could feel its rough, calloused surface, and he thought of what his mother had said, after Jerry went to the store, about Jerry wanting more than anything to be able to strike a match on the bottom of his foot, like Big Bill Henry. Danny smiled in the dark.

Danny had dreaded seeing the Chief. But now he thought that it had not been anything to be uneasy about. Maybe he had forgotten the bitter things that he had said, a long time ago. Big Bill Henry had always been a part, a towering part, of all their lives. He had been in and out of the house as long as Danny could remember, roaring and swearing, laughing in a vast tumult of sound, and as often being strangely gentle, especially with Jerry.

Remembering it now in the dark, Danny could almost see Big Bill Henry standing there, completely filling the door ... the time he came in when Jerry was being washed. That was before they had this house. Danny expected the big man to laugh that terrible laugh of his and make fun of him. Instead, Bill Henry had come, with amazing lightness, and squatted down on the heels of his monstrous bare feet on the other side of the tub. Danny had felt mite-small.

"Here, let me give you a hand with this launchin', boy," Big Bill Henry had said, and even now Danny marveled at the gentleness of his voice. The Chief took hold and Jerry gurgled with infantile delight when the massive man set him in one hand and sluiced water over him. Jerry was a big baby, even then, and from the day of that bathing there had been a strange bond between the growing Jerry and the big, boisterous, gentle Bill Henry.

And it's stronger now than it ever was, Danny reflected, smiling a little and remembering the massive man's plaintively mocking contention that Jerry had threatened to jab him with the ceremonial sword. As for himself, Danny had always liked this tempestuous friend of his father's — and his mother's — but there was something overwhelming about him, something that Danny could not quite cope with.

Life had not been very good to Bill Henry, Danny mused, but it had never beaten him. There were a lot of men — some right here in the Woods — who couldn't have stood up under some of the battering that had come to Bill Henry. He had married three times. Danny could not remember his first wife. The last one had died, his mother had written him, while he was away. The second marriage had gone on the rocks, and Bill Henry never mentioned it to anybody . . . not even to Polly Gray.

There had been two sons. One of them, the second wife's, had gone off with her when she left. Nobody knew what had become of either mother or son. He was a weakling, as Danny remembered him. The older boy had joined the Service when he was eighteen. He elected the sea, and his ship had gone down early in the war, somewhere off Greenland. No, life had not been gentle with Bill Henry, but he had lived it, by his own rules and on his own terms, and nobody had ever heard him complain.

But he had been especially explosive when he heard that

Danny had, after his father was dead, determined to go away and join the Army. He had come roaring to the house. He had called Danny hard, ugly names, and he had said bitter things about his being a quitter and going off out of harm's way when the Germans were right there in sight of home. His words had hurt. Danny had carried away with him a bitter resentment that knew no softening.

But, surprisingly, it was softened now, and lying in the dark Danny wondered if, after all, the Chief's bitterness had not come from his own private grief, from a feeling of frustration that there would not, now, be a son of his own to carry on the tradition of his race in the Service. There had always been a Ragland in the Service, and if there were a pre-eminent passion in Ragland's life it was that heritage.

Even the other day, when he was talking from the Twenty-nine, that had been almost the first thing and the last thing that Big Bill Henry had said to him. But then, there was Jerry, and it was plain enough that if things went on like they were headed, Jerry would join as soon as he was old enough, and that by then, the boy would already know all that the Chief could teach him. Bill Henry was not as young as he used to be, and he was already long past the thirty years that would, in ordinary times, have meant retirement. Herein must lie most of the vehement urgency that drove him.

The Light moved in endless rhythm against the wall . . . on . . . off . . . on. . . . Danny lay utterly still in the dark, and his thoughts revolved, with the placid rhythm of the Light, around Big Bill Henry. He was almost startled when Jerry's voice, muffled against his shoulder, came to him. The boy had not stirred.

"What you doin' awake, Danny?" When Danny, taken unaware, did not immediately reply, the boy went on, "Ain't nothin' the matter, is there? I didn't kick you or snore or anything, did I? How long you been awake?"

Danny held his wrist in the path of the Light when it came
again before he answered. He had been awake almost two
hours.

"Oh, not long," he answered. "No, you haven't moved all
night as well as I can see, and you've not snored. I guess I just
woke up."

"Don't you sleep good, Danny? Does my bein' here bother
you?"

"Sure, I sleep good, and you don't bother me. How long
have you been awake?"

"I just woke up, and I sort of knew you were awake, too.
It ain't time to get up."

"No, I guess it isn't. I was just lying here watching the Light
and thinking about this and that."

"What this and that, Danny? Do you wake up thinkin'
about — about the war? Some of the boys was tellin' me about
a movie they saw down at Hatteras. It was about a feller that
had been to the war and he would wake up yellin' like — like
all hell was after him."

"No, nothing like that. I was just watching the Light, I
guess, and going around and around like it does — only not
making much light myself."

"It's company to have you in here with me. I've watched it a
lot of times when you were gone."

"You've grown a lot bigger, Jerry."

"Yeah, I reckon I have," Jerry said indifferently. "What
you suppose would happen if the Light — if they was to forget to light it some night, or it went out?"

"Somebody might pile up on the beach."

"Then Bill Henry would have him a time, wouldn't he? I
guess he misses wrecks like they used to have when boats had
sail on 'em and they didn't have any radio."

"I guess he does, but there'll always be wrecks off there."

"He's sure pulled a mess of people out of there," Jerry said.
"They give him another medal — Legion of Merit or some

such. Mailed it to him this time. He told 'em he didn't have time to go after it. Guess he didn't want to put on his shoes." Jerry's laugh was half smothered.

Jerry yawned deeply and stretched his legs, planting his toes against the foot of the bed. He turned toward the wall, half on his side and half on his belly, one arm under his chest and the other crooked above his head. In a moment Danny knew that he was asleep again.

Danny watched the Light come, go, come back again. There were things that he had to think about, urgent things that he had, sometime or other, to make up his mind about, things that had ridden with him through strange skies, paced to the drumming of the four great engines of the Twenty-nine. No matter how far he had gotten away from this point of land, from these tranquil Woods that were immemorially a haven from the sea, Big Bill Henry's bitter words had kept pace with him.

There were times when his mind was made up. He would never come back. There were, to be sure, times when it looked as if he would not survive to come back. Death would come so close that he could feel it brush his face, freeze the blood's flow in his veins. There was one time, in the instant before he set the battered Twenty-nine — the first "Polly & Jerry" — down in the water off Iwo that he had really believed his number was up.

Even then, in that instant that was the length of eternity — he remembered now his thoughts, those last thoughts — he had been thinking about being precisely where he was now, in this bed with Jerry asleep beside him, with Polly Gray asleep in the room at the other end of the house and, outside, the whole of the Woods asleep beneath an untroubled sky . . . and the Light watchful above them.

The Twenty-nine had hit the water with a fearful impact, and in that instant Danny had let go the controls, doubling his forearms across his face and his head. That must have been what saved him from being knocked cold. The big ship, already ripped almost to shreds, did not wholly disintegrate. Danny could never be very sure what happened after the ship hit the water, but they told him — it was mentioned in the citation — that he went back through the water and dragged out the young gunner who had been badly hit . . . that he did not leave the wreckage until the last man in the crew had been hauled out. Nobody had been seriously injured. Sergeant Dragonnetti had a knot on his head and was talking incoherently. Danny could never quite remember what he was saying.

But after that, Danny was sure that he would come back, that things would happen just as he had seen them in that flashing instant, as he had felt them when he committed the staggering bomber to the hazard of a crash landing in water. After that he had never worried about a mission. Nothing had worried him — except the echoing of Big Bill Henry Ragland's bitter accusing when he took leave of the Outer Banks.

Danny Gray, after that, knew that he would come back. But would he stay? That was the perplexing thing that he had to think about. It had been almost miraculous, the way things had happened as he pictured them. The house had not changed. The Woods had not changed. His mother had not changed . . . and he found her in almost the precise spot where he had left her when he went away.

Jerry had grown unbelievably, and that was the only thing that Danny had not taken into account in his pictured homecoming. When he went away Jerry had been not quite twelve, big-framed but somehow scrawny and not promiseful of becoming the clean-limbed, healthy young animal now wrapped in untroubled sleep beside him. Animal is not the word, Danny amended his thought, and anyhow he is a lot better adjusted right now than I am.

Danny lighted another cigarette, and the flame of the match blurred the outline of the patch of light that came and went on the wall beyond the foot of the bed. He thought irritably that he would never get anywhere with thinking things out if he let his mind flit from one thing to another like this. The point was that he had always wanted to fly, even before that day when he had slipped into the boat down at the little dock when his father was taking somebody out to the big lumbering seaplane that had landed in Pamlico Sound.

The man, whoever it was — Danny could never remember — was awfully sick. They had him on a stretcher brought from the Station, all covered up with blankets so Danny could see nothing but his face. His face was a sort of ash gray and his breath was coming in short, noisy gasps. When they got to the seaplane, some men took one end of the stretcher and Daddy took the other and they lifted him aboard. Daniel Gray had not seemed to realize, until he turned away, that Danny had stowed away on the boat.

When they got the stretcher aboard, the boat had stood by while the big plane turned into the wind, its engines roaring. It was almost out of sight before it lifted from the surface, and all Danny could see was a cloud of white spray. His father said maybe they would get there with him alive and Danny said, with childish eagerness, that he was going to fly like that someday. His father smiled, a little sadly Danny thought now, and after a little added that he was afraid of the things himself. Danny puzzled over his father being afraid of anything . . . and it was years before he understood what his father meant.

But Danny had always wanted to fly, and throughout his boyhood he was puzzled and troubled by the fact that the ships that came down to take sick people to the hospital had "U. S. Navy" in big letters on their wings. Didn't the Coast Guard have any airplanes, he would demand of his father. And he remembered now the delight, the pride, that had welled up inside him the day he saw the first plane with "U. S. Coast Guard" in very large letters under its wing.

There were not so many of them, and people like Big Bill Henry Ragland were tolerantly disdainful of them. "They may be all right in their place," the big man would say, "but their place is up there. This country here is boat country, and there's nothin' like an oar and a good arm to pull it when you've got to go somewhere important, like out yonder when she's in a bad humor."

Always they spoke of the sea as a woman, and of her moods as they would of a woman's moods. They would look at her and say, "She's sort of riled this morning," or they would say, "She's in a good humor today." The sea was a woman, and sometimes she smiled like a mother smiles when she looks upon the face of a child in sleep, like Danny remembered his mother's face when she let him look at Jerry the first time.

And sometimes she was terrible in vituperation, like old Mrs. Daniels on the other side of the store when she was in a bad humor with her husband. . . . Danny had been passing there one time when he was a little boy and, wonderingly, had seen a saucer fly through the window, followed by Mrs. Daniels' voice uttering a strange word. He had told his mother about it, pronouncing the strange word, when he got home, and his mother had said never to mention it and never to say that word again, either. . . . It was the first time he knew that a woman could cuss like Bill Henry.

But Danny had always wanted to fly, for no reason that he ever undertook to analyze. He had just wanted to fly, and even now, after more than three years of it, years that had carried him above and across strange oceans, into battle in far places and back again, the sky's fascination was as compelling as it had ever been. There was still nothing — or almost nothing — that could touch the feeling he had in that instant when he felt the ship lift its first inch off the ground.

Never, after that first day when he saw the seaplane carry away an old man to save him from dying, was the awareness of flight quite out of his thoughts. Through long indolent hours he would watch the gulls above the surf, big lumbering cranes above the marshes and, in winter, the endless squadrons of geese that came in their arrowed formations out of the north and wonder what it would be like to fly.

But mostly Danny had liked to watch the pair of bald eagles that had a nest down in Trent Woods, which was not a separate woods exactly but an extension of these next to the Light. He had seen their nest many a time when he went with his father to Hatteras or somewhere down the Banks. It was in the top of the biggest pine in the whole woods and it looked as big as a house. There were some sticks in it so big that Danny couldn't see how even an eagle could move them.

It was when they flew, hovering above the Open Ponds beyond the Station, that Danny had loved to watch them. There were lots of fish in the Open Ponds, fresh-water fish that nobody cared about eating. But Papa Eagle would hover above the ponds until he sighted a fish in the water, swoop down on him with a rush of wind through his feathers that you could hear above the beat of the tide against the beach, and then come up with a fish wriggling in his claws and head like a streak for his nest. . . . Danny had wanted to fly like an eagle, and not like a gull or a goose or a crane.

There was not much about the little ship to remind anybody of an eagle when it came down the beach on that afternoon that became, for Danny, the most eventful and remembered of his life. It was flying low, lower than he had ever seen one fly. It was September, the September after Danny was thirteen, and the sea, she was in a good humor, as smooth as the Open Ponds and tranquilly blue: blue with the deceptive peacefulness that people like Daddy and Big Bill Henry saw with foreboding.

Danny and some of the other boys from the Woods had come out swimming, but the sea was in such a somnolent humor that there was not much fun in swimming. They were lazily sunning themselves, their sun-browned bodies stretched full upon the hard sand left by the ebbing tide. Danny's ears were the first to become aware of the low hum of the engine, and he turned over on his side to scan the haze to the north-ward.

When it came it looked like a yellow beetle, its wings awk-wardly long and its engine just a little nub sticking out in front. But it could fly. It came puttering down the beach and some of the boys laughed derisively at it when it swept low over them. But not Danny. He watched it, fascinated; and his heart came up in his throat when it pulled up, pivoted on the tip of a wing, and came back in a narrow circle. It straightened out and — oh, wonder! — it glided down with its engine just able to mutter.

All of them scrambled up and stood, watching. A gangling fellow got out of the little plane. He had a curious, cumber-some-looking camera in his hands, and he started looking at the Lighthouse, glancing down into the bulging bellows of the camera and moving first to one side and then to the other. At first all the boys held back, hesitating about whether to go where they would be in the way of the man, but after a little, one of them, and then all of them, broke into a run toward the plane.

At first the man with the camera paid them no attention at all, didn't even glance around to see if they were bothering his ship. He was intent on the picture he was taking of the Light-house. Nobody touched even a wing of the little ship, and the man must have noticed that when he turned back and came slowly toward them, glancing back at the Lighthouse over his shoulder. He smiled, and when he got to them he said, cas-ually, "Good afternoon, gentlemen."

When he said that, a little pulse of astonishment rippled around the knot of boys. It was the first time that Danny, or any of the rest of them he supposed, had ever been called "gentlemen." Then he wanted to know if they'd mind gather-ing around the ship so he could get a picture with the Light-house in the background. He took their picture and then he set the camera inside the ship and sort of flopped down in the sand and drew out a pack of cigarettes. He lighted one and asked if anybody would join him.

One or two of the boys said they didn't mind if they did. He didn't say where he was from, or what his name was, and nobody asked him. Somebody did ask him how fast a ship like that would go, and he said about eighty miles. And then he asked them if this was the first time anybody had ever landed on the beach, and Danny spoke up and said it was the first time, but the Coast Guard landed big ships over in the Sound to take off people who were sick.

Danny could never quite remember what more was said, or whether anything was said; but he knew, suddenly, that the man had turned curiously upon him and was looking at him speculatively, and presently the man was asking him if he had ever been up in an airplane, asking him, friendly and casual, if he would like to go.

"I'd like to get a picture of the Lighthouse from the air, and maybe you could hold her steady for me while I take it," the man said, and in a sort of trance Danny found himself inside the ship. He heard the engine sputter and then start purring. The man told him to "hold back on this stick" and then went around to the front and spun the propeller. The man got in and the little ship went down the smooth strand of the beach, lifted . . . .

When they were almost down to the Cape, past the Old Station and higher than the Lighthouse, the man pulled the thing marked "throttle," and the engine was quieter. Half turning in his seat, he called back to Danny to take hold of the stick between his knees and just let his hands follow its motions for a minute. Danny felt it out, sensing and linking the cause in his hands with the effect of the ship's movement.

"Now when we come past the Lighthouse, just hold her steady and I'll try for the picture."

It was as simple as that — easy — like the eagles. When the man set his camera down, he said, "Thanks, fellow — do you want to look at where you live from up here?" Danny nodded and the man said for him to point it out. Once Danny had climbed the Lighthouse and looked out, and he knew where to find the house. But he scarcely saw it; he was too busy letting his hands sway with the movement of the stick between his knees.

When they were back on the beach the man asked him his name and put it down in a little book. In a week or so a plain envelope came. There were the pictures, the one of the Lighthouse from the air and the one with the whole gang on the beach. But there was nothing to show what the man's name was. Danny had the pictures put into a little frame that his father made for him. They were over there on the bureau, now, just as he had left them when he went away, only now they were more yellow, fading.

Danny had always known that he was going to fly. . . . Well, now he had flown, if not quite around the whole earth, anyhow across its biggest oceans, and he had touched all of its continents. Now the question was, what now, what next? There had been a lot of talk among the fellows about how they were going to keep on flying after they got out of the Army. All of them were going to get out of the Army — all except the Dragon.

Some of them were so sick of flying, they said, they'd never get in an airplane again as long as breath and sanity remained, but most of them — there were all sorts of plans, and some of them had the sound of sense in them. They were going home and fly the mail, the airliners; or they were going to China, going somewhere and start an airline of their own. But they were through with the Army.

Some of them, of course, would stay in the Army. They were making more money than they could ever make when they got back to their jobs of soda-jerking. Often enough he had heard fellows reminded of that. The trouble was, Danny realized, that he just didn't like the Army. Too much shoving and pushing, too many people climbing all over you to get to where they wanted to be — and climbing down your throat because they were afraid you might climb on their backs.

He had had enough of it . . . or he was sure he had until the other night when the General . . . . Danny put the thought out of his mind, as firmly and as definitely as he stubbed out the burning coal of his cigarette in the ashtray, a flat sea-clam shell, on the table beside his bed. He turned over on his side, closing his eyes against the pillow. But above him, slanting across the bed, he knew that the long finger of the Light was probing the darkness, making a blurred patch on the wall beyond the foot of the bed.

"I'll think about that tomorrow," he told himself and wondered, sleepily, where he had first heard that phrase; it had come so handily, of late.

A flat beam of sunlight fell across Jerry's feet, projected nakedly from under the bed covering, with their darkly calloused soles uppermost. The sun warmed through the thickened skin and Jerry stirred, raised himself on his elbows and, remembering that he was not any longer alone in the bed, grinned and glanced at Danny. He started to speak but stifled the impulse when he remembered that Danny had been awake awhile ago. He glanced out the window and with practiced precision calculated the time of day by the way the shadows lay on the grass. He moved his head to look at Danny's watch.

"He's slow," Jerry said to himself, with a seafaring man's feeling of self-approval at being able to tell the time of day by the sun. Although he secretly wanted a watch, Jerry openly disdained them. Big Bill Henry had never had a watch in his life and he always knew what time it was. Never even bothered to look at the ship's clock above his desk.

Jerry watched Danny's sleeping face intently for a while, hoping that he could sort of wish him awake. He put away an impulse to give him a rousing poke in the ribs. "Guess he needs some sleep, where he's been and all," Jerry concluded and began to move himself soundlessly toward the foot of the bed. His feet found the floor and he stood up, stretched himself, and sent an exploring foot under the bed in search of his dungarees. Balancing himself with his weight on his hands on the foot of the bed, he picked up the dungarees with one foot and extended the other down through its proper trouser-leg. He wished that Danny were awake to see this trick — if he could make it work.

Still Danny did not stir. Jerry glanced at him, at his neatly folded clothes on the back of the chair. He crossed over to the bureau where Danny had put the things he had in his pocket: his wallet, a small knife, some loose change. The little metal disc lay apart from the other things. Jerry examined it briefly — the same one that Daddy used to tote in his pocket. Danny's dog tags made a small, tinkling sound when he picked up the colorless plastic cord on which he wore them. There was something else beside the dog tags on the cord — something shiny, like silver.

Jerry held it up to the light at the window. He had seen a lot of fellows over at the Station with little things like that around their necks. Catholics, mostly. Jerry turned the object in his fingers, looking at the reverse side of it. His brow furrowed as he deciphered the fine script lettering. He turned toward the bed as if he were about to say something, but he laid the dog tags and the little silver thing down where he had picked them up, making no sound.

Sunlight was streaming in at the window now, reaching almost up to Danny's chin. Jerry went to the window and pulled the shade down, shutting out the sun. Then he moved silently around the bed to the other window. The room was in a sort of twilight, and the brightest thing in it, Jerry saw when he turned back from the door, was the blond cloud of Danny's hair above the pillow.

11

IT WAS MIDMORNING WHEN DANNY CAME INTO THE KITCHEN. His eyes were heavy with sleep, and his voice, when he greeted Polly Gray, was murky. He felt almost as if he had been drugged. He rubbed his eyes with his fists and looked around, smiling a faintly apologetic smile.

"Gee, whiz, Mama — why didn't somebody wake me up? Where's Jerry?"

"There was no need for you to be up," his mother said mildly. "Jerry said he left you sleeping with the shades down so the sun wouldn't bother you."

"Guess I am a little behind with my sleep," Danny said, "but where's that young pup?"

"He went out to the Station as soon as he swallowed his breakfast," Polly Gray said, and her tone suggested, though uncritically, that most of Jerry's absences from the house were accounted for.

"How did he go — walk?"

"No, he rode his horse."

"His horse? Didn't know there was a horse left in the Woods."

"It isn't much of a horse," his mother said. "It's the banker pony that Mr. Quidley had, and I guess it must be the last horse on the Banks. Jerry traded Mr. Miller out of him."

"What did he trade for him?"

"Words, mostly, I expect," Polly Gray said with her slow smile. "I do believe Jerry could wheedle anybody out of his eyeteeth if he set his mind on it. He was a pretty poor sight when Jerry got him, but he's trimmed his mane and his hoofs. He ordered a currycomb and a brush and he has him looking almost like a horse. He calls him 'Bos'n.' "

Danny laughed tolerantly. His mother had turned up the flame in the oil-burner range and set the percolator above it. She went to the pantry and Danny heard the door of the oil-burning refrigerator open. . . . So Jerry had a horse. . . . Danny could remember, far back, when almost everybody along the Outer Banks had a horse, most of them scrawny and unkempt and mostly making their own living grazing in the marshes, even in the wintertime.

There was a legend about the horses: A long time ago, two hundred years ago, a ship loaded with horses foundered on the Inner Diamonds and some of the horses swam ashore. People said they were fine Arabian horses being shipped to Edenton or somewhere up the Sounds where fine folks wanted them for saddle horses. None of them ever got there. Like any other castaways — like the dark-skinned Arab who came ashore from the same ship — the horses settled down on the Outer Banks and adapted themselves as necessity compelled them.

Once every year, on the Fourth of July unless it happened to be Sunday, they had a horse-penning. Mostly the horses ran wild, and on penning day they would round them up into a corral and everybody would draw lots for choice. Pieces of paper were put in a hat and whoever got Number One got first choice of all the colts in the pen. The colts were as wild as rabbits . . . as wild as the young deer that lived in the outer reaches of the Woods.

Danny could scarcely remember them, but his father's tales of the pony-pennings were vivid enough. The pen was out by the Lighthouse, and after the penning there would be a picnic and racing. There was a regular race track laid out on the flats between the Lighthouse and the ocean. Nobody had saddles and they all rode bareback. The Coast Guard had horses, too, but they were kept in regular stables and fed oats and hay. They used them to haul the lifeboats.

But all the horses were gone now. The Coast Guard had been completely motorized, and other folks, too. Most people had got rid of their horses back in the years when somebody, somewhere — in Raleigh or Washington, or maybe in both places — had wanted everybody to dip his cattle, his horses, in some kind of vats to get rid of the ticks. Something about cows having some disease. There was a lot of complaint about it, and some of the vats the government people built were blown up at night. But most people just got rid of their cattle, shooting them and letting them lie. The last one, they said, was shot by some sportsman. . . .

"Has Jerry got him a saddle?" Danny inquired when his mother came back from the pantry. She had two eggs and some strips of bacon in her hands.

"No, he rides bareback like your father used to do when he was that age." She was silent for a moment and then she added, with a note of anxiety, "Sometimes I'm afraid he'll hurt himself. He does such outlandish things — like standing up to ride. I guess it's something he must have heard some of the boys talking about when they came back from the moving pictures in Hatteras."

"Doesn't Jerry ever go to the movies?"

"I don't believe he has ever seen a picture — just doesn't care about it. Bill Henry lets some of the boys at the Station go every night they have a picture, twice a week. Sometimes Bill Henry goes, too, but that seems to be one place Jerry won't go with him."

"He and Bill Henry seem pretty thick," Danny said; and, when his mother glanced at him sharply, he wished he hadn't said it. He added, a little hastily, that he thought it was a good thing for Jerry to have somebody, someone who was older, to look after him.

"You still like your eggs scrambled, Danny?"

"Any way you fix 'em, Mama."

"You must be hungry. It's a long time since supper last night."

"Starved," Danny said lightly. He moved around to the place she had set for him, settled himself in the chair, and spread the napkin across his lap. His mother poured his coffee — two spoonfuls of sugar and two of milk from the can she brought from the refrigerator. She poured a cup for herself before she sat down across from Danny.

"There's some fig preserves," she said. "Sugar has been so scarce that I haven't made any in two years. We've saved some of what we had until you got home."

"That's swell, Mama," Danny said. He ate hungrily and Polly Gray watched him, her eyes tender, brooding. But deep down there was a remote shadow. The years had changed him, matured him. They had taken from him, and from her, the last years of his youth. Now there was a little furrow between his eyes. It had not been there when he went away. The youthful looseness was gone from his mouth. His lips were straight now, and firm. His nose was somehow sharper, leaner, and there were faint lines that came down from it to the corners of his mouth. One corner, the left, was tilted upward.

There were wrinkles in his forehead, too, and the eyes under the blond brows were darker, less brightly blue than they had been when . . . when he went away. There were hollowed places at his temples, and his ears seemed to cling more closely to his head. They used to stick out, somehow. Polly Gray remembered how Jerry used to pull at Danny's ears when he frolicked with him before bedtime. As if he might have sensed his mother's thoughts, Danny looked up from his plate, grinned.

"That's from having them pinned back so much when I was in the Army — at first, I mean. I'm still in it and I guess they'll go right on pinning 'em back."

"Pinned back, Danny?"

"Yeah," Danny said, "my ears. It's a saying they have in the Army, but I guess wearing earphones on my head, flying, maybe made 'em stick closer to my head." His smile was patient, disarming.

"It's good, so good, to have you home," his mother said presently.

"You don't know the half of it, Mama."

"What do you want to do today, Danny?" Polly Gray inquired when she had poured a second cup of coffee for him and for herself. There was no urgency in her tone, no sense of hurry. She was not, today, a busy housewife, hurrying through breakfast toward things that needed doing. Nothing mattered, today, nothing except the fact that Danny was home again. He was thoughtful for a moment before he answered her. The sunlight was bright outside; the leaves of the yoepon on the hill back of the house glistened as if they had been freshly waxed. Red was beginning to show on its berries.

"Nothing, Mama; just plain nothing," Danny said slowly. "I used to think about it a lot, back yonder, planning what I would do the first morning after I got home. I thought I'd like to take off my shoes and roll up my pants halfway to the knees and just get out and walk in the sand."

Polly Gray smiled an indulgent, happy smile.

"I thought I'd just like to feel the warm sand coming up between my toes and the warm sun poking down the back of my neck. I'd have my shirt open, or off, and the wind would be blowing. . . . But now that I'm here I guess I'm just lazy."

"Everybody will be wanting to see you," Polly Gray said. Danny protested, but his mother, gently insistent, said that he ought to put on his uniform and — and let people see him. Pride lighted her eyes when Danny stood up. He had filled out, had grown actually taller. He turned to look out the kitchen window, and Polly Gray, with a little shock, seeing him in profile against the sharp light of the window, knew that his chin must have changed more than anything else. It had a squareness — a hardness that she had not noticed. She was the mother of a grown-up man now. Danny took down the dishcloth when he turned from the window.

"Let's get through with these few dishes and go outdoors and maybe just sit in a deck chair and — well, let's just sit."

After they were through with the dishes Polly Gray told him to go along; she would come presently. When she came down the front steps and turned toward the deck chairs beside the oleander, Danny was not there. She glanced around the yard, along the beds of flowers against the cedars, and along the road beyond the hedge of palmetto palms. He was not in sight. She started to call out to him but put the impulse away. She crossed over to the chairs, pausing to pick off some blossoms that had faded. She sat down, waiting. . . .

Today there were soft clouds, woolly and white against the blue, wandering like grazing sheep across a meadow, shepherded by an uninsistent wind. Down the hill, in the marsh across the road, the foxtails stirred, rustling faintly in the small wind; and the hibiscuses, on stiffer stems, nodded to each other. Their colors — white, red, and all the shadings between — were bright under the flawless sunlight. Now and then a shadow fell upon them.

Sensing his approach rather than hearing him, Polly Gray turned to watch Danny when he came toward her from the little hill above the house. He came through the screen of cedar and fig, came slowly down the smooth grass. He sat down without a word, stretched out his legs and crossed his ankles. His hands were folded behind his head and his long-lashed eyelids drooped over his eyes, shielding them against the sunlight.

"We'll have to get a marker for Daddy," Danny said presently.

"Yes," Polly Gray said. She was thoughtful for a moment before she went on. "It has worried me, not doing it before now. But everybody has been so busy with the war. I just

couldn't bring myself to stop what they were doing for that.
. . . It was his war, too."

"Yes, I know," Danny said. "You've kept his grave nice —
the grass around it must have taken a lot of work. He would
have liked that Cape jessamine bush you've planted."

"He always liked them," Polly Gray said, musing, remembering. "And I wanted to wait until you got home so we could
decide, all three of us, what sort of a stone to buy."

"He'd like something simple, with just his name and the
date of his birth and — and his death on it, I guess. But it will
be whatever you say, Mama."

"That's what I had thought — something simple. But do
you suppose it would be — it would be proper if we were to
have them carve — the cross on it? It's something that — that
I want people to know and remember."

"I think it would be okay for him, Mama."

"We'll have it that way, then, Danny. Jerry spoke of it at
breakfast. I'll write to them about it today — but I'd rather you
did it."

"You'd better do it, Mama. Any idea what it will cost and
— and, well, just how are you — are we fixed for money?"

It was something that he had been intending to ask, something that he had worried a lot about. His mother had not,
from the day he left home, mentioned money in any of her
letters. Always her letters were cheerful, always they said that
she and Jerry were faring well. He had made her the usual
allotments, and besides that he had had them send his pay to
the bank on Roanoke Island to be deposited to her credit with
the provision that both his and his mother's drafts on the account would be accepted.

Danny had never known very much about money. Until he
entered the Army he had never earned any money, and there
was nothing, at home, to spend it for. Sometimes they used to
go fishing, his father and Jerry and he, when his father was

on liberty, and they would sell the fish, if they got any, at the docks in Hatteras or at the little fishhouse at the head of the creek. Daniel Gray had always divided what they got, share and share alike, with a share for the maintenance of the boat. It was never any very great amount, Danny realized now, but to him and Jerry, then, it was a lot. He had never had to ask for money.

"Yes, I've had prices," Polly Gray was saying. "I guess we could afford a higher-priced one than we've planned to get, but your father would not like that." She fell silent, but after a while she went on.

"There's no need for worrying about money, Danny," she continued. "We were, as I've written you, mighty grateful to you for sending home your allotment, but we've not used it. Your father's insurance, some outside his service policy, has been enough for Jerry and me to live on. Jerry has never asked me for a penny — he still fishes at odd times."

"You mean you haven't spent any of what I've sent you?"

"No, Danny — we haven't needed it. I told them at the bank to buy war bonds for you but never to fail to have enough there to take care of any check you might send in. Your father's insurance is there, too, but most of it is in war bonds."

"You mean all the money they've paid me is right there — now? I cashed a few small checks here and there, but where I've been we didn't need much money."

"Yes, Danny, I know you haven't spent much. The bank sends a statement every month, and sometimes I've worried because you were not taking enough. I was afraid you were denying yourself things you needed."

"No, Mama, I got along fine, but I still don't like it — you ought to have spent my money and saved yours. You may need it one of these days."

"No, Danny, I'll never need anything — and you won't, either. It's — it's ours — yours, Jerry's, and mine. I'll get the last statement and see how much it is." She started to get up.

"Don't do it now, Mama," Danny protested. "It's too comfortable here to bother. We'll look at it sometime. Do we still have Daddy's boat — the one we used to go fishing in sometimes?"

"Yes. Jerry has taken care of it. He hauls it out and scrapes and paints her bottom. Sometimes he gets Bill Henry to go fishing with him, and sometimes some of the boys in the Woods here go. There have been so few left to go that fish have been scarce and they bring a good price when they do get any."

"I'd like to go fishing in it again. I wonder if I've forgotten how."

"Well, if you have," Polly Gray laughed, "Jerry hasn't, and I'm surprised that he hasn't already mentioned it. What were you boys talking about so long after you went to bed last night? It sounded like old times, only Jerry's voice has changed so."

"Nothing — or anyhow nothing that I can remember. I guess we were just talking. Jerry remembered the times I used to wash him before I put him to bed. What became of Daddy's old car? Did it just fall apart?"

"No; it didn't fall apart, but the tires had just about rotted off. We sold it, and it amazes me what people will pay these days for even an old car. I put the money away to start paying for a new one — if you want it. You'll be sort of lost without a car, won't you, Danny?"

"I hadn't thought about it," Danny said. "I guess I've mostly just thought about getting back here — getting home — and finding things just like they were. They are, pretty near, Mama."

Throughout the long sunny morning they talked, contentedly, sometimes idly, sometimes with surges of eagerness from one or the other. Polly Gray made no effort to guide their talk into any channel, toward any objective, though there were things that she wanted to talk about. No particular things, but in her heart she wanted to explore, and to possess again, every byway in the heart of this — this new man who had come home in place of the boy who had gone away.

Questions kept bubbling to the surface of her awareness and sometimes they almost bubbled over, but she put them purposefully back into their place. Today she would not ask anything of him, demand anything of him. She would let him come back to her along paths of his own choosing, in times of his own choice. It was enough to have him there, smiling lazily at her, his face placidly content just to be there.

The sun climbed toward the top of the sky and the wind lay still along the sweep of the marsh. The foxtails quit nodding to each other, left off their remote secret whisperings together, and the hibiscuses — the marsh mallows — stared fixedly at the little clouds that seemed now to be standing still in the sky's wide blue meadow like sheep resting at noontime. In the deck chair Danny, too, seemed almost asleep. Presently he stirred.

"What time do you reckon Jerry will get back? Does he stay all day when he goes over there?"

"Sometimes he does, but today — I forgot to tell you — he said that he would be back by the time you were awake, and for you not to do anything until he saw you. He tried to sound mysterious, but I think he had in the back of his mind that he's going to parade you up to the store. Jerry's awfully proud of his big brother."

Danny grinned comfortably, pleased.

"What does he want to do — put me in a cage like a bear at a carnival?"

"No; it isn't that. It's sort of hard to get it into words just what he feels. It isn't reflected glory, or anything like that — I think I hear him coming now."

Across the somnolent marsh there came a sound which, to an uncritical ear, could have passed for a cowboy's whoop, or which might have been, more accurately, interpreted by a more energetically co-operative horse as an urging to expanded and enlarged effort. Polly Gray smiled to herself. Danny listened and after a little could make out the clop of the horse's hoofs crossing the little bridge over the ditch that led from the marsh to the Sound.

Danny watched, fascinated, when the horse came within sight. The animal's head was down and it plodded methodically in the sand. Jerry was hunched over the animal's neck. He rested his weight on his hands against Bos'n's shoulders. The horse paid him no attention nor did he alter his gait when Jerry's legs came up his sides. The boy's feet felt out the horse's back and his long toes dug in just back of the shoulders.

And suddenly Jerry was standing upright, with the reins in one hand. Altogether the sight was definitely ludicrous. The horse moved like a dejected automaton, and only Jerry seemed actually alive. Bos'n and his upright rider plodded along the palmetto palm hedge.

Danny could not see all that happened in the next instant. He could see Jerry balance himself tensely, but he could not see Jerry's two big toes dig down into Bos'n's hide, exploring until they found a sensitive spot. Danny saw the horse's hind legs suddenly double under him and then extend outward and upward. Danny started from his chair, but his mother told him, quickly, to sit down — nothing was wrong.

When Bos'n's hind legs reached the top of their arc Jerry dropped lightly to the sandy roadway, and with an imperceptible twist of his arm the halter came off and the horse turned placidly toward the marsh. Without a backward glance and with elaborate unconcern Jerry came casually up the walk, cut across the grass toward Polly Gray and Danny. He dropped the halter on the grass and sat down, cross-legged, facing them.

"Hi," Jerry said casually.

"Hi, Jerry — how'd the boat drill go?" Danny greeted him.

Jerry was silent for a little, and in his silence there was more disdain than he could have measured in words.

"Them lugs," he said after a while. "Ain't a one of 'em —
leavin' out Scarborough — that's got any more idea what an
oar's for than — than that dam' horse would know what to do
with a hymnbook."

"As bad as that?" Danny said lightly, and then he sensed
that this was the wrong tack to take with Jerry. The boy
glanced at him in questioning surprise.

"Yeah, as bad as that," Jerry said aggressively and then,
mollified, when Danny's face was properly serious, he went on.
"They just ain't from — from nothin'. I think Bill Henry
ought to quit messin' with 'em before he gets himself a stroke.
They make him turn right purple in the face. What time did
you wake up, Danny? What you been doin'?"

"Just fooling around here — thought I'd wait until you got
back and see if you had anything on your mind." Jerry looked
relieved.

"Not a thing, special," Jerry said. "Ain't it most time to eat,
Mom? Need anything from the store?"

Polly Gray appeared to weigh the matter judiciously, and
Jerry watched her with covert eagerness. His mother said that
she really did need a jar of salad dressing if he thought they
had any at the store. She was planning to have a salad for
dinner. "And if there's any cheese, that would go good with
some canned pears I thought we'd as well open and use."

Jerry got up from the grass and stood for a moment eying
his brother speculatively. He sat down on the arm of Danny's
chair and, balling up his fist, rolled it upward along Danny's
chest until it was under his chin. Then he boxed Danny's
ears lightly, placed a forefinger on his nose and a thumb under
his chin, and pressed, not too gently. He grinned.

"How about walkin' to the store with me, Captain?" he
said, half-teasing, but with a note of pleading in his voice.

"Oh, I don't know — I'm not in uniform."

"What's that you've got on if it ain't a uniform? Ain't no
zoot suit."

"Oh, I mean my tie and my — my bars. You're not in uniform unless you've got on everything you're supposed to wear
— including shoes."

"How about your ribbons and them wings?"

"You don't have to dyke yourself out in ribbons, especially
if it's just a shirt you're wearing."

"Don't, huh?" Jerry's hand lay loosely across Danny's
shoulder. "Come on, Danny."

"Okay, Jerry," Danny relented, "but how about some service for your elders, varmint? How's for running in the house
and bringing me my tie and my cap, and look in that leather
case in my bag and bring me a set of bars and a collar wing and
that set of wings that goes here on my shirt."

Jerry went toward the house in a loose-jointed lope, reappeared almost at once with the small leather case in his hands.

"I brung 'em all, so's not to make any mistake. Here, is this
the wings that go here?"

Jerry's fingers were eager and surprisingly efficient.

"You forgot my cap, Jerry."

Jerry went back toward the house.

"Put these things back on the dresser in the room when you
go in, will you, Mama?" Danny said, handing his mother the
case. Polly Gray smiled gratefully up at Danny.

"I'm glad you would go with him," she said. "He's waited
a long time for this to happen. Be patient with him."

"I will, Mama — I've always tried to be — remember? But
he's grown in so many directions since I left here. In some
ways he's older than I am."

Polly Gray watched her two boys move off down the walk
and turn into the road toward the store, Danny erect, quick
and alert, and Jerry moving with loose-jointed, effortless ease.
Jerry's quick laughter drifted back to her through the soft, still
sunlight.

12

ALTHOUGH IT WAS LATE OCTOBER, AUTUMN HAD LAID NO IN-
timation of itself across the Woods. Down in the marshes
thick grass was turning brown, and on the far reaches of the
hills beyond the marsh, where the low hills rolled toward the
sea, toward the south beach that turned sharply westward
from the Point of the Cape, there were glints of color. The
dogwoods, first to greet the spring when it came up from the
south, were hanging out their russet-leaved flags of welcome
for autumn.

But along the sandy road that followed the slope above the
marsh there was no hint of autumn. Sunlight came down in
warm patches on the sand, slipping past the canopy of interlaced limbs of the live oaks overhead. The leaves were always
green. Next spring, when new leaves came, the trees would
somewhat absent-mindedly shed their old leaves.

So also would the yoepon and the cedar, but not until after
they had been prompted by the appearance of new grass along
the marshes, and the hibiscus was sending up tender young
shoots out of the muck, and the crows were brawling over their
nest-making in the tops of the taller pines on the ridge beyond
the marsh, and the snowy egrets, in their secretive fashion,
were carrying sticks for new nests in the green myrtles.

Pendants of Spanish moss hung from the limbs of the live
oaks and no breath of air stirred them. Under the trees there
was a cathedral quiet, and the shadows, out of reach of any

prying of the sunlight, were cool and remote and secretive. At the turn of the road, where it began to slant upward toward the top of the ridge, the ancient holly tree, its branches heavy with berries that were beginning to redden, its trunk rough with the whittled initials of generations, leaned at an unfamiliar angle above the road.

"That old holly tree's been listin' to port ever since the hurricane last year," Jerry said. "That was some hell of a wind, Danny. First it hit us from the ocean side and then it whopped us from the Sound side. Water was six feet deep here in the marsh."

Jerry, walking in the left wheel rut, moved up the incline with effortless ease, his bare feet touching the warm sand soundlessly. In the right wheel track Danny was finding the going surprisingly arduous. The sand gave way under his booted feet and he felt as if he were slipping backward. He wondered, glancing at Jerry's feet, if he had forgotten how to walk in the sand. Of course he hadn't . . . it must be these boots. . . .

Buying these boots had been one of the few times in all the years he had been away that Danny had let himself go in what seemed like extravagance. He was not, as they called it, stingy; he was just unused to spending money. He bought the boots in Brazil when they were on the way to North Africa. They had landed for an overnight rest and Danny saw the boots in a window. He bought them. They came halfway up the calves of his legs, but the leather was soft as a piece of silk. He had worn them a lot, but now — well, he wished again that he was barefoot like Jerry.

When they came to the top of the ridge both stopped, Jerry because Danny had halted, and Danny because he was a little out of breath and because he wanted to look at something that had ridden with him across the world and back again. Below him, westward and northward, was the now glassy blue of Pamlico, with the little harbor, white-dotted with small boats, each loosely tied to its stake. There was no dock for them, except the little one at the fishhouse. . . .

Yonder stretched the miles of the Woods, with here and there the roof of a house showing through the hazy green of the treetops. Yonder was the store, the little mite of a post office, the clean whitewashed picket fence, the schoolhouse with its acre of white sand in front of it where the boys over at the Coast Guard had helped to clear away the yoepon and make a playground. Here and there the white trail of the road showed through the trees, where it climbed across a ridge. . . .

"They got post cards of it down at the store now," Jerry said casually, but Danny scarcely heard him. He looked slowly around, his gaze swinging northward where the haze that hangs above the beach was thick under the noonday sun. He turned in a slow circle, his scrutiny lingering on the Lighthouse, its white-and-black, candy-striped spirals seeming almost to vibrate with life in the intense light of midday. Beyond it the sun danced on the Outer Diamonds.

Nothing . . . nothing here . . . had changed; it was all as he had seen it always, as he had remembered it he couldn't begin to think how many times and in what strange places. It had been a sort of anchor, he had thought, something to come back to. . . . Yonder he could see the remote white gleaming walls of the Station against the haze that curtained the Cape itself from his vision. . . . Danny turned back to the road and moved down the slope.

"You've never been sick a day in your life, have you, Jerry?" Danny said.

"Don't know as I have — unless it was maybe colic when I was a baby," Jerry replied, looking at Danny doubtfully. "Why?" he added.

"Guess I was thinking about the worst sickness there is — worse than seasickness or anything like that."

Jerry walked along in silence, a little puzzled, waiting for Danny to continue.

"I mean homesickness," Danny said.

"Oh," Jerry said, relieved. "I thought maybe you were talkin' about some disease you might have caught from them Japs."

"You've never been away from here, have you, Jerry?" The boy shook his head and said, doubtfully, that he had been to Norfolk that time — didn't Danny remember?

"Well, I guess all this sounds like darned foolishness to you," Danny went on, "and you'll never know how sick you can get until you are off somewhere away from everything you've ever known, from everybody you've ever known. Sometimes I'd get so homesick I'd — I'd cry myself to sleep."

"Nobody didn't see you, did they? There wasn't nobody sleepin' with you?"

Danny shook his head, laughing at Jerry's alarmed concern.

"What you mean is, you're glad to be back here," Jerry said reasonably. "Well, you ain't any gladder'n I am. I used to cry, nights, too, while you were first gone. Maybe I had the same ailment you had."

There were houses along the road now, each set back a little way, most of them screened from the road by plantings, or natural growth, cedars or yoepon and Cape jessamine. None of them were kept so neatly or painstakingly as Polly Gray's house, her yard, but all of them were clean, tidily painted. They were sturdy houses, square-built to withstand the shock of wind when hurricanes came roaring out of the south — or worse, when northeasters came howling down the coast in winter.

As if they might have been waiting for him, people seemed just to happen to be on the front porch, or out in the yard, when the two passed by.... Zenova Westcott, stouter — fatter — than Danny remembered her, came bustling down to the picket fence that guarded her flower beds, exclaiming breathlessly and flapping her arms like an alarmed goose trying to get off the water.

"Why, Danny Gray!" Her voice mounted into a breathless squeak of pleased excitement. She wiped her hands on her apron and reached across the fence to shake Danny by the shoulders. She held him off at the length of her plump arms. "My, my — how well you look! And you've grown!" All Zenova Westcott's utterances, everywhere and for all occasions, seemed to end in double exclamation points.

"Have you come home for good, Danny? Don't tell me you're going back to that Army — haven't you had enough of it? You just don't know how Polly Gray has missed you. We all have. We've been hearing about you — Eph heard all about you on the radio the other night and he said it was no more'n he expected. We're all mighty proud of you, Danny."

Zenova — she had been named for a schooner that was being pounded to bits off the Diamonds the day she was born — was still in full cry when Jerry interposed to say that they had to get along to the store and get back home. "Mom's waitin' for somethin' she needs for dinner," he said. He took Danny's elbow and they went on, leaving Zenova leaning against the paling of her fence, exclaiming after them. Danny must come up and see them right away.... "Eph will want to hear all about the war...."

"She's harder to stop than an east wind — pops off like a volcano," Jerry observed when they were out of hearing. "Did you see any volcanoes when you were gone, Danny? Did you see that one there's always pictures of in Japan?"

Before Danny could answer that he had flown over it a good many times, they were coming past another house, receiving another greeting. Jerry took no part in these encounters, or no active part. Nobody paid him the least attention, and for that he was secretly glad. These women were too —

they talked too damned much! Danny was polite enough. He took off his cap and stood there smiling, and, when he could, getting in a word or so edgewise. . . .

It took them a long time to get to the store, and when they got there it had all to be done over again. Mrs. Grady came around from behind the counter and put her arms around Danny's neck, and for a minute Jerry thought she was going to kiss him. But she just hugged him and exclaimed over him, said that he looked so grown-up and, of course, how proud Polly Gray must be of him. "And Jerry, too, of course — I know he's glad you're home."

This time of day the store was almost empty. Jerry glanced around, almost as if he were looking for somebody in particular, while Mrs. Grady was taking on over Danny. . . . She wasn't there: Jerry was relieved, and a little let down, too. He'd felt certain that she would be hanging around, like usual, waiting for Danny, or somebody. . . . He knew it had to happen sometime and it might just as well happen and be over with.

Danny glanced appraisingly around the little store. Mrs. Grady's eyes followed his glance and she interposed with "Times are not like they used to be, Danny. It's so hard to get anything now, and most of the time we're out of everything." The shelves did look pretty bare. The places where she used to have a lot of canned stuff — peaches and things like that, tomatoes, canned salmon — were empty. Mrs. Grady turned to Jerry.

"I got some more lemons, Jerry, and knowing Danny was likely to be home, I put away a whole dozen for your mother."

"Gee, thanks — thanks a lot," Jerry said. He had better tell her what else they wanted so he and Danny could get out of there and start for home. Jerry was beginning to feel an emptiness in his middle — and Danny must be tired of these goings-on about him. Mrs. Grady, even, couldn't keep her eyes off

Danny. Nobody could, for that matter.

Jerry glanced out the door to measure the time of day by the sun's shadow on one of the posts that held up the little porch in front of the store. It was mighty near twelve o'clock, and Mom always had dinner at twelve o'clock. He shifted his weight from one big foot to the other, waiting for Mrs. Grady to sort of run down so he could tell Danny it was time to be going. Jerry never interrupted older people when they were talking — nobody except Big Bill Henry, sometimes, but somehow the Chief never seemed like older people. But Jerry never interrupted him when he was busy with something that had to do with the Service, something that was official. . . .

Mrs. Grady continued. Jerry was not listening but he was conscious of the uninterrupted flow of her words. She was nice and friendly, always doing things for somebody, especially Mom — things like saving lemons for her, or a piece of beef for Sunday dinner when she had it. Jerry gazed out the door, off across the lowering Woods to where the blue of the Sound began. The Sound was still, without a breath of wind to stir its surface into any sign of life, except that now and then a fish broke the water out beyond where the boats were tied to their stakes. . . .

The sound of their voices, Danny's and Mrs. Grady's, with now and then one or another of the few people in the store breaking in, flowed around and past Jerry and out the door. Their humming almost made Jerry sleepy and he closed his ears utterly to the sound of it. He leaned indolently against the counter where Mrs. Grady kept the candy, when she had any, and the tubes of shaving soap and little bags of salted peanuts. He reached over the showcase with a long arm, explored until his fingers encountered peanuts, and withdrew them. With his other hand he reached down in his pocket, brought out a nickel, and laid it on top of the showcase.

Outside the door the jeep halted with a backward jerk, only

its front wheels showing through the narrow door. Jerry could tell by the way the body creaked who was in it, who was getting out. His eyes kindled when Big Bill Henry's bulk filled the narrow door.

Big Bill Henry Ragland ignored him and went past him, his enormous shoes creaking against the planking of the floor. His booming voice swallowed up all lesser sounds in the store when he demanded to be told if Jennie Grady had any such thing in that, in a manner of speaking, store as a mess of thumbtacks.

"It's got to be so it takes more thumbtacks than it does beach gear to run a Station," he rumbled. "Every day there comes a passel of paper from somewhere with directions that it be stuck up on a bulletin board so everybody can read it. And I'm plumb out of thumbtacks, and unless you got some I guess we'll just shut down the Station, even if a whole ocean full of people drowns."

Winged and brought down in full flight, right in the middle of something she was saying, though her sentences mostly had no beginning, no middle, and no end, Jennie Grady looked around helplessly.

"Why, Bill Henry — let me think. Seems like we did have some tacks like you mention around here somewhere. I believe I ordered them for something — I can't remember now what — about — I just can't think when it was — but I know we had some. But where did I put — no, they're not there. Jerry, have you ever noticed any thumbtacks around here anywhere?"

Jerry's grin was tolerantly stoic. He knew exactly where the thumbtacks were. They were in that showcase, under the box of assorted spool thread. Without moving anything but his arm, he reached around, felt for the tacks, and brought them out. He tossed them to the Chief with a flick of his wrist and returned to his contemplation of the shadow made by the sun against the post that held up the front porch.

"Goin' back to the Station, Chief? How about a ride as far as home — for me and Danny?"

The Chief grunted, pocketed the box of tacks, and strode toward the door. Jerry motioned Danny to come on, picked up his small parcels, and went out. He got into the back seat, leaving the front for Danny. The wheels groaned in the sand and the vehicle lurched around, turned back along the rutted road, its narrow tread making a havoc of the established ruts. They rode in silence until they topped the rise and the road slanted down toward the Gray house.

"When you comin' over to the Station to see us, Danny?" the Chief rumbled. "How about this — this afternoon?" He always hesitated over the use of what he called a store-bought word like "afternoon" — the first half of daylight was morning, the second half of it evening, and the rest of the time was night. Danny was about to say something, he was not sure what, when Jerry broke in.

"Can't," he said briefly, "We're goin' fishin'. Ought to be some mullet foolin' around out there in the Sound."

Danny glanced at his brother gratefully. There had not, until now, been anything said about fishing. He knew that he would have to go over to the Station sometime, that he would have to face something out with the Chief . . . but not today. He didn't want his first day of home spoiled. . . . The Chief let them out in front of the house and drove on, with a silent wave of his hand.

"Somethin' gnawin' on him," Jerry said speculatively. "He breaks out in a rash every time he gets a letter from Headquarters. He thinks the whole Service has gone plumb to hell since they 'bolished the ratin' of surfman."

"I didn't know they'd done that," Danny said, carelessly.

"Guess it's on account of the Navy," Jerry said. "They didn't have any, and the Coast Guard's got to be just like the Navy — a lot of 'em think."

Nothing was said about washing the dishes when they had eaten, but neither Polly Gray nor her sons thought for a moment about it. They had told her about the fishing trip while they were at dinner, and that had settled it. Domestic matters like washing the dishes, or anything else around the house, never interposed themselves into a man's world. If there was fishing in prospect, or duty at the Station — well, nobody ever thought about housework then. Men left women to their work just as naturally, just as automatically, as they helped them with it when they were about the house with nothing to do.

"Better have a spider hot when we get back," Jerry said to his mother with easy confidence when they left the kitchen, and to Danny he said, when they came to the bedroom, "I got a pair of sneakers around here somewhere. You'd better wear 'em if they're not too big for you. You'll mess up them boots in the boat. Better wear a pair of my dungarees, too."

"Think I'll go barefooted," Danny said.

"Better not — your feet's too tender. Sand'll burn hell out of you. Take these sneakers and lace 'em up tight." Danny put on the sneakers and dungarees.

This time they went purposefully along the road and Danny did not stop to look back at the sight of home. They did not talk as they went along the road, and now nobody came down to the fence to delay them with welcoming. Here and there somebody lifted an arm to wave, or a voice to call out in greeting, but they stopped nowhere. They were going fishing.

Nor was there any talk while they fished. Danny was surprised that the engine started so easily. Jerry had a way with engines — and with an oar, too, he observed. He untied the boat from the stake and shoved it out toward deeper water, poling it with the oar thrust against the sandy bottom. The engine sputtered when he cranked it, and went silent. Jerry cranked it again, swearing at it with no inconsiderable eloquence. The engine took hold, docile, even-tempered, and the boat went out along the channel.

"There ought to be some fish along here," Jerry said after a while. He stopped the engine and dropped the small anchor over the bow of the boat. He went back to the stern and lifted the cover of the small compartment built into the boat and took out the neatly bundled net, examined it briefly, and dropped it at his feet. Then with the same economy of movement he shook off his clothes, stripped down to his shorts.

"Keep on them sneakers and dungarees," he directed Danny. Danny stood uncertainly on the bow of the boat. It had been a long time since he had been fishing and he dreaded it a little for no reason that he could think of. Maybe it was because Jerry was so sure of himself, so casually competent about everything that he did. Jerry was waiting astern, with his feet trailing in the smooth water. He looked around to see if Danny was ready.

Danny's back was deeply freckled across the shoulders and along the upper part of his arms. . . . Danny had got hairy-chested while he was gone, Jerry observed, and he was a little taken aback. He glanced down at his own chest, wondering if anything had happened to it that he hadn't noticed. It was smooth and hairless.

"Hey, Danny," he called, "you take this end and hold it against the boat and I'll take the other and walk out along this shoal and bring it around to you. Keep them sneakers on — there might be a broke bottle around here somewheres. Lot of clunks think they can't fish unless they got beer in 'em."

The net was empty when they examined it after Jerry drew it in to the boat, and Danny felt a sense of disappointment. Jerry was unruffled. "Guess I made too damned much noise," he said, and when he waded out again, with the water coming almost to his armpits, he went without leaving a ripple on the surface. This time there were two stout, fat mullet in the net. Jerry, with his middle finger through the gills, tossed them into the boat. They wriggled, silver in the sunlight, and after a while they lay still against the box that housed the engine.

They fished throughout the afternoon. Not steadily, but intermittently, with long, lazy intervals between. They talked, sometimes about nothing in particular, sometimes with eager surges of animation. They lay on their backs up forward with their heads toward the sun that went lower across the Sound.

"Gimme one of them things," Jerry said when Danny was lighting a cigarette.

"Sure it won't make you sick?" Danny questioned with a small note of concern in his voice.

"Heck, no!" Jerry said. Danny watched him light, watched him as he smoked, drawing the smoke deeply. He wondered, but he did not ask, if Jerry had been smoking regularly. He wondered whether their mother knew he smoked. But he asked no questions. Jerry thumped the butt of the cigarette in a wide arc, his eyes following it until it plumped into the smooth water.

"Feel grown up now?" Danny said. He hoped he made it sound light and not concerned . . . or big-brotherly.

Jerry grinned, but said nothing. He rolled over on his side, balled up his fist and poked Danny's upper-arm muscles. A little frog came up under the skin.

"I smoke sometimes — just for the hell of it, I reckon," Jerry said lazily. "Bill Henry raises hell when he sees me." His voice trailed off into a comfortable silence. Jerry was easy to have around, Danny thought. But a little later he wondered if he might be wrong about that — he had such an uncanny way of getting right inside your mind.

"Danny," Jerry said, stretching himself lazily and turning on his back. Danny waited for a little to see what was coming next, and when Jerry did not continue, he said, "What's on your mind now, Jerry?"

"Goin' to take her that package you brung her tonight, Danny?"

Somewhat taken aback, Danny did not answer immediately. He had, at that moment, been thinking about the same thing and rather dreading to think about it. Thinking about it involved making up his mind to do it and — well, there was no avoiding Jerry; he would have to know about it. Maybe he was dreading the actual thinking more than he would the actual walking up the road with it in his hand and seeing her. He wished he had left the damned thing in Tokyo.

There was, he told himself, no reason why he should bring Sally Tillett anything from Tokyo or from anywhere. There was nothing, there had never been anything, between them. They were about the same age, they had started to school the same year, finished the same year. She had never been "his girl" or anything like that. They had sat next to each other in class, and on fish-fries and things like that they had sort of paired off.

But there was nothing to it, nothing more than that. He liked her, in the casual fashion of — of the young. Danny was somehow shocked to be thinking of "the young." After he went to State in Raleigh he had sent her some post cards, pictures of buildings at school, the Capitol, things like that. It was all just foolishness . . . a blurred sort of a mess, he thought unhappily.

Sometimes he would think about her when he was by himself, or when the fellows were talking about their girls . . . their women. They talked a lot about their women. . . . They talked mostly about their women, but Danny had always the feeling that they were just talking and that they, like himself, actually didn't know very much about girls . . . about women. Only, Danny was never very much of a talker.

Not that he was shy or — well, it was always a mystery to him why the fellows, or so many of them, made so much of — of sex. There had never been any mystery about sex, not to Danny. He had always known about it — or anyhow since

Jerry was born. Daddy had told him about it, like he would have told him — like he did tell him — about how to run a boat. There was nothing ugly about it, the way Daddy made it sound, nothing to be secretive about, to be ashamed of. . . .

It was just something that happened, naturally, in its own time. Danny had never linked Sally Tillett and sex together — or he hadn't until he listened to so much of the talk about women that seemed always to be eddying around him. The piece of silk, when he saw it, had just somehow, there in that shop in Tokyo, reminded him of Sally. Danny knew that Jerry was looking at him, not expectantly, nor speculatively . . . just looking at him.

"Yeah, I guess I'd just as well," he said, and he knew that he had not made it sound as careless as he had intended to make it sound. "Let's make another haul and go home, what do you say?"

"Okay," Jerry said and dropped soundlessly from the end of the boat.

The mullet were running better and there were ten of them when they hauled the net back to the boat. Jerry hauled the anchor and started the engine, swung around in a comfortable circle, and headed into the channel. Jerry appraised their catch.

"We've got a lot more'n we can eat," he said. "We could sell 'em — there's nearly four dollars worth here but, heck, let's give Zenova a mess — she always liked fish — and Miss Jennie Grady's mouth will be just waterin' when we pass there."

"Suits me, Jerry," Danny said.

Jerry reached inside the wooden box that housed the engine and pulled loose the wire that led from the coil. The engine stopped and the boat nudged its stake gently. He knotted the bow line around the stake. He hauled the skiff alongside and tossed the mullet into it. He hauled the net together and tossed it into the skiff.

"This thing's got a hole in it — guess I better take it home and fix it before we use it again," he said.

Zenova Westcott surpassed even herself in breathless exclamation when Jerry laid the three mullet on the steps at her kitchen door. She had been, she said, wishing all day that somebody would bring her a mess of fish. She had been after her Eph — her Ephriam — all week to get off'n his bottom and get her a mess of fish, but it seemed like he just couldn't get around to it and she would be glad when her Little Eph got home from the war so she could have fish whenever she wanted them.

"Since he got out of the Coast Guard, Eph, he ain't done nothin' but just set," she went on placidly and with utter dispassion. "When it's cool he sets in the sun and when it's warm he sets in the shade and I can't get a thing out of him."

Her round, creased smile cushioned her words, and Jerry knew, as a matter of fact, that if Ephriam Westcott so much as stirred out of his chair, Zenova would be right after him with admonishment not to strain himself or anything. She would be reminding him that the doctors, three of them, had told him to take care of his heart.

When they got home Jerry was very casual about the fish. He called to his mother to know if she had the skillet hot like he told her. He laid the fish on the grass outside the kitchen door and went inside to get the scaling knife. Surfman came down the slope from where he had been asleep under the fig tree. He sniffed each fish and sat down. He extended a tentative paw and touched the largest of them.

"You lay off'n them fish, Surfman," Jerry said from the kitchen door, and the cat withdrew his paw, waiting. Jerry put the fish on the cleaning board set against the wall outside the door. The cat hopped nimbly up, settled himself, and waved his long, bushy tail, watchfully.

"Where you been the last two days, cat?" Jerry demanded.

The cat looked at him with fixed, unblinking eyes. "Don't you try to play dumb with me, cat," Jerry went on, his voice stern. "You been off gallin' and — where'd you get that scratch on your face? Somebody beat hell out'n you, didn't they? Told you to watch yourself when you got to foolin' around among those woods cats, didn't I?"

Jerry shoved the severed head of a mullet toward the cat, and Surfman, after smelling it daintily, pushed it away with his paw.

"So you don't like your fish raw, Surfman? Hell of a sea-farin' cat you are." The cat regarded him without emotion, and Jerry turned toward the kitchen.

"Say, Danny!"

Danny answered him from the kitchen.

"If you are goin' gallin' you better go wash yourself and put on your gear before supper. Pitch my sneakers and dungarees out the window and I'll hang 'em up to dry. Guess I'll fix this net while Mom's cookin' these fish."

"He thinks of everything, doesn't he, Mama?" Danny said to his mother, relieved that Jerry had so casually divulged his plans for the evening. "I guess I'd better go and do like he says."

Polly Gray's smile, above the bowl in which she was mixing the batter for the muffins, was as serene as the sunset that brightened the sky beyond the window. Danny went, whis-tling, toward the bathroom. When Polly Gray called them to supper, Danny came first. His face was ruddy and clean-shaven and no wrinkle showed anywhere in his uniform. The ribbons and the wings outspread under them made a bright patch against the dark olive of his blouse.

"Danny, how nice you look!" his mother exclaimed. "I guess I was so busy looking at you last night that I just missed your uniform completely."

"Aw, Mama," Danny said, embarrassed, pleased.

Jerry came in from the kitchen after washing his hands at the sink. They heard him addressing the cat with mild blasphemies, and when he came into the dining room the cat's long body drooped resignedly under his arm. In his other hand Jerry had the three-legged stool that Daniel Gray had made for Polly's kitchen. He placed the stool beside his chair at the table and sat Surfman on it.

"Now you sit there, Mister, and behave yourself. And I don't want to hear a word, not nary word, out of you until I get ready to feed you — hear me?"

Surfman blinked and sat still. Jerry tumbled into his chair. He smelled faintly of raw fish. His thick hair, curling a little, fell across his forehead. His shirt was open, all the way. He grinned engagingly, disarmingly, and Danny wondered if Jerry could be as unaware of his own charm as he seemed to be.

"You ain't met Surfman, have you Danny?" Jerry inquired. "He's been off havin' himself a spell of romance. He's a good cat. Castaway. I got him over on the beach. He was just a kitten when he come ashore in one of them lifeboats that was full of bullet holes. He was all there was alive on it. How about sayin' grace so we can eat, Danny?"

All through supper Jerry appeared to be preoccupied with Surfman. From time to time he took a piece of fish between his thumb and forefinger and held it out to the cat. When Surfman took it in his jaws and made as if to put it down on the stool, Jerry clucked reprovingly.

"That's no way for a good-mannered cat to eat, Mister," and the cat seemed to conform obediently to his master's notions of what constituted suitable table manners.

Jerry pushed his chair away from the table and stood up. He held open the kitchen door and Surfman departed, replete and full of dignity and contentment. Jerry looked at Danny and said, "I'll walk as far as the post office with you, Captain, and get the mail — Gee, Mom, we've not been after the mail in two days, have we? It don't seem to matter much whether we get it or not, now that we've got Danny home, does it?"

Danny went to the bedroom to get his hat and Jerry followed him. "Think I'll hit the sack as soon as I get back from the post office, but you can wake me up when you get home, Danny."

Danny was arranging his cap before the mirror, and when he had it at an acceptable angle he started for the door. Jerry watched him for a moment, then went to Danny's unlocked bag and took out the flat parcel.

"You ain't about to go off and leave this here, are you, Danny?"

13

THE CLEMATIS VINE THAT SPRAWLED IN BILLOWING GREEN OVER
the porch roof, spilling over the eaves in a cascade of loose,
undisciplined luxuriance, was the only hallmark of distinction
about Mahala Tillett's house. The paling fence that sur-
rounded the yard sagged and the whitewash on it was flaked
and unkempt. Sandspurs rioted across the white sand of the
yard, their sharp spikes biting at the ankles of anybody who
went along the walk. The walk was bordered by rows of listless
Cape jessamines.

There had been no paint for the weather-roughened boards
of the house for a long time. The house had a sad, wilted look,
very like Mahala Tillett herself. Above the first floor a chimney
leaned away from one end of the house as if it might be re-
coiling from too close association with it, and the lightning
rod that ran upward along its center line was bent outward.
It looked like the wilted stem of some tall flower.

But the clematis vine, planted in shaded ground at one end
of the porch that ran the length of the front of the house, was,
summer and winter, riotously healthy. About the only time,
nowadays, that people ever glimpsed Mahala Tillett was when
they saw her coming up from the marsh that stretched away
from the foot of the slope back of her house. She would have
a big pail in her hand and her shoulders would sag from the
weight of the black muck that sloughed up over the rim of the
pail.

Mahala Tillett's whole life, now, seemed somehow to be

centered in the clematis vine. Nobody knew where it had come from or how it came to be there. It was akin to, but more delicately flowered than, the wild clematis that grew at the edge of the marshes. When people thought about it at all they supposed that it must have been something that her husband had brought from somewhere when he came home. He was never at home very much; he was on a ship somewhere — a seagoing ship.

Older people could remember when Mahala was — well, not like she was now, not like she had been for a long time. She had been young and pretty, they remembered, and lively . . . the very image of Sally. That had been when she was young, right after Vance Tillett had brought her to the house that had been his father's. He had fixed it up, put on a new cypress shingle roof. He had built with his own hands the picket fence and a new cistern to catch rain water. He and Mahala had brought with their own hands the muck from the marsh to enrich the planting of Cape jessamines along the walk.

And then Vance Tillett went away to his ship, went away to the sea again. People knew that Mahala was going to have a baby, and the women of the Woods were very gentle with her. But Mahala Tillett, who was so pretty and so gay and lively, became still and silent; and there were lines between her eyes that were deeper every day. She never said much, but all the women of the Woods knew that she was afraid . . . afraid that the sea would not let Vance come back to her . . . afraid that her baby might be a man-child.

There was nothing so very strange about that and the women of the Woods understood it. They resented — passively, most of them — the sea. It took their men from them and sometimes never let them come back. Mahala Tillett, when they showed her the newly-born, covered its male nakedness with a sheet. She pushed it away from her and turned her face to the wall.

Nobody could remember, after that, ever seeing Mahala

Tillett smile again. She was very tender with the baby and it thrived and grew, but the women of the Woods were puzzled at what she had named it. They were puzzled, when the child grew and walked and began to talk, that she never put a man-child's clothes on it. She dressed the child like a girl and kept it always within sight of her own eyes, within reach of her own hands.

Vance Tillett came home from the sea, but his visits were shorter, with longer intervals between them; and he was silent most of the time, he who had been so boisterous and friendly with everybody. He went back to the sea. Once a month Mahala went to the post office, where there would be a letter for her, a thin letter, but always it had a blue piece of paper in it, and Mahala would get money for it at the window. Then she would go to the store to buy things, and sometimes she would go to the post office to buy a money order, which she put in an envelope addressed to a place in Chicago.

More and more Mahala Tillett lived to herself, withdrawn and silent. She never went to church. She was not un-friendly. She just did not go around much; and nobody ever heard her laugh, ever saw her smile. Then it was time for the child to start to school. Nothing happened the first year; but the second year, after he was seven, he appeared at school one morning, dressed in a neat gingham dress. Nobody said any-thing. The women of the Woods were silent, and Mahala's secret was safe with them. The children didn't know, and Jessie Tillett always went straight home from school. Mahala Tillet would be waiting, outside the gate, her eyes remote and brooding; and light would kindle in them when she caught sight of the bright gingham dress coming toward her. . . .

Vance Tillett came home that fall, but he stayed just one day. When he passed the store on the way to the dock where the mail boat landed every day, he didn't look at anybody and he spoke no word to anybody. It was five years before he came back again, but the envelope came on its appointed day every month. Mahala Tillett never opened the envelope where anybody could see her, but it was plain enough to anybody that there was no writing in it, no letter — just the blue slip of paper that Mahala took to the window and got money for.

When Jessie Tillett was not quite twelve years old he discovered that he was not a girl, that he was a man-child. He appeared at the store, his face swollen and ashamed. He had on one of his father's old shirts, with its folds clutched together about his middle. He held some crumpled money in his hand, held the bills out to Mrs. Grady without a sound. His eyes were dry and hot and hard, and his mouth was grimly set.

Mrs. Grady was an understanding woman. One glance from her choked off the ribald laughter that began where a little knot of people were clustered around the stove. She went to the door and held it open. Without a word the idlers left. When Jesse Tillett walked out of the store again, he was wearing blue overalls and a denim shirt. The havoc that he had done to his long, girl's hair, coarse and dark, had been remedied; his head was close-cropped and he wore a boy's cap.

What happened when he got home nobody ever knew, but after that he could be seen almost any time during daylight wandering the remote ridges of the Woods; or standing on a dune out by the Lighthouse, staring at the sea; or sitting, alone and silent, down by the little dock where the mail boat tied up when it put off and took on mail or chance passengers. He would be staring out across the Sound. He never spoke to anybody, except to Mrs. Grady when he came to the store. Mahala Tillett didn't come to the store any more.

Jesse Tillett was big and sturdy when his father came home the next time. Sometimes, during that visit, which lasted longer, the father and son came to the store together. Vance Tillett was not so taciturn as he had been. He spoke to people when they spoke to him, but mostly he was preoccupied with the boy. He was at home for more than two weeks that time. When he went down to the dock to go away on the mail boat, the boy trudged beside him and carried a small bundle under his arm. He did not come back from the dock and people knew that he was gone. He was big for his age now, and there was nothing unusual about a boy going to sea when he was no older than that. Jesse Tillett had never come back to the Woods.

After that Mahala Tillett was more remote, more withdrawn, than ever. Some of the women, in compassion, went to see her, but she was listless and silent; and she never mentioned her husband or the boy who was gone from her. After a while people who glimpsed her, who saw her when she came to the post office or to the store, knew that there would be another baby; but it was not until they heard her scream in the night that anybody knew her time had come. Some of the women of the Woods, when they hurried through the dark, forgetful of their lanterns and thankful for the great pointing finger of the Light, found her, senseless and bloody. The newborn child wailed in the dark.

The women of the Woods washed the baby and attended the mother. By dawn Mahala Tillett had come back into consciousness, and when they showed her the child, wrapped in a blanket, she seemed not to care. Zenova Westcott laid back the wrappings so she could see that it was a woman-child, but Mahala Tillett gave no sign that she knew or cared. The women were trying to be cheerful and Zenova Westcott asked her what they should name it. Mahala Tillett seemed not to hear them.

"Let's name it Sally," Zenova persisted in determined cheerfulness. "My Eph come home last night and he was telling me about a little schooner that was ashore on the Inner Diamonds. It was named 'Sally' and I'm named for a boat that was being wrecked while I was being borned — let's name her Sally."

And so they called the child Sally. By the time the child was able to walk, all the women who could remember when Mahala came into the Woods as a bride knew that the baby would look just like her. She was a pretty baby, but Mahala seemed never to care; nor did Vance Tillett seem to care when he came home the next year and saw this daughter for the first time. He was as silent as ever, and he said nothing to anybody about what had become of Jesse. Nobody quite dared to ask Mahala — nobody knew how she might take it. No letter from him ever came to the post office. It was on that trip home that Vance Tillett must have brought the clematis, and before long it began to climb up the pillar at the corner of the porch.

Sometimes the cold killed it back, and its billowing green leaves were black and dead. But nothing could kill it down through the wrapping of sacks and muck that Mahala put around its roots in winter, and by spring it would be climbing back over the porch. Most winters the cold did not amount to enough to bother it at all. About the only times anybody ever saw Mahala were when she watered the roots of the rioting vine, or worked at its climbing tendrils, or lugged muck from the marsh.

The vine was the only fresh and vibrant thing about the whole place — the vine and Sally. The child grew into a healthy, laughing baby. When Mahala came to the store or the post office, she brought Sally in her arms and the baby cooed and laughed — almost flirted, Mrs. Grady thought, as she waited on the silent mother who never said anything beyond mentioning the things she wanted from the store's shelves.

Sally started to school when she was six. She was bright and clean, with her bright silky hair in neat braids and tied with blue ribbon. The gingham dresses she wore to school seemed, to the older women who saw her go past toward the schoolhouse, a little faded; and they wondered, mildly, if they were not, maybe, the same dresses that poor Jesse had had to wear when he started to school. They were not even a little alike, Jesse and Sally. Jesse was dark, like his father, and his hair

152152152152152 *sand roots*

grew close around his head; the ends of it were always wriggling
out of the braid into which his mother had bound it, and the
ribbon often came loose. But Sally's hair was like silk and
almost the color of thick cream. Her forehead was broad and
low and her eyes were a shining blue. There was something
elusive and beckoning and a little challenging about her smile,
even that first day when she came to school with two of her
front teeth missing.

Sally was, everybody said, smart in her books. She learned
easily and eagerly, but there was nothing ostentatious or too
self-assertive and superior about the child. Always she knew
the answers when nobody else knew them. The little dimples
on each side of her wide little mouth twinkled, and the other
children, even the more dour among the boys of the class,
remembered the dimples and forgot that she was smarter than
they were. . . .

Danny was thinking about, remembering, Sally's dimples
when he came to the gate that hung from one hinge. He
tucked the flat parcel snugly under his armpit to free one hand
for the spare handkerchief he had brought to clean the dust
from his newly-shined shoes, and to lift the gate. Its single
hinge groaned disconcertingly when he let himself through
and he wondered if it would be amiss to leave the gate open.
He could close it when he started home.

Light from an oil lamp, blurred and diffused by the thin
lace curtains, came through the two windows of the room at
the left of the hallway that ran through the house, the room
that Sally used to call the parlor. Danny tried to remember
what the room looked like, but he could not recall that he
had ever been inside the house. Sometimes, during their last
year at school, he had walked home with Sally from one or
another of the festivities they were having at school, or from
prayer meeting on Wednesday night.

But Sally always said good night on the front steps, and it
never occurred to him to wonder why she didn't ask him to

come in, or to wonder why it was he never saw Sally's mother. Always he could feel her presence when he came to the front steps with Sally, as if she were looking at them from behind that vine, or from somewhere in the house. It gave him an uncomfortable feeling, this sense of being watched, but then — well, everybody liked Sally, and she couldn't help it if her mother was sort of queer. . . .

Sometimes, especially during that last week of school when they were rehearsing a play they were going to give, and Sally had to practice reading her valedictory, Danny came to the front door and walked with her to the schoolhouse. Sometimes he came in the car, and then he stopped out front and blew the horn. By the time he got there the car was usually filled with boys or girls who climbed aboard as he came down through the Woods. But always there was that creepy feeling that Sally's mother's eyes were brooding upon him.

As he came along the sandy road toward the house with the curious vine climbing all over it, Danny had tried to remember when he had seen Sally last. He had not come to say good-bye when he left; and the one time that he was at home, when he got leave after finishing primary flight training, he could not remember that he had even seen her. They had given him just three days and he hadn't had time. He hadn't even been to the store.

As Danny went up the walk the air was heavy with the scent of Cape jessamine, and in the blurred light that came through the leaves of the clematis he could see that there were a few waxy white blossoms at the tops of the bushes on each side of the walk. He remembered Sally's dimples; and he remembered the uneasy feeling that he had always had when he came up that walk, or when he turned back away from the house and toward the road — the feeling that Sally's mother's eyes were following him.

Without seeing anything, actually, in the gloom beyond the vine, Danny sensed that something, somebody, had moved along the porch; and then the light that streamed through the windows was obscured for a brief moment; somebody was moving along the porch toward the steps — or was it toward the door that opened into the hallway? Danny could not be sure. Maybe Sally was coming to meet him, or maybe her mother had been sitting on the porch and now she was going into the house to avoid seeing him. He could not remember that Mahala Tillett had ever spoken to him in all his life. The moving shadow stopped and Danny knew that it was Sally, waiting for him at the top of the steps.

"Hi, Sally," Danny said, "I was just wondering if your dimples still show."

"Danny!"

Danny stood at the bottom of the steps and looked up at her. The diffused light from the window caught her hair and made it shine with a luminous glow. There was a blur of white in her hair and Danny caught the odor of a Cape jessamine. He could not see her eyes, nor her dimples, if she still had them, nor tell the color of her dress. But he could see that she was still lithely slender.

"Danny!" she repeated and then her voice lost that soft, blurred huskiness that Danny remembered. It was higher pitched, almost nasal — and not Sally. "Danny darling how nice to see you!" The words ran together. She reached out with her hands, came down a step toward him. Danny felt her hands take hold of the sleeves of his blouse, pulling him upward. He felt her hands tremble, heard her breath come in little, unsteady — unreal — gasps. He knew he ought to say something, do something — anything would be better than standing there dumb. He shifted his feet unsteadily on the bottom step.

"Danny," Sally breathed against his shoulder, "it's so wonderful to see you."

It sounded like something Danny had heard in a moving picture somewhere, maybe one of those USO places where they brought girls out in busloads and turned them loose, in a fashion, among airplane drivers. It just didn't sound like Sally — or like any other girl Danny had ever heard, here in the Woods.

"It's nice to see you, too, Sally," he said, and he wanted to kick himself for sounding like that. Then, managing a lighter note, but with his voice still a little shaken, he said, "Aren't you going to ask me to come in — after all these years?"

"Of course, Danny darling — come on in — I've been just breathless to see you ever since I heard you were home."

She slipped a slender hand under his arm and turned toward the door that opened into the hallway.

"Come on in where there's light so I can look at you." She led him through the hall and into the room that they had always called the parlor.

Sally took his cap and dropped it on the table that stood beside the door and turned back to him. She came close and took him by the shoulders and turned him slowly about. Her lips were parted breathlessly and her long, surprisingly dark lashes drooped over her eyes. Her eyelids, Danny thought, looked blue. She made small, secretive cluckings in her throat, exclaiming to herself over him. Uncomfortably, Danny thought: this is all very pretty, very like moving pictures — but it isn't Sally.

"You look simply wonderful," Sally said, drawing the last word out until each syllable sounded like a complete word in itself. She clasped her hands between her breasts and leaned backward, her head to one side, and looked at him. Danny noticed, with a little shock, that her breasts looked hard and pointed, with her dress, dark red, stretched tight across them like that. Danny was obscurely ashamed of himself for even noticing or thinking a thing like that . . . about Sally.

"Here's — here's something I brought you," Danny said, and once more he wanted to kick himself for being a blundering idiot. The parcel, still flattened under his armpit, fell to the floor when he loosened the pressure of his arm. Bad co-ordination, he thought, as he stooped to retrieve it; if some flight surgeon caught you he'd ground you just like that! Danny picked up the package and handed it to her awkwardly, his face red.

"It's just something I saw in a window in Tokyo, one of the windows that I guess we didn't smash, and somehow the color of it reminded me of the color of your eyes and I thought it might make you a nice dress."

Sally took it in her hands and with a lingering, speculative look into his eyes turned toward the lamp on the table before the fireplace. Danny followed her, hesitantly.

"I brought Mama some of the same stuff, only a different color," he said.

Sally's fingers ripped the paper. Her nails were dark red, the color of her dress. Her fingers tore at the paper, and Danny remembered with what slow carefulness his mother — was it just last night? — had undone the wrappings of her parcel when he gave it to her. He fumbled for a cigarette, lighted it.

"Light me one, too, will you, Danny?" Sally murmured. Her voice had regained its soft blur, its native huskiness. A thick lock of her shining hair fell across her forehead. She turned her mouth toward him, opened her lips. Danny put the cigarette between her lips and smoke curled upward through the lock of her hair.

The paper wrappings fell away and the shimmering cloth, blue and almost incandescent where the light touched its folds, seemed alive in her hands. She laid her cigarette in the clam-shell tray on the table and held the cloth at arm's length away from her. She held it draped across her body, against her breasts, around her slender waist, let it fall in soft loose folds about her ankles. She looked into Danny's eyes and the dimples at the corners of her mouth came and went and came again. She gathered the cloth in both hands and laid it across the back of a chair. She picked up her cigarette without looking at it and inhaled deeply, stubbed it out against the clam-shell.

"Danny," she said, her voice almost a whisper, "I'll just have to kiss you."

Danny stood, still, awkward, wishing that she wouldn't, hoping that she would, and wondering what crowning stupidity he would be guilty of next. Sally came toward him, her eyes shining under her long, unaccountably dark lashes.

She slipped one hand under his arm and Danny felt her arm, warm against the small of his back. The other hand went up, above his shoulder, and her hand was against the back of his neck, the finger tips exploring his hair. She stood on tiptoe and drew his head down. Her lips were warm and moist against his mouth. Danny could feel her whole body pressing against his own. Her thighs lay warm against his, and he could feel her breasts pressing against his breast. Her lips clung to his, and Danny could feel the tip of her tongue against his lips, against his teeth.

All volition, even the power of breathing, seemed somehow to seep out of Danny's body, and he stood, his hands limp against his thighs, but with a strange tingling in the tips of his fingers. And then, without any awareness of what he was doing, his hands came up and his arms were around the girl's waist. His hands, moving with little trembling spasms, explored her back. His arms held her tightly to him, and he could feel her heart throbbing, her breath coming in quick, jerky gasps, until he was set aflame with a blaze that rolled like a marsh fire, down through his stomach, flared out across his loins.

With a little breathless cry Sally loosed her arms about him, put her hands on his shoulders and pushed him away, gently at first and then not so gently when Danny's arms were tight about her waist and his mouth fumbled against her cheek. His breath came in deep, hungry gusts.

"Danny," Sally said without looking up at him, "I don't

believe you've ever kissed a girl before in all your life — but I believe you could learn without much trouble."

"In one easy lesson," Danny replied and was surprised at his own boldness and at some curious sense of assurance, of confidence that had driven out, put to flight, his feeling of awkwardness and indecision.

The girl glanced at him, seemed about to say something, but she turned away, with her back to him while she lighted a cigarette at the table before the fireplace. Danny was too confused, too wrapped in his own tumult, to notice any change in her. When she had lighted the cigarette and tapped the match against the tray, she turned back to him, cool, smiling.

"Gosh, Danny, you've got lipstick or something all over your mouth — have you been a bad little boy?" Her tone was light, remotely mocking. Danny reddened, fumbling for his handkerchief. He could feel sweat popping out along his brow, and his armpits felt cold and clammy. Sally said, "Here, let me do it," and she took his handkerchief, touched his lips, lightly and then more firmly.

Danny could feel the pressure of her finger tips on his mouth and he tried to lay his hands on her shoulders. She shook them off with a little gesture, avoiding him. When he tried it again she shook her head, laughing a little provocative laugh. Danny felt the marsh fire sweeping down out of his breast again. He wanted to get his hands on her naked shoulders but, his face ruddy-red, he thrust them deep in his trouser pockets.

"There — that will do, I think," Sally said, pushing him away.

"Let's sit outside where it's cooler," Danny proposed.

"Is it hot in here — I hadn't noticed," Sally replied. "I guess it's this lamp. I wish we had electric lights. These lamps heat up a room so." She was cool, casual.

Outside, in the deep shadow of the clematis vine, they sat in the cushioned porch swing. Sally's hands lay inert on the cushion and, in the dark, Danny laid his hand over hers, searching for her fingers with his own. She drew her hand away, slowly, and in the gloom Danny could see that both her hands were folded in her lap. After some hesitation Danny tried again to take hold of her hands, making, he knew, an awkward, fumbling mess of it.

This time she pushed his groping fingers away, not ungently but definitely, firmly. With her toes against the floor she rocked the swing back and forth, gently, withdrew into a meditative, detached silence. Danny sat with one arm along the back of the swing, his face turned toward her, his hand drooping downward toward her shoulder, not quite touching it. He wished that he could think of something to say.

"I thought —" Her voice trailed off into silence.

The house was still, and in the silence Danny remembered how he used to feel that Sally's mother was watching him, secretly, from somewhere in the house. He moved uncomfortably away from the girl, and his arm came away from the back of the swing.

"What did you say, Sally?"

"Oh, nothing."

"You must have said something. What did you start to say?"

"Oh, skip it, Danny," she said, with a little gesture of impatience. "Let's talk about you — have you come home for good? And who all have you seen since you've been back? Peggy? You must have gone to see her, surely."

Danny protested that he hadn't even thought of Peggy, much less gone to see her. He said he hadn't even wondered if she was still around. She might have married somebody, some of those fellows who had come down to the stations along the Banks about the time he went away.

Sally's silence had a sort of stoniness about it, and Danny decided to say no more about Peggy. He told her about going fishing that afternoon and, with more enthusiasm kindling in his voice than he was quite aware of, about what a good boatman Jerry had come to be while he was away.

"I've never seen anybody grow like he has while I've been gone — he's almost as heavy as I am."

Danny felt Sally's eyes searching his face in a brief, measuring glance, but she said nothing. Presently she asked for a cigarette, reached for it in the dark. He felt her fingers touch his but there was no answering pressure from them when he held the match for her. She inhaled deeply and lapsed again into silence.

Danny talked on, a little desperately, but there were only intermittent responses from the girl. She seemed withdrawn, remote, brooding — like her mother, almost. Not hostile exactly, but withdrawn from him, as if he were not really there. A feeling of frustration began to gnaw at Danny, a frustration that transformed itself into irritation. Sally made only desultory comment upon anything he had to say, but now and then Danny could feel her glance searching his face. After a while he said that he guessed it was time for him to be going.

"So soon, Danny?" Sally said, but she did not protest, did not insist that it was early. She stood up dismissively, and went into the house and brought out his cap. Danny stood, hesitant, puzzled, confused. She walked with him to the top of the steps and he turned, impulsively, and tried to put his arms around her. She eluded his arms and stood, cool, composed outwardly. All the artificiality of her welcome, the "Danny darling" mood, all the wanton passion of her kiss, and all the sunny naturalness that he remembered — none of these things were left. It was a stranger to whom he said a curt good night.

Danny went down the walk without a backward glance. He did not see Sally start, with a little convulsive lift of her arms, as if she wanted to reach out and bring him back. He left the unhinged gate hanging crazily open and went down the sandy road through the Woods. A little shudder went across his shoulders, and he wondered if Mahala Tillett's eyes had flicked him.

Danny walked faster than he realized, he almost ran, until he was over the ridge that separted the house with the clematis vine sprawled across it from the other houses in that end of the Woods. His thoughts were a tumbled confusion as he went down the slope toward home. He couldn't think just what it was he had expected when he saw Sally Tillett again, unless it was the same girl he had gone through all the grades of school with, the girl with blue eyes and shining hair and twinkling dimples.

Something funny had happened to her, Danny's thoughts went on as he plodded the deep-rutted road. He didn't like it — and he did like it. He felt his face redden when he thought of how he — how he had behaved when she kissed him like that. He excused himself with thinking that he hadn't expected it, that she had taken him without any warning. He knew that she had kindled a fire, that she had set burning a flame that he had never felt before — felt with any sort of purpose.

He knew, now, that he wanted Sally Tillett. He did not try to analyze it, appraise it. His mind was too filled with bewilderment at why she, having kindled the flame, had smothered it, killed it with cold, inexplicable silence. He wondered if it was something that he had said, that he had done, that had changed her so suddenly from her mood of provocative ardor to a mood of cool — cold — dispassion. What was it she had started to say?

Well, he would find out, Danny told himself doggedly, the next time he saw her. He would ... well, he would show her that he didn't need but one lesson ... when he saw her again. But when would that be? She had said no word about his coming back to see her, and he had not, himself, proposed it. But he would see her, he would show her. ...

Danny let himself into the sleeping house in silence, closed the door behind him without a sound. The door to the bedroom, he could see by the coming and going of the Light, was half open; and beyond it he could see the opal blur of the windows against the moonlight. He went in and started to undress without turning on the light . . . no use waking Jerry, or disturbing his mother. He took off his blouse and hung it over the back of a chair, sat down to take off his shoes. He fumbled in the closet for his pajamas and decided, since he couldn't find them, he would sleep in his shorts, like Jerry.

Accustomed now to the dark in the room, he could see, when the Light flickered along the wall, Jerry sprawled across the bed. He had on the fantastic pajamas that were fashioned from a red parachute, the upper half of them open. Jerry's breathing came even-paced, soundless. Danny stood hesitant, wondering whether it would wake the boy if he moved that sprawled leg to make room for himself on the bed. He was startled when the light at the head of the bed clicked into life. Jerry rolled over on his back, toward the wall. He grinned, wide awake.

"Hi," Jerry said. "Light hurt your eyes, Danny Darling?"

Without a word Danny sat down on the edge of the bed, kicked off his socks and stretched himself out on the bed. The calves of his legs ached from walking in the sand.

"How'd you make out?" Jerry said presently, and Danny felt a fleeting sense of irritation. He wished that Jerry had not awakened, or that, now that he was awake, he would go back to sleep and not — and not ask questions. Danny said nothing for a minute, and then he tried to make his voice sound tired and sleepy and careless when he said that he had made out all right. Jerry moved a little further toward the wall. He held his foot up in the path of the Light and watched its grotesque shadow flick against the wall.

Surfman stood up beside Jerry's pillow and stretched himself, yawned. He sat down on his haunches and considered Jerry meditatively, purred softly when the boy reached up and scratched him under the chin. Surfman extended a paw and touched Jerry's cheek lightly. The boy's foot moved across the bed to the window, and the great toe felt for the hook at the bottom of the screen, pushed upward. The screen came up.

"Want to go outdoors and wee-wee, Mister?" Jerry said. Surfman went sedately down the bed to the window and stood for a moment with his forefeet on the sill. He disappeared into the darkness outside.

"Surfman's a good cat," Jerry said. "Sleeps with me regular when he's home. When he wants to go out he just pokes me in the face with his paw and I let him out."

"Will he come back in? Do you leave the window open like that?"

"Don't reckon he will," Jerry said. "Guess he's sort of jealous — you bein' here." He reached with his foot and hauled down the screen.

Jerry turned toward Danny, raised himself on one elbow, and studied his brother's face appraisingly. He grinned. Danny folded his arms across his eyes, shielding them from the light.

"Got that stuff all over your mouth, Danny Darling," he said. "Hold still, dammit."

Jerry moistened a finger with the tip of his tongue and scrubbed, holding the finger to the light to examine the result. He reached under his pillow and brought out a handkerchief, making clicking noises with his tongue against his teeth. He scrubbed Danny's upper lip and tossed the handkerchief away, sending it across the room. He clicked out the light and rolled over against the wall.

"Did she lay you, Danny Darling?" he asked presently, and his tone was as casual as if he had mentioned the passing of a heron across the sky at sundown. Danny was glad that he had turned off the light before saying it, that darkness hid the scarlet tide that engulfed him, flowing down from his face until it tingled off the end of his toes, leaving him cold. Danny started to exclaim in denial, but Jerry's soft laugh intervened.

"Night, Danny," Jerry said.

14

OCTOBER WANED. IN THE MARSHES THE MALLOWS STOOD WITH-out moving and stared at the sun, and the sea drowsed under a sky unvexed by any wind. The sea slept, murmuring contentedly in her sleep like a woman who has been loved to her satisfaction, serenely like a woman who has slipped from the arms of her lover to lie, still and content, beside him, knowing that the ebbing tide of his ardor will turn and awaken her to new ecstasy when the dawn comes.

October waned and the sun, when it came up out of the green water of the Gulf Stream swirling past the Lightship at the rim of the Outer Diamonds, shook off the mists, like a woman taking off her night gown. The sun was a little further to the south each morning. In the hour before dawn vagrant winds came and stirred the sea and the leaves of the live oaks and the pendants of moss that hung like draperies below their limbs.

But when the sun had come up and put off her night dress of mist, the winds hid themselves deep in the woods and the sea drowsed again and the leaves of the oaks were still. The valances of moss that hung from their limbs drooped in the shadows. The tides ebbed sleepily and almost forgot to come back. The whole earth seemed to sleep beneath a sky that was iridescent by day and that was purple velvet by night.

The tide's coming and its going were like the earth breathing, gently in sleep, measuring out two deep breaths of time in the space of the earth's turning. The wild fox grapes along the ridges in the Woods turned purple, and the air was heavy with the scent of scuppernongs that ripened into a ruddy brown above the trellis anchored against the kitchen wall, and Polly Gray was busy by day with marmalade. It took less sugar to make marmalade and her menfolks liked it almost as well as they did grape jelly.

Danny and Jerry painted the house. It was Jerry's persuasion that moved Mrs. Grady to negotiate with the dealer in Norfolk for paint. He ignored the first message she sent him by the driver of the freight truck, but on the next trip he grudgingly sent down all that she had asked and a little more. It was not quite the shade of cream that Polly Gray had wanted for the house, but it would have to do.

Busy over a kettle of marmalade simmering on the range in the kitchen, Polly Gray smiled in serene contentment when she heard the murmur of her sons' voices, or their silence, or Jerry's ebullient laugh, or the muffled thump of paintbrushes against the walls of the house. There would be long intervals of silence outside, unbroken save for the sound of the brushes against the house, and then Jerry's laugh would surge upward like a rocket.

Danny scarcely ever laughed, but that did not trouble Polly Gray. She knew that he was smiling, his eyes lighting up. Danny had never been a noisy boy. Not that Jerry was noisy, or that Danny was morose. Life just seemed to bubble up out of Jerry; not boisterously — it just flowed out of him, out of some bottomless spring of vitality. But Danny was quiet . . . like the Open Ponds deep in the Woods, where there were water lilies and where the eagles watched their shadows in the still mirror of the water.

Sometimes Jerry would call briefly from the yard, "I'm goin' over to the Station awhile, Mom — be back in time for dinner." Polly Gray would hear his whistling as he went down the front yard toward the marsh where Bos'n made his own living on the tender grass that grew down next to the muck, and she would glimpse him as he went along the road toward the sea. That would happen on days that she knew Bill Henry had set apart for boat drill over on the beach. . . .

Sometimes other boys in the Woods stopped by on their way to the beach. They would whistle, or call out to Jerry if he were not in sight, and he would answer them. There were all sizes and ages of them, but their ages didn't seem to matter when they were going to the beach. There were not so many, now, of Danny's age. So few of them had come back from the war. But the younger ones accepted him and he went along with them without any feeling of self-consciousness.

Sometimes Danny and Jerry went off toward the beach by themselves and lay sunning themselves on the sand or walked along the wash of the beach, stopping to examine something that had come in with the tide — a curious bottle, a bit of driftwood, a shell, or a bit of coral that had broken loose south of the Cape, where the water always was warm, and washed ashore.

Once they walked northward until they came to the place where they had brought Daniel Gray ashore and laid him on the sand. Danny, taking his bearings from the aft rail of a schooner broken to bits long ago, scattered and half-buried along the beach, calculated the precise spot where they had laid him. He stood there, looking down at the clean sand . . . sand that he had seen stained with red. The schooner's rail was buried deep in the sand. For generations it had been a guidepost, a milepost, for people who went that way.

"Is this the place, Danny?" Jerry asked after a while, and Danny nodded. "I never knew exactly where it was before. I was little then."

"A lot of things have happened since then — to me — you — everybody," Danny said.

On another afternoon they walked down to the Point where Cape Hatteras poked a blunted finger into the side of the drowsing sea. They stopped to look at the stranded lifeboat, half-filled with sand. Jerry poked exploring fingers through the bullet holes that riddled the starboard side of it from bow to stern.

"There's fifty-three of them," Jerry counted, "and I guess there was nobody left alive. There was two fellers in it," he went on. "I didn't see 'em but Bill Henry told me. They're buried up there in the pines. One of 'em was a Britisher. They had a regular funeral."

"Didn't they for all of them?" Danny asked.

"Heck, no. Some days there were a dozen of 'em washed ashore. If they had their dog tags on and were not rotten they shipped 'em out of here. All except the Germans."

"Germans?"

"Heck, yeah. There was abouty twenty of 'em washed up here and around on the other side of the Point in one night. They didn't get any funeral and nobody bothered to make 'em a tombstone either."

Danny sat down on the gunwale of the boat, looking out across the Diamonds. Jerry sat down on the sand, resting his back against the steel hull of the boat.

"And that wasn't near all of 'em," Jerry went on. "Bill Henry went out and picked up some of 'em before they was drowned and some feller named Burke — he's Coast Guard — landed a plane out there and picked up some more. Bill Henry wanted to make a cage and keep his live ones in it like — like snakes. But somebody come and got 'em and carried 'em off. Wanted to ask 'em questions."

Danny waited for Jerry to go on, and when he said nothing more Danny asked if anybody knew just where the submarine was sunk and who had hit it.

"Them Army fellers," Jerry said. "Bill Henry was up in the tower yonder lookin' right at 'em when it happened. He seen the hull of the sub out yonder on the Outer Diamonds, seen her plain as day. He's seen her since then, lyin' right there on the bottom. If we was out there now, with the sea slick like it is, bet we could see it, too."

Jerry picked a flattened piece of shell out of the sand and sent it spinning upward toward a gull, whose curiosity had brought him down close to them. The gull squawked, ducked out of harm's way, and went back to his surveillance of the surf.

"Bill Henry was sure mad as hell when they took his prisoners away from him," Jerry went on with a laugh. "When the spies come he didn't take any chances."

"Spies!" Danny exclaimed.

"Didn't you know about 'em?" Jerry's tone was suddenly guarded.

"No, I didn't. What —"

"Get Bill Henry to tell you," Jerry answered shortly. "Or maybe he'll tell you without you askin' him." He was thoughtful for a while and then he added, "Don't you ask Bill Henry — wait. Let's walk down to the Point — what you say?" Jerry got lightly to his feet.

They walked the half mile to the Point in silence. The sun was warm on their shoulders and the sea scarcely murmured in its drowsing sleep. The Point poked its finger out into the sleeping water where scarcely a ripple broke the surface. No fleck of spray rose anywhere as far out as their eyes could reach. They sat down cross-legged in the sand and neither of them said anything for a long time. It was Jerry who broke the comfortable silence.

"She's like an old harlot takin' a nap," Jerry said.

"Harlot? Where did you get that word?"

"Ain't it a nice word? Sounds better'n 'whore,' anyhow," Jerry said, unabashed. "That's what Bill Henry calls her," he added, as if that settled the matter, once and for all.

"She is like an old harlot," Jerry went on, with no hint of argument in his voice. "Like an old harlot with two sailor friends. One of 'em, Bill Henry says, is the South Ocean and the other is the North Ocean."

Jerry looked around at Danny wondering if he — and Bill Henry — were making themselves clear. Danny's faint smile encouraged him, and he went on.

"Her South Ocean friend — he's gone now. All summer he's been comin' up from this way —" Jerry waved an arm toward the wide expanse of water to the south and west — "and now it's her other boy friend's time. Almost any time now he's due to come hellin' down from yonder —" he extended an arm to the east and north — "and when he does he'll wake her up and start a roughhouse with her, just like a dam' sailor."

Danny, smiling to himself, waited for Jerry to go on.

"You can tell what time of the year it is by the shape of this Point, tell which one of her fellers is stayin' with her. When her boy friend from up yonder comes, the Point crooks around to the west; and when her feller from down yonder gets back next spring, he'll twist it around the other way."

"I never noticed that," Danny said.

"I never neither until Bill Henry showed it to me," Jerry conceded, "but heck, there's a lot of things that old bitch can show you. Especially times when one of her fellers gets here before the other one leaves and they start whammin' hell out each other."

"Don't you go to school any more, Jerry?" Danny asked suddenly.

"I can read and write, can't I?" Jerry parried.

"But —" Danny began, protestingly.

"Teachers ain't got much sense," Jerry broke in. "They think this here ocean is just a lot of pretty water for the sun to wash his face in of a mornin' or to make poetry about. Let's go home before Mom gives us out and puts supper away."

Most of the time Danny was content to let Jerry take the initiative in all their talk. The morning after he came back from his first, his only, visit to the house where the clematis vine sprawled its disorder across the roof of the porch, Danny had dreaded to face his brother, fearful of his wickedly provoking grin, fearful of the moment when Jerry might, again, call him "Danny Darling" . . . in daylight, before their mother. The dark had saved him that night.

At first, when Jerry gave no sign of having remembered anything that was said after he got home that night, either before their mother or in the company of other boys, Danny had an uneasy feeling that his brother was waiting, biding his time, until he had him alone. He turned over in his mind the reasonableness of moving into the other room, but that might seem like he was dodging Jerry, avoiding him. And Jerry had not, by any word or look or gesture, given any hint that he even remembered.

But Jerry, Danny knew, had not forgotten anything. He had just pulled down a black curtain over the thing. Danny tried to put all thought of Sally Tillett out of his mind, but that didn't work. He would lie awake after Jerry rolled over against the wall, asleep. Resist it though he would, the smouldering marsh fire would sweep over him and his arms would ache for the feel of her shoulders, and his lips would burn, remembering that kiss. . . .

What was it that had changed her so suddenly? What was it that he had said or done that was wrong? What was it she had started to say when she suddenly changed her mind, changed herself from warm — too warm — eagerness to remote, cool, almost hostile indifference? He got nowhere asking himself the same questions over and over again, and there was nobody else he could ask . . . unless it was Jerry, and not again would he face that derisive smile, even though it had in it a certain gentleness.

He couldn't make up his mind whether he ever wanted to see Sally Tillett again or not. Sometimes he told himself that the sensible thing to do would be to go back and have it — whatever it was — out with her; that the thing to do would be to go back and take her in his arms and hold her until she — until . . . well, until she what? At other times he told himself that he wanted never to see her again, and he wished that he had thrown that damned bundle overboard in the middle of the Pacific Ocean. . . .

What was it that had changed her so, Danny asked himself over and over and over in the dark. And why was it that nobody ever mentioned her name to him any more? None of the boys, even when they were in their most jocular mood, teased him about her, or even mentioned her name. But there was nothing surprising about that . . . it was just the way of the people in the Woods — they let other people's business alone, anyhow until they were asked. And, after all, was there any reason for anybody to think that there had ever been anything between him and Sally Tillett?

Danny wondered whether this was what people called being in love. Sometimes he wished that it were Sally Tillett there in the bed beside him; and he would imagine himself turning toward her, his arm across her breasts, and his mouth searching for her mouth in the dark, and his legs warm against her legs; and the marsh fire would sweep across his loins and its smoke would fill his eyes with tears. . . .

And Danny wondered if this were some sort of sickness that had come upon him yonder in the Pacific where strange things happened to so many. And he wondered, over and over, what it was that had made Sally Tillett act so funny that night — kissing him one minute as if it were something she had waited for a long time, and the next minute turning away from him as if he were somebody with something terribly wrong with him. . . .

Why . . . why . . . why? He would groan in the depths of confusion like . . . like somebody sinking into the maw of the marsh where it was black and underlaid with quicksand, and he would be asleep . . . and awake. The Light would come and go and come again, making its glowing patch against the wall. Sometimes Danny would pull down the shade, shutting out the Light, but the insistent finger flattened itself against the curtain, unrelenting . . . like the questions that went their heavy-footed way across Danny's consciousness. Midnight. . . . Dawn would soon be at the windows, and at breakfast Polly Gray would look at Danny. She never asked him if he had slept. She had no need to ask.

"Reckon it's about time you tell me, Danny — get it off'n your mind."

Jerry's voice came out of the dark, casual, detached, undemanding. Danny started as if somebody had flicked him with a branding iron. He glanced apprehensively toward Jerry when the Light flicked across the room. The boy had not moved. He had awakened, as he always did, without stirring and was just lying there. Danny could feel the boy's eyes searching him.

"Tell you what, Jerry? Was I — talking in my sleep?" Danny tried to keep the tremor in his voice hidden.

"Naw — you weren't asleep," Jerry said.

"Well, what are you talking about?"

"Not talkin'," Jerry said. "You can, though, if you want to."

Danny felt his face turn scarlet in the dark, and he was thankful that Jerry had not clicked on the light. He opened his mouth, and angry, bitter words trooped to the end of his tongue. He kept them back with an effort; he would ignore this intrusion upon his misery. Still . . . in so many ways, it seemed to Danny, Jerry was the older, wise with a wisdom that he had learned from — from the old harlot . . . from Bill Henry Ragland . . . from his own blood. . . .

"You mean about going over yonder the other night?" Danny said hesitantly, and he was irked because his voice would not sit steady in his throat.

"That's what's botherin' you, ain't it?"

Haltingly, with long gaps of embarrassed, groping silence between, Danny began to tell Jerry; and then the sentences came rushing out, sometimes so hard, one on the heels of the other, that he was almost incoherent. He left none of it out and now and then repeated himself out of the confusion of his own mind and out of a recurrent feeling of shame to be talking about a girl, about any girl, like that, and about himself.

"What made you call me 'Danny Darling' when you woke up the other night?" Danny ended his narrative with a question.

"Just did," Jerry said amiably. "Figured she must have — she might have — called you that. She used to call 'em all that. Guess it was a word she picked up on some of them visits to her aunt." Jerry's voice coiled in scorn around the last word.

"Her aunt? I didn't know she had any kinfolks like that, away from here."

"No law against inventin' aunts if you need 'em, is there?"

"Quit being specious, Jerry, and out with it."

"What's 'specious'? Okay — okay, if it'll do you any good. I ain't much of a hand at messin' in other folks's business, but I reckon somebody's got to tell you. After you left here there was a lot of fellers come in here — Bill Henry said he guessed it must have been as bad as when the Yankees come in here back in 1862 I think he said it was. The Woods was just crawlin' with 'em — some Coast Guard, some Army, some Navy, and some others that nobody knowed what they were. They was goin' to do somethin' about submarines and spies and such.

"Mostly it looked to me like they expected to find everything they was lookin' for up here in the Woods. Some of 'em was right nice and some of 'em were sort of lousy. A lot of 'em, all of 'em I guess, was woman-hungry, and they started makin' passes at all the girls and some that ain't been girls for so long they can't remember it. Some of 'em even had their cars down here and some of the girls fell for 'em.

"Some of these gals here in the Woods are pretty smart. They got theirselves a husband. But maybe they were not so smart at that. Sally didn't land hers, none of 'em."

"Did — did anything happen?"

"You mean did she get knocked up? Hell, no — not that I ever heard of. She just run around with one feller a lot, and after he left it was another feller. One time or another I reckon she had about all of 'em. They'd get stuff for her, stockin's and that stuff she puts on her mouth — like you had on your'n when you come back.

"Anyhow, she was always dressed up like somebody you see in a picture, and she started puttin' on a lot of airs like callin' everbody 'darling' — I even heard her call Mom that one time she was here.

"After the submarines was gone, these fellers sort of thinned out around here, and after a while there wasn't anybody left for Sally to play around with. Then she'd visit this aunt up in Norfolk. . . . She wasn't ever your girl, was she Danny?"

"Not — not what you'd call my girl, Jerry. I used to sort of pair off with her at school — you know how that is — but —"

"Yeah, I remember how it was, 'specially that last year. Still, I thought she was sort of your girl and she ought to have behaved herself better'n that. She ought to have waited. I guess she knew I thought dam' little of the way she was goin' on, and I wouldn't be surprised if that was what she had on her mind when she clammed up on you — thought I'd been tellin' you things."

"Why didn't you tell me, Jerry?"

"You got better sense than that, Danny. The only way you can find out about things — about a woman, about an ocean — Bill Henry says, is to find out yourself."

"Did she — did she ever make a pass at you, Jerry? You said she came over here a lot."

"Hell, naw," Jerry said, disgusted. "I didn't have any of them nylons she was always talkin' about and not much else, either. Besides —"

"But what I still can't understand," Danny broke in, "is why she was one way one minute and just the other way the next. What did I do that was wrong?"

"Didn't do nothin', I reckon, Danny . . . she just got her bearin's mixed. Guess she figured you'd been gone so long maybe you'd got like all them other service fellers she's been foolin' with, and then she found out you hadn't changed much. Gimme one of them cigarettes if we're goin' to talk all night."

Danny reached for a cigarette, lighted one for himself, and held the match for Jerry. They smoked in silence, until Jerry, hearing Surfman outside, reached out with his foot to raise the screen. The cat's luminous eyes surveyed them from the window ledge, and Jerry tickled him under the chin with his toe. Surfman was in no playful mood. He got down from the window sill, curled himself in the puddle of Jerry's clothes under the bed, and went to sleep.

"Who's this Judy, Danny?"

"Why — why, how did you know about her?"

"Name's on that thing you wear with your dog tags."

"She's a girl I met down in Florida that winter I was down there training on the Twenties. She —"

"Let's save her for some other time, Danny," Jerry said sleepily. "One woman a night is enough for me. Night, Danny."

Jerry turned to the wall, pillowed his cheek on a loosely balled fist, and went to sleep. When he awoke again the sun was slanting across the bed, warming the bottoms of his feet, and Surfman, sitting on his haunches beside them, reached out a soft paw and touched them lightly. Jerry turned, raised himself on an elbow, and studied his brother's face thoughtfully. . . . Danny, somehow, reminded him of a little child asleep. The little furrowed lines between his eyebrows were gone. Jerry got out of bed, slid out of his red pajamas and into his dungarees and shirt. At the bedroom door he looked back, returned to pull down the shades to keep out the sun. Danny awoke at noon.

15

OCTOBER WANED AND IT WAS NOVEMBER, BUT STILL THE SEA drowsed under skies that were cloudless. Sometimes, before dawn, the winds came, irresolute, and flecked the surface with little purposeless waves. But they were vagrant winds, now out of the north, now shifting to the opposite quarter; and when the sun had come up they went away and hid themselves. The sea slept.

They finished painting the house. Jerry carried home the ladder they had borrowed from Mrs. Grady while Danny put away their own ladder, hanging it on the rack back of the car shelter. Danny remembered that he had helped his father when he built the rack for the ladder; Daniel Gray had been a man who wanted things shipshape around the house. And Danny wondered why it was that so many of the men of the Woods were, really, better housekeepers than the women.

There was enough of the white paint used for the window frames left over, and before they cleaned their paintbrushes Danny and Jerry painted the kitchen walls and the bathroom. There was still paint left, and Polly Gray proposed that they touch up the woodwork in the spare bedroom. She wished that the plastered walls could be papered; she had seen a pictured pattern of a paper in the catalogue that she liked, but . . . .

"You must be expectin' company, Mom," Jerry said cheerfully. Polly Gray was thoughtful before she said anything.

"Well, you never know when somebody might come. Why,

176

some of Danny's friends that he knew in the Army might come down, when the hunting starts."

"He ain't said anything about it, has he?"

"No; but you know he must have a lot of friends in the Army, and some of them might come down, when the geese and ducks come."

"If it's goin' to stay summer all winter there won't be a goose between Hatteras and Oregon Inlet. Besides, where's anybody goin' to get any shells? Ain't been any since the war started, and if we get any geese I reckon we'll have to fire-light 'em."

"Why, Jerry," Polly Gray said reprovingly, "you know they don't allow that any more — the very idea."

Jerry grinned and returned to his painting. Presently he said, "Mom, instead of thinkin' about havin' company, why don't you think about goin' off somewhere and bein' company yourself? You ain't been off the Banks since before the war started."

"Go away when Danny has just come home, Jerry — the very idea! And besides, there's nowhere I want to go."

"Shucks, Mom, there's plenty of places to go. You and Danny could go together. Go to Norfolk. I got a notion Danny's sort of achin' to go up there and see if he can find himself a car. You could find a lot of stuff in the stores."

"It would be a treat, Jerry," Polly Gray said, "but what about you, Jerry? Don't you want to go — you and Danny?"

"Heck, I don't care nothin' about it. I can stay out at the Station — me and Surfman, and I can come over here every day and look after things. You and Danny could bring me all I want."

"What would you want us to bring you, Jerry — if we were to go?"

"Some boots," Jerry said promptly. "My feet's growed so I can't get 'em in the tops of — of them of Daddy's that I've been wearin' ever since . . . you could tell 'em my size."

"It would be better for you to be there and try them on," Polly Gray said, "and maybe there would be something else you would want after you saw it."

"Some boots and some shells is all I want," Jerry insisted. "You'd have a big time, Mom, you with that new dress you made out of that cloth Danny brung you, and him all rigged out with all his ribbons. He'd be proud as hell of you, Mom — you'd have a big time." Jerry's enthusiasm effervesced.

"Jerry!" Polly Gray was gently reproachful.

"Oh, 'scuse me, Mom — I just forgot," Jerry said, his face reddening. "And you could get you a new hat to go with that dress."

"But maybe Danny wouldn't want to go. He's been away from home so long," Polly Gray said, doubtfully.

"Oh, I've done fixed that — he's just waitin' for you to say the word. I told him I'd get you to go."

"Jerry, you are more like your father every day you live. You sound just like he used to when he would set in to persuade me to take a trip with him."

"Nothin' wrong with that, is there?" Jerry demanded shortly, his face serious. But in a moment he brightened, continued. "Besides, I got a notion Danny's been gettin' sort of restless. He's about caught up on his sleep and we've about worked ourselves out of a job around here unless we take to fishin' regular. You can go up on the bus and come back in the car. I know Danny can get a car."

Because she was a woman, and because she liked instinctively to be coaxed into doing something she wanted to do — and because, though she was scarcely conscious of it, she could, if she closed her eyes, almost feel that Dan Gray and not her son was persuading her — Polly Gray began to marshal excuses, reasons why she couldn't possibly leave her house, her yard, her kitchen; she just couldn't think of it, not for a minute.

Jerry listened with skeptical silence. He plied his paintbrush, not stopping until he had finished the last window sill and the paint can was, this time, really empty. Then he turned to his mother.

"Day after tomorrow, Mom — I got to take Danny over to the Station tomorrow mornin' for a while. But after that there's nothin' in the way."

Jerry crossed the room to where his mother, who by now had talked herself out of breath and out of resources for invention, was waiting in a state of helpless indecision. He crooked a finger and hauled her chin up until he could look down into her eyes. . . . That was the way Daniel Gray used to end all sorts of discussions. . . . Jerry grinned.

"Day after tomorrow, Mom. I'll tell Danny. He didn't think you'd go. Naw, I guess — well, you tell him."

Polly Gray surrendered. "You sure you'll be all right over at the Station with Bill Henry? I've never left you a night in your life."

"Sure," Jerry said. "You just bring me some boots and some shells. I got to go clean these paintbrushes now."

Jerry went out, whistling. He encountered Danny coming into the kitchen door, poked at his chin with a drying paintbrush without saying anything. Polly Gray, following him to the kitchen, came upon Danny and for a moment avoided his glance. She waited until Jerry was out of hearing.

"Danny," she said with what was, for her, almost severity, "what have you and Jerry been scheming? Here he's practically driven us both out of the house and off to Norfolk."

"Oh, so you've decided to go, Mama?" Danny's voice rang with his pleasure.

"No, I didn't decide," Polly Gray said, at once rueful and happy. "Jerry decided. Seems like he decides almost everything around here. Do you suppose I've spoiled him — while you've been gone?"

"Maybe you have, Mama," Danny said. "But you've had a

lot of help — good help, too, I should say."

"What do you mean, Danny?"

"Well," Danny said, "he's just like Daddy in a lot of ways — looks like him, talks like him sometimes. But there's a lot of Bill Henry in him, too — and a lot of just himself, and some of you, too. But, fortunately maybe, not much of me."

"If he would just go to school," Polly Gray summed up.

"I asked him about that the other day and he said he could read and write, couldn't he? And that settled that. I didn't argue with him."

"No; there's no use arguing with him. He just looks at you and grins, and when he does that I'm just helpless — like I was when he got after me to go off to Norfolk. Do you — did you really want to go, Danny?"

"Not particularly," Danny said, smiling, "but after all it doesn't seem like a bad idea. Do you good to get away and — you know — buy things. And maybe we can find us a car up there."

"Well, there are some things I've been wanting. But shouldn't we take Jerry, too? I hate to go away and leave him here just by himself."

"I thought about that, too, but he said he didn't give a damn — excuse me, Mama, but —"

"Yes, Danny, I know." Polly Gray's smile was gently tolerant.

"Well, he said, you know, that he could live the rest of his life without ever leaving these Banks, and I think he would if he could just stay over at the Station — with Bill Henry."

Polly Gray nodded her head slowly and was silent for a moment. "He has never stayed over there all night," she said, "never stayed out from under this roof except that time you and your father took him to Norfolk. But what's this he's planned for you to do over there tomorrow morning? He said we couldn't get off on our trip until the day after."

Danny's face showed his surprise.

"Why, I don't know anything about it. He hasn't mentioned it to me."

"Danny, you haven't been over there since you've been home, have you?"

"No, Mama, I haven't. Somehow I've just dreaded going. It was Daddy's station and — well, you remember all the things Bill Henry said when — when I didn't stay here and join up."

"Yes, I remember that; but you must go back, sometime." She was thoughtful for a little before she went on. "Don't let on to Jerry that I said anything to you about it. He'll tell you, in his own way. I expect this is something else that Bill Henry is at the bottom of, or something they've cooked up together."

"They do seem to get a lot of cooking done, one way or another," Danny said. "Is there anything that needs doing that can't be left until we get back from our trip — anything I can help you with?"

Jerry went past the window outside, his white sailor's hat at a negligent angle over an ear. He whistled. Surfman came down from his place under the fig tree and they went toward the road. During the rest of the morning, when she glanced out across the marsh beyond the road, Polly Gray could glimpse Jerry's white hat above the browning foxtails, and she could hear him when he admonished or cajoled Bos'n, or, when these expedients were unproductive, threatened him with immoderately profane consequences.

When he came to dinner at midday he ate in silence for the most part, taking no part in the conversation and paying little attention to his mother and Danny, who were, by now, infected with anticipatory excitement about their trip. He did mention that he intended to teach that horse to let Surfman ride if he had to pull his ears out by the roots. As soon as he was through eating he pushed back his chair and left the table. He said that he thought it might be a good idea to take the horse and the cat over to the beach where he could have more room to maneuver.

"There's still mosquitoes down there in that marsh," he said, and when he reached the door he turned and added casually, "I'll go down to the Station when it's suppertime and maybe I'd just as well stay out there tonight and see how I'll like it while you all are gone to Norfolk." Without waiting for comment or protest, he was gone. Surfman was waiting for him at the front of the house.

"Just like that!" Danny said when Jerry was out of hearing. "Does he never ask if he may do something — just always tell you he's going to do whatever it is he wants to do? Doesn't he know anything about discipline?"

Puzzled and a little troubled by Danny's vehemence, Polly Gray was thoughtful for a moment before she answered him.

"He always tells me, Danny, what he is going to do, and if it seems . . . seems reasonable, he will say why he's doing it." Her voice took on a slight edge. "Do you think — I've been negligent?"

"No, no, Mama. I didn't think that at all," Danny protested.

"I've never tried to be like some of the women of the Woods — you know that. I've never switched either one of you, and I've never demanded that you do anything. Your father and I expected a lot of you — and both of you've been — I know he would be proud of you both if he were here."

Danny's face flushed and he started to speak. His mother looked at him quietly, waiting.

"We tried to let you boys discipline yourselves," Polly Gray went on when Danny's silence went unbroken. "Jerry has puzzled me a lot since you went away. He moped like a sick, lost kitten at first. It was lonely here for him. Everything happened so suddenly, and then you weren't here. He missed you more than you can ever know. I used to listen outside his room door. I could hear him crying. I wanted to — you'll never know how I wanted to go in there, but he would never let me see him cry.

"I used to think that you, wherever you were, must be as homesick as Jerry was. He never said much — never said anything, really. Sometimes I knew that he was trying to comfort me. He knew that I was — well, I never thought about discipline, as you call it. He disciplined himself.

"That first year was pretty bleak for him, but he started to grow; and then he got so he would take the boat out. He would always tell me — but, as you say, he never asked me. He had some trouble with the engine at first, and that's when he and Bill Henry started, as you might say, going together. He got Bill Henry to help him with the engine and ever since then . . . well, you must have seen how it is.

"Both of you boys were sort of torn up by the roots. You had always been so close to each other. I used to worry too much about being so trifling after Jerry was born and leaving so much to you. There were — I'm ashamed to say it, Danny — times when I must have been actually jealous of you — Jerry depended on you for so many things."

Polly Gray fell silent. Danny stirred uneasily in his chair across the table from her, ashamed of himself for having spoken. Presently she went on, her voice gentle, a little sad.

"No, Danny, it's — I don't think there's much to worry about as far as Jerry is concerned. His roots were torn up, back there, but he — but they have taken hold again. I wish I were as sure about your own roots . . . in a lot of ways it's been harder for you than it has for Jerry. I'm not very handy making figures of speech, but they moved you so far from home, and they moved you around so much — well, sometimes I'm afraid for you, Danny."

"For me, Mama?"

"Yes, Danny. I want you to be happy, and happiness comes only for people who have their roots in the earth somewhere. We have been here a long time — your father and his father and my father and my father's father. Our roots are here, Danny."

"So you're like — like Bill Henry and all the others — I shouldn't have gone away." Danny's voice was thin, bitter.

"It's not like you to say that, Danny," Polly Gray said gravely, "because it isn't true. It isn't true about any of them. Bill Henry said hard things, I know, and I resented them. It wouldn't have made any difference. You couldn't have stayed here; you would have gone, like all the other boys in the Woods.

"No, it isn't that. You went where they sent you, did what nobody in these Woods or anywhere could do any better, and I'm proud of you. But the thing that troubles me is that I'm afraid it may be harder for you — to come back, to put down your roots again."

"But — but what can I do here? What is there for me to do? Fish — join the Coast Guard — get me a truck and haul fish and freight? I've been thinking about it a lot, Mama, and I don't know what the answer is. I — I wish that there'd never been a war and — and things were like they used to be."

"I know, Danny," Polly Gray said gently. "But there has been a war and it's robbed you — no, I can't like that word — it has taken three years of your growing-up time. You'd have grown up anyway — only with roots in the same earth, like Jerry."

"Darned if I know what to think — what to do," Danny said, wearily, unhappy.

"Don't fight it, Danny, and don't worry about it. There's plenty of time for that. And don't fret, especially about Jerry. I know he'll vex the life out of you sometimes. But just keep in mind the fact that he loves you better than anything on the earth."

"Except maybe Bill Henry," Danny said.

"Not excepting anybody, Danny. Bill Henry is — different from you."

"That's something, anyway."

"No, Danny — that's not the way to think about it. I know the things he said still rankle, but give him time — give Jerry time. I don't know what the child is up to, but when you get acquainted with him again, you can trust him."

"I know that, Mama. He — he set me straight about something the other night, something that had pretty near driven me nuts, I reckon."

"You mean about Sally, Danny?"

"How did you know? Did he tell you?"

"Of course not, Danny — you ought to know him better than that. I don't know — and I expect you'd better not tell me now — what the trouble was about that poor girl. I guess I can imagine enough. It's too bad, Danny. She was such a nice girl when you all were young. I still can't feel like she's really bad."

"Did you think — I was in love with her, Mama?"

"I didn't know, Danny, and so I didn't think. You were both so young when you went away."

"We're both a lot older now."

"Wiser, too, I hope, Danny."

16

AS CASUALLY AS HE HAD TAKEN LEAVE, JERRY CAME BACK THE next morning. He came into the kitchen where Polly Gray and Danny lingered over their coffee, greeted them with a casual "Hi," and crossed over to lay a parcel on the table beside the sink. Polly Gray started to get up from the table, saying that she would get him some breakfast. Jerry stopped her with a gesture.

"I've done eat," he said briefly. "Sit still — I'll get me another cup of coffee." He took a cup from the shelf.

"We got sugar," he announced and began to unwrap the parcel. "Bill Henry sent you his sugar, Mom. Said he didn't have any use for it, now that he's not livin' at home. Said you might have used up all you had cannin' figs and you might need it, what with Danny home."

Polly Gray exclaimed over the windfall of sugar, and then she wanted to know if Jerry had fared all right over at the Station, if he had slept, if he was not just a little homesick.

"You know this is the first time you've ever been away overnight, Jerry."

"Heck," Jerry said, dismissing the matter. He drank his coffee in silence and with the spoon gleaned the last bits of partially dissolved sugar from the bottom of the cup.

"How'd you and Danny get along without me? You sleep all right, Danny?"

Danny said that he had never slept better, and Polly Gray said that she did, too, after she got to sleep. "I did lie awake awhile wondering how you were doing out yonder."

"Heck," Jerry said. He looked at Danny speculatively across the table, a sun-whitened eyebrow lifted quizzically.

"How did you come out with Bos'n and Surfman, Jerry?" Danny inquired. Jerry grunted noncommittally.

"That's a dumb horse," he said after a while. "Dumber'n some of them clunks out yonder at the Station. He don't like cats."

"What happened, Jerry?" Polly Gray said when the boy fell into a ruminative silence.

"Nothin' much," Jerry said absently. "He throwed me in the ocean."

Danny's laugh echoed throughout the house. Polly Gray's face was anxious.

"Did you get hurt, Jerry?"

"Naw," Jerry replied indifferently. "Just wet. Heck, I was as wet as one of them recruits when Bill Henry sends 'em out for boat drill. We were doin' all right, but when I thought I'd sort of see if he would take a sea, it must have worried Surfman a little and he started to get a good tight hold on Bos'n's neck. Guess he must've found a tender spot in his hide somewhere and got his claws in a little too deep. Bos'n slewed around so quick I went overboard, but Surfman — you ought to have seen that cat jump. Didn't even get his feet wet. That cat was same as an airplane, Danny."

"What became of the horse?"

"Oh, he wallowed a little, and righted himself and come out. But he didn't seem like he wanted to associate with me much after that. Bill Henry come down to the beach in his jeep and we chased him. That dam' horse can run when he puts his mind on it. I reckon he must have made it back to the marsh before night."

"Must be a lot of life left in him yet if he can outrun a jeep," Danny suggested.

"Couldn't have if I'd been drivin' it," Jerry said, his tone suggesting that he was stating a fact and not boasting. "Bill Henry just can't get used to 'em, somehow. When he gets in a tight place, he starts yellin' at it, like it was a horse, and forgets to step on the gas, and when he wants to stop it all of a sudden, he yells 'woah' instead of settin' his foot on the brakes."

"How long have you been driving, Jerry?"

"Ever since they got 'em down here, I reckon. Anyhow, since Bill Henry got his. Did you ever drive one of 'em, Danny?"

"No. But I've ridden in them a lot. They used to take the crews down to the ships when we were ready to take off somewhere. I used to think I'd like to have one of them down here — they ought to be swell on the beach. Can't stick one, can you?"

"Can if you don't watch yourself. There ain't nothin' that won't get stuck in this sand if you don't handle it right." Jerry got up from the table. "Want to ride back over to the Station, Danny?" He tried to make himself sound very casual, indifferent even, but his voice betrayed something of his eagerness. Polly Gray glanced at Danny quickly, nodding silently.

"You got a jeep out there? Do they let you drive it off by yourself?"

"Heck, yeah — sometimes. Comin', Danny?"

"Sure, I'll come. Let me get my cap." Danny went out through the dining room and in a moment came back with his cap. Jerry surveyed him with a little impatience, disappointment.

"Why don't you wear your wings and them bars that go on your collar, Danny?"

"You think I ought to wear 'em, Jerry? Won't some of them think —"

"Wear 'em," Jerry said shortly.

Danny turned back to the bedroom and Jerry went down

toward the road where the jeep, with its top off, was parked. Only, neither Jerry nor any other dweller along the Outer Banks would have used the word. He — they — would have said, "She's layin' yonder," as if they were speaking of a boat. Jerry slid into the front seat and waited.

Danny came down the shell-paved walk from the house.

"Like to take her, Danny?"

Danny stopped suddenly between the gateposts, his eyes fixed on the lettering of the jeep's name, stenciled under the windshield.

"She drives like any other car, only you put her in four-wheel with this thing here if you need it."

"Who named this thing, Jerry?" Danny demanded.

"Bill Henry and me named her. What's wrong with it?"

"Nothing, Jerry — not a thing. But 'Danny' seems to me a queer sort of a name for something you call a 'she.' Anyhow, I'm sure obliged to you if it's me you've named her for. Is she a good jeep?"

"Best one on the Banks. Want to try her?"

Danny hesitated a moment before he said, "No, Jerry — I might get her stuck in the first streak of sand I came to." He went around to the other side and got into the seat; Jerry slid under the steering wheel.

The vehicle moved off smoothly and Danny watched Jerry out of the corner of his eye as the boy drove. He sat under the wheel, relaxed and unconcerned outwardly, and his driving was effortless. Only the broad great toe of his right foot, the toe with which he hoisted the screen at the window for Surfman, rested on the accelerator, and it seemed as dextrous as a finger. He managed the gear-shift lever without seeming to move his hand and his eyes never deviated from the road ahead as he calculated the hazard of every doubtful spot in the road.

"Did you ever think about flying an airplane, Jerry?" Danny inquired when they were come out of the Woods and on to the open, treeless reach of grass-studded sand that stretched southward toward the Station.

"Guess I could — or anyhow I could learn. But I'd rather have me a boat. One airplane flyer in the family ought to be enough. I'd like to ride in one, though, sometime — if you was flyin' it."

"I think you'd like it, Jerry."

"Guess I would," Jerry said with no more than polite interest. "They're all right in their place, like a boat's all right in its place. . . . Heck, the ocean is as slick as a saucer today. Maybe them clunks can get a boat launched without wettin' theirselves this mornin'."

When they drew up before the Station, Chief Ragland was standing at the top of the steps at the entrance. He was barefooted. He stood with his feet wide apart, with his hands laid flat against his hips. His shirt was open at the neck, revealing the hairy, mighty chest. Only the cap that he wore on the back of his head gave any indication that here was a Chief Warrant Officer, commanding one of the strategic stations in the Service.

Ragland's wide face was impassive. He smiled briefly when Jerry lifted an arm in casual greeting as he slid from under the wheel and, without a backward glance, crossed the space of grass toward the boathouse where the boat crew was idling, waiting, beside a rugged weapons-carrier. Behind the truck there was a trailer with a dory lashed to its floor, its bow and stern projecting beyond the ends.

Danny got down from the jeep and stood, uncertain and hesitant. He started to call out after the departing Jerry, irritated at being left abandoned, at not being told what to do with himself. But Jerry was moving purposefully toward the group around the truck. As he approached them their lethargy vanished. They stood up, looking at him expectantly. Danny would not have been surprised if somebody had saluted the confident youngster — there was just something about him, some instinctive quality of leadership, some inborn will to lead, to command. . . .

"Well, Danny."

Big Bill Henry's voice behind Danny was low-pitched, almost soft. Danny turned. He had almost forgotten that the big man was anywhere around. The Chief put out his hand and Danny was surprised at the gentleness of its grip.

"I'm glad to see you back at this Station, Danny."

Endless times, in far places, in the long monotony of flight above trackless waters, Danny had wondered how this first meeting, at this Station, with this man, would come about. He knew, always, that someday he would come back, that he would face this man in this place — this man who had been his father's teacher and friend; this man who had, in the bitterest hour of Danny's life, turned upon him with bitter, deriding disdain.

"I'm glad to be back," Danny said simply.

The big man stood in that posture that was natural to him, that was almost the hallmark of him, looking down at Danny; there was no avoiding the intensity of his eyes. Danny, inwardly unwilling, looked back at him, his gaze unwavering. The big man's eyes softened and a rare, unaccustomed smile lighted them. He fumbled in his shirt pockets for cigarettes and a match. He handed one of the cigarettes to Danny without a word and placed the other between his own lips. He brought up the sole of his foot and struck the match.

"You first, Captain," he said, holding the match for Danny, but his effort at jocularity withered on his lips.

"Thanks, Chief," Danny said.

The big man's voice rumbled. "I've got a mess of crow to eat, Danny," he said, blowing out an enveloping cloud of smoke. "It's a worse mess because it's seasoned with some of my own words."

Danny wanted to say something, wanted to put off, to postpone this ordeal, for himself and for this man who had been his father's friend. Ragland anticipated him.

"Not a word out of you, Danny — this is my dish and I'm goin' to eat it.

"Maybe it would go down easier," the big man said after a pause, "if we were to go over yonder on the beach and watch my boys do their stuff, such as it is, with that boat. You ought to see 'em anyhow, or leastways, you ought to see that young hound that's growed up while you were gone. Mind?"

"I'd like to," Danny said. "But Chief, about this —"

"Shut up, Danny," the Chief ordered.

Across the open space the boat crew were coupling the trailer to the truck and the group climbed aboard. Danny noticed that Jerry had climbed into the dory while the rest of the crew were at their places in the weapons-carrier. The truck moved slowly out of the areaway and turned toward the beach. The Chief moved toward the jeep and Danny fell into step beside him.

"Drive," the big man said, waving a hand toward the driver's seat.

"But, Chief, I've never driven one of these things. About all I guess I know how to do is drive an airplane."

"Drive," Big Bill Henry repeated, and Danny slid under the wheel. "I just can't get used to these damned things," the Chief said. "Jerry, he thinks I'm the worst driver on these Banks — and I guess he's about the best. They're good things, though," he conceded.

Danny started the engine and put the vehicle into gear. It lurched forward. Danny's face reddened and he eased his foot on the accelerator. On the second attempt things went more smoothly and Danny turned eastward, following the truck as it lumbered across the flat sandy waste with the dory in tow.

Ahead of them the weapons-carrier stopped halfway in the circle that its wheels had made on the flat sand of the beach, backed up until the wheels of the trailer were almost within the reach of the rising tide. The truck stopped and the crew, except for the driver, got down and uncoupled the trailer, raised its tow shaft until the bow of the boat touched the sand. The truck pulled away, climbed the beach until it was past the normal reach of the tide.

Danny halted the jeep alongside the parked weapons-carrier. The nine men of the boat crew were rolling up their dungarees, making them into a tight band midway their thighs. Some of the men kicked off their shoes. Danny looked for Jerry and for a moment was unable to determine with any certainty which one of the group was he. Jerry had merged himself with the crew and, Danny thought, put away his own individual identity. He was part of the crew.

Some of the group seemed no older than Jerry. Two or three of them, it seemed to Danny, were not sure what to do with themselves, or with the boat. They moved about uncertainly, looking sometimes at Jerry standing almost inert at the port bow of the dory, waiting until the truck driver came down. The boat rested with its stern projected past the forward end of the trailer. Big Bill Henry Ragland reached for the ground with one foot, balanced his weight on it, and stood up. He moved with as much easy assurance as ever. The fifty-eight years he had lived had left no burdening weight upon him. His hair was thinner, with a lot of gray in it. The crew glanced inquiringly at the truck driver and he, in turn, sent a questioning glance toward the towering figure half a hundred feet away. Ragland nodded.

Now the leader turned back to the boat. There were no orders that Danny could hear. The leader — he was not much older than the other members of the crew, Danny observed — said, "All right, fellows," and the crew took their stations on each side of the boat. Danny saw Jerry's blond, tousled head at the port bow. He had taken off his shirt and tossed it carelessly toward the dry beach. The boat slid forward, its bow in the thinned-out wash of the tide, its stern on the sand.

Oars were unlashed, a line looped at the stern, and an oar passed through the loop for a tiller. Ranged on each side of the boat, facing seaward, the crew waited. A breaker hit the beach, sending a wall of white foaming water toward the boat.

"Let her go!" The helmsman's voice was scarcely audible where Danny watched. The crew slid the boat forward; its bow came up on the crest of the breaker. With split-second timing the helmsman projected himself into the boat at the instant the water was about to touch his feet. Danny's eyes searched for Jerry. He was already aboard, with his oar in its lock, its blade reaching out, poised, waiting. One of the younger crewmen, on the starboard side, had lost his footing when the foaming water climbed up his legs and now he was pulling himself aboard with his arms. The helmsman, standing with the steering oar grasped in one hand, reached down with the other and hauled at the man's belt. He flopped into the boat and fumbled for his oar.

For that moment the dory was off balance. It lost its headway and swung broadside to the following wave that was now beginning to break in a white froth. The helmsman swung his oar. Three of the rowing oars were still fumbling for their locks, their blades dragging. Danny saw Jerry's oar thrust downward, saw his shoulders hauled backward. The dory's bow came into the wave almost head-on; it rose, bucked the roller, and dropped out beyond it.

Now the oars came up in unison, swung downward, and the dory rode seaward, rising on the next breaker before it began to foam. The helmsman swung the boat to ride it head-on, and the little craft now moved steadily seaward, the oars rising and descending in smooth, measured beat until the boat was out beyond the first shoal where, at low tide, the swell broke the surge of the sea and the waves reformed them-

selves to sweep shoreward. The boat turned in a wide circle
and came back.

The Chief stood, as he always stood, with his feet planted
wide and his hands flattened on his hips just forward the after
pockets of his blue trousers. His eyes had not left the dory
from the moment when he nodded briefly to the helmsman
and he had uttered no word. The lines around his mouth were
set in a fixed, unchanging pattern, grim, sardonic; but under-
neath and in the shadow of his eyes there was the fierce, rugged
pride of a race of men who deal with the sea with their naked
hands. When the dory rode past the final hazard of the shoal,
he took out a cigarette, lighted it without glancing at it.

Danny had got down on the other side of the jeep to stand,
watching the drill. In the instant when it looked as if the dory
were going to be swamped and its crew sent sprawling into
the surf, some of them perhaps to be trapped under it when
it overturned, he felt the sweat popping out in the palms of
his hands and under his armpits. It was like — the intensity of
that instant when an aircraft is committed to the air, that
instant when daylight shows under the landing gear.

Now the dory was coming in for a landing and Danny again
found himself reaching back into his pilot's lore for something with which to compare it. It came to him with something of incredulous surprise that this was, in reality, the first
time he had ever actually watched a boat drill from the beach
or from anywhere. It was something that he had always taken
for granted.

The dory rode the swell of the breaker. It swung off when
the helmsman judged that he could not ride it all the way in
to the beach. The oars were poised, still, their blades just
above the surface, and for a moment the boat idled. The
helmsman's eyes were seaward, measuring the lift of the following sea. Danny could not hear whether any orders were
spoken, but he saw the helmsman's arm sweep downward.

The oars bit down into the water with the sweep of his arm, and the dory's bow swung toward the beach.

When the dory came through on the crest of the swell as it broke into white foam on the flat sand, Jerry and the youth at the starboard bow oar shipped their oars and swung their legs over the side. They took the dory's gunwales in their hands and steadied it against the backward lash of the receding wave, and the boat grounded lightly, its bow even with the wash of the tide. The other crewmen dropped over the side and took hold, and on the wash of the next wave they swung the dory around until its bow again pointed seaward. They turned and looked expectantly toward the Chief.

Ragland strode across the intervening sand and looked into the dory. He shook his head without saying anything and the crewmen glanced uneasily into the boat. There was water in it — too much water. Ragland turned directly to the youth who had lost his footing and said, not unkindly, "That's your water, Iowa. You stood with your legs stiff and you had to limber 'em before you could get goin', and that takes time. Next try, get your legs limber and jump just before — just when you feel the water touch your toes."

"Yes, Sir," the boy called Iowa said uncertainly. "I'll try, Sir."

Without any further word the Chief turned his back on the crew and walked slowly up the slant of the beach. The crew tilted the dory on its side and decanted the water they had brought back. When Ragland regained the dry level of the beach he sat down in the sand, with his shoulders planted against the bumper of the jeep. He motioned Danny to sit down beside him.

From appearances the Chief had, for the moment, lost interest in the activity on the beach below him. His glance was only casual when they righted the dory after pouring the water out of it and the crew took their places, watching the waves as they rode the shoulder of the making tide.

"It's a marvel to me what a country this must be," he said presently, with seeming irrelevance. "And all the different kinds of people there is in it. I remember when we had that first war there was some few come here from far-off places, back yonder in the country, from places I never heard of. Of course, I'm used enough to people that come from that way." He gestured widely toward the sea.

"This time, it's just been more than I could do to keep track of 'em, the different kinds and the different places they come from." He fell silent when the crew was poised for the launching. This time the boy they called Iowa jumped an instant too soon, a fraction of a second ahead of the man next to him, and again the dory's stern dragged as the foaming water flowed under it.

"It takes time and it takes practice," the big man said, a fugitive smile hovering at the corners of his mouth. "But it takes somethin' else that these fellers they send here from Iowa and some sort of a place called Idaho just don't bring with 'em. Your daddy had it, and Jerry yonder, he's got it. I reckon you've got it, too, Danny — I don't see how you could help it."

"What is it, Chief — this thing you're talking about?"

The big man was thoughtful before he answered. He looked seaward where the dory's oars were rising and dipping smoothly. Sunlight glinted on the blades of the oars as they rose, dripping, from the water. His scrutiny quickened and his eyelids narrowed when the helmsman swung the dory to bring it broadside to ride a swell, and the oars on the port side, with the exception of the bow oar, were reaching for water that was, for an instant, not there.

"That's what I mean — yonder," he said. "Did you see that Jerry's oar when the dory was settin' on top of that swell? He knew where to find water to dip it in — these other ones don't.

And," he added a little morosely, "I don't know whether they'll ever learn. Jerry, he don't have to learn."

Offshore the dory rode the long swell of the sea, now disappearing from sight altogether as it went down into the trough beyond a rolling hill of water and again rising until it perched, for a fleeting instant, seemingly motionless, on a crest. It turned and came shoreward. This time the helmsman calculated his approach with more precision, and the little boat rode in without losing headway. They swung it around, bow-on to the sea.

Danny knew that they were, all of them, this time, looking directly at the Chief. But he was not quite prepared for what happened next. With one upward swing of their arms the men, moving now as one man, swung the dory off the sand, lifted it slowly until it was even with their shoulders. The men on the port side bent their knees and the port gunwale tilted downward. No water came out of it. They set the dory down, but now they looked at one another and not at the Chief. There was a moment's silence.

"Take time out!"

The Chief's voice rolled down to them. Danny wondered if that were all the commendation they were to hear. The crew slid the boat a little way up the beach, out of the way of the reaching tide. They moved away from it, some of them dropping down on the warm sand. One or two went to the parked weapons-carrier and got cigarettes where they had left them to be sure that they would be dry when they needed them.

Their voices came in muted murmuring across the sand. Now and then Danny could make out a sentence or two, though he was not trying to hear. The talk was about how to get a boat launched without shipping so much water that she would sink. The Chief waited in meditative silence. After an interval the crew went back to the dory, and this time the boy from Iowa managed his timing with exactness and the dory rode lightly into the rising tide. The Chief watched them, his eyes undeviating.

"And now, Danny, I'll eat my crow." The big man's voice cut across the silence.

"I wish you wouldn't, Chief," Danny protested, almost pleading.

"No, Danny." The Chief's voice was patient. "In my lifetime I've talked a lot — too damned much — and too many times I've said things that may have hurt somebody."

"But, Chief, you've always made up for it, one way or another, and more besides. Just the way you've looked after Jerry since — since — well, while I've been gone."

"Don't argue with me, Danny. I'm goin' to say what I'm goin' to say if I have to sit on top of you and make you listen to me." He leaned away from the jeep's bumper and turned to face Danny directly. Danny kept his gaze fixed, unhappily, on the bobbing dory now well out beyond the shoal.

"I reckon I don't have to remind you of what I said when you went off from here," the big man went on. His voice lost its explosive vehemence. "I told you that you were runnin' away from here when times were pretty bad with us.

"This is our country here, Danny, and this is our ocean. It belongs to us and we belong to it. I don't know just how to say it — me that talks too damned much most of the time — I can't find words when I need 'em.

"My folks and your folks, away back yonder, were cast up on this beach and we've stayed here. I don't begin to know how long it's been — since the first of us come here. I don't guess anybody ever just settled here willin'-like, or on purpose, but when they got cast up here, they — we — stayed. There were good times and there were bad times, but where we were cast up we stayed.

"My daddy and his daddy — your daddy and his daddy —

as far back as anybody knows — they've been here. We have belonged to this here Service. My granddaddy and your great-granddaddy helped drag the crew of that old 'Monitor' out of the ocean yonder between New Christmas and Old Christmas, what there was of 'em left alive. It was not more'n a cable-length from where your daddy was when they got him.

"I may be sort of mixed up about this business, Danny, but it was me that let your daddy go out that night when he didn't come back. He wanted to go and I ought to have gone myself. But it was his turn and we were pretty busy in them times. Remember? There was one night when there were eleven ships afire off there at one time and you could read the palm of your hand by the light of 'em, standin' on the shore here.

"I'm not excusin' myself for bein' a damned fool, but I reckon I figured that the end of the world was about to pop down on us and there was nobody to hold it off except them of us that know this beach and this ocean. When I saw your Daddy lyin' there on the beach where they laid him it was like my own son dyin' all over again, only where I could see it.

"Your daddy was in my boat crew up the beach from the time he joined just before he was eighteen, back yonder in that little war. Times was bad then, with them damned sub-marines poppin' up all over the ocean. He joined up. He was with me when we picked up them nine men off'n a schooner out there. This is not the first time I've seen this ocean afire.

"I wanted you with me, Danny.

"You looked just like your daddy looked when he joined up with me back yonder in the little war. Of course he had wanted you to go off to school, and I did, too. Times are changin' around here and a boy that's had schoolin' will have a better chance.

"I reckon I thought the whole war was goin' to be fought right here, and it looked like it was goin' to be lost right here. They had taken all the old men we had, fellers like 'Lonzo

Burrus and Palmer Midgett and Dorland and the rest of 'em, away from here. . . . Did you ever run across any of 'em out yonder, Danny?"

"Yes, I did, now and then," Danny said, "and I was sure glad when I ran across somebody from here. They had it pretty bad, and anybody will tell you if it hadn't been for them and a lot like 'em there would have been no landings on Guadalcanal and a lot of other places."

"I know about them, Danny, and I know about you, too. They come home and they brought me news and I knew that I'd been — well, I knew I'd as well get to work on this here dish of crow."

"They never saw me do anything, Chief," Danny said helplessly, wishing that he could, somehow, stem the flow of this big man's confessional.

"Maybe they didn't see you, but they know that it takes — it takes — hell's fire, Danny! I been wantin' to just put my hands on that scar on the back of your head. Jerry told me about it. Lean down here."

The Chief's great hands were gentle when they touched Danny's head. He held the cap in his hands when Danny sat erect again and a forefinger moved caressingly over the bright surface of the double bars that attested Danny's rank. He was silent for a while after he handed the cap back to Danny, and then he went on, his voice slow, low-pitched.

"That's all I got to say, Danny. I wish I knew how to say I'm proud of you — as proud of you as I'm ashamed of myself for ever thinkin' that Dan Gray's boy would run away from anything between here and the bottom of hell."

"Thanks, Bill Henry," Danny said simply.

Ragland's face was suffused with a smile that began at the corners of his mouth and wrinkled his bronzed face upward to his ears.

"You know this is the first time in your whole damned life

you've ever called me that, Danny. Now that squirt yonder —" his eyes were soft as they searched for Jerry among the crew, who were now beaching the dory again — "he's always called me that from the time he learned to talk. And, damn me, I've always liked it."

Now the big man uncrossed his folded legs and stood erect. Danny noticed that he did it without effort, without the help of his great arms lifting him, and his hands pressed down in the sand. He strode swiftly across the sand to the dory and, by custom, looked to see how much water it had shipped. The bottom of the dory was scarcely damp. His smile beamed.

"That's better — that's damned good," he rumbled. "You're learnin', Iowa, but the tails of your shirt are wet." He glanced upward at the sun. "About time to go in. Williams, take her in, and when you've washed her and put away your gear, you and the crew take the rest of the day off."

Ragland turned and walked back toward the jeep, but Danny lingered, watching the crew balance the dory on the trailer, lash it down, and couple the trailer to the truck. Its wheels were deep in the rising tide, half embedded in the sand, and the crew put their shoulders against its weight to get it under way. Danny walked slowly back up the beach to where the Chief was waiting.

"Does Jerry ride back with us?" he asked idly.

"No," the Chief said shortly. "He rides with the crew where he belongs. Not," he added, "that he ain't welcome to ride with me, but when he comes out with 'em he goes back with 'em. You boys will stay to dinner."

Danny started to protest but the Chief silenced him with a wave of his hand. They climbed aboard the jeep and started toward the Station. Danny drove more evenly, but still he hoped Jerry was not watching him too closely when he almost stalled crossing the big wind-built dyke that held back the sea when — when she was in one of her ecstasies. The weapons-carrier, the dory in tow, lumbered past them. Jerry did not glance in their direction.

Ragland stood, waiting, at the head of the long table until all of the crew except the man on watch in the tower outside and the man at the communications switchboard came in and took their places. He indicated to Danny that he was to sit in the first place on his right. Danny noticed that Jerry, when he came in, went down to the far end of the table, to a place to which he seemed accustomed. No word was spoken by any of them until they were all in place. The Chief intoned the blessing, his voice sonorous — and it sounded as natural as it did when he shattered the air around him with roaring blasphemy.

When the "Amen" was reached, the men around the table lifted their hands to the backs of the chairs behind which they stood, glanced toward the head of the table. The Chief had not moved but stood, his glance traveling from face to face down the right side of the table, crossing over to the opposite file of faces, and coming backward until, again, his gaze rested on Danny's face.

"This," the Chief said with a nod toward Danny, "is Captain Daniel Gray of the Army Air Forces. Some of you have known him all your lives. Some of you who are new to this Station and to this Service have heard of him. His father was my friend, and a member of the crew of this Station until —" the Chief's voice hardened, was frozen in an involuntary silence for an instant — "until his death. I am glad to have Daniel Gray's son — his other son — back at this Station, if only as a guest. Sit down, men."

Throughout the meal Danny could feel their covertly appraising glances directed toward him. Some of the men — boys, really — at the table he knew, if not directly, by family resemblances . . . the lanky youth with red hair must, surely, be a Scarborough from Avon . . . the blond youth with sharp gray eyes would be one of the Midgetts . . . and he could pick out the native-born by their voices, if not by family favor. . . .

The boy who had missed his footing at the first launching during boat drill was sitting next to Danny. He was eating with a concentration of purpose that indicated a healthy appetite. Danny asked him, casually, if he were from Iowa. The boy, with a hasty, surprised glance at Danny, said, "Yes, Sir," and returned to his eating.

There were no mess attendants. Each man helped himself from the platter nearest him and passed it along to the next. Big Bill Henry Ragland dipped mightily into every dish that came to him, heaping his plate with boiled beef and cabbage, with mashed potatoes and a half dozen stalks of celery. Coffee was poured into pint-size china cups. Danny helped himself more sparingly. At the other end of the table Jerry helped himself with impartial generosity from every platter that passed him.

When the men finished eating they got up from the table, picked up their plates, and went past the garbage can that stood just within the kitchen door. They scraped any fragments of food left on their plates into the can and dumped the utensils into the sink, plates and cups in one compartment and knives and forks in another. Danny and the boy from Iowa came to the garbage can at the same time. The boy held back.

"You needn't have done that, Sir," the boy said diffidently. "Some of the fellows would have brought your plate. I'd have been glad to, myself."

"Thanks, Iowa," Danny said easily, "but this is the last place on earth that I'd have thought of RHIP — if that's what you had in mind."

"What's that, Sir?" the boy asked.

"RHIP? It's a saying they have in the Army — in all the services, I guess — 'rank has its privileges.' But it seems somehow out of place here — and anyhow that wave that got you by the legs this morning wouldn't have stopped to see if I had these things on my collar."

"I don't guess it would, Sir," the boy said, still doubtful and not quite at ease, "but still — oh, thank you, Sir! I got mine wet out yonder when that sea hit me, and they've been pretty hard to get here lately. My matches got wet, too, Sir."

"So you come from Iowa," Danny said. They had come back through the mess, the young seaman walking hesitantly beside Danny. "My navigator was from out there somewhere. He'd never seen an ocean until he got in the Army, but he was a good navigator. Being where I was supposed to be was never any worry when he was along."

"Gee, that's swell, Sir. It's — it's almost like seeing somebody from home, hearing you say that. I've not seen anybody from home since I've been here. Was he in the ship the other day, Sir, when you flew over here?"

"Yeah, and I had him worried when I got off course to come by here. How did you come to join the Coast Guard, Iowa?"

"I guess it was because I always wanted to see the ocean, Sir, and I thought I'd maybe get to fly, or maybe be around one of those helicopters. There was a picture of one on a poster in front of the post office back home, where they enlisted me. Can you fly one of them, Sir?"

"Never saw one until I got to Dayton the other day. There were three or four of them outside a hangar when I landed."

"I've never seen one, either," the boy said, "but I'd sure like to fly one."

Williams came through the screen door behind them. He held back for a little, waiting as if to see if Danny and the Iowa boy were talking about anything in particular before he spoke.

"Captain — Danny, some of the fellows are going down to

the Point and do some surf casting — somebody saw a school of drum playing around there this morning. Want to come along?"

"Sounds like a good idea," Danny replied. "Is the Chief going?"

"Don't guess he will," Williams said. "Just us that was in the boat crew this morning. The Chief's up to his ears in his paper work — hear him grumbling over it?"

Danny started to protest that they ought to be getting back to the Woods but remained silent when he saw Jerry's eyes fixed, almost pleading, on his face. Other members of the boat crew were waiting inside the door. Danny glanced down at his neatly-creased uniform, at his polished Brazilian boots. The Chief's towering figure loomed suddenly in the background.

"Go on with 'em, Danny — wish I could go myself," he rumbled, "but they've got this outfit so bogged down in paper now that some of these days they're goin' to haul me up yonder and court martial me." He turned to the boy with red hair. "Get him a pair of dungarees — that's all he'll need, Scarborough."

"You could use my locker to stow your stuff in while you're gone out, Sir," Iowa said.

"Heck, he don't need no locker. Ain't nobody goin' to bother his stuff," Jerry interposed. Locks keep only honest people out, Danny thought, remembering a native adage. . . .

When he came out of the Station a few minutes later, clad only in a pair of loose-fitting dungarees and a sailor's hat set insecurely on the blond mass of his hair, the boat crew had backed the weapons-carrier out of the equipment building. The crew were aboard it. Danny noticed that the seat beside the driver had been left vacant, the crew ranging themselves along the seats that ran lengthwise the body.

RHIP, Danny thought, and without hesitating he went to the rear of the truck and climbed aboard. "Slide over into that front seat, will you," he said casually to the man nearest the front. "I'd like to sit back here where I can get a good look around. It's been a long time since I've ridden down to the Point."

The Chief watched them go and there was a smile of content, of serene satisfaction on his broad face as he turned and went back toward the office and the mountain of paper work that awaited him.

17

JERRY GRAY SAT ON THE FRONT STEPS, ELBOWS ON HIS KNEES, chin cupped in his hands. Surfman sat erect beside him, immersed in some remote feline speculation; he had touched Jerry's elbow with a tentative paw. When there was no response he settled back on his haunches, waiting.

November twilight was thick in the low places of the marsh across the road and under the big live oaks at each end of the yard, and the sand along the rutted road had turned a dull gray. Above the marsh the sky was drained of all color except for a tinge of red that lingered in the west. The leaves and the moss on the trees and the grass in the marsh were without any sort of motion. . . . By tomorrow it would rain.

It was about time for the bus, Jerry thought, with a small kindling of hope, and maybe it would stop and Mom and Danny would get off. Maybe Danny had not been able to get a car after all, and they would have to come home on the bus. Or maybe they had got a car and had crossed over on the same ferry as the bus and they would come along together, almost any minute now.

Two days had gone by — three counting today — and it seemed to Jerry like a lifetime. The first day it had been a lot of fun having the whole house to himself, and late in the evening the boy they called Iowa had come. He had liberty coming to him and Big Bill Henry had let him off to come and stay two nights and a day. The day and the two nights had passed quickly enough. Iowa, Jerry discovered, was a pretty good sort of fellow after all. Only, he wasn't much good around a house, cooking or things like that. But Jerry hadn't minded that.

Not going over to the Station to stay while Polly Gray and Danny were in Norfolk had been Jerry's idea, and he had kept it to himself until the bus was out of sight. The idea was born of impulse after supper when Iowa offered to help him wash the dishes behind a dozen people who had eaten. It had been a swell supper, Jerry reflected now. Mom hadn't batted an eye when he and Iowa called her from the back yard to come out and look at the huge fish they had caught. When he told her about asking the whole crew over to eat it she had just smiled and got to work. . . .

Jerry couldn't remember when there had been so many people in the house at one time, or when he had heard so much laughing and going on. The table in the dining room would not hold all of them at one time, and they had had to eat in two shifts. Jerry and Iowa and Bill Henry and Mom and Scarborough had waited until after the first lot of them had eaten. There was plenty of fish and Mom could do a swell job, even with a tough old drum. She could cook anything so it would taste good, Jerry thought now, unhappily hungry.

Afterward he and Iowa had washed the dishes. It was funny about Iowa; he seemed just like a kid, the way he talked about landing the fish. He didn't boast when he told about it and he laughed at himself for flopping over so many times. He assured Polly Gray and the Chief that if it hadn't been for Jerry the fish would have come and swallowed him, like Jonah and the whale. Jerry was not very clear about Jonah. He remembered looking down the throat of a whale that got stranded on the beach one time. Gosh, how the damned thing stunk!

Jerry couldn't remember when he had seen the Chief in such a good humor. He almost purred like Surfman. Jerry absently stroked the cat beside him and Surfman purred dutifully, contentedly. Bill Henry got to telling tales about wrecks they had had away back yonder. They were old tales to Jerry, but Iowa sat there with his mouth popped wide open, forgetting to eat.

Right after supper they had all gone back to the Station but not before Iowa had promised, privately, to come back the next day and stay out his liberty. Jerry had intended to tell Polly Gray and Danny about changing his plans, but both of them were so busy, after everybody had gone, with last-minute things they had to do before leaving that — well, anyhow it might bother Mom or even make her change her mind about going at all. Nobody could ever tell about women, and Jerry didn't want to have to start all over again persuading her to go.

It had worked fine.... Almost before the bus was out of sight, before Jerry could start missing his mother and Danny, Iowa, all rigged out in his best uniform, had come up the walk. He had a pair of faded dungarees rolled into a bundle under his arm, with a toothbrush in the middle of the bundle. He put on his dungarees and all day they had just fooled around. They got the horse out of the marsh and before night Iowa could ride him standing up. But nothing would persuade Bos'n to let Surfman get near him.

Iowa talked a lot about how things were back where he came from, how the cornfields were as big as the ocean, pretty near, and how they turned first one color and then another when the corn was green and growing.

"It looks just like the ocean, sometimes," Iowa persisted, and Jerry said that he had never seen corn growing, except maybe a row or two in somebody's garden down on the edge of the marsh where the ground was rich and there was always plenty of water.

"And you never have a hurricane come out of your corn ocean," Jerry maintained.

"Yeah, but you ought to see a tornado strike sometimes. Ever have a tornado around here?"

"They ain't nothin' but little pint-sized hurricanes, Bill Henry says."

Where to put Iowa to sleep presented Jerry with something of a puzzle when bedtime came. He didn't know whether he wanted anybody sleeping in Danny's place or not, or even whether it would be right to ask somebody if he wanted to sleep with him. Iowa settled the problem casually enough.

"Heck, no use having to make up two beds in the morning. I sleep with my brother all the time when I'm home. He's about your age, I guess, but not as big."

Iowa had been just like homefolks, and Jerry had puzzled over that for a while after they had gone to bed and turned out the lights and after Iowa's breathing told him that this fellow who thought corn patches looked like the ocean was asleep. Up to now he had never had much to do with these strange people who had come to the Outer Banks after the war started. But Iowa was all right, Jerry conceded, and now, in the gathering twilight, he wished that he had asked the Chief if he couldn't stay until Mom and Danny got back. . . .

But he put the thought away. Not for anything would he ever let on to Bill Henry that he was — that he could be afraid to stay by himself. Iowa had not been in any hurry to get back to the Station. He had brought up the matter out in the Sound, while they were fishing. Iowa, as it turned out, was a pretty good hand at fishing with a net, once he got the hang of it, only he kept talking about how much alike the engines in a tractor and a boat were. They came back by the fishhouse and unloaded the boat.

"This here's your share," Jerry said when they came away from the fishhouse.

"My share for what?" Iowa demanded, not taking the two crumpled dollar bills Jerry held toward him.

"Take it, dammit," Jerry insisted bluntly. "That's the way my daddy always divided up — one share for each man and a share for the boat."

"Gee, thanks!" Iowa stammered.

"Thanks, hell; you worked for it, didn't you?"

"The Chief would let me stay, if you were to ask him," Iowa suggested hopefully.

"That's all right, Iowa," Jerry replied. "Mom and Danny'll be along, and if they don't come I'll be okay; and besides, the Chief don't like anybody to get their liberty extended. You can come back another time, if you want to."

"Gosh, I'd like to — I've had a swell time."

Iowa went down the walk toward the road and stopped, waiting. His white cap made a blurred patch against the gathering gloom above the marsh. The jeep's horn sounded at the top of the rise down the road and Iowa crossed the road. The jeep slowed almost to a stop and Iowa climbed aboard. The long finger of the Light cut across the gathering twilight. The jeep moved off toward the Station.

Jerry continued to stare at the tunnel in the yoepon after the red taillight blinked past the turn. Any minute, now, he was sure the headlights of the bus — or maybe the car, if Danny could get one — would cut through the dusk and Mom and Danny would be home. He wondered if he ought to get up and turn on a light in the house so they could see, before they got there, that he was at home waiting for them.

When he had turned the impulse over in his mind he decided against it, telling himself that there was no need of wasting current out of the storage battery burning a light when there was nobody in the house. Besides, it was not dark yet, up there on the hill. They could see the house plain enough. Its newly-painted walls were bright against the dark of the cedars and the yoepon. He would just sit there where he was and wait for them. He stroked Surfman's neck, and his fingers explored the cat's chin, rubbing it gently. Surfman purred, stretched himself in luxurious content along the step, and turned his paws upward. Jerry scratched the cat's belly and Surfman took the tip of a finger in his mouth, biting gently. . . .

Jerry stretched his legs, letting his heels rest on the lower step. He considered the magnitude of his feet, wondering if the boots they were bringing him from Norfolk would be big enough. He rubbed his two big toes together and then ran the roughened sole of one foot along the skin of the other leg. He smiled abstractedly. His fingers searched the pocket of his shirt until they found a long-stemmed match. He brought it out and looked at it.

"Wonder if it would," he said half aloud. He looked at the head of the match, smiled uncertainly. He brought the foot up until the heel rested against the knee of the other leg. He held the match against his forefinger with his thumb and, with sudden decision, scraped the match along the bottom of his foot.

The match burst into flame.

"Damn," Jerry said softly and then, as the flame climbed along the stem of the match, his face was suffused with a smile of contentment, of achievement. The match burned itself out and Jerry dropped it. His fingers moved along the bottom of his foot where there was only a faint tingling from the friction of the match. He put his foot flat on the gravel in the walk and rubbed it. His fingers searched for another match, found it. Jerry looked at it and put it back in his pocket. The sole of his foot itched a little.

Jerry felt a lot better. The sole of his foot was warm against the ground, with a warmth that flowed slowly, contentingly up through his legs, his thighs, and spread across his belly into his chest until even his face glowed. . . . He could strike a match on the bottom of his foot — like Bill Henry. He was not lonesome, now. His hand moved out and lay crooked along Surfman's soft jaw on the step beside him.

Lights gleamed from the darkness of the tunnel through the yoepon. Absorbed in the contemplation of his massive feet, Jerry was first aware of the light when the shifting beam cut across the yard before him, caught the whitewashed pillars at the foot of the walk. He brought his eyes to focus on the approaching lights, wondering whether the bus would stop, but somehow, now, it didn't matter so much whether it stopped or not. Anyway, it was not the bus. Jerry recognized the familiar exhaust of the jeep's engine.

The Chief got down from the jeep when it halted at the foot of the walk. He came around behind it and toward the house. Jerry stood up, waiting. Surfman got to his feet, rubbed his back against the bare calf of Jerry's leg, purring. The Chief came up the walk, his massive legs unhurried. . . . He walks like he might not be more than just grown up, Jerry thought, like he was no older than — than me.

"All by yourself, Jerry?" the Chief said.

"Yeah, Bill Henry," Jerry answered casually. "Just waitin' to see if the bus would come."

"You all right?"

"Yeah, I'm all right."

"That boy could have stayed with you if you'd wanted him to."

"Didn't need him," Jerry said. "But he's all right," he added.

"Just goin' to the post office and thought I'd stop by and see if Polly and Danny had come home."

"Want to go in the house?"

"No — sit here on the steps a little."

The Chief settled himself on the top step, his massive feet planted flat on the bottom step. Jerry sat down beside him. For a while neither of them spoke. Surfman sat down between them. The Chief scratched the cat's ear with a massive forefinger and the cat purred softly.

"He likes you, Bill Henry," Jerry said.

Ragland said nothing. With the fingers of his other hand he began to search in his pockets for a cigarette. Presently he found one, placed it between his lips. He sat there with it drooping loosely.

"Got a match, Jerry?" he said presently.

Jerry took out a match, started to hand it to the massive man beside him. Instead, he brought his left foot up until its heel rested against the knee of his right leg. He took the match between his thumb and forefinger, flicked its head along the sole of his foot. The match broke in half. The Chief waited. Jerry took out another match. This time he held the head of it nearer the tip of his finger. It burst into flame. The Chief lighted his cigarette.

"Much obliged, Jerry," the Chief said presently.

"Welcome," Jerry replied casually.

"You're a good boy, Jerry," the Chief said.

Jerry did not answer him. The Chief smoked in silence until the cigarette's glow inched up toward the tips of his fingers. He sent the butt in a wide, glowing arc above the lawn. Two short blasts of a horn cut across the stillness of the evening and lights glowed far back in the tunnel through the yoepon. Jerry got up from the step, stood with feet wide apart on the walk. Surfman came down, arched his back and rubbed it against Jerry's leg. The bus was slowing down. Jerry started down the walk. He must not, he thought, run, or even walk too fast. The walk was warm against the bottoms of his feet.

The bus stopped and its door opened even with the space between the two white pillars at the end of the walk. Jerry could make out the driver's lean young face in the light from the dashboard. He was looking backward, up the aisle. He didn't get out and, Jerry thought with quick disappointment, that must mean that Mom's not along; he always gets out when there's a woman passenger to get off.

Jerry could see, dimly, somebody moving along the aisle, coming from somewhere in the back, toward the front. It couldn't be Danny — too big, too tall, for him. His shoulders were up past the top of the windows and his head was hidden. He held a small bag in his hands, held it above the seat backs. Jerry could see the driver's face turning as his eyes followed the dismounting passenger toward the front.

"He's got on a uniform, anyhow," Jerry said over his shoulder.

The Chief sat still on the step, his elbows on his knees and his massive hands clasped in front of him. Without looking back at the bus driver the man in uniform turned toward the open door. His head was bent forward and Jerry was unable to see anything of his face except his chin as he stepped down into the road. He straightened up and looked quickly around and the bus door closed behind him. The driver waved briefly at Jerry before he put the vehicle into gear and gathered speed up the hill.

The man in uniform just stood there. After what seemed to Jerry a long time, the man's eyes found him. He shifted the little bag from his right hand and started slowly forward. Jerry waited. The man came up the walk.

"That driver," the man said slowly, "said this is where Captain Gray lives." His voice was half questioning.

"Sure," Jerry said. "This is where Danny — Captain Gray lives. But he ain't here — he and Mom went to Norfolk and they ain't back yet."

The man half turned, his eyes searching the gloom into which the bus had disappeared. He moved, Jerry thought, with a heavy slowness, almost as if he were half asleep. Jerry shifted uncomfortably on his feet. He felt the gentle push of Surfman's back against his leg, heard the soft vibration of his purring. Jerry glanced around at the Chief. He was looking at the man intently.

"They — they might be back any time," Jerry said, his voice not quite steady. "I was sort of lookin' for 'em on the bus — or they might be comin' home in a car. Danny was goin' to get a car, if he could."

"You must be Jerry," the man said, turning back to look at the boy directly in the half-light. His voice was low-pitched, tired. He added musingly, "Captain Gray spoke of you often — if you're Jerry."

"Sure, I'm Jerry."

"My name is Dragonnetti," the man said slowly.

"Sergeant Dragonnetti — Danny's crew chief?"

"Yes," the man said simply. He shifted his glance from Jerry to the massive man behind him on the steps. "Good evening, Chief," he added.

The Chief nodded briefly. Jerry stared at the man for a minute, his lips apart and his eyes wide. The man regarded him with aloof appraisal and a smile came slowly into his eyes. He didn't offer to shake hands, and when Jerry came out of the haze of uncertainty and bewilderment that encircled him, neither of them thought about it. The Chief stood up, towering above the man. A match flamed in his hands and when Jerry glanced around, the Chief was looking intently at the man by its light. It burned almost to his fingers before he lighted his cigarette.

"I'll have to get along now, Jerry," the Chief said. "You and the — Danny's sergeant can come on out to the Station, if you want to. Plenty of room for you, Sergeant," he said, addressing the man directly. The man looked uncertainly from the boy to the Chief, and back again at the boy.

"We can make out here, I guess, Bill Henry," Jerry said. "Mom and Danny might be along any minute — did you see anything of them on the ferry, Sergeant?" The Sergeant shook his head.

"Gosh, I know Danny'll — come on in the house — maybe they'll get here any minute now. Maybe they caught the last ferry. Gimme that bag. You come on in, too, Bill Henry . . . well, good night, and see you tomorrow, maybe. Surfman acts like he knows you, Sergeant — he's funny about people. Why in heck didn't you let Danny know you were comin' to see us?"

"I should have written," the Sergeant said, "but it seemed like a waste of time. Just took a sudden notion to come. . . . Good night, Chief."

"You can stay until he gets back—we've got plenty of room,"

Jerry went on. "When he gets back he'll make you stay — how much leave you got?"

"More than I've known what to do with," the man said slowly.

"Well, come on in and make yourself at home. You ain't had any supper, have you?"

When the Sergeant did not immediately answer, Jerry went on. "Mom left a whole ham cooked and — you can cook, can't you, Sergeant? Danny told me how you used to bring him coffee. I can cook some. We'll make out."

Jerry went into the spare bedroom and snapped on the light. He set the Sergeant's bag down and opened the windows, remarking that the room smelled like hell of paint. "We just finished it before Mom and Danny left." The man stood, looking about him, his eyes blinking in the light. "Bathroom's yonder — take a shower if you want to. That's a swell shower — I fixed it. I'll get the stove goin' while you get fixed."

Jerry lighted two burners on the oil stove, filled the percolator and set it above the flame. He took the baked ham from the refrigerator, wishing that he and Iowa had not been so generous with themselves and so untidy with the carving knife. He got the knife from the drawer beside the sink and was cutting thick slices when the Sergeant came into the kitchen. The man moved slowly and there was something about him that made Jerry feel that his thoughts were far off. He went to the window and, holding back the curtain, looked out into the night sky, at the sweeping finger of the Light.

"Sorry Mom's not here to fix you a good supper," Jerry said, "but maybe we can make out until she gets home. How about — do you want a drink, Sergeant? Danny's got a pint in his bag that's never been opened."

"Thanks, Jerry," the Sergeant said, "but no — you're not taking one, are you?"

"Heck, no — don't even know what the stuff tastes like. But it's okay if you want to take one. I'll bring it."

"No, Jerry — not in this house unless the Captain were here."

"What difference would that make?"

"He's Captain Gray — and nobody ever had a better skipper. But —" the Sergeant's voice trailed off into silence. He looked closely at the boy, now bent over the stove where the percolator was beginning to bubble into life. "You look a lot like him, Jerry," the Sergeant said meditatively.

"Gee, thanks," Jerry said. "Even if you had sent Danny a letter," the boy went on, when they were seated at the table and their plates heaped with sliced ham, with peas and a helping of fig preserves, "I guess it wouldn't have done any good. I just remembered I ain't been after the mail in three days."

Sergeant Dragonnetti ate in silence, pausing now and then to look straight at the boy across the table. More than once he seemed to be about to say something and Jerry waited expectantly. But every time the Sergeant turned back to his plate. He ate, not hungrily, but more like, Jerry thought, it was just something he was used to doing. He did it without thinking, maybe without even tasting what he was eating.

"These preserves," Jerry said, "are some that Mom saved all durin' the time Danny was gone. Said she couldn't bear to think of Danny comin' home and not findin' some fig preserves in the house. He sure likes 'em."

The Sergeant smiled a little, nodded appreciatively, but said nothing. They finished eating in silence and Jerry poured a second cup of coffee. Dragonnetti drank slowly, and between sips at the cup drew deeply on a cigarette, inhaling it and sending the smoke out of his mouth in long, thrusting jets. His eyes were, most of the time, brooding, remote . . . as if he might have been looking at something on the other side of the world. . . .

Jerry watched him from across the table, studying the immobile face above the drab uniform with an intent fascination. The man's hair was dark, not quite black, and here and there, above the temples, flecks of gray were showing. A lock drooped over his forehead. When he brushed it back into place, Jerry noticed that his hands were brown and the fingers were long and they shook a little. He wore a curious sort of a ring on his third finger.

But it was the man's eyes that held Jerry's scrutiny. They were hidden, well back, under thick eyebrows. They were dark, almost like a smoked glass, but beyond them burned an intense, hooded light. His face was lean and brown and his mouth was wide, with one corner of it pulled down and sort of to one side. The Sergeant rested an elbow on the table and leaned his face against the palm of his hand. The tips of his long fingers were hidden in the thick hair above his temple.

"Guess I'd better get these dishes washed," Jerry said when the Sergeant stubbed out his cigarette in the clamshell ashtray. "Mom's funny about dishes — she never lets one stay dirty all night. Says something might happen in the night and people would come in and find her kitchen out of whack."

"Lend you a hand," the Sergeant said. He got up from the table. "I used to be a pretty good hand around a kitchen a long time ago."

"Heck, you'll get your uniform all messed up," Jerry protested. "You just sit and I'll get 'em done in no time."

The Sergeant hesitated for a moment and sat down again at the table. His eyes did not leave Jerry's face while the boy washed the dishes at the sink, dried them, and returned each to its place in the cupboard. When the dishes were washed and put away, Jerry put the ham back in the refrigerator. He wondered if his mother would think that he'd fed the whole neighborhood while she was gone, if she looked at what was left of the ham when she got back.

"Shipshape," Jerry said when he had finished putting away the remnants of supper. He went back to the refrigerator and cut off a small slice of the ham, holding it in his fingers as he turned to the light switch beside the door. He looked at the Sergeant inquiringly and the man got to his feet.

"This is for Surfman," Jerry said, and when the Sergeant's eyebrow lifted slightly, he added, "He's my cat. Come ashore in a lifeboat back durin' the war."

When they came again into the living room the Sergeant stopped indecisively, looking around him. His glance roved around the room, came to the framed photograph of Danny, moved away and came back to it. He crossed the room slowly and stood looking down at the photograph. He moved a hand as if he were about to pick it up and examine it more closely but instead he moved away from the table.

"I didn't realize he looked so young," the Sergeant said presently, as if speaking to himself. He turned away from the picture and moved toward the front door, opened it and went out across the screened porch to the door above the steps. Jerry followed him, wondering uneasily if somewhere he had done something, said something, that made the Sergeant seem so restless, so like he might be thinking of something a long way off.

Wind stirred among the leaves of the palms at the end of the slope, moving them into muffled protest at this disturbing of their sleep. Jerry could hear their rustle, feel the wind cool against his face; and above, when he glanced up, the stars looked as if they were wearing thin veils over their faces. The wind was out of the southwest, and tomorrow or the next day there would be rain and the wind would veer into the north, into the northeast. . . . It would be winter. . . . Beside him the Sergeant drew a deep breath into his lungs, exhaled slowly.

"Like to stretch your legs, Sergeant?" Jerry suggested. "Trip on that bus must tie knots in you. We could walk up to the post office and get the mail. It's not far."

"Might be a good idea at that," the Sergeant replied, rousing himself out of the silence that wrapped him about. "I'll get my cap." He went back into the house. When he came out his manner was eager, almost urgent. They went down the walk toward the road.

When they came down to the road, the Sergeant turned to the right without hesitating, Jerry observed, turned as if he knew already the direction of the post office. They came to the top of the rise and the Sergeant stopped and looked around. Above them the long finger of the Light revolved against the sky, flicking one house and another with the brief intensity of its beam. Against the skyline the trees stood out starkly as it passed them.

He spoke to the Chief like he knew him, Jerry reflected while the Sergeant lingered there on the crest of the rise . . . but anybody would know his rate on account of his cap. He couldn't remember whether the Chief had been wearing his collar insignia, but he was sort of dressed up. . . .

When they came to the post office the Sergeant waited outside while Jerry went in, peeped through the little glass window in their box to see if there were anything in it before he went to the bother of turning the combination dial and opening it. There were the papers and some letters, and these Jerry thrust into the back pocket of his dungarees without glancing at them. . . . There was never any mail for him, now that Danny was back home. Still, they might have sent him a post card from Norfolk. He took out the thin bundle of letters and riffled through it. . . . Nothing for him.

"What you say we walk to the store long as we've come this far, Sergeant? You need cigarettes or anything?"

Without replying, the Sergeant fell into step beside him, and they went off toward the store. Lights glowed from the front windows of most of the houses, and from the front windows of the store. Jerry glanced again at the man walking in the opposite rut. His shoulders were up and his head back, and Jerry thought that the Sergeant was almost as tall as Bill Henry.

Outside the store the Sergeant hesitated in momentary uncertainty, in indecision that Jerry could feel rather than see, but when he held open the screened door Dragonnetti went in without glancing around. Jerry followed him, blinking his eyes against the naked light of bulbs hanging from the low ceiling. Mrs. Grady smiled behind the counter where she was waiting for somebody to make up his mind about what it was he wanted. There were two or three people in the back of the store, gathered around the cold drink box.

Sally Tillett was across the store, with her back turned, examining — pretending to examine, Jerry thought — something in the showcase. She turned around when the Sergeant came in and Jerry could feel her eyes exploring the Sergeant's face. . . . And that ain't all, either, he thought disgustedly. . . . When she saw that Jerry had a stranger with him Mrs. Grady left the customer and moved along the counter.

"Mrs. Grady," Jerry said, "this here's Sergeant Dragonnetti — he was Danny's crew chief on his ship. He come down on the bus."

Mrs. Grady smiled and held out her hand across the counter. Her voice was soft and gentle, as always, Jerry thought, when she spoke to the Sergeant, saying she was glad to see him.

But the Sergeant just stood there looking at her for, it seemed to Jerry, a long time before he moved or said anything. And when he did move, his hand came up jerkily, and when he spoke, his voice was down to almost a whisper. But it lasted just a second before the Sergeant got hold of himself, and when he shook hands, his hand did not tremble any more and his voice sounded almost as big as Big Bill Henry's. . . .

"I'm delighted, Mrs. Grady — I've heard Captain Gray speak of you and the store."

Cedric Baum came from the back of the store, and several others came along, slowly, holding back and looking at the Sergeant who, somehow, looked a lot taller now. With his shoulders back and his head up, he almost touched the ceil-

ing. Mrs. Grady introduced them, telling the Sergeant that
Cedric was one of Danny's close friends, that they had never
been separated until they both went off to the war. She introduced the others, too.

"Have a drink, Sergeant?" Cedric Baum invited. "Mrs.
Grady's got some Coca-Colas hid away back there."

The Sergeant, smiling now and showing strong white teeth,
said sure, he would like to have one with them, only they
would have to let him pay for it. They went back to the
cooler together and brought the bottles back. The Sergeant
held one toward Jerry. They stood around talking, with Mrs.
Grady sort of the center of the group. The customer forgot
whatever of urgency there might have been in his buying and
joined them.

"Where are you from, Sergeant?" Mrs. Grady asked, and
that look of unwilling surprise came back, fleetingly, to the
Sergeant's eyes. He lifted the bottle to his mouth and drained
it before answering her.

"I've been in the Army so long I've almost forgotten that I
was ever from anywhere else," he said. "I joined the Army in
New York before I was eighteen and before that I'd knocked
around some on ships."

Mrs. Grady was about to say something more when her attention was diverted. Sally Tillett turned and moved away
from the counter across the store, and Jerry's glance, following
Mrs. Grady's, saw the girl's eyes searching the Sergeant's as
she moved slowly — too slowly for Jerry — toward the front
door. The Sergeant turned half around and his glance met
Sally Tillett's. Mrs. Grady's hesitancy was just barely perceptible before she spoke.

"And this is Sally Tillett, one of our local girls, Sergeant
Dragonnetti," she said evenly.

Smiling slightly and lifting two fingers to the edge of his
cap, the Sergeant murmured perfunctorily. The girl stood still,
slowly bowing, but her glance held the Sergeant's eyes. She

looked up at him through drooping lashes, a faint smile tinged her mouth, and her dimples came out.

"Won't you have a drink with us?" the Sergeant invited. "I think there's another back there." His voice was smooth . . . silky, Jerry thought.

Sally Tillett's veiled glance moved slowly, almost defiantly, around the group and came back to the Sergeant's face before she spoke. She felt Jerry's eyes, hard, forbidding, staring at her. Cedric Baum did not look at her.

"No, thanks very much," she said, her voice husky, drawling. She moved slowly toward the door, her glance lingering fleetingly on the Sergeant's face. He moved, lightly, to the door and held the screen open while she went through it. Her shoulder, lifting, brushed his arm. He murmured "Good night" and let the screen close behind her. He turned back to the group around Mrs. Grady. His face was expressionless. Nobody said anything for a moment and then Mrs. Grady's soft voice dissipated the silence.

"You must stay with us for a good long visit, Sergeant," she urged. "I know Danny will be disappointed because he wasn't here to welcome you, but I'm sure Jerry's looked after you. We're mighty proud of Danny." She turned to Jerry. "Can't you bring him over to breakfast in the morning, Jerry? We're going to have smoked herring and corn cakes."

"We'll make out all right," Jerry said, "but thanks, just the same. Wait until Danny gets back and they can come over together."

Some of the group drifted out; others came on one or another errand. All of them, departing, invited the Sergeant and Jerry to go home with them for the night. And Jerry knew that all of them meant it, that none of them would have been surprised, or put to any conscious inconvenience, if they had gone with them. He was in no hurry to go home; the Sergeant seemed to be enjoying himself. He talked to everybody as if he had known them all his life. Finally Mrs. Grady glanced at the clock and Jerry knew it was time for them to clear out and let her shut up the store.

Outside the store the Sergeant — Jerry wondered why it was they called him "The Dragon" — stopped again. His head was up and he looked at the sweeping finger of the Light, moving in unending vigilance across the sky. He turned his body so that his eyes could follow it through the whole sweep of the circle. Jerry waited, his own eyes following the mesmeric sweep of the beam above the sleeping Woods.

"Feel like walking some more, Jerry? Let's see what this end of the road looks like, if you're not too tired."

"Sure — okay with me," Jerry replied and fell into step along the rutted road. They walked westward along the trail, neither of them saying anything. Now and then the Sergeant paused, waiting until the Light flecked one or another house with its brief, intense illumination. Then he moved on, walking slowly. His hands were deep down in his pockets and sometimes, Jerry could see by the Light, he shook his head, quickly, like he was trying to shake off something.

At the top of the hill where the road slanted down past the house over which the clematis vine sprawled, the Sergeant stopped again, waiting until the sweep of the Light touched the expanse of Woods below them. The Light came, and for an instant Jerry could make out the billowing white of the vine, now come to the last of this year's flowering. . . . Tomorrow it would rain and after that the winds out of the northeast would tear at the tresses of white flowers. . . . Yellow lamplight glowed through the windows of one of the rooms on the second floor and, more dimly, through the windows of the room below, the room shadowed by the vine.

A mosquito whined, brushed Jerry's cheek with her wings, settled on the back of his neck. The boy waited a second until she got herself anchored and set; then he brought his cupped hand down with a little crack. . . . Wind will get all of them out of the marshes by tomorrow, Jerry thought. . . . He glanced at the Sergeant. He was just standing there; he hadn't moved, except that now his hands hung limp.

After a while, when the Sergeant spoke, his voice trembled, broke into little fragments. The sound of it ran off in a thin stream into a pool of silence, and Jerry could not be sure that he had spoken at all . . . maybe he had stood there until he was asleep and this was something that he had dreamed the Sergeant had said. . . . How could he have been born in that house? Didn't he say . . . no, he said he had joined the Army in New York, not that he was born there. . . . The yellow lamps behind the windows in the house went out. Only the billowing white of the vine showed when the Light flicked it.

"I was born in that house."

Jerry was sure, now, that he was not asleep, that he was not dreaming. The Sergeant had said it — again — and he must say something back, make some sort of a sound, if just to let the Sergeant know that he had heard him, that he was not asleep or that he didn't care and wasn't paying him any mind. He felt the Sergeant's hand on his shoulder, the long, strong fingers clinch, felt the muscles in his shoulder twinge, felt the leaden weight of the hand drop away.

"I'm sorry, Jerry." The Sergeant's voice was low, almost a whisper, but it didn't break up into little lumpy fragments. "I'm sorry," he said again. "I didn't . . . bring you out here to — to get mawkish."

Jerry was not sure what the word meant, but he could feel the terrible intensity with which the Sergeant was speaking, the bitter anguish in his voice. He wondered if the Sergeant were going to cry . . . or if he would start cussin'. Danny said there was no man in the whole Army who could cuss like the Dragon when he had something to cuss about.

"That's all right, Sergeant," Jerry said weakly. "You mean — I mean it's all right about me. You mean you were — that's the Tillett house and she and her mammy have lived in it — nobody else ever lived in it."

"You must know about me, now, don't you, Jerry? My name is not Dragonnetti — it's a name I borrowed from a man . . . the only man who was ever good to me when —" The Sergeant's voice trailed off again. Jerry waited.

"She's your mother — down there?" Jerry said after a while.

"Yes." The Sergeant waited a long time before he said it.

"And — Sally — she's your sister? That was her back yonder at the store."

"Yes."

"Don't — don't you want to go down there and see her — see your — see Miss Mahala?"

There was no answer. Jerry wished that it were light so he could see the man's face and he was glad that it was dark so he could not see it. He waited, saying nothing. After a while he reached out, felt the Sergeant's wrist in the dark, moved his hand up the arm until it was past the elbow. He could feel the Sergeant's arm muscles, taut, hard, under the sleeve. He pulled gently, turning the man around, away from the house.

"Let's go back to the house, Sergeant — let's go home," Jerry said.

No word passed between them as they went back along the road, past the store, past the post office. When he was sure the Sergeant understood that they were going away from the top of that hill, Jerry let go the arm that he held in his fingers and moved across to the other rut. The walking was easier. The Sergeant, Jerry could see when the Light flicked his shoulders, was walking with his head bent down.

Surfman was waiting for them at the top of the steps, and he walked into the house ahead of them, his tail stiffly erect. Jerry hesitated with his fingers on the light switch before he turned on the light. At first he did not look at the Sergeant when light flooded the room. The Sergeant's back was toward him and he was fumbling in his pocket for a cigarette. He lighted it before he turned around. His face was calm, except for the tightening of the lines around his mouth. Jerry went to the bedroom and then to the kitchen. When he came back he had a glass in his hand, almost filled with amber liquid. Two cubes of ice floated in it.

"Danny would make you drink it if he was here," the boy said briefly. The Sergeant took the glass without a word, raised it to his mouth, hesitated for a moment, and set it down on the table without tasting the whiskey. He sat down, pushing his chair out of reach of the table.

"I'm acting like a damned fool, Jerry," the Sergeant said. There were a lot of other words.... Some of them, Jerry thought, not even Bill Henry could have known about. "Maybe it would be a good thing if I was to be struck dumb in my tracks. I'm sorry again, Jerry."

"That's all right — wait until I take you down to see Bill Henry. You know some words maye he ought to learn." Jerry grinned.

"Maybe we'll do that, Jerry. I've been wanting to see Mr. Ragland — again. I remember him, but not very well.... Maybe you'd better sit down, Jerry, and let's get this thing over with. I'm ashamed as hell I let myself get out of hand over yonder on that hill. I didn't intend to — it just, what I said, sort of popped out of me."

"Ain't no harm done, as I can see," Jerry said.

"But somehow I'm glad it was you and not Captain Gray that heard me. I wouldn't want him to see me making a fool of myself."

"Didn't make any fool of yourself," Jerry said encouragingly. "Go ahead and take your drink — make you feel better."

"Not yet, Jerry. I'd better be cold sober if I'm going to say any more."

The Sergeant smiled, and Jerry thought it made him look like a different man. He moved his chair back over toward the table. His long fingers touched the glass tentatively but did not close around it. He motioned to Jerry to sit down and the boy crossed over to the deerskin rug at the hearth. He sat down, cross-legged. Surfman came and poked a tentative paw against his thigh. The Sergeant lighted another cigarette. This time the smoke did not come out of his mouth in a spurting jet; it curled lazily past his face, spreading in a little cloud above his head.

"I was born back there, like I said," the Sergeant went on presently. "I guess you know the story — such things never die in these Woods."

"I guess I've heard it," Jerry admitted, "but I didn't think much about it, one way or another."

"Nobody remembers such things, here, with any feeling, I guess," the Sergeant said. "But I went away when — when I found out I was not a girl. I went with my father. Mrs. Grady cut my hair off, what I'd left of it, and put boys' clothes on me."

"She didn't even know you, did she?" Jerry put in wonderingly.

"No, she didn't — and I guess that made me feel too damned cocky — made me want to go down there and look at that house. But, as I started to tell you, I went away from here with my father. He took me on the ship with him, but he never had much to do with me. I know, now, that something must have died inside him.

"But I didn't know it then. When I was about fourteen I jumped ship and I never saw him again. There was a man on the next ship I was on, and he was good to me, in his fashion. He was the first friend I ever had, outside of Mrs. Grady. Somehow he understood that something had happened to me. Anyhow, he was gentle and kind with me. He was a seafaring man but he wanted me to stay ashore and go to school. I didn't want to leave him, and I didn't — as long as he lived.

"After that I joined the Army. Mr. Dragonnetti was an engineer and he wanted me to follow that trade. But I was sick of the sea. I guess I've always hated it. Maybe it was born in me — hating the sea. There was nothing in the world I hated so much. Except this place. But much as I hated it, I've always known that I'd come back here someday. Well, I've come."

Jerry sat, unmoving, cross-legged on the floor, his eyes not leaving the Sergeant's face. Surfman squirmed himself through the space between Jerry's arms and his body and curled himself in the boy's lap. Jerry waited, his eyes questioning, but the Sergeant had lapsed into meditative silence. Questions crowded across Jerry's thoughts, demanding, insistent, but he kept silent. After a while the Sergeant stirred, as if emerging from a dream.

"Maybe there's something about this place that just brings you back. Maybe I don't hate it, like I've made myself believe all these years. Maybe I don't hate — my mother, like I've believed all these years. I just don't know. All I know is that I've known, maybe from the time I left here, that someday I'd come back. I never thought it would be ... like this."

"It's funny you got to be on the same ship as Danny — what do you call it? A co — co — what the hell is it?"

"Coincidence, Jerry? Is that the word you're after? There was no coincidence about it, and it took a lot of wire-pulling to get me on the same ship with him. It may have been just chance that I saw his picture in some paper over in Italy, with his name and his home town, but the rest of it I did myself."

"Gosh, I bet I got that paper — Danny sent it to me and I got it put away."

"I've got it, the clipping, in my wallet."

"You mean — did you tell Danny you come from here? He never said anything about it."

"Danny — the Captain doesn't know," the Sergeant said somberly. "I could never see any point in telling him, but after I saw his picture, well — I used to see your father around here back when I was a little girl —" the Sergeant's voice was sardonic, bitter — "a little girl down here. And then, after that day when Mrs. Grady put dungarees on me, your father was the only one that didn't laugh every time he saw me.

"One day down at the dock when I was waiting for the mail boat to see if my daddy might be on it, your father spoke to me, pleasant and natural-like. Called me by my boy-name of Jess. Anyhow, I always remembered him, and when I saw the Captain's picture — he was just a second lieutenant then — I worked it first one way and then another until I got to where I could look at him.

"And then when he got ordered home to train on the big ones — I was crew chief on A-Twenties then, same as he was flying — I got transferred, too. After that it was easy enough. He finally asked for me as crew chief, and I've been with him ever since."

"Danny sure thinks a lot of you," Jerry said. "He said he'd asked you to come down sometime. You're the only man in the crew he asked."

"Yes, and I'm ashamed of that, sort of," the Sergeant said. "I guess I sort of wangled the invitation out of him when he was off his guard. It was when I took him coffee after we left here that day we flew over. I knew he was tired, but I just wanted to be where I could talk to him. Well, that's all there is to the story, Jerry."

This time the Sergeant's fingers closed around the glass, and when he lifted it to his mouth he drank; the glass was half empty when he set it down.

"There's just one thing more, Jerry — I know I don't have any right to ask it, because I made a fool of myself right there in the middle of the road where anybody could see. But — but could we keep this thing between the two of us until I get my head clear?"

"You mean you're not goin' to tell even Danny?"

"I'd rather not — not yet."

"He'd sure like to know."

"I could tell him if he were just Danny," the Sergeant said slowly, "but you see, he's two people. He's Danny Gray and he's Captain Gray. I'm still going to fly with him."

"Okay, Sergeant," Jerry said. "I ain't heard nothin' and I ain't seen nothin' and I ain't sayin' nothin' to nobody."

Jerry set Surfman on the deerskin rug and got to his feet. He crossed over to the table and took the half-emptied glass, moved around the chair, and sat down on its arm. He pressed the glass in the Sergeant's hand, half lifting it to the dark man's mouth.

"Finish your drink, Sergeant," the boy urged, "and then what you need is a night's sleep. . . . You know, Sergeant, you remind me of Danny in a lot of ways. Bill Henry says there's some places inside of Danny that just got stunted in their growth while he was off in the war and we got to give him time for 'em to get loose and grow up. I expect Bill Henry would say the same thing about you after he got a good look at you."

"Maybe he's right," the Sergeant said, "about me. But not about the Captain. He comes as near being a grown man as anybody I've ever been off the ground with and I've seen him in some mighty tight places."

"Danny's okay, but he's awfully young about some things," Jerry said with his most disarming grin. The Sergeant drained his glass.

Jerry pulled on the light at the head of the bed in the company room and turned toward the door. From the door he said good night and told the Sergeant not to get up until he felt like it in the morning. He went toward the door of his own room, pulled on the light, and when his dungarees fell in their accustomed puddle around his ankles he was aware of an unaccustomed thud. . . . The mail. . . . He picked up the garment and removed the flattened bundle from the back pocket.

The door of the spare room flew open and Jerry stood, breathless and naked except for his shorts. His eyes danced with excitement and his voice vacillated indecisively between baritone and falsetto.

"Look here at this, Sergeant! Does that mean they've promoted Danny to a major?" He bounded toward the bed, holding out the envelope in his hand.

Sergeant Jesse Tillett Dragonnetti took the missive in his hands. It was addressed to Major Daniel Gray. The Sergeant's fingers trembled a little as he laid the letter on the bed covering across his stomach.

"It doesn't mean anything else, Jerry. Somebody up there must aim to keep him in the Army."

"Gosh! Is that the way they let you know — just mail you something with 'Major' on it?"

"One way is as good as another — and he ought to have had it long ago. What's the other letter you've got there? Is it addressed to the Major, too?"

"Oh, I'd clean forgot it," Jerry said. He examined the square blue-gray envelope. "Nope, it's to Captain Gray. . . . Gosh, it smells!" He held the letter to his nose, sniffing. "Some woman." He turned it over.

"Say, Sergeant, who is this Judith Hale, and what's she writin' to Danny about?"

18

JUDITH HALE FLICKED THE KEY IN THE IGNITION LOCK AND LET her shoulders go limp against the russet leather cushion at her back. Her gloved hands lay inert in her lap. Under its long hood the engine, as if unmindful of the fact that the ignition had been cut, continued to run in a series of convulsive sputterings, and from somewhere under the radiator there was a sound of hissing steam.

After a while the engine quieted itself. The hissing under the radiator continued, but with lessening intensity. Judith Hale tugged absently at the fingers of her gloves, and when her hands were freed of them she folded the gloves on the rim of the steering wheel. Leaning forward she pressed a thumb against the latch of the compartment at the right of the instrument panel and explored it with her hand. It came away empty.

In silence the woman beside her in the convertible put out her left hand, palm upward, stiffened fingers flatly extended. Judith Hale, without looking directly at the extended hand, took the compact. It was square and yellow, with an H outlined in square-cut aquamarines. The younger woman opened it and, without glancing at her reflection in the mirror, powdered her nose lightly, scrubbed her cheeks until they glowed. She snapped the fragile case shut and dropped it on the cushion. The older woman's hand, again flatly extended in silence, this time had a single cigarette lying across its palm.

"I wonder, Miss Gussie," Judith Hale said, "how females

used to sustain themselves when they got in this sort of a mess — before somebody invented the device of powdering the nose."

The older woman remained stiffly silent. The only indication that she had actually heard Judith Hale was in the tightening of the thin line of her lips. She stared fixedly in front of her angular, pointed nose. Her chin was set at a lifting angle, and her hands, with their fingers tightly interlaced, lay rigid against the black cloth of the dress that covered her narrow lap. Her feet were planted flat on the floor of the car. Her knees were held rigidly together. Judith Hale considered the woman. Her smile was amused, lazily tolerant.

"Relax, Miss Gussie," the girl said sweetly. "You might try powdering your own nose just for this terrible once in your life. And," she added, "we do seem to be in rather a mess."

The woman addressed as Miss Gussie unclasped her fingers, but only, apparently, to take a firmer grip. Her hands worked agitatedly in her lap and the thin line of her lips parted as if she were about to let words past them. Her eyes darted a glance at Judith Hale but went back instantly to their fixed staring through the windshield. Judith Hale half turned in the seat and rested an elbow on the lower rim of the steering wheel. She continued to look at the older woman, a little smile playing about her mouth.

None of the company of reporters and the custodians of gossip columns who, with dismaying regularity, had occasion to mention her had ever found a convenient or consistent adjective for Judith Hale. Some of them, in a sort of desperation, had spoken of her as being beautiful — or beauteous — and at once deplored their own inaneness. Judith Hale was not beautiful. Nor was she pretty; sometimes they made it read that she was handsome, but looking at their adjective in cold print they continued to feel, unhappily, that she had some quality that persistently eluded them.

Mostly they had settled upon the phrase, "Judith Hale, the

elusively handsome daughter of Seymour Hale." After a while they left her father's name out altogether, to that continually dismayed man's not inconsiderable relief. Being Seymour Hale, he found it increasingly convenient not to have his name in the public prints at all. There was something about people that made them fearful of a bank whose head got his name in the papers too often.

Judith Hale was not beautiful. It was easy to call her red-headed, though her hair was of no authentic shade of red. It came nearer to being a warm russet, the russet of the leather upholstery of the long convertible. It was as easy to call her green-eyed, though her eyes were not green. Not always, at any rate. They were a sort of aquamarine, most of the time — like the square-cut stones in the vanity case, or the shining blue-green of the convertible.

More than one syndicated wholesale merchant of gossip, savory or unsavory, had mentioned that Judith Hale's nose was generously flecked with freckles and that, sometimes when she laughed, she wrinkled her nose. Some of them said she wrinkled it provocatively, and others said that her nose was impudent. Photographs that sometimes accompanied these items of literary merchandise indicated a broad forehead, but one not quite high enough to be described as "intellectual."

Judith Hale's mouth, they said now and then, sometimes with pictures to confirm it, was wide. Sometimes they said it was a wide, generous mouth, and sometimes they contented themselves with just measuring it longitudinally. Her chin, they were agreed, was both rounded and firm, and her complexion was warm and smooth. But, of course, there were freckles of an exuberance that made them wander off the reservation of her nose. They said, also, that she was clean-limbed. One of them, in the course of a disconsolate morning after, was able to think of no better word than rangy.

But if they were unable to agree upon any conclusive and comprehensive adjective, there was one particular in which they were all in agreement about Judith Hale, daughter of Seymour Hale, the banker. She frustrated them wholly and utterly. She never seemed to mind what they said about her. They could have called her knock-kneed, and she would have smiled that same lazy, indifferently tolerant smile, her wide mouth parted a little, showing strong white teeth. Sometimes somebody would think, or say in print, that her teeth were too big. Almost always they said her voice was throaty, and that would suggest that her throat was long. They spoke of her long throat, and a good many would have, pleasurably, wrung it for their own peace of mind.

Still, Judith Hale did not confuse and frustrate them utterly. No matter how vexatious might become the task of finding the right adjectives for the external Judith Hale, there was abiding comfort in the fact that, when it came to the internal Judith Hale, there was just one word that covered all with a suffusing compensation. None ever lingered doubtfully, fingers poised above the keys of a typewriter. It was virtually automatic when their fingers tapped out "willful."

"But Miss Gussie, you haven't told me!" Judith Hale's throaty voice cut across the grim silence that gripped the older woman beside her. "What *did* women do, before there was machinery for nose-powdering anywhere, when they got themselves in a fix?"

Miss Gussie stirred. She opened her mouth and closed it in a succession of snapping contortions of her lean cheeks. She clasped and unclasped her hands, finally bringing them upward and outward in a gesture of despair and disavowal. She made incoherent chirping noises that sounded, Judith Hale thought amusedly, like the offspring of an unholy union between a nervous hen and a frightened rat might sound, half-cluck, half-squeak. The sounds gradually took on a sort of coherence.

"This is the end of the world and we'll die right here and

drown in the ocean and nobody to save us," Miss Gussie screeched. "No woman, not even you, ever got herself into such a fix before, and powdering your nose is not going to help any."

The girl patted Miss Gussie's shoulder, and the older woman looked up, her lips trembling. She looked as if she were about to cry.

"I — I wish you wouldn't call me — that name," she said forlornly. "You know I just can't — I'm sorry, Miss."

"Never mind, Augusta," the girl said consolingly. "Please forgive me. I guess I was just being mulish. That's a nicer word than they usually call me, don't you think? Doesn't it sound nicer than 'willful'?"

"I could never abide mules," the woman said primly.

"Now, now, Augusta," Judith said. "You ought to just adore mules. They're neither male nor female, and when you get pouty — oh, let's skip it. We've got to get out of here, somehow."

Judith opened the door of the convertible and got out. She shrugged off the loose-fitting sports coat of cream-colored wool, thrust her hands deep down in the pockets of the green slacks she was wearing, and stood back to look at the car. Her russet hair, held in place at each ear by a small comb, rioted down to the collar of the shirt she was wearing. She closed the door and walked slowly around the car.

"It looks as if it's made up its mind to go native right here, Augusta," she reported. The long, low-slung convertible had its rear wheels embedded in the loose sand, engulfed so deep that the rear bumper was out of sight. The burrowing tires had packed sand under the rear fenders.

Augusta McGarrah peered cautiously over the rim of the door at her sparse shoulder. She glanced backward toward the girl standing irresolute, looking down at the back of the car. The woman shuddered and resumed her fixed scrutiny of such of the world as she could see through the windshield directly before her eyes, as if by fixing her gaze upon some spot ahead she could, somehow, hoist herself toward it.

Such of the earth as she could see ahead looked little more inviting to her than the spot they were engulfed in. Above the waste of sand the sky was leaden, and off to the left the ocean was no less dreary. It was made of lead, like the sky, but not the still, lifeless metal of the sky. The ocean writhed in a misery that reflected, echoed, the misery that engulfed Augusta. The unhappy woman could almost feel waves of misery flowing upward through her legs, breaking suffocatingly under her chin. Augusta McGarrah just knew that she was going to be seasick.

"It's going to rain," the miserable woman announced. "Is there any way we could put up the top of this thing?"

When Judith did not answer, Augusta peered around, gripped in a sudden panic, sure that the girl had vanished, leaving her here to become the prey of — of pirates, highwaymen, or of unimaginable monsters that would come creeping up out of the ocean. Judith was some little distance away. For the first time Augusta noticed the battered hulk of what had once been a ship . . . a very large ship, as large as the ship that had brought her, Augusta, from Ireland . . . a very long time ago. Augusta had been very wretchedly sick.

It was this piece of wreckage that had brought them their own irrevocable disaster. Augusta was sure that it was irrevocable. Despite the premonitions that had weighted her shoulders from the moment they rolled off the ferry, they had made good time. The convertible's tires fairly sang along the hard sand of the beach, and now and then Augusta had shut her eyes tight to keep from them the dismaying sight of the speedometer's finger reaching past seventy.

Her eyes were tightly shut when Judith Hale slowed down suddenly. Augusta could feel the car swerve under her thin limbs, slacken its speed, and finally grind to a dead halt. It must have been that battered hulk of what had once been a ship that caused Judith to stop. It lay at an angle across the beach, half buried in the sand. Its bow was well up the slant of the beach, and in order to pass it a vehicle had to climb through the soft sand of the top of the bank. There were in-dications that other cars had passed that way. Some of them had been, like themselves, embedded. Judith turned from the derelict and came slowly back to the foundered convertible.

"We'll have to wait until somebody comes along, I'm afraid, Augusta."

"Nobody will come," Augusta replied somberly. "And when they do they'll be pirates and highwaymen. They will cut our throats and — and —" The woman's imagined horrors choked her into silence.

"You're illogical, Augusta," the girl said drily. "There can't be highwaymen because there isn't any highway, and all the pirates in the world abandoned the sea long ago. Father is a pirate — or do you ever read the papers? Somebody will come. Somebody always does, Augusta. And it won't be pirates."

"Not always," Augusta said grimly. She saw with a little glow of prim satisfaction that the color in Judith's cheeks deepened with a flush.

"All right, all right, Augusta — the trick is yours," the girl said. "Could you maybe spare me a cigarette? I know I'm not due one for nineteen whole minutes, but I can't spend all the time powdering my nose."

Augusta grudgingly opened her handbag and took out a cig-arette. This time she held it in her fingers instead of laying it in her flattened palm. Judith lighted it and slid into the seat, letting her hands lie loosely on the rim of the steering wheel. As if sensing Augusta's anxious mistrust of the weather, she laid the cigarette across the ashtray, clicked the switch, and started the engine. Cooled by now, it started without effort. The girl held her thumb against a button and the top of the convertible came up. She fastened it to its moorings at the top of the windshield, observing as she did so the first flecks of rain dotting the glass. Augusta exhaled a sigh of relief and relaxed against the cushion.

Removing the combs above her ears and dropping them loosely in her lap, Judith shook out her hair and laid her head back against the cushion. Her eyelids drooped over her eyes, which now, had any adjective-hungry beholder been observing them, could have been put down as a soft, luminous blue. Her lips were parted in a contemplative smile. After a while, when Augusta saw the half-burned cigarette drop from Judith's relaxed fingers, she leaned down and picked it up, poked it into the ashtray. She pulled the cover over the ash receiver, dusted her fingers carefully, and returned to vigilance over the landscape, or such of it as she could see through the rain-blurred windshield.

Judith came out of her half-sleep with a start. Augusta's lips were close to her ear and an agitated hissing came from them. The girl rubbed the sleep out of her eyes and sat up. Augusta was jabbing the space between herself and the windshield with an agitated finger, and her eyes were darting back and forth between Judith and the windshield in an ecstasy of agitation. The hissing crystallized into a half-whispered word, repeated until it finally burst in a hysterical verbal rocket.

"Pirates!"

The girl lowered the window at her shoulder and looked out. Beside her Augusta lapsed into silence and slid far back against the cushions and the opposite door of the car. Her thin hands clasped and unclasped around the door handle as if she were about to open it and take refuge in flight. The girl laid a restraining, reassuring hand on her arm and turned an unbelieving scrutiny upon the apparition that had emerged, by some magic, out of nowhere.

For a moment she was sure that here must be a fugitive from some museum devoted to vehicular antiquities. It was, in a manner of speaking, an automobile. Or it had been, once. It belonged to a genre that had come upon a palpitant world fifteen or eighteen years earlier. Once it had been a shiny coupé, no doubt the pride of somebody's life before the world of 1929 collapsed about its ears.

But now . . . there was not much of it left. Its fenders had been lost somewhere, as had its running board. About all that was left now were four wheels, a radiator, and a hood that must still conceal an engine. All the after part of the body, that part that people called the baggage compartment, had been sheared away, and in its place a rude structure of miscellaneous tin and plyboard had been erected. Its radiator hissed, and beyond it were distracted mechanical sounds. One side of the structure back of the windshield detached itself and fell off in the sand.

Now a figure materialized, the figure of a being as archaic, Judith thought, as the vehicle. He was wizened, and he looked as if, without the loose denim trousers and shirt that he wore, his frame would just fall apart. His skin was like old leather. His face had long since collapsed around toothless gums. His nose and chin were kept apart, Judith surmised, only by sheer determination and constant vigilance.

But when Judith saw his eyes she forgot the rest of him. They were warm and bright, smiling and friendly, confident and reassuring. And they were very blue, the sort of blue that the sky has sometimes when it is newly washed with warm rain. He came loose-jointedly toward her, and a leathery hand moved up past his face to remove a battered seafaring cap that might once have adorned the pate of a yachtsman. Thin wisps of damp hair drooped across his forehead.

"Looks like you're stuck, Ma'am," he observed cheerfully.

"Doesn't it?" Judith Hale replied. Without further notice of her he went around the car, circling it completely. He came back to the window.

"How much air in your tires, Ma'am?"

"I don't know," Judith Hale's voice was impatient. "The usual amount, I suppose."

"Didn't anybody tell you, Ma'am?"

"Tell me what?" Judith demanded, her voice edged with truculence. She half-opened the door, wondering if she couldn't better cope with things, with this apparition and his questions, if she were on her feet.

"I'd just take it easy where you are, Ma'am, if it was me," the man said. "No use you gettin' out here and gettin' yourself all wet. They should have told you to let some air out of your tires." He went on ruminatively. "Shame to mess up a car like this on this beach."

"But what can I do?" Judith demanded. "I'm here now, and —"

"Don't believe there's a single thing we can do, Ma'am — unless I had me a shovel and some rope, and maybe some boards. You're just plumb out of sight." And he added irrelevantly, "My name's O'Neal."

From the gloom at the other side of the car Augusta McGarrah emitted choking sounds which Judith, rightly, interpreted as sounds of relief. The man took a limp cigarette from his trousers pocket and placed it between his lips. It disintegrated and he got rid of the debris by thrusting his tongue against the end of it and letting the mess fall away from him. Augusta stirred. She burrowed into her handbag. Judith pressed the lighter on the instrument panel and when it glowed red she held it out the window.

"Thank you kindly, Ma'am," Mr. O'Neal said. He drew deeply on the cigarette and let the smoke curl upward out of his nose. "How far were you aimin' to go tonight, Ma'am?"

"They told us to turn right about a mile this side of some lighthouse," Judith said, "but I guess we'll never make it, now."

"Don't guess you will, Ma'am," Mr. O'Neal said cheerfully.

"Not like the weather's turned and the wind kickin' up a tide like this." He surveyed the dripping sky, tested the wind with his cheek. He turned back to the improbable vehicle and took up the door from where it lay on the sand. He got into the structure and pulled the door after him, but after a moment it opened a scant hand's width and Mr. O'Neal's cheerful eyes beamed.

"You just set here, Ma'am," he said. The door closed upon him and the calamitous vehicle moved forward. It groaned, it screeched, it growled; but it moved, and the murk of a rain-filled twilight engulfed it. Judith Hale slumped back against the cushions and for the first time since she was a child Augusta McGarrah saw the girl's chin tremble.

"Would it be all right, Augusta, if I said one small-sized 'damn'?"

"Savages! Maybe cannibals!" Augusta McGarrah exclaimed. She sat forward briskly, half-turned in her seat to glance backward in the direction Mr. O'Neal had taken. "The very idea — calling himself by an Irish name! He's no more an — he's a bloodthirsty pirate, and if he shows that face here again I'll — I'll take his nose and his chin in one hand and wring 'em off and throw 'em at him, damn him!"

"Why, Augusta!" Judith Hale said. "Do you realize you've sworn? You've said 'damn.' "

"Where's that gun you brought to shoot geese with?" Augusta demanded, ignoring the girl's shocked amusement. "We'd best be ready for 'em when they get back."

"Weren't you just going to wring his chin off, Augusta?"

"Wouldn't get my hands dirty touching one of them," the woman exclaimed. "Never get them clean as long as I live. Where's that gun?"

"Oh, let's be hopeful about it, Augusta." Judith laughed. "He can't be that bad. Didn't you see his eyes? And what could he do anyway? Where's that thermos jug of coffee you had them fix at that restaurant?"

Augusta continued to mutter of vengeance and of the terrible price at which she would sell herself, her life, her belongings; but, half-erect, with her knees on the cushion, she searched for the jug of coffee. There were sandwiches, too. The girl flicked on the car's lights and they ate the sandwiches, drank the still-steaming coffee.

Rain drummed on the heavy canvas top and it sagged slightly under the weight of water collected overhead. Judith flattened her palm against the canvas, and the water cascaded over the windshield, momentarily clearing it. Augusta maintained a vigilant silence. The hands of the clock on the instrument panel moved, slow, inexorable. . . . Mr. O'Neal had been gone forty minutes . . . forty-three minutes . . . forty-five minutes. . . .

Augusta's neck lost its vigilant rigidness and her head drooped against the cushion at her back. Judith, wide awake now, opened the window. The rain was cool against her cheek. In the reflected glow of the car's lights she could mark the surge of the surf. After a while, she calculated, it would come past where they were stranded, and waves would break through the window if the wind kept rising. She glanced at the dozing Augusta beside her and closed the window.

Then the flat beam of what Judith knew must be a searchlight slashed across the sand outside the window, and in a moment a thing like a behemoth lumbered past, scarcely moving. It swung in ahead of her car and stopped, came slowly backward. Figures in black oilskins appeared at the stern of it, leaped lightly to the sand. One of them came toward the front of the car, paying out the lengths of a cable coiled around his forearm.

Augusta awoke with a start. She emitted alarmed sounds, but not even Judith's accustomed ears could have translated them into words. At the stern of the behemoth ahead Judith caught sight of a gleam that could have come from nowhere except the depths of Mr. O'Neal's eyes. Augusta must have, Judith thought, caught the same gleam, since she had, apparently, fainted with a swiftness and completeness that would have had the unstinted approval of any surviving custodian of the Victorian tradition. Judith lowered her window.

Ahead the behemoth moved. Judith could see the black cable take on life, its loose coils writhe into a straight line. Then she felt the convertible straining against the taut line of the cable. It moved forward, slowly, its frame dragging. And then she knew that the convertible was riding on an even keel again. Judith wondered if Augusta had actually fainted or was just playing dead as a defensive expedient.

The forward motion of the behemoth and convertible stopped, and the oil-skinned figures came back toward the car. One of them stopped and took hold of the cable and the other came around to the window. Judith was sure, now, that she had seen Mr. O'Neal at the stern of the behemoth, but it was not his face that loomed in the murk outside the window. This one was young — awfully young, Judith thought — from what she could see of his rain-streaked face. He was bare-headed and his hair fell in loose, damp waves across his forehead.

"Evening, Ma'am," he said. "I guess you're all right now, but the Chief said we'd better bring you back to the Station."

"The — the Station?" Judith said uncertainly.

"Yes, Ma'am. We're from Chicky." And then, as if he sensed the girl's mounting bewilderment, he added, "Chicamicomico, that is, Ma'am. Coast Guard."

"Oh," was all that Judith could think of to say.

"Chief would have come himself, but he went over to his house to tell his wife to fix you some supper and a place to sleep."

"But — but couldn't we stay — won't that be an awful bother for her?"

"Not a bit, Ma'am. She'll be glad to have you. We ain't fixed up so good at the Station for ladies. Don't believe I've ever seen one inside the Station — not since I been down here."

Mr. O'Neal's voice was cheerful from somewhere behind

the youth at the window and Judith could feel the warmth of his gleaming eyes.

"You'll be all right now, Miss, but — bein' it's so dark and everything, maybe you'd better let one of the boys drive your car back up."

"Oh, Mr. O'Neal, I was afraid you'd — we'd not see you again."

"They didn't need me," Mr. O'Neal said modestly, "but I just sort of come along. Nothin' else to do."

"We brought him," the youth at the window said. He turned to Mr. O'Neal. "Pop, you'd better drive this wagon." He turned back to Judith and for the first time noticed Augusta's slumped figure. "One of you can slip into the back seat. Pop's the best driver that ever hit this beach."

"Got your tire gauge, son?" Mr. O'Neal asked. "Better see how much air she's carryin' before we try to move her."

The youth dropped back beside the rear wheels and there was a sound of air hissing through valves. He came back.

"She ought to be okay now, Pop. Get in and ride her."

Mr. O'Neal came out of the shadows and toward the door of the convertible, paused in uncertainty. Judith without a backward look at Augusta swung her feet out and stood on the sand.

"She's all yours, Pop," Judith said, almost gaily. She turned to the youth. "How about riding back with you in — that?" She waved an arm toward the bulking shadow ahead.

"It's okay with us, sure, Ma'am — but a duck is the roughest riding piece of plunder anybody ever dreamed up."

"Well, let's go," Judith said, "and happy motoring, Mr. O'Neal."

Mr. O'Neal turned diffidently to the convertible, looked at it wonderingly, and got in. He glanced toward the crumpled figure at the far side of the cushion. He was astonished when a lean hand materialized out of the gloom. From the ends of the fingers dangled a cigarette.

"Thank you kindly, Ma'am," Mr. O'Neal said. Augusta did not answer him.

"Who is this amazing Mr. O'Neal? Augusta was sure he was a pirate right out of the book," Judith said with a little laugh that tinkled pleasantly above the rumble of the behemoth as it circled and fell in behind the convertible's taillight.

"Pop? He's no pirate. He's retired now, but in his day he was the damnedest — excuse me, Miss — surfman there ever was on this beach, unless it was Mr. Ragland down at the Cape. He was back in service during the war but they've retired him again now."

"But —" Judith's voice wavered.

"You mean his face — the way he looks?" the youth interposed helpfully. "Looks don't mean anything to him. He does look different, though, or he used to when his wife was alive to remind him to wear his teeth."

Judith laughed aloud.

"Maybe that would be a good way for Augusta to spend her time — to employ herself from now on."

"Augusta, Ma'am?"

"That's Augusta up there." Judith nodded her head toward the convertible's taillight. "Father found her in Ireland when I was teething age and she was my nurse, almost my — my mother. She raised me. She doesn't approve of me."

"Don't see how that could be, Miss," the youth said politely. "Is she — she's not out of a job, is she?"

"No, she isn't," Judith said with some emphasis, "but things might work out, down here, so . . . ." Her voice trailed off in silence, but the youth, when he glanced at her inquiringly, was sure that her smile was the smile of someone in love. He sighed regretfully, and the duck's rumblings were intensified as it began to gain on the convertible's taillight.

19

IN BANNISTER O'NEAL'S PHILOSOPHY, WOMEN AND THE ATLANTIC Ocean, and especially that part of the ocean around Wimble Shoals, were sisters; and it would never be possible to say, with any fixed certainty, what either of them might make up its mind to do next. They had their vagaries, women and the Atlantic Ocean, and you just had to take them as you found them, taking nothing for granted and trusting neither completely.

Mr. O'Neal's dealings with women and the Atlantic Ocean were characterized always by an amiable and outwardly tolerant wariness, but both his late wife and the continuing ocean were in no sense nor in any degree fooled by him. Both the late Mrs. O'Neal and the continuing ocean were, in their ways, as tolerant and as amiable as he.

But in any case Mr. O'Neal's marriage to his wife and to the ocean had been eminently satisfactory adventures, not only to him but to both his wives. Mr. O'Neal was no polygamist and it would have been surprising indeed if he had ever heard the word mentioned. Actually there was no difference between his wife and the ocean; each was somehow the extension of the other, though Mr. O'Neal never bothered with thinking of such abstruse matters. Mrs. O'Neal had ignored the ocean with silent resignation. She did not approve of it.

Both were moody, sometimes, but rarely concurrently. There were times when Mr. O'Neal avoided Espindola O'Neal's — she was named for a barque that had foundered about the time of her birth — kitchen as if it were plague-ridden; and there were other times when he avoided the ocean for a kindred reason, when the sea was in a cantankerous mood. When either of them, or both of them, were merely truculent, Mr. O'Neal knew how to deal with them, how to coax them into a show of reasonableness, and he knew how to be stern and demanding. Also, he knew when to leave them both alone.

Had it not been that Mr. O'Neal was preoccupied with the chromium complexity of the instrument panel of the convertible, and a little dazzled by it, he might have taken note of Augusta McGarrah's wordless gesture when she handed him the cigarette. It was at that moment when he had, with no inconsiderable diffidence, settled his thin haunches on the soft leather of the cushion and reached out for the ignition switch.

Actually the woman had been, until then, only an obscure thin shadow on the far side of the seat. Mr. O'Neal's glance in that general direction had been shyly quick and he had uttered a somewhat neutral "Good evenin', Ma'am" when he got into the car. He wondered mildly why the lady had continued in her rather discouraging silence. He could feel her eyes searching him, and he supposed that she — as his late wife certainly would have — disapproved of his wet presence. Mentally he braced himself to weather a brief squall of reproving remonstrance.

And so it was, astute though he was in dealings with women and with the ocean, that he missed the significance of Augusta McGarrah's gesture. To be sure, his late wife, after a suitable interval of admonition and remonstrance about coming into the house all soggy from exposure to the elements, would have got him a dry cigarette from somewhere; and if she had been especially vigorous in wifely declamation, she would have included a dry match in her dispensation.

Augusta McGarrah was as surprised herself as Mr. O'Neal would have been had he possessed experience with her gestures. Any of the very limited coterie of people who knew her would at once have perceived in the gesture a complete index to the workings of her perceptions, reflexes, and other emotional and cerebral phenomena. Judith Hale would have bubbled inwardly and, very likely, outwardly as well.

As for herself, the woman was wholly unaware of providing an outward index to the inner workings of her feelings. All her life she had been handing things to people. If she approved of the person so served, and of the service itself, she held this thing or that thing in her fingers. If she was vexed about something — and since she had left New York two days before she had been continuously vexed — she laid whatever was needed or required of her flat on her palm.

The earth contained an incalculable number of things that Augusta McGarrah did not approve of, and the people who inhabited the earth were given to innumerable practices from which she withheld any least approbation, no matter how persistent the necessity of accommodating herself to them might be. She especially did not approve of Judith Hale smoking cigarettes — but if she had come upon any who shared this attitude she would, most likely, have stoutly denounced them. Disapproving of Judith Hale was something that Augusta McGarrah tolerated in none except herself.

Judith Hale had been not quite two years old, twenty years before, when Augusta McGarrah came to the Hale household as nurse for the child. It was not a happy house, nor a tranquil house. Too much of all the things that could be had for money and too little of the things that could be bought in no market place, the woman told herself before she had been in the house a day. Newly come from North Ireland, she was herself . . . but then, she never told her age to anybody.

Elizabeth Hale, Judith's mother and Seymour Hale's second wife, had been one of those women who make a life's work out of not being contented with life, and before Judith was four years old she — Augusta McGarrah always thought of her as "that woman" — had removed herself from the household. By now Augusta McGarrah never thought of her except when she saw in the papers that the one-time Elizabeth Hale had taken another husband.

Judith Hale had scarcely missed her mother and there was nobody to mention her. From the day she departed from the house, her name, in so far as Augusta McGarrah knew, had never passed the tight lips of Judith's father. And, of course, Augusta never mentioned her, though at first it needed effort to be silent.

When he knew that his wife was irrevocably gone, Seymour Hale sent for Augusta to come to the library after dinner one night. He was smoking in bitter, vengeful silence, and Augusta stood, waiting — waiting and wishing that he would say whatever it was he had to say and let her go back to the baby abovestairs. It was time for the child to be put to bed.

After a while Seymour Hale spoke through the murk of smoke that hung like a pall around him. All he said was, "You'll be her mother, McGarrah. You will continue to be her mother. You are the only mother she has ever known, and don't you ever leave her!"

Augusta McGarrah had never left Judith Hale. Apart from the child she had no life, no separate existence. The Hale household was not small, but Augusta lived somehow apart from it. She was not a servant in the sense that the housekeeper, the cook, the maids were servants. These came, they went, but Augusta seemed scarcely aware of them execpt as they contributed to the well-being of Judith Hale. Nor was she any closer to Seymour Hale.

The child adored her father and, in another way, she adored Augusta McGarrah. Only once had she ever undertaken to appeal to her father from Augusta's judgment. Neither she nor Seymour Hale had ever spoken of the matter to Augusta, but she knew, instinctively, what had happened. After that — it was about some trifling matter that did not really matter —

there was never in any of their minds any question about where final authority lay.

It was Judith's good fortune, Augusta was sure, that she was not like her mother, that she took after her father. She had his coloring, she had his usually tranquil disposition — and she had his placid determination to have his own way. He was never — nor was Judith — stubborn or what Augusta called "contrary." When he wanted something, he took it. When Judith wanted something, she took it. But he was kind and he was gentle, especially where Judith was concerned.

Seymour Hale had not married again, and that was something Augusta was thankful for. He was in his late thirties when she came to the house, and now, in his late fifties, Augusta was sure that he worked too hard. The war had taken the last of the ruddy glow out of his hair and it was beginning to turn a wan white. When he could get away he spent more and more of his time at the country place on Long Island. They spent all their summers there.

But Augusta's life revolved, not around the household, but around Judith Hale; and since she had "come out" at eighteen the center of her detached universe had spun dizzily along a widening orbit. Augusta had known, always, of course, that the time would come when Judith would . . . when there would be men in Judith's life. But most of the time she shut her eyes against that eventuality. She would just not think about it.

There were a lot of things, Augusta told herself often enough, that were beyond her comprehension, but the most perplexing of all the bewildering aspects of wartime was where all the men — old, young — fat, lean — came from. And often it seemed to Augusta that the entire armed forces were organized just for the purpose of laying siege to her Judith. New York swarmed with them and they covered Long Island like locusts.

Often enough Augusta told herself, and sometimes she told Judith, that if these people would get out of the house and go about their business there were, surely, enough of them to get through with the war in no time whatever. And, moreover, she would continue, how did they ever expect to get the war over with if they spent all their time laying siege to the Hale house? Judith would laugh her placid, throaty laugh.

In so far as Augusta could discern, each of them looked — whether he were soldier, sailor, or marine — about like all the others, and seemingly they looked that way to Judith, too. But as the war went on and the siege of the Hale house continued, Judith had grown increasingly restless. She went out continually, she smoked more than was good for anybody, and she drank sometimes at home, but always without, in so far as Augusta could see, its having the least effect on her.

Sometimes Augusta was troubled at her own surmise that Judith might be taking this one or that one more seriously than there was any safety in, but these moods passed. Or all of them had passed except the one that had, on sudden impulse, taken them to California. It had been, of course, unthinkable to either of them that Judith could go anywhere alone. Seymour Hale had, somewhat grudgingly, managed reservations for them, and Augusta had grimly resigned herself to travel by air.

But the thing that really concerned Augusta was not whether she and Judith and the airplane were likely to take up against some unheard-of mountain. For the first time in her life Judith was keeping her own counsel. She had never mentioned this particular fellow to Augusta. Always, until now, she would come home, bubbling inconsequentially about this one or that one, and Augusta would listen with no great concern about it, knowing the mood for what it was — an effervescence common to girls of that age. Only, Augusta herself had never effervesced, outwardly, at any age or about anything or about anybody. . . .

But now Augusta was sure that Judith, at last, was heels-over-head in love with some vague somebody who piloted an airplane. It had begun that winter in Florida, Augusta thought, though she had never seen him, nor even a picture of him. The most that she knew about him, beyond her certainty that Judith was in love with him, was what she could sense with her ears. Once or twice she had answered the telephone, during that week in San Francisco. Not more than that; Judith had been quick about answering the telephone . . . that week.

It was a curious sort of voice, this pilot's, and nights when she lay wakeful, waiting until she could hear Judith's foot on the stair, she would try to recall every soft inflection of it. It was a pleasant voice to hear, especially the way it said, "Good evening, Ma'am, may I speak to Miss Hale?" It fell pleasantly on her ears, as Augusta remembered it in the long darkness of waiting. In the months that had become a year she had built up, like a figure of coral, a personality to fit the voice.

There was little else she could use for her building; by no syllable did Judith contribute to the picture. She just never spoke of the possessor of that voice that fell so pleasantly upon Augusta's ears. Sometimes, she knew, there were letters, and once she caught sight of the name in the upper left corner of an envelope, a Lieutenant Daniel Gray, APO San Francisco.

Then the name had been in the papers, the picture. That evening, instead of going out as she usually did — Augusta could never be sure just where she went, and she had only the vaguest notions of the places that were mentioned in gossip columns — Judith had stayed at home. She developed an unaccustomed interest in the radio. Augusta had heard the broadcast from Washington and then Judith had gone to her room. Through the closed door Augusta knew that she was, with an unaccustomed determination, sitting beside her telephone.

More than once during the long evening Augusta's hand had almost touched the extension of the telephone. Not that she wanted — or had she ever wanted — to pry into what might be said. Actually, Augusta knew, she wanted to hear again that voice, at once diffident and shy and confident, out of which she, in her loneliness, had contrived a person. She put aside the impulse and waited. After a long time in her room Judith came out. Her face was lighted with an inner glow that Augusta had never seen there before. . . .

And when Mr. O'Neal settled himself diffidently on the cushion, took hold of the steering wheel, and turned to say, "Good evening, Ma'am," Augusta knew that she was hearing, not the voice out of which she had fashioned a young man for Judith, but, surely, an echo of it, older — and formed without the proper help of teeth — but still possessing the same peculiar quality.

And hearing it, Augusta Hale burrowed into the reticule where she kept the cigarettes to be rigorously rationed to Judith for her own good, and taking one in her finger tips, she held it out to this man whom she felt she knew, somehow. And for the first time in her career of handing things to people, she reached forward and pressed the lighter in the instrument panel; when it glowed red she removed it and held it for Mr. O'Neal, who said, "Thank you kindly, Ma'am," and thought, obscurely, of his late wife in her most favorable aspect and glanced appraisingly at the sea.

"We'll have a shift of wind before mornin', and you'll have a good beach when you come back along here, Ma'am."

20

"THAT SHIRT," CHIEF WARRANT OFFICER WILLIAM HENRY RAG-land stated gloomily, "looks like your mammy and Danny might have took it off'n some feller in a circus." He regarded Jerry Gray with truculent disapprobation. "Or maybe," the Chief continued, "they run across that feller Joseph up there and took his coat off'n him. Ain't there no buttons to go with it?"

Jerry grinned. The shirt, a thing of soft, thick wool, did, as a matter of fact, virtually exhaust the spectrum. Mostly it was red, but there were stripes of yellow, of green, and of black. It fitted with comfortable looseness, and he was wearing it open at the collar. It irritated his shoulders a little, and he explored that area with palliative fingers.

"It's got what they call zippers," Jerry stated.

"Didn't they bring you any shoes, or couldn't they find any in all Norfolk big enough to cover them feet?" the Chief continued with an asperity which, the boy knew, was largely simulated. "In God's holy name, ain't they ever goin' to get you civilized?" The big man's voice rumbled.

"Sure, they brought me some shoes and some boots, too. Take me home and I'll show 'em to you," Jerry said.

The Chief made explosive sounds and for some minutes ignored the boy. He shuffled papers on his desk, piled them into a heap and pushed them disgustedly away. He glared at them. Then without a word he stood up and started toward the door, not looking back to see whether Jerry followed him. When they came to the side entrance before which the jeep was parked, the Chief stood silently looking up at the rain-blotted sky.

The sweeping finger of the Light, diffused by the falling rain but strangely intensified, flicked the weather vane above the flag tower; they could see the wind arrow pointing into the northeast. The wind sang through the stay-wires of the tower, and out beyond the low dunes the tide pounded in reverberating diapason, muted, softened somewhat by the intervening distance and by the rising obligato of the wind.

"She's kickin' up her heels," Jerry said.

The Chief listened to the roar of the surf, the song of the wind, analyzing and appraising the night's sounds. He nodded absently. Presently he demanded, "How much wind, Jerry?"

The boy considered for a moment before replying. . . . It would not do to be too cocky about it. . . . Such things had to be weighed gravely and computed precisely. Jerry listened to the wind as it sang through the stay-wires, to the tempo of the surf piling itself on the beach.

"Twenty-two — twenty-four knots."

"That damned gadget in yonder would maybe make it twenty-three," the Chief said. "Go look at it — you just as well begin young to look at gadgets."

Jerry re-entered the Station, and when he came back a moment later he said, "Twenty-three it is, Chief." The Chief nodded. They went toward the parked jeep.

"Drive," the big man said briefly. Jerry looked at him gratefully and slid under the steering wheel. At the end of the driveway, where it forked into the trail leading toward the beach and another leading northward past the Lighthouse and into the Woods, the Chief with a brief wave of his hand directed the boy to turn to the right, toward the ocean.

When the vehicle climbed the low dune and slanted down seaward, the beam of its headlights reached out above the writhing foam of the surf. Wind-driven spray, mixed with the rain, lashed across the windshield and licked at the curtains. The wind hit them in gusts. The Chief's glance at the roiling tumult of the water before them was casual, detached, remotely calculating, as if he were weighing the expedients that would be necessary if he had to put the lifeboat out. . . .

Jerry turned northward, driving along the level, relatively smooth top of the beach just beyond the long, running tongues of frothing water that nipped at the tires of the vehicle as it went forward against the quartering wind. Ahead, presently, loomed the Lighthouse. The surf pounded in mounting intensity and the spray flashed white across the windshield occasionally. The Chief rode in silence without glancing seaward again after his first appraising scrutiny.

"Heave to, Jerry," he said suddenly.

If he was surprised, the boy gave no sign of it. He swung a little to the left, to the top of the beach, and brought the vehicle squarely into the wind, well out of reach of the thrusting tide. He halted the vehicle, disengaged the gears, letting the engine idle. The wipers on the windshield wrestled with the driven rain and flying spray that reached them, even here. He did not look at the Chief, but waited, without any uneasiness, without wondering, even, what Bill Henry might have on his mind. Some minutes passed before the Chief spoke, and when he broke the silence his voice was at first hesitant, doubting.

"This sergeant of Danny's over at your house, Jerry —"

He glanced at the boy searchingly, but all the change he could see was in Jerry's fingers when they tightened around the rim of the steering wheel. It was just for an instant. The fingers relaxed, and the boy looked around at him, meeting his eyes squarely.

"What about him, Bill Henry?"

The Chief studied the boy's face for some time before he replied, and then he swore corrosively. Jerry's stolid face was warmed by a slow, appreciative smile. "Go ahead, Chief, what's on your mind?"

"If you were any other one of the two billion people they say infest this world, you would think I was meddlin' with something that's none of my business," the massive man rumbled.

"I've been turnin' this thing over in my mind, such as it is, ever since I first saw him. There's two ways to figure it — either you don't know nothing, or do know it and ain't sayin' nothin' because you told him you wouldn't. If you don't know nothin' I thought I might tell you."

The boy had turned back. He sat staring through the windshield where the rain slanted down along the length of the beam of light that reached out ahead. He started to say something, bit his lip in silence. He glanced quickly, appealingly, at the big man beside him.

"I'm bein' a blunderin' fool," the Chief went on, "but I don't want to make any worse mess than I have to, and I don't want anybody else to make a worse one. That's why I'm talkin' to you — I want to find out where I'm at.

"As soon as I got a good look at him I knew him. I've known three generations of his folks along these Banks and he's got the markin's of damned near all of 'em. I knew his daddy. He come and talked to me about his troubles, back yonder.

"And I've had a notion ever since you come to the Station before supper you had something on your mind you wanted to talk to somebody about, Jerry, and you couldn't. I'm not tryin' to pry anything out of you, but I did sort of figure that he might have told you — and I thought maybe we'd better get together on it. Danny don't know anything, does he?"

"You're pretty smart, Bill Henry." Jerry's voice was not steady.

"That all you goin' to tell me, Jerry?"

"I — I guess it is, Bill Henry."

The boy turned again to look squarely into the Chief's eyes. His mouth trembled. There was a pleading look in his eyes.

"You're a good boy, Jerry," the big man said gently. "And

you got sense. We've got to look out for Danny."

"Yeah — if he needs it. And he might."

"Hoist anchor, Jerry," the Chief said shortly. The boy drove forward. Beyond the Lighthouse he swung off to the left, re-crossed the dyke, and went along the road toward the entrance to the Woods.

"All you can hear around our house now is airplanes," Jerry said as they approached the Woods. The Chief grunted.

"From what the — from the way he and Danny talk, you'd think that there Twenty-nine Danny flew is plumb out of date now and they're goin' to have bigger ones. Without engines in 'em. The Ser — he talks a lot about helicopters, and stuff like that, too. He stayed around that place in Dayton after Danny come home and looked at a lot of stuff Danny hadn't even heard of."

The Chief grunted again.

"He keeps talkin' to Danny about jet ships and says when he goes back Danny ought to try out on 'em."

"So he talks about Danny goin' back, does he?" There was a note of bitterness in the big man's voice.

"Yeah, and you ought to have seen him salute Danny when Danny and Mom got home from Norfolk this mornin'. It looked sort of funny, him bein' what you might call an old man standin' up there with his hand like that. Danny, he was so surprised to see him he must have forgot to do what he ought and kept him standin' there for the longest kind of time." Jerry's laugh crackled.

"Calls Danny 'Sir' all the time, too," the boy went on. "Or he did until Danny told him to skip it and relax." The boy lapsed into silence for a time, and then, "Mom's a funny woman, Bill Henry — or did you ever notice?"

"Yeah, I noticed it a long time ago. What's she done now?"

"When I got around to showin' Danny that letter addressed to Major Daniel Gray and askin' him if he had any idea who it was for, she started blushin' and sort of laughin' and fumblin' around in that bag she totes when she goes off. Damned if she hadn't bought a pair of them leaves like a major wears."

"She did, did she?"

"She did. She said she just saw 'em in a store window and thought they looked nice. And then she said she had a sort of feelin' that they'd maybe come in handy, sometime."

"She did, did she?"

"She did. Two pairs of 'em."

"What'd she do with 'em?"

"Dragonnetti — the Sergeant — he took a pair of 'em and — but Danny didn't seem to notice him. He took the other set and give Mom one and me one and we put 'em on his shoulders, after we took off them little bars. He looks nice. Mom kissed him. It's the first time I can ever remember her doin' it. She ain't much of a kisser."

"What did you do, Jerry?"

"Heck, I didn't do nothin' — except maybe I poked him in the gut. I started to kiss him like I used to when I was little, but then I thought if Mom had learned how, he didn't need me kissin' him any more. The Sergeant, he saluted and Danny shook hands with him. Mom, she was cryin' and laughin' all at the same time."

Jerry brought the jeep to a halt when he reached the gate.

"Come on in, Bill Henry — they got a fire in the fireplace — and sit around awhile. She ain't kickin' her heels so high you need to worry about her."

They fastened the curtains of the jeep in place when they got out, and both stopped instinctively to contemplate the weather before turning toward the house. The sky was black. Muffled by the mile of intervening dunes and trees and marsh, the sound of the pounding surf came more dimly, with a far-off roar that echoed against the westward hills. Jerry cocked an ear, listening.

"You hear that, Bill Henry? Geese!"

High overhead, somewhere beyond the gloomy night, faintly

heard above the surge of the wind through the live oaks and above the remote roar of the sea, the haunting cry of the wild goose came down to them. In a moment the cry was repeated, re-echoed above the clouds.

"There's a lot of 'em," Jerry said. "These woods ought to be full of 'em by daylight."

"Don't get any old-fashioned ideas in your head," Bill Henry said gruffly. "When there's geese there's game wardens — more wardens than geese, and you can't shoot a goose until they say so."

"That's what they think, Bill Henry," Jerry answered. "Let's go in the house. Show you my boots."

But the Chief held back. When the Light flicked his face Jerry saw that he was not, as he supposed, looking skyward at the weather and listening to the migrants above it. He was, instead, staring moodily at the lighted windows of the house above the road. Jerry waited. After a while the Chief reached out a ponderous hand and laid it on the boy's shoulder.

"Jerry," he said soberly, almost wistfully, "I guess I got my foot in my mouth out yonder. I was goin' by dead reckonin' and maybe I hit a shoal. From here on, I aim to keep my mouth shut. But if anything comes up — people are curious animals — you come let me know. You hear me?"

Jerry met Big Bill Henry's eyes steadily when the Light flicked them again and then, with boyish impulsiveness, he put his arm under the Chief's elbow, poked his loosely balled fist against his ribs.

"Come on in out of the rain, you big porpoise, before you get yourself a cold and start sneezin' — I told you out yonder you are pretty smart, didn't I? Maybe if I'd been raised right I'd tell you thanks or — or — hell! come on in out of the rain."

Jerry greeted the group around the hearth with boyish exuberance. "Hi, Mom — Hi, Major — Hi, Sergeant! You and Danny still talkin' about airy-o-planes? Bet neither one of you could row yourselves across the creek in a skiff."

"Jerry!" Polly Gray smiled reproof. "Danny, let's let Bill Henry have the chair next to the fire — he must be soaking wet! Where have you two surfmen been this time of the night?"

"Geese are comin' Mom — we could hear 'em — a whole lot of 'em. Marshes will be full of 'em before daylight. Say, Danny —"

"No you don't, you lawless limb of Satan," Danny said good-humoredly. He turned to Big Bill Henry, insisted that he sit down in the chair that had once been his father's. He crossed the room to bring another for himself. The room was lighted only by the fire on the hearth. The flames crackled, sending up spurts of blue, red, and yellow as they fed on dried driftwood brought from the beach.

The Chief settled himself in the big chair and crossed his knees. He glanced at the Sergeant, reluctant at first to meet the soldier's eyes directly. The Sergeant had resumed his chair and was staring, moodily reflective, at the spurting flames licking their blue and red tongues around pieces of wood that had been, once, parts of heavy ship's timber. Before he settled himself on the deerskin rug before the fire, Jerry spoke briefly to Danny, who disappeared in the direction of the kitchen.

"It's a good night for a toddy, Chief," Danny said when he came back from the kitchen. He set a tall glass on the table at the Chief's elbow and the big man's eyes spoke his thanks as he sipped at the glass slowly. Surfman followed Danny into the room. He went toward the fire, settled himself on his haunches, and sat, staring at the fire. The big man's fingers began their search through his pockets. He placed the cigarette between his lips, but he did not immediately light it. He held the match loosely in his fingers.

Jerry, his legs stretched toward the fire, toasted the soles of his feet. He glanced around, saw the unlighted cigarette drooping between the Chief's lips. Reaching out he took the match from the Chief's fingers and with elaborate casualness scraped the head of it against the sole of his foot. It burst into flame. He leaned backward, with his shoulders against the Chief's knees, holding the match upward. Big Bill Henry lighted his cigarette in silence. Danny laughed.

"Have you two been rehearsing that act?"

"Naw," Jerry said cheerfully, "but it ain't a bad act, is it, Danny?"

Polly Gray and the Sergeant joined in Danny's amusement, but the Chief sat silent, his eyes brooding on the boy's face. He sipped his drink in silence and only Polly Gray saw what was in his eyes.

"Trouble with you avvy-a-tors," Jerry said, making the word sound gently derisive, "is you get your calluses where they ain't much good to you. You sit down too much."

"Jerry!" Polly Gray tried to make herself sound shocked, but she was unable, quite, to keep the amusement out of her voice. She went on hurriedly, covering her momentary confusion. "You must wear your shoes, Jerry. It will be cold by morning."

"Heck," Jerry said ruefully. He sat, staring at the fire, withdrawn from any awareness of the talk that went on, somewhat desultorily, around him. He drew his feet under him and relaxed on one elbow, his head against the Chief's knee. Surfman purred contentedly against the boy's breast and now and then Jerry pulled abstractedly at the cat's ears. After a while he yawned sleepily. He picked up the cat, holding him loosely under his arm, and went off toward his bedroom without a word.

Silence held the room, loosely, without constraint, after the boy closed the door, a silence of the quality that falls among people who are content with one another's presence and who have nothing in particular that they feel they must talk about.

Polly Gray and Big Bill Henry Ragland sat at opposite ends of the hearth, each looking at the fire that was, by now, burned down to a heap of coals that now and then sent up spurts of blue flame.

Danny and the Sergeant sat directly in front of the hearth. Each of them seemed wrapped in his own private thoughts. Danny's face was tranquil, his lips slightly apart, and his eyes had the look of remote dreaming upon things not sharply defined, upon things wrapped in a speculative bright haze. His fingers tugged absently at the tip of an ear, and now and then he smiled, softly, as if in greeting to some image that moved, with lazy leisure, across his vision. . . .

The Chief sat utterly still, his face immobile and the lower half of it hidden behind a great hand flattened across his mouth, its thumb along his nose. Only his eyes were speculatively alert, and they were almost hidden beneath the shaggy line of his brow. His glance traveled meditatively around the half-circle before the hearth and came back to rest on the Sergeant's dark, remotely brooding face, outwardly calm but with a smouldering light, far back, in his eyes. The Sergeant lighted a cigarette and let it burn almost to his taut fingers before he took it to his lips again.

As if he felt the big man's eyes searching his own, the Sergeant glanced at him quickly, so quickly that the Chief was taken by surprise. He withdrew his gaze in some confusion but not before he saw the Sergeant's hand move convulsively, fingers clenched against the palm. The man looked distractedly at Danny, and when he saw that the Major's thoughts were far off, his glance moved, in a little panic, toward Polly Gray.

It needed conscious effort for the Sergeant not to look at the big man in the chair again. He swallowed hard and his hands shook when he lighted another cigarette. He inhaled deeply, and the smoke came back through his lips in a long, sharp jet. The draught into the fireplace caught the billowing smoke and sucked it sharply up the chimney. Outside the wind roared in quickening gusts and the rain beat against the windows.

Somewhere in the back of the house a shutter slammed against the outer wall, cracking the silence like a sudden shot. Polly Gray started in small alarm and Danny came out of his detached abstraction. They got up at the same time, each looking inquiringly at the other. The Chief sat immobile, moving his head slightly to bring his ear in range of the chimney above which the wind rolled.

"It's that shutter at the east window in my room," Polly Gray said. "The hinge has been loose and I'm afraid the wind has broken it off."

She turned toward the door of her room. Danny followed her, leaving the Sergeant and the Chief alone, marooned in a pool of uneasy, uncomfortable silence. When the door closed behind Polly Gray and Danny, the Sergeant turned to the Chief. Resignation and relief were mingled in his voice when he finally spoke.

"So you know me?"

"Yes."

"Did he —"

The Chief stopped him with a gesture that carried something of a quick threat.

"He didn't," the Chief said, and his tone made the Sergeant shiver inwardly. He went on, not unkindly. "I knew you when I first laid eyes on you. I've known three generations of your people."

The Sergeant stared at him bewilderedly. He started to speak.

"Keep your shirt on, Jesse," the big man interrupted him. "And until you've had time to do some thinkin', keep your mouth shut. I learned that much on the way over here tonight. You come over to the Station if you find out you want to talk and it's me you want to talk to."

Danny and his mother came back into the room, Danny with his hair and the sleeves of his shirt rain-splashed.

"Nothing serious," Polly Gray said, "but it's getting to be a rough night out of doors."

"Must be pretty rough along the beach, Chief," Danny said. "What sort of storm warning is up?"

"This won't amount to much," the Chief said carelessly. "Blow itself out before daylight. Everything's quiet along the beach, nothin' happenin' all day that I know of. The boys up at Chicamicomico did go out right after dark and haul in a car buried in the sand abreast the 'Kohler.' "

"Who were they?" Danny inquired without much interest.

"Didn't hear," the Chief replied. "Couple of women in a New York car — one that's too big for drivin' around here, even if they knew the beach."

"Beach was getting pretty rough when we came down this morning," Danny said, "but it ought to be smoothed out after this blow."

"Yeah," the Chief said, adding that it was time for him to be heading back to the Station. "Something might happen," he added. He turned directly to Danny. "Bring your sergeant over to the Station tomorrow, Danny — let him look around some."

"Okay — thanks; we'll do that, Chief," Danny said.

21

A CLEAR-EYED DAWN AWOKE THE SEVEN VILLAGES OF THE OUTER Banks. During the night the wind had shifted to the east, then to the south, and finally, when the tide turned, to the northwest; and when it had driven the last laggard cloud out to sea, the wind slept. The stars looked down upon the sleeping villages and upon the sandy waste that linked them together and, at the same time, held them apart, each in its own orbit.

Backward from the storm, now far out beyond the horizon, came long sweeping swells that wasted themselves on the beach in an impotent froth, with diminuendo roaring. Now and then they smashed on the beach with vengeful, staccato crashes, and here and there, in the Seven Villages, one or another man started out of his sleep, remembering other mornings, not so long ago, when the detonation of ships writhing in death broke the dawn's quiet.

It must have been one of those exploding swells that brought Augusta McGarrah awake in the big square house behind the Station at Chicamicomico. For a while she lay still beneath the heavy covering of the bed, lost in the strangeness of her surroundings. Last night she had gone to sleep without dallying, in her unvarying custom, over the day's events, arranging them in her mind, deploring, approving and, in some vague fashion, rationalizing them.

She had known, in her own mind she was sure of it, when she went to bed that she would not sleep so much as one wink throughout the night. Her thin legs had trembled under the covers. Never, she told herself, in all her lifetime had there been such a day; and never had she been so helplessly beyond the reach of anything that was secure and accustomed, so preyed upon by strange terrors, including pirates. And then she had remembered the softness, the almost Gaelic softness, of Mr. O'Neal's voice. When she awoke she remembered it again.

Through the opened door that connected with the next room Augusta could see, against the glowing light of sunrise outside the window, the soft ebbing and flowing of Judith's breathing. The girl lay on her back, her arms stretched loosely along the pillows; her mouth was smiling, as if she had gone to sleep thinking about something that pleased her and had, through the night, dreamed upon it. Augusta looked out the window beside her. The sun's yellow rim was lifting out of the sea. She got out of bed. The floor was chilly beneath her bare feet until she found her slippers, and her thin shoulders shivered.

In Waves and in Salvo and Avon, the dawn stirred the villagers of the Outer Banks, and under the shadow of the towering Light the ocean heaved and the sound of its crashing against the Cape reverberated across the Woods. Jerry Gray came awake. He sat up, letting the cover fall away from his bare shoulders, and glanced at the sky, now turning from luminous gray to glowing yellow. Surfman, curled in sleep at the open window, opened one eye and looked out, opened the other and considered his master. Somewhere in the marsh a goose greeted the dawn with a long-drawn honk.

Jerry glanced at Danny, hoping that he would awaken. He started to reach out and poke his brother in the ribs but, instead, tucked the cover under Danny's shoulder. He got quickly out of bed, searched beneath it with his foot until it encountered his dungarees. He put them on and picked up his shirt, folded across the back of a chair in a sort of acknowledgment of its newness and of his esteem for it. He combed his hair with his fingers and set the white sailor's cap above one ear.

Surfman got down from the bed and stood expectantly, swishing his tail. Jerry went to the closet and took out a single-barreled shotgun, breached it, and looked down the barrel. He put a half dozen shells in the pockets of his dungarees and, with a backward glance at Danny, went out and closed the door softly behind him. In the living room he stopped, irresolutely, looking at the closed door beyond which the Sergeant slept.

"Sleepy-heads," Jerry said to himself with mild disdain. He opened the front door and went out without making any noise. Surfman followed him with eager swishings of his tail.

Above the marsh beyond the road a gray mist hung suspended above the brown grass, but even as Jerry looked at it, the wind, stirring now out of the north, pushed it gently, moving it until it flowed soundlessly among the live oaks and the pines along the ridge at the other side. The palmetto palms at the end of the sleeping yard stirred with faint noises, and from the marsh came the sounds, clear and unmistakable, of geese feeding.

Jerry went along the road, with the sun falling warm across his shoulders, until he came to the rise where he could look down across the Sound. Beyond the rim of trees and low-growing yoepon and myrtle along the water's edge he could see the Sound, stretching, mile upon mile of it, into the west and north. The wind, freshening now, came down out of the north, cool, flicking the blue water with wisps of white.

There they were, hundreds of them, Jerry saw, like little brown boats riding at anchor. Nearer the shore, now and then, a big goose lifted himself against the shallow bottom and, with a mighty sweeping of wings, looked as if he were about to launch himself into flight. But he would settle back in the water, probing the bottom with his long neck. . . . Guess they're sort of stiff after flying so long, and hungry, Jerry thought. . . .

Out of the north, high and riding a freshening wind, came a long pointed arrow of geese. Now and then their leader honked and one or another of the geese on the water answered him. Jerry smiled and his forefinger moved along the stock of the gun caressingly until it came to the trigger guard. He brought the piece to his shoulder, sighted along its barrel. But he made no move to load the gun. For now it was enough to watch them.

High overhead, the flight of geese, early sunlight glinting on their wings, circled, coming lower. The flight circled again, this time just above the treetops, and disappeared above the marshes that lay back of and away from the Lighthouse. He glanced down at Surfman, sitting erect at his feet. The cat looked up at him inquiringly.

"Let's go look at 'em, cat," Jerry said, and they turned away from the wide reach of the Sound. They went down a little path that cut across the woods toward the marshes back of the Lighthouse. A low causeway, made when they had opened the place to drain the marsh of flood waters that sometimes came out of the Sound when the wind was in the northwest, crossed the nearer marsh.

Here and there, as they made their way through the Woods, a single goose, with loud, alarmed squawkings, would lift himself in awkward flight. Jerry would raise his gun to his shoulder, with cheek against its stock, and take aim, following the bird's flight until he was out of range. Once his hand moved, as if involuntarily, toward the pocket where the shells were, but it came away empty and the boy sighed regretfully.

Now the sun was well up, its light slanting across the woods, bright, clear and, with the freshening wind out of the north, almost cold. Jerry rubbed the sole of one bare foot against the shin of the other leg, warmingly. The cat, as if sensing that the boy might be cold, rubbed his thick fur against the calf of a leg. When they came to where there was shallow water, the boy picked up the cat, carrying him loosely under his arm.

There were geese everywhere, Jerry discovered; but, he thought regretfully, not as many as there used to be. Or, he wondered, was that just something that he had heard so often that he had come to accept it as part of his own experience? Anyhow, there were a lot of them and he wished he could . . . why, he could have brought down a dozen before now — six, anyway. . . . He wondered if he could wait until the season opened . . . or if he could get away with killing one. . . .

Skirting the rim of the marsh until he came to the low hill south of it, the boy climbed to its top and looked about him. He was beginning to feel a little empty and he wished that he had waited, anyhow, for a cup of coffee before leaving the house. Yonder was the Station, and he could walk over there in mighty near no time. . . . He decided against it and turned back toward the Lighthouse.

Ahead, along the ridge, the tall sea oats stirred. The boy knew that there was no wind stirring them, nor any goose. No goose would sit still in the grass here. . . . He reached into his pocket for a shell and slipped it into the breech of the gun, moving forward carefully, watchful. The cock pheasant's gaudy feathers caught the sunlight when he catapulted himself into flight. Jerry brought the gun to his shoulder and laid his cheek against the stock. The pheasant dropped, heavily.

"Nope, cat," Jerry said when Surfman, stirred by some atavistic instinct, uttered a low growl and made for the bird. "That's for Mom. Maybe we'll get you a rabbit before we get home. I wish the mate of this feller would show up."

Jerry missed the second pheasant when it whirred into flight just beyond the range of the gun. With the cat at his heels he turned homeward. The wet sand was beginning to be a little cold under his feet. Surfman, with grateful growls, retrieved from beneath a clump of yoepon the small rabbit that

Jerry shot and would have begun his breakfast there, but Jerry picked it up, carrying it by its long ears.

"Damned if you eat ahead of me, cat," he said. "Wait until you get home and you can have a whole day at it."

Surfman trotted ahead, his tail stiffly erect. Now and then he looked back to be sure that his master was coming. When they came to the little railed bridge across the ditch that drained the marsh when there was need of it, Jerry stopped, looked out again over the expanse of blue Sound water, flecked with white waves and dotted with resting geese. He laid the rabbit and the pheasant on the top rail, leaned the gun loosely against his hip. Surfman leaped lightly to the top rail and sat, looking inquiringly at his master, and at the rabbit hungrily. . . .

Meanwhile Judith Hale and Augusta had departed from the northmost of the Seven Villages, resuming their journey. Leaving the big square house, the girl found herself in a state of troubled confusion. Her face, as she drove along the beach, was still flushed with an embarrassment that she could not, altogether, define or account for. But the feeling that she had, somehow, violated some local ground rule of hospitality would not be put completely out of her mind.

And the worst part of it all, she reflected as she drove — confidently now and in accordance with what they had told her at the Station — was that her hostess had been as ill at ease as she herself had been. When Judith, opening her bag, inquired how much she owed for the night's lodging for herself and Augusta, the woman had flushed uneasily. Judith, a cigarette drooping between her lips, took out some folded bills held together flatly with an elaborately chased silver clip.

The girl misconstrued the woman's hesitation and with an irritated shrug separated a bill of larger denomination than she had, somewhat idly, surmised that the woman would mention. She held it toward the woman with what, she thought, would be just the right air of — Judith's face reddened as she drove when she remembered her manner. The woman had stammered.

"Why, Miss — there's no — we were just glad to have you."

"But I insist," Judith broke in. "It's ridiculous — you must take this."

But the woman had made no move to accept the money and her face was not happy when she looked away from Judith's eyes. Augusta had begun to feel the moment's tension and to wonder, unhappily, what had gone wrong and why Judith had to act so — so superior. She wished, in a little panic, that Mr. O'Neal would come and — well, do something. Mr. O'Neal did, just then, come through the front gate. Not only were his eyes gleaming like two bright marbles, but his teeth were shining through his lips. His chin and nose, this morning, were utter strangers. Augusta McGarrah breathed a sigh of relief.

"Mornin', Miss — mornin', Ma'am," he said and, turning to the woman in whose house they had slept, "mornin', Aggie." He turned to Judith.

"Put away that money, Miss — we just ain't used to seein' it around here. Not this time of the day, anyhow."

Judith, in no inconsiderable bewilderment, returned the bill clip to her bag and snapped it shut. Before she could begin to formulate some word of thanks, and to cover her embarrassment, Mr. O'Neal was going on.

"Ought not to be a bit of trouble now, Miss. Sand's good and wet and that little blow we had last night ought to have smoothed out the beach. Ought to make it down to the Cape now in — why, you can just scoot along. It's not but twenty-four miles, and with that car you could make it, if you had to, in mighty near no time flat. But what's so pushin' about gettin' down there? Why don't you spend the day here with us?"

Judith flushed, but if Mr. O'Neal was aware of it, he gave no sign. He continued.

"Just one thing to remember when you're drivin' the beach — keep your headway. Don't ever let her stop goin' ahead. But you won't have any trouble now. Some of the boys over at the Station will follow you until you get past where you got stuck last night, and after that it's all open beach. Better get goin', too, if you want to make it on this low water. But why don't you all spend the day here?" Mr. O'Neal looked pointedly at Augusta, and Augusta made a disturbing discovery. She could blush.

Judith put down the top again when she saw that the day was clear and, to her, not more than just crisp. She glanced now and then into the mirror at the top of the windshield, saw that she was leaving the slower-moving Station jeep too far behind. She slowed the car, watching every yard of the beach ahead, as they had told her, appraising its stability. The jagged hulk of the wreck loomed ahead; she put the car into second gear and swung it toward the top of the beach as she approached. The car labored in the sand but it maintained headway. In a moment she was around the obstruction and the car began to pick up speed on the hard sand.

Confident in her driving now, Judith halted the car and leaned over the door to look back at the jeep. It came past the wreck, now only half-immersed in the surf. The same youth who had driven the duck last night was at the wheel. He turned in a wide circle and, without stopping, waved an arm in farewell and continued north.

"He's damned casual," Judith said with an irritated little frown. "Or would you say impersonal, Augusta?"

"Good a word as any," Augusta said shortly, "and better than some. After all," she continued with surprising spirit, "what did you expect him to do — come over and kiss us good-bye?"

The girl ignored Augusta. Before she put the car into gear she looked at the speedometer.

"Six miles we've come — eighteen to go. Isn't this a glorious, gorgeous day, Augusta?"

"I've seen worse no longer ago than yesterday," Augusta conceded. "But it would look better if I had a good cup of coffee inside me."

"You ought to be coffee-logged right now, Augusta — three whole cups of that good woman's coffee."

"Too much chicory in it," Augusta said glumly. She was thoughtful for a moment before she went on. "I wonder whether Mr. O'Neal was serious when he said what he said about money. And anyhow, you'd better keep yours out of sight until you know more about the customs of the — of these people."

"Why didn't you stop me? You let me make an utter fool of myself."

"Learn the hard way — stays with you longer," Augusta said grimly. She appeared to be pondering something, turning it over in her mind, reluctantly approaching a conclusion. "I guess they're communists," she said.

"Augusta!"

"That's what Mr. O'Neal said."

"Mr. O'Neal said they were communists!"

"Something like that. He explained it to me before you came back from wherever you went — over at that Station."

"But communists, Augusta!"

"It's all right the way he made it sound," Augusta insisted. "If you get stuck in the sand, somebody helps you out. And if they get stuck, you help them out. Same way with — with a bed. If you don't have one, you sleep in theirs; and if they don't have one, they sleep in yours. It sounded fine, to hear him tell it."

"You and Mr. O'Neal seem to have got down to fundamentals," Judith said, lightly accusing. "Communism . . . beds."

"Mr. O'Neal is a nice gentleman," Augusta said.

"You must have noticed that he was wearing his teeth this morning," Judith said mildly.

Augusta ignored her. She retired to the far corner of the seat, and when the clock on the dash indicated that it was time for Judith to have another cigarette, she looked persistently away from it, ignored it altogether. But Judith, busy with her driving, was unaware that she was being ignored or neglected punitively. Low dunes flitted past on the right, and on the left the ocean danced in long, sinuous measures, like a waltz. . . .

"That's the Lighthouse, Augusta! We must be almost there."

Augusta considered the Lighthouse while she fumbled at the clasp of the bag that held Judith's cigarettes.

So intense was Jerry Gray's scrutiny of the Sound and so far off were his thoughts — and so smoothly did the convertible move along the wet sandy road — that he was startled when a voice yanked him back into an awareness of his immediate surroundings. He turned around. The cat, in sudden alarm, started to jump down from the rail and take flight down the road toward the security of home.

Never in his life, except in pictures, had Jerry seen such a car, he told himself. And also, never in his life, not even in pictures, had he seen a woman who looked just like this one peering at him over the rim of the door nearest him, not more than five or six feet away. Her black eyes seemed as if they wanted to bore right through him, and her mouth was set in a grim, straight line . . . like that of a schoolteacher.

"Young man!" Augusta's voice was primly sharp.

"Yes — yes, Ma'am," Jerry stammered and was then ashamed of himself for letting somebody slip up on him like that. This was the second time she had spoken, and this time it was sharper. He leaned back against the rail, with his elbows on it, the fingers of his left hand fondling the muzzle of the gun resting against his hip. Surfman, reassured, considered the woman without any emotion.

"Young man," Augusta said for the third time and, without knowing why she did it, she added, "Haven't you got any shoes?" Then she reached out her hands in a helpless gesture, as if she would grab the words out of the air and stuff them back into her mouth. She laid a hand over her lips.

The boy shifted his weight to one foot and held the other up to where she could see it plainly. Now he was aware for the first time of the other woman in the car . . . and again, he thought, he had never seen such a girl, except in a picture, maybe. He grinned at his naked foot and smiled at the woman who, even if she did look like a schoolteacher, was sort of funny. The young woman laid a restraining hand on the old woman's arm.

"Is — is this Buxton?" Augusta asked, and when she glanced down at the preposterous naked foot she knew that she had been rebuked.

"Yes, Ma'am. It's up there in the Woods." Jerry waved an arm inclusively.

"Where does —" Augusta began and then looked uncertainly at Judith. The girl was smiling . . . smiling as if she enjoyed the older woman's obvious discomfiture. Augusta returned to what, she knew now, was an uneven encounter.

"Is there anywhere we could find a cup of coffee, young man?" she asked weakly.

"Most anywhere — Mom's probably got a pot goin' by now," the boy said. The older woman gave up in resigned bewilderment, glanced helplessly at the girl beside her, and leaned back against the cushion. Judith leaned forward toward the open window.

"She means is there a restaurant or hotel or boarding house or any place like that where — where —" And now Judith gave up. At least she gave up trying to make herself intelligible with words. Judith smiled.

"Don't know of any such place but Mom's got coffee. Most anywhere you'd be a-mind to stop they've got coffee this time of the day."

"We were — I was looking for Captain Daniel Gray," Judith said. Her purpose was to be casually bold about it, but she ended with a suffusing blush. Jerry's eyes narrowed in surprise but he continued to smile.

"There ain't any Captain Gray," the boy said. He saw the quick alarm flit across the girl's face, and he saw the old woman's mouth drop open. "Danny's a major," he added after a pause.

"Oh, how wonderful!" the girl exclaimed. And then she added, her face quizzical, "You must be Jerry."

"Yeah, I'm Jerry."

"This is just marvelous," the girl said, but Jerry couldn't see anything marvelous about being Jerry. Who else would he be? . . . The girl went on, "I should have known you — Danny used to talk a lot about you. But you've grown, haven't you?"

"Some," Jerry said neutrally, and then confusion sent his thoughts whirling. He couldn't see the old woman, only the young woman now, and she was leaning forward, across the old woman, with one hand on the door, and she was smiling. Jerry stammered, "You must . . . . Are you Judy?" And he knew that his face had turned red for no reason that he could think of, and that his voice was croaking . . . like a goddam frog. The girl nodded, smiling.

"So you know about me, too?"

This — this won't do, Jerry thought muddily; it won't do at all. Here is Danny's girl . . . and here I am half naked and lookin' like a castaway . . . and Danny asleep yonder in bed — up all night talkin' about airplanes . . . and this old woman here yowlin' for coffee . . . and Danny's girl . . . . Jerry's head felt light, as if it might be going to float off his shoulders in a minute. The girl's hand drew back from the door and Jerry came out of the haze that wrapped him. He took a confident step toward the car.

"Come on up to the house — Mom'll have a pot of coffee and I'll wake Danny up."

The girl's hand flicked the handle inside the door and it came open. The hand dragged at the old woman's lap, motioning her over and making more room in the seat.

"Come in," the girl urged, glancing past Jerry at the railing where Surfman sat impassively, guarding the pheasant and the rabbit. "But don't forget your — is that a pheasant you've shot there? And don't forget your cat."

Jerry turned back to the rail precipitately, picked up the bird and the rabbit and dropped them on the floor of the car. Augusta moved her feet jerkily. Jerry took the gun in one hand and scooped Surfman off the rail with the other. He slid into the seat and pulled the door shut with an elbow.

"All set — just keep goin' on this road. This sure is a fine car. Got room enough, Grandma?"

Augusta McGarrah bristled, but when the boy looked at her, smiling in boyish friendliness, she relented, smiled feebly and then with more warmth.

"Plenty of room," she said, "but you ought to have shoes, young man."

"Oh, I got shoes," Jerry said easily. "Brand new ones — Mom and Danny got 'em in Norfolk. But I didn't wait to put 'em on — not cold anyhow. I was in sort of a hurry to get out and look at the geese. They just got here last night."

"Here," Jerry said briefly when the convertible came to the gate. Judith brought the car to a halt and Jerry hunched the door open with his elbow. He got out. Surfman wriggled out of his arms and went halfway up the walk. He sat down watchfully.

"You all get out and come on in the house. You must be cold out here — Mom'll have coffee."

Augusta got down, somewhat stiffly, and looked around doubtfully. Judith opened the other door and got down effortlessly, with complete composure. Jerry ran ahead of them toward the house, gun in one hand and game in the other. He left the door open behind him, and as they moved up the walk, Judith and Augusta could hear him call out.

"Hey, Mom, you got any coffee? There's two ladies out here."

Judith glimpsed Polly Gray's figure in the shadowy room as she came toward the front door. Jerry fell in beside her. Judith studied Polly Gray's face with quick apprehension, but when she saw Danny's mother's face light with its slow smile, warming it as a lighted lamp warms when the wick is turned up, the girl went up the steps, calm, reassured.

"I'm Judith Hale," she said simply. "We shouldn't be bothering you, I know, but Jerry here — well, it isn't hard to let him persuade you."

Polly Gray held out her hands. Jerry, with something of surprise, saw his mother and the girl go through the door, into the living room, leaving the older woman standing on the steps ... as if to shift for herself. Not, Jerry saw, that she seemed to mind; but, after all, it didn't seem right to leave an old woman standing there by herself.

"Come on in the house, Grandma," Jerry said. He held the door open for her and she ducked past him. Judith and his mother were standing there talking a little, but mostly just looking at each other. The girl was tugging at her gloves. She looked around at him and smiled.

"That's mine and Danny's room there," he said, nodding toward the closed door of the bedroom. "He's in there, still asleep. I'll get him awake, though."

The girl's glance made a leisurely circuit of the room; it stopped when it got to the door of the other room.

"Danny's sergeant — he's in there," Jerry said. "He come down on a visit — to see Danny."

"Would you mind if I just took you back to the kitchen?" Polly Gray put in. "Breakfast is almost ready; I've been waiting for Jerry to come in, or for Danny to wake."

"I'd love it, but may I just wash my hands before we go in?" Polly Gray nodded and went to show her the bathroom.

"This here's Grandma, Mom," Jerry said when his mother turned back to the living room. "Don't guess that's her name, but she ain't told me what else to call her. She thinks it's scan'lous for me to be barefooted." Jerry grinned.

"I'm Augusta McGarrah, Ma'am," the older woman said. She made a stiff-kneed little curtsy, wondering, as she did it, why. "I'm — I'm, well I just don't know how to tell you what I am. I — I raised her."

"It's nice to have you here," Polly Gray said gently. She turned to Jerry. "Son, bring them out to the kitchen when they're ready. I'll get some more coffee going."

Judith Hale came into the kitchen a moment later. After a glance around she murmured, "How nice that coffee smells! It must be something in the air — Augusta has been hysterical for coffee all the way down."

Augusta, when she came, with Jerry trailing her, moved warily, looking uneasily about until her roving gaze came to the percolator bubbling above the blue flame. She sniffed and the upward sweep of her nose came down in a widening smile. Unconsciously she rubbed the palms of her hands together. Jerry was busy setting the table.

When they were well down in their second cups of coffee — the third for the older woman — after disposing of generous helpings of smoked herring and corn cakes, Jerry leaned backward, his hand exploring the space beside his chair. He had a piece of herring between his thumb and forefinger. He felt the cat take hold gently, felt him sit down on his haunches. He didn't look down. His eyes were finding it increasingly difficult to leave the glowing face of the girl at the table. She acted as if she had always been there . . . or maybe as if she intended, now, always to be there.

Such a prospect, Jerry thought to himself, didn't have anything wrong with it. And he could tell that Mom liked the girl, too. She was . . . friendly. Grandma, now, maybe she was different, but then, she was old. She put her head down to the cup when she drank out of it, instead of lifting the cup to her head. Bill Henry had a saying that you could tell people's age and raisin' by the way they took their coffee. Now and then she looked at the girl, and then she looked at Mom, and then she glanced backward over her shoulder, as if she were expecting somebody to slip up on her.

Augusta was looking over her shoulder toward the door when it opened without any sound and Danny stood there, rubbing his eyes sleepily. He hadn't combed his hair yet, his shirt was open, and his mouth was half open in the middle of a yawn. A thick lock of his blond hair straggled across his forehead. Augusta looked, transfixed, but Jerry . . . was looking at the girl.

22

FOR A LONGER TIME THAN SEEMED CREDIBLE AFTERWARD WHEN
he tried to reconstruct the scene, to repossess it, and perhaps
to refashion it more to his own liking, Danny Gray stood
there inert, unbelieving, and without any volition to say anything or to move. He stared at the girl, saw her cool, smiling
eyes looking into his own. One eyebrow, he could remember
afterward, was lifted a little out of line with the other, questioning.

Danny's eyes blinked and he wondered if this could be
something that he was dreaming; if he, after all, were not still
in his bed, unawake but still not quite asleep. His glance
wavered around the table, saw his mother's placidly smiling
face, saw the strange older woman with her eyes darting back
and forth between him and the girl, saw Jerry's enigmatic,
half-jeering, half-pleading grin. . . .

"Hi," he managed, the syllable almost choking him. He
smiled thinly, rubbed his fists against his eyes, and shook his
head jerkily.

Judith got up from the table, lightly, unhurriedly. She came
around the older woman's back, toward him. He knew that
the others — his mother, Jerry, the old woman — were looking
at him intently, expectantly. . . . The girl came closer, and
Danny could smell the elusive perfume that, he remembered,
she used to dab lightly back of her ears.

"Hello, Danny," Judith said.

She was holding out her hands. Not well out, as if she were going to take hold of his, but ... invitingly. Her smile was steady, unabashed, but not bold or challenging ... waiting. Danny took her hands in his, a deep flush suffusing his face.

"Judy!" Danny's voice was almost a whisper. And then, "Gosh — am I still asleep? Is this something I've just dreamed up?"

"You may be asleep, Major," Jerry put in quickly, "but you ain't dreamin'. Come on, Grandma, let's me and you get out of here and make room for Danny. I got to wake up the Sergeant before he sleeps himself sick."

Augusta, emitting strange clucking noises, got up hastily, spilling some of her last cup of coffee on the table. She started toward the door, turned back for another searching look at Danny's flushed, boyish face and at Judith, calmly smiling. Jerry's hand under her elbow urged her, not without gentleness but firmly, through the door. He propelled her toward the living room and into a chair.

"You just make yourself at home, Grandma," he said. "I got to get Danny's sergeant out of bed, and then I got to clean that pheasant, and then — oh, I got a hell of a lot to do."

"Young man," Augusta said distractedly, a little absently, "you put on your shoes before you go out of this house."

"Heck, it ain't cold," Jerry answered and went toward the Sergeant's room. The Sergeant was already awake, had been awake for some time Jerry judged by the number of half-smoked cigarettes in the ashtray beside the bed.

"We got a lot of company, Sergeant," Jerry said. "Danny's girl's come, and she's got a grandma with her that can't think of nothin' but me not havin' on no shoes. You better get up."

The Sergeant avoided looking directly at the boy. Jerry took hold of a toe projected upward against the bed covering, wrung it gently. The man seemed to be unaware of it. He lay staring at the ceiling.

"Mr. Ragland knew me, Jerry," he said presently. His voice was tired, lifeless. In a moment he sat up, looked at Jerry directly.

"Did he tell you?"

"Yes. Last night, after you went to bed. I want to apologize to you, Jerry. Without thinking, I asked him if you had told him. Or I started to ask, and he stopped me. I believe he'd have broken my neck if I had really said it."

"That's all right," Jerry said.

"I just wanted to tell you . . . and thank you."

"That's all right," Jerry said again. He shifted his feet uncomfortably. "You ever seen Danny's girl?"

The Sergeant shook his head. He lighted another cigarette, sat smoking moodily.

"Mr. Ragland invited me to move over to the Station for a few days," he said presently. "Maybe it's a good idea."

"No need to do that unless you want to," Jerry said. "You're welcome here long as you want to stay."

When Jerry went back to the kitchen to tell Polly Gray that the Sergeant would be along as soon as he got dressed, Judith and Danny were at the table. His mother was busy about the range, making fresh coffee and cooking a new lot of corn cakes. Danny, Jerry saw, would look at the girl, and his face would turn red, and he would look away. She was smiling her soft, cool smile.

"May I have a cigarette, Danny? Augusta rations me, thinks I smoke too much," Judith was saying. Danny fumbled in his pockets. His hands came up empty.

"Jerry —"

"Okay, Major — comin' right up." He brought Danny's cigarettes from the bedroom, tossed the pack across the table. Danny picked it up and held it toward Judith. She put a cigarette between her lips, waited. . . . Danny's still in a fog, Jerry thought — why don't he give her a light? The boy took out a match, hesitated for a moment before he brought his heel up even with his knee. . . . The match flamed and he held it for the girl.

"My goodness," she said through a little cloud of smoke, "do you —"

"It's an act he and the Chief — you must meet the Chief, Judy — put on. They think it's pretty good."

"It is good," Judith said, smiling up at the boy. "You must show it to Augusta, and maybe then she'll let you alone about wearing shoes."

"Heck," Jerry said, "Grandma's all right. She don't mean any harm — just likes to nag a man." He smiled disarmingly. "You're goin' to nag Danny, ain't you, Judy?"

Danny's face flamed and Judith, for once in her life, found herself without any easy rejoinder. Her own face flushed.

"I don't mean a whole lot — just some," Jerry amended.

"Jerry!" Danny's voice was sharp, his face a deeper red, angry.

But the girl had recovered her composure. Quick laughter bubbled in her throat and she got up from the table. Her strong, slender hand lay along the boy's arm below the elbow, and his eyes widened at the size of the green-looking stone in the ring on her finger.

"Not . . . too much, Jerry," she said easily.

"You aimin' to marry him, ain't you, Judy?" Jerry said.

Beneath the careless boldness of his words there was a note of pleading. Danny, more confused than ever, and his face now almost dark, started to get up from the table. Polly Gray, at the stove, looked around, her face losing something of its placid calm. The girl moved her hand from Jerry's arm to Danny's shoulder, pressed it gently. Danny slumped back in his chair. Jerry stood, irresolute, flushed and ashamed, wishing that he could, somehow, get hold of the words and stuff them back in his mouth.

"Sit down, Jerry," Judith said, "and won't you, Mrs. Gray?"

The boy slumped uneasily into a chair at the table, stared

fixedly, unhappily, past Judith, at nothing beyond the window. Polly Gray came to the table and sat down, a troubled, placative smile hovering around the corners of her mouth. Judith looked directly at Jerry.

"Thanks, Jerry," she said. Her voice had a little catch in it. "It makes it easier, now. Of course I have to account for my being here like this. I know all of you must be wondering — and Heaven knows what you must be thinking."

She was silent then, her eyes softly meditative, as if she were collecting her thoughts, scattered by the boy's blunt directness, and putting them together again in some sort of order. Presently she went on.

"Neither one of us —" she glanced at Danny — "has ever mentioned it. I doubt that Danny has ever — well, I don't know." Now she looked directly at Polly Gray. The mother was looking at her hands, folded in her lap, below the level of the table.

"I'm afraid I'm a spoiled creature," the girl went on. "I'm not — I didn't come down here to pursue Danny. I'm not very clear about why I came, but there's one thing I've always been very clear about, in my own mind, and that is: when I marry, it has to last.

"Somehow my family hasn't ever been able to make a go of marriage. My mother has been married five times. I've never seen her that I can remember. My father has been married twice — the last time to my mother. His father and my mother's father . . . well, none of us — none of them — ever had any gift for marriage.

"I'm afraid all this must sound awfully . . . wicked, to all of you," she went on, "and I'm afraid I must look, must sound, like a brazen hussy — or worse. There have been a lot of boys — men — you know how it is, Danny — and some of them — maybe a good many of them — have proposed to me. Some of them I liked, but ever since I was a child and Augusta started looking after me, I've wanted, when I did marry, to know that once would be for keeps.

"Then I met Danny. Somehow I felt that — well, I couldn't be sure. But I did want to see him again and — on his own grounds, against his own background. It wouldn't do to measure him against my own.

"That's about all I can say, Mrs. Gray, Jerry," Judith said slowly. "And you, too, Danny. I'm not proposing to you. I didn't come down to — to throw myself at you. When you went to the Pacific, I thought . . . we thought . . . well, what did we think? Or did we?"

"Judy —" Danny began.

"Not now, Danny," the girl interrupted. The voice that people who wrote pieces about her described as throaty was now calm, almost detached. "And maybe never: we'll start from here — or maybe we'll stop where we are."

"You must stay with us," Polly Gray interposed quietly. "You must stay, until . . . ."

Judith Hale turned her quiet eyes directly toward the older woman as if seeing her for the first time. Her eyes, Jerry thought, were sort of misty. Danny sat in a daze, and his hand trembled when he reached out for his cup.

"Where'll everybody sleep, Mom?" Jerry demanded. "There's Judy and Grandma. The Sergeant, he's goin' to move over to the Station and visit with Bill Henry some."

"Isn't there a boarding house or hotel or something like that — or a house we could take?" Judith suggested.

"Can you cook, Judy?" Jerry asked.

"Not much, I'm afraid, but Augusta would dote on it. She loves it and she never gets a chance when we're at home."

Danny had recovered somewhat from the apparent state of shock that had settled over him while Judith, with numbing directness, was saying why she had come to the Outer Banks. She had not mentioned, Danny reflected, the letter she had

written, or that he had not answered it. He was relieved at
that. But she had given no least intimation that she proposed
to come. She had, rather casually, invited him to come to New
York. . . .

"What about those cottages on the hill above the Station,"
Danny asked with quickening energy. "Are any of them empty, Jerry?"

"Most all of 'em are empty," Jerry said. "Why don't you and
Judy go up and see if Maude White will let her have one of
'em? They're all furnished and everything except sheets for
the bed. Maybe Miss Maude or Mom could let you have
some."

"You could be very comfortable there, but I hate not to
have you here in the house with us," Polly Gray said.

"It would be better over there, don't you think, Mrs. Gray?"
Judith turned to Danny. "Could we go and see about it?"

"Sure," Danny agreed. He got up from the table. "Where's
the Sergeant, Jerry? How about taking him over to the Station? The Chief wanted him over there about something."

"Sure, I can take him. You goin' to use the car? We can
walk."

"There's mine," Judith suggested.

"You ought to see her, Danny!" Jerry exclaimed admiringly.
"There ain't ever been one like her on these Banks."

Danny's face clouded. . . . It wouldn't do, he thought, to
be riding around in a car like that — her car — especially if it
was so fancy. His own — their own — the one they had bought
in Norfolk, was not such a fine one, but it would do. He had
wanted a new one but there were none to be had. They bought
the best they could find, and both Danny and Polly were
appalled at the price they had paid for it. Danny wanted to
forget about a car, but his mother insisted that he needed it.

"We'll go in ours." Danny's voice was decisive. Jerry looked
at him wonderingly. It was not like Danny . . . anyhow, not
like he had been lately. He sounded like he might sound when

he was giving orders . . . like a major, maybe. Jerry looked at Judith. She was looking straight at Danny, and her eyes were wider than they had been. Maybe she had noticed it, too. . . .

"We'll go in yours, of course, Danny," she was saying, "but Jerry can use mine to take your Sergeant over to the Station. You drive, don't you, Jerry?"

"I can drive a jeep but I don't reckon I could navigate a craft like that one of yours," the boy said doubtfully.

"Of course you can. They all drive alike, and if they don't I'm sure you could solve any little puzzle that came up."

Jerry grinned self-consciously.

"Won't you call Augusta? She can help your mother here, Jerry. Or better still, you come along with us, Mrs. Gray, and let's leave the kitchen to Augusta. She'd love it, and she can feed the Sergeant when he's ready."

Polly Gray hesitated, began to protest that she couldn't leave her kitchen, that it was unthinkable to make a stranger wash dishes in a strange kitchen.

"Nonsense," Judith laughed. "She grew up in a kitchen in Ireland, and I think she bemoans the day she ever left it — especially when I've dragged her half the length of the country."

"Back the car out for me while I get my cap, will you, Jerry?" Danny said. "And if you drive her car, you be careful with it. Maybe you'd better walk."

"Don't think of walking, Jerry," the girl told him. "The car keys are in there with my gloves. And don't let Augusta put shoes on you, either — not until it's good and cold."

But when Judith and Danny drove away they were alone in the car; Polly Gray, nor any woman of the Woods, would ever leave her own house when there were guests in it, or when the men of it were gone. . . .

Chief Warrant Officer William Henry Ragland's voice rolled along the corridors of the Station; and when Seaman

Scarborough, cooling a midmorning cup of coffee in the galley, was able to pick out fragmentary syllables of his own name among the reverberations, he was sure that for once in his life anyhow his name had rattled the windows of a building. He set the cup down hastily and went through the door toward the Chief's office.

"Yes, Sir," he said, with what breath there was left in him, when he came to the door.

The Chief's arm swung in a wide gesture that ended with a finger pointed at the chair beside the desk.

"Sit," the Chief rumbled.

Seaman Scarborough sat down, his feet flat against the floor and his arms poised on the arms of the chair. It would be better to sit so — the Chief might, as unpredictably as he had ordered him to sit down, order him to get up again. "*Semper paratus*," the youth murmured under his breath. He smiled a little to himself, at his own secret, somewhat rueful jest. The Chief looked stonily at a sheaf of papers on his desk.

"You can read and write, can't you?" the Chief demanded.

"Yes, Sir," Seaman Scarborough said tentatively, as if he had considered that it might, presently, become expedient for him to deny that he had ever so much as learned his letters. The Chief was restless this morning.

Few of the Chief's next fifty-some words were completely coherent, and none of them were printable. When he stopped for a long breath his face was mildly purple. He stabbed the pile of papers with a forefinger.

"You see that, boy?"

"Yes, Sir."

"Paper work!"

"Yes, Sir."

"Two hundred and twelve — " the Chief here became unquotable for some sixty words — "pages of it, and that's just for one week."

"Yes, Sir."

"And do you see this instrument of misery and damnation here?" The Chief indicated a typewriter on a smaller desk against the wall.

"Yes, Sir."

"You're sort of crazy in the head, ain't you? All your folks have been for all the generations I've known 'em."

"I guess so, Sir," Scarborough said, again tentatively.

"No harm in 'em — and some of 'em were good surfmen," the Chief said, relenting a little. "But some of 'em read books," he went on accusingly.

"Yes, Sir."

"Well, me — I just wasn't made for it. It's drivin' me stark crazy. Like as not fifteen people could drown right out yonder and I'd not be able to do a thing about it because I'm behind with my paper work."

"Yes, Sir."

"It's comin' to the time of the year when I got to think some about what this outfit's for — or used to be. I got to get rid of this mess. Reckon you could take that thing there — " he accused the typewriter with a finger — "and this garbage here —" he indicated the stacked papers — "and take 'em off somewhere where you wouldn't be in a man's way and where I couldn't hear that —" he was extendedly unquotable about the typewriter — "and make some sort of sense out of 'em?"

"Yes, Sir."

"You can't be one bit wronger than I manage to get most of the time. You will make a godless mess of it, same as I do, and they'll send it all back here to be amended and corrected and improved. But they'll be educatin' you — not me. I just plain don't want no such education, and it might do you some good, years to come, if this whole damned Coast Guard don't choke to death on paper."

"Yes, Sir."

"Take 'em and get out of here. And when you work your way down through that mess there, if there is one sheet of paper left in this whole damned station and you can figure out how to do it, put down on that piece of paper that I want 'em to make you First Class. Now get the hell out of my sight."

"Yes, Sir."

"Somebody'll have to sign 'em, I reckon, but I don't want to see 'em. I can sign my name blindfolded, if somebody'll set my fingers on the place. You come in here and blindfold me when you have to. Git!"

"Yes, Sir."

Seaman Scarborough departed, burdened, but before he was halfway down the corridor the Chief's voice shook the windows again.

"Scarborough!"

"Yes, Sir?" Scarborough said from the door.

"Don't you get any notions in that damned skull that this gets you out of boat drill. There'll come a day when that damned typewriter you got there won't be good for a damned thing unless you made fast a line to it and dumped it over for an anchor. The oar, boy, the oar — that's what brings people out of yonder and don't you ever forget it."

"Yes, Sir."

Seaman Scarborough went away, and the Chief, with a relieved sigh, turned his gaze out the window. It was no day to be cooped up in a house. November sunlight lay bright along the tops of the low pines, and beyond them the sea sparkled like . . . like a woman's eyes when she is laughing. It was past ten o'clock, the Chief knew without glancing at the ship's clock on the wall above his desk, and time for Danny and that Sergeant to be showing up if they were coming.

The Chief was by no means sure that Dragonnetti would come. He heaped anathema upon himself silently for having allowed himself the moment of weak-kneed curiosity, as he now considered it, about things that did not, in any remotest particular, concern him. Unless, he reflected, it might somehow work to the disadvantage, or the unhappiness, of Dan Gray's boys . . . his boys. Why couldn't the fellow, once gone, stay gone? And if he had to come back, why didn't he come back aboveboard and in the open? The Chief stared moodily out the window. . . .

After a while his eyes narrowed. Down the road, where it wound crookedly through the low-growing pines, the sunlight caught something that gleamed, something that moved, disappearing and reappearing through the dense growth. He watched it stolidly, and when the green convertible came clearly into range no muscle in his heavy face moved. His eyes followed it, nearer, until it moved past the corner of the Station toward the parking area at the side of the building.

He had not moved and he did not make immediate response when Jerry and the Sergeant appeared at the door. He ignored the presence of the man in uniform and fixed Jerry with a cold glare, halting the boy in mid-flight of a tumbling ecstasy of words about the car.

"I saw it," he said grimly.

"It belongs to —"

"Don't I know it? Think I keep my head buried under a stack of papers all the time? Every man between here and Oregon Inlet past teething age, and most of them that's lost their teeth forever — they been whickerin' like a stud pony ever since daylight about 'em. Didn't I have to send out a patrol to follow 'em in here? Think I don't know what goes on along this beach?"

Crestfallen, Jerry was silent, with a hurt, questioning look in his eyes. He glanced uneasily at the Sergeant. He wondered if Bill Henry was never going to say anything to him. This was not like the Chief.

"Ain't you feelin' good, Chief?" he asked, puzzled. "You sick or somethin'?"

"Sick!" the big man exploded. "Yeah, I'm sick — dying. Dying of what you might call paper fever, among other things."

"What sort of fever's that, Chief?" the boy said placatingly, but with a note of apprehension. The Chief ignored him and returned to his contemplation of the world outside the window. After a while he spoke, but over his shoulder, without looking around. The Sergeant had dropped into a chair near the door. Jerry stood, leaning against the door.

"You're ignorant, Jerry," the Chief said. The boy waited, wondering what else would be coming.

"Yes, Sir," he said, tentatively.

"I could launch a boat in the surf before I could read or write my own name," the Chief went on ruminatively. "But it's got so now when there's anything to be done you've got to take an oar in one hand and a God-damned book in the other, and if you can't manage 'em both at one time you put down the oar."

"Yes, Sir," Jerry said.

"You've got to have book-learnin' now. You ever read a book, Jerry?"

"Yes, Sir, I reckon I have," the boy said doubtfully. "Part of one, anyhow."

"Got any idea what it was about?"

"Don't know as I have, specially," Jerry said, mystified. "It was some sort of poetry. Had in it about some marshes — 'bout the tide comin' in on 'em. Some of it wasn't so bad. I can remember some of it — about marsh grass sendin' down roots. Want to hear some of it?"

"I don't," the Chief said somberly. He looked around at the boy, fixing him with a stern glare. He spoke slowly, somehow reluctantly. "Jerry, you've got to go to school. Monday."

The boy's face slowly took on a stricken, horrified look. He stared at the Chief, unbelieving. . . . He'll bust out in a grin in a minute, Jerry thought. . . . The Chief's face remained stern.

"This — this here's Saturday," Jerry said dully, and then, more eagerly, "and goosin' season's just comin' in."

"Monday," the Chief repeated grimly. Then he smiled, thinly, as if he were ashamed of himself. He went on, almost gently.

"That's how it is, Jerry. You got to have book-learnin' in this outfit now." His voice rose to a half roar. "And I'm goin' to make a surfman out of you if I have to drown you, if I have to crack that damned thick skull of yours and stuff books inside it with my naked hands. Now get out of here. Get back to that damned sex-wagon you're drivin'. Take it down to the beach and see if it can take a sea any better'n that damned horse. Git!"

After the boy was gone the Chief returned to his gloomy contemplation of the bright world outside the window. The Sergeant, who had got to his feet when Jerry went out, stood, waiting. Once he turned as if to follow the boy down the corridor and out of doors but he turned back, indecisive. Finally the Chief spoke two words against his thick hand, flattened across the lower half of his face. An elbow rested on the arm of the chair and the big man was half slumped against its back. "Sit down," he repeated.

"I'd be a damned sight easier in my mind if I'd kept my damned nose out of your business," he went on wearily. He continued his contemplation of the crisp, sun-lighted world beyond the window.

"That's — that's all right, Mr. Ragland," the Sergeant said. "I laid myself open for it."

"That's not the point," the Chief said gloomily. "The point is that I put in an oar where there was no need for me to do it, no excuse that I can see. This here's a free country. I used to tell my first wife there's enough ways to do a thing for everybody to have a way of his own. If that's the way you want to come home — well, that's your way of doin' it."

"Home." The Sergeant's voice was half bitter, half musing.

"I've thought a lot about you," the big man went on, almost as if he were speaking to himself. "I knew your daddy and I used to know your mammy. All of us got married about the same time. She used to hate that ocean yonder. She was afraid of it."

"I guess she was," the Sergeant said dully.

"Most of these women here in the Woods are afraid of it, and they hate it — takes their men away from 'em. Polly Gray never seemed to do either one. She didn't hate it, and she didn't fear it; but it took her man, just the same. You're scared of it, too, ain't you — what do you want me to call you?"

"It doesn't make any difference — anything you like. Jesse, if that's how you remember me."

"I've always thought your daddy did the best he knew when he took you away from here, but it didn't settle anything. You knew he was dead, didn't you?"

"No, I hadn't heard." The Sergeant's voice betrayed no feeling.

"Somewhere in the Atlantic. Torpedo. But you got off to a bad start, and no fault of your own. You've done pretty well, and I'm damned proud of you."

The Sergeant waited, his face flushed slightly . . . pleased.

"But what now?" the Chief went on. "I don't know as I've got any right to ask you that but . . . since Dan Gray got butchered by them damned swine out there, I've felt like his two boys were mine. Does all this touch Danny anywhere? Is it likely to bother him? It's already touched the other one, but nothin' bothers him."

"I — I hadn't thought about that."

"Is there anything wrong — anything that's not natural — the way you feel about Danny?" The Chief's voice was cold, grim.

The Sergeant's face went white, and then dull red in anger. His hands clenched and he started slowly out of his chair. His eyes smouldered and for a moment the massive man at the desk wondered if he had hit too hard . . . maybe too low. The

Sergeant sat back in his chair and his eyes met Ragland's evenly.

"No," he said simply.

"I wanted to know," the Chief went on. "I am an ignorant man and the only way I know to find out about things is to ask. But there are some things I know without asking. One of them is when a man is lying to me." The Chief's face warmed with a sudden grin. "I'm obliged to you for not tryin' to knock some sense into my damned head with your fists, Jesse."

Both men were quiet for a time. Then the Sergeant, with long gaps between sentences and sometimes abandoning sentences altogether when he was half through them, began to retrace the years. He came back to the day Mrs. Grady had, salvaged his adolescence.

"You know, Mr. Ragland," the Sergeant said wonderingly, "when she didn't recognize me that night I thought nobody in the world would ever know me. And then, in less than an hour when I was standing up there, it all just sort of slid out of me . . . onto that boy."

"Go on — if there's any more you want to tell me."

"There isn't much more. There isn't any more to tell, I guess. Major Gray — Danny — was — he *is* the best skipper I've had in all the years I've been in the air. There have been times when I don't believe any other pilot could have brought us out, but they never turned a hair on his head. Every man on the ship worshiped him, sort of, young as he was."

"He's a good boy," the Chief said, "but I don't know as I understand him like . . . well, not like I do that Jerry."

"They're a lot alike," the Sergeant said.

"In a lot of ways Jerry is older than Danny. But maybe that's because he's been around here so much while Danny was gone. He's — he's handy with an oar. But what now? What about you?"

"I don't know," the Sergeant said. "I've never put down

any roots anywhere. Since Mr. Dragonnetti died I've been on my own in the Army. When I got furloughs I didn't have anywhere to go. Mostly I'd save up my money and take a trip somewhere . . . mostly to where there were more airplanes, and stay as long as my furlough lasted, or my money."

"Women?"

"No, Sir. There have never been any. Somehow I've — I've always been afraid of them. I guess something must have died in me that day — when Mrs. Grady put overalls on me and cut my hair. I've never been around any. Danny's mother is the — it's the first time I ever had much of a notion what it would be like to have a mother."

"Your own mammy is up yonder in the Woods."

"Yes. I remember. I've tried for twenty years not to remember."

"You have a sister — born after you left."

"Yes, I saw her. She . . . almost made a pass at me."

Both men were silent for a lengthening interval.

"Would you — I think maybe it would make sense if you talked to Polly Gray some, Jesse. She's got sense. Jerry, damn him, gets a lot of whatever it is he's got from her."

"I've thought of that, but the more I think about the whole thing the more I believe the best thing is for me to go back . . . somewhere. I don't belong here."

"Maybe you don't," the Chief said musingly. He sat up with sudden energy. "Do you see them oaks up yonder on the top of them hills? They look like they might topple over with the first change of wind — but they got roots that go down through that sand and they've been standin' there ever since — well, some of 'em saw the Spaniards when they started wreckin' themselves out yonder four hundred years ago. They can't leave — they got roots. You can't leave — you got roots. No, nor Danny, neither. Your roots are here. Maybe they've got knots in 'em — scarred places on 'em — but they're down in the ground. Talk to Polly Gray."

"Yes, Sir," the Sergeant said humbly, "but I'm afraid it might —"

"Hell, ain't that Danny's car comin' yonder through them pines? I guess I don't see as well as I used to."

"Yes, Sir, I believe it is."

"Girl with him?"

"Yes, Sir."

Danny was turning into the last place at the far end of the parking line when the Chief and Sergeant Jesse Tillett Dragonnetti came through the entrance. The green and chromium convertible was at the opposite end of the line, with Jerry, disconsolate and brooding, seated on the railing against which the front bumpers of parked vehicles usually rested. He glanced up quickly and looked away when the Chief's glance crossed his. Danny and Judith got out of the sedan and started toward the entrance. The Chief appeared not to have seen them.

When they were almost within greeting distance of him the big man turned and walked, with measured deliberation, toward where Jerry was seated on the rail. When he came to him he reached out with both great hands, took the boy by his shoulders and pulled him upright. Jerry looked unhappily away. Then the Chief put both hands under the boy's armpits and lifted him until his feet were level with the top of the flat parking rail. He looked at him searchingly, his mouth grim. The boy looked past him, beyond his great shoulders.

"After we've eat dinner, Jerry," the Chief said casually, but loud enough to be heard as far away as the galley, "I want you to see if you can't borrow this here sex-wagon. I want to go ridin' in it, up and down the village. Here I've been a widower for goin' on four years and nary a female woman has so much as laid one little eye on me. Maybe if they was to see me ridin' in this contraption, maybe they'd — come on here and make me acquainted with this girl that's come to teach Danny some things me and you never got around to and ain't qualified for. We've neglected the hell out of him."

It was not exactly what Jerry had made up his mind to do or to say when he got the Chief's attention again — if he ever even bothered with him again — but his slightly pouting mouth relaxed. The shadows went out of his eyes. He grinned.

"Okay, Chief," he said. "She's a damned good girl. I think we're goin' to like her, whether Danny does or not. He's acted pretty dumb, so far."

23

THE FIVE COTTAGES ON THE CREST OF THE ANCHORED DUNE THAT
looks down upon the Point of Cape Hatteras were the residue
of the sometimes rudderless dreaming through which men
everywhere, in the mid-thirties, escaped from uninviting, sometimes intolerable, reality. So also were the pine and live oak,
the dogwood and yoepon, the nodding acres of browning sea
oats, now in the mid-forties beginning to cover the thousand
acres of flat sand that stretched away to the Point.

They were sturdily built, these cottages, as Judith Hale could
see when, with Danny, she came toward them along the road
that twisted itself into veritable knots, for no very obvious reason, past the area where there were still rusting vestiges of the
camp in which, a decade ago, rudderless youth had been mo-
bilized to do something about erosion on the Outer Banks.
They had, with painstaking and unhurried patience that was
possible in that decade, planted grass, planted trees.

And they had built, also, these houses. They were designed
as pleasure cabins where people with leisure and reasonable
means might come and stay while they fished in the surf off
the Point or, in season, while they tenanted the shooting
blinds that dotted the quiet waters of the Sound. The men
who occupied themselves with dreaming in the mid-thirties
had pictured here a sort of sportsman's haven.

Before the echoing roar of the first torpedo had ebbed into
a silence that was immediately ripped apart by the groans of
a ship in death agony, the men who dreamed and the youths

305

who planted and built had hurried away to battle. . . . Sometimes, when he looked out above the now wooded flats and to
the dune which these lads had anchored and upon which they
had built the five houses, the Chief wondered about these
dreamers . . . how many of them had died . . . and if, in the
evening, they might come back to brood above the hill they
had anchored, above the trees they had planted. . . .

When she came to the crest of the hill, where the houses
were and from which she could see the spreading land below
and the Point beyond, where the Two Oceans, even now, were
white with the froth of their immemorial wrestling, the girl
stopped, breathless. Maude White had said she might have
her choice of the houses, had recommended the second in
the line because it had two bedrooms and a comfortable living
room with a wide fireplace.

"This is perfect, Danny!" Judith exclaimed. "I never
dreamed there could be such a place — inside and out. Augusta will just have fits when she sees that little kitchen. When
can we move in?"

"I guess you've moved in already, if you like it," Danny
replied. "All you need now is to get some stuff from the store
and — well, that's all you need to do."

"Lovely," Judith bubbled.

"They took the electric light plant away during the war;
you'll have to do with oil lamps," Danny said. "It's a lot different from what you're used to."

"Lovely."

"It'll — you'll find it pretty rugged. There's no telephone,
and when you want something you get up and get it. There
aren't any buttons to push."

"I'm not bedridden, you know, Danny."

"And you may find it lonesome out here. The Station is
your nearest neighbor, yonder. It's nearly three miles up to
the village. Of course, the boys yonder at the Station can al-

ways see you from the tower, and if you need them, they'll come."

"How would they know whether I needed them, Danny — and what would I need them for?"

"Oh, nothing in particular," Danny said vaguely. "And the weather gets pretty rough around here from now until spring. You just can't ever tell what the weather will do next — except that, whatever it is, you won't be expecting just that."

"Don't overdo it, Danny," Judith said with a laugh. "I don't discourage very easily."

Danny's face reddened. "Oh, I didn't mean it that way — of course I didn't. I just wanted — the Chief, he'll look after you, and — and I'll come over if —"

"If, what, Danny?" Judith prompted.

"If you don't mind," Danny added lamely.

"I won't mind, Danny."

The girl was silent for a little and then she went on. "But let's not be less than frank, Danny. Don't you ever feel that you have to come, or that I'm sitting here pining away for you. I'm not going to pursue you — not one inch — and I'll not compromise you or do anything foolish and terribly unmaidenly." She looked at him levelly, not smiling. "It seemed worth while to get acquainted with you — on your own grounds. But I've told you that."

They were standing on the little platform before the entrance. Danny turned now and looked at her, and it was as if he were seeing her for the first time. She was not looking at him but out across the wide reach of what men had planned to make into a park, toward the Point where, even at this distance, she could see little white geysers of froth leaping upward . . . as if they wanted to take hold of the sun with their hands and pull it down. . . .

Here it was that the two oceans met, the southern ocean sweeping up from the south and west and the northern ocean coming down, jubilant and confident on the shoulders of its own wind. They met yonder, the surf rolling in from opposed quarters, meeting at the Point. One breaker would, she could see from where she watched, smash almost at right angles against another rolling down from the northeast. . . .

Judith felt Danny's eyes searching her face, and without looking at him she knew that his hands, his arms, moved without his knowing it. . . . She could almost feel his hands take hold of her elbows . . . move upward toward her shoulders . . . and she knew that his face was flushed, shyly eager. She smiled and turned toward him; when she saw what was in his eyes she shook her head slowly. She touched his elbow with a light hand.

"Let's go, Danny," she said cheerfully. "Don't you suppose Jerry is still down there at the Station? Didn't we tell him we'd see him over there?"

"I guess we did, Judy," Danny said.

Leaving the door of the cottage open, they went down the slope toward the car. Danny's face wore a puzzled frown, but when he glanced at Judith, her answering smile was quiet . . . friendly, Danny thought.

"I think all of us were a little mad that week in San Francisco, Danny," she said presently. "Maybe hysterical would be a better way to put it."

Danny's step slowed and he started to speak, but it was Judith who went on, after a moment.

"I suppose everybody everywhere was a little mad then, as if they were grasping at something that they were afraid might be slipping out of reach forever. I guess we were a little delirious that week, too. I've tried so many times to recapture it, but it always eludes me."

"I used to think about it a lot, too, when we'd be flying, especially at night," Danny said. "I'd think so hard about it that it seemed to slip out of my hands . . . like a cake of wet soap when you hold on to it too hard."

"Do you remember that last night, Danny — when you kissed me?"

Danny's face reddened. "Sure."

"It was the first time I had ever been kissed . . . like that."

"What do you mean — like that?"

"You had never kissed a girl before, Danny. Now don't turn red like that, because —" Judith felt her own cheeks warmed by a deepening scarlet. "It was somehow the first time I'd ever — ever felt kissed. Of course there'd been — I'd been pawed and mauled and kissed — oh, you know, Danny — routine."

Judith's voice was not quite steady.

Danny stopped still in his tracks. He turned slowly toward the girl, a shy, uncertain smile on his lips. Judith stopped, too, and turned to face him.

"I think we're both just a pair of children, Danny," she said, a little breathless at her own discovery. "But," she added cheerfully, "maybe there'll be room for us to grow up down here — if it doesn't get too rugged." She glanced backward at the cottage at the top of the hill, gleaming white in the sunlight. "But isn't it time we went and found Jerry and Augusta? Isn't it marvelous how he calls her 'Grandma'? I think I'll adopt it when I break the news to her that she's got herself a kitchen to cook in."

Danny was about to agree without any enthusiasm. He was thinking how pleasant it was just to hear Judy talk, how softly warm her voice was when it trickled into his ears and went singing through his head, leaving a sort of glowing warmth in its wake, sending little tingling waves down his back. He was not thinking, actually. It was just something that he was aware of when another sound cut across his consciousness.

Far off, northward, muted in the distance and diffused by the unending roar of the surf pounding against mile after mile of the beach, the exhaust of engines and the beat of propellers came to them. Danny listened with an airman's intentness, forgetful for the moment of all else. The texture of the sound was not quite familiar; Danny's brow furrowed as he listened.

"Can't quite make out what it is," he said, half to himself.

"Could it be something like a Navy blimp? Don't they do a lot of patrolling down this way?"

Danny looked at her with quick surprise. "I didn't know you knew about airplanes," he said.

"How could I help it, unless I'd had my head unhooked from my shoulders and buried in the sand somewhere? Did I ever tell you, come to think of it, that I can even fly one, in a certain limited fashion? That is, I can stagger off the ground and flop back."

"You never did, Judy." Danny's voice was reproachful.

Judith laughed lightly and went toward the car. As they drove down toward the Station Danny's attention was divided, half on the girl beside him and half on the beat of the engines in whatever it was, up the beach and coming nearer. It was Judith who sighted the craft first.

"It's over there, just beyond the Lighthouse," she said casually. "I've never known whether they're of any use or not, but they do make a nice show, don't they, Danny?"

The dirigible was low above the surf, flying at scarcely half the height of the Lighthouse. Midday sunlight fell squarely on its blunt, bright nose. Its engines were at half-throttle and the big craft moved with slow, almost majestic leisure. It rolled lazily on the breast of the breeze that now, at midday, was dying out.

Danny turned the car into the short driveway that led from the road to the Station. The dirigible, with muted engines, moved slowly down the shore line to the Point, idled above it, and with a sudden spurt of power swung around and headed into the wind. Danny pulled into the space at the far end of the line of parked vehicles.

"Well, here we are," Danny said. "That's the Chief standing over there on the steps."

"They didn't skimp when they designed him, did they?" Judith observed when she saw the massive figure standing in his characteristic posture. He was looking above and past her, toward the dirigible now coming northward from the Point.

"They didn't," Danny said, getting out of the car. "Not in anything they put in him."

"He must be the God of the Mountain around here." Judith laughed.

"Don't! Wait until you've had a closer look at him, Judy," Danny said. His voice was tinged with impatience. Judith saw the man turn away from her, from the dirigible, from Danny, and move off in the opposite direction, as if he were deliberately ignoring her. A litte jet of resentment kindled in her eyes.

"Isn't he going to speak to us, Danny? Or is this the way they deal with intrusive females?" Judith stopped and stared at the deliberately turned back.

"I know it isn't that, Judy," Danny said, perplexed. "That wouldn't be like him — not at all. Just something else on his mind. Look at him."

Judith watched with mounting fascination while the Chief went down the line of parked vehicles to Jerry, picked him up by the shoulders as if he weighed no more than a baby, and stood him on the railing. As the Chief's rumbling voice came to her ears a smile began tugging at the corners of her lips.

Judith watched while Jerry's countenance lifted, brightened with its restored good humor. She was smiling when the massive man and the big, awkward boy came toward her. The Chief's eyes were smiling, too, and when they were a good six paces away Jerry started to say something, but whatever he was saying the girl was not ever to know.

Halfway between the Point and the Station the lumbering dirigible seemed scarcely to move against the faltering wind. Out of the sun came the screaming wail of an aircraft diving under the full power of its engine, its roar blotting out whatever words were forming on the boy's lips. Involuntarily Jerry looked up. Out of the corner of her eye Judith saw the face of the man in a sergeant's uniform grow suddenly tense.

Judith saw the clumsy dirigible shudder when the screaming black-winged fighter shrieked upward, climbing like a winged arrow. She heard the blimp's engines sputter under throttles shoved open suddenly. Its speed quickened, and in the same instant another fighter plummeted toward it. The dirigible's speed accelerated and it came toward them steadily while fighters cascaded out of the sun, screaming, diving, until it seemed inevitable that they would smash into the bulging walls of the craft. The whole earth seemed to rock under the impact of their screaming roar.

None of the group around the entrance of the Station attempted to say anything while the simulated battle raged just above them. The Sergeant, through habit become instinct, counted them off on his fingers, measured the interval between them. Danny's breathing seemed to suspend itself, and the Chief studied the sky grimly. Only Jerry regarded the scene with somewhat skeptical aloofness. The fighters climbed almost vertically until, for a moment, they looked like the tail of an enormous and invisible kite. The dirigible plodded along on an even keel, bland and unhurried.

Big Bill Henry Ragland wiped sweat from his forehead with the flattened palm of his hand, dried the palm against the flank of his trousers.

"Play-pretties," he said in an aside to Jerry. He turned to Judith. "Looks like everybody's too busy gapin' at them idiots to think of their manners, Ma'am," he said. "But anyhow, my name's Ragland."

Judith turned at the sound of the surprisingly soft, burry voice, turned slowly and looked up at the face of the man towering above her.

"I'm Judith Hale," she said.

Danny, flushing with embarrassment at his own preoccupied negligence, stammered, "This is Judy, Chief."

High above the Point the squadron of fighters had re-formed now and were moving in a wide-winged arrow. The arrow slanted down for a massed sweep toward the droning dirigible. They came low above the Station, in so tight a formation that their wing tips seemed to be interlocked. In a moment they were gone, climbing sharply beyond the dirigible and leveling off into the north.

After them came the lumbering bulk of a big Mariner, whose comparatively slow presence beyond the Point had, until now, passed unnoticed. The radioman, whose name always confounded the big man when he undertook to pronounce it, materialized silently at his elbow. The Chief glowered at him.

"That's one of ours, Chief," the radioman said, indicating the Mariner. "I just spoke to him. They've been out ninety miles to take a man off a tanker. Got appendicitis."

The Chief grunted skeptically and turned to contemplate the big ship with a band of yellow encircling the after part of its hull. Its wing pontoons were painted in the same color, which was repeated in a wide section of the wings.

"That's the first of them we've seen down here, Sir," the operator offered. "That color is the identification of Search and Rescue."

"Good color," the Chief grunted. He turned again toward Judith, and Jerry nudged him.

"There's somethin' else comin' down the beach, Chief," Jerry said, "but it don't sound like anything that's been flyin' around here before. You hear it?"

The Chief grumbled, cocked an ear northward. "What do you reckon they'll bring next, boy?"

"Maybe Danny knows," Jerry suggested, "or the Sergeant."

"She's tearin' up a lot of air for the speed she's makin' from the sound of her."

"Sounds like a helicopter, Mr. Ragland." The Sergeant spoke, trying to make himself sound unobtrusive.

The sound came in expanding volume. The group around the entrance turned expectantly toward the north, watching the sky line above the low, grass-studded dunes. It came, with a wide sweeping of its rotors, but with a certain confident assurance mitigating its ludicrous awkwardness. It was flying at an altitude that brought it level with the dome of the towering Lighthouse. It circled the Light, hovered above it, seeming to stand dead still.

The Chief watched it through narrowed eyelids. Jerry glanced around at the group, at Danny, whose face showed something between amused disdain and newly-born wonder; at the Sergeant, whose face was impassive. Judith was frankly astonished. Jerry wondered what had become of Iowa. He ought to be out here to see this gadget, he thought . . . joined up so's to get to fly one of the things.

This fugitive windmill, the Chief reflected, must belong to us, too, since it carried that yellow bellyband. He wondered grimly what next would be coming out of — out of nowhere. He watched the thing as it came nearer, saw it swing in a wide circle around the Station, moving no faster than a lively man could walk . . . as if whoever was flying it was deciding whether to risk a landing. . . .

Apparently the cumbersome craft had made up its mind; it narrowed its circle around the Station until, just above the open space at the end of the parking line, it stopped, with its rotors flailing the air. It hovered, and then it came slowly down until its landing gear almost touched the ground. Men came tumbling out of the Station, and in the tower the man on watch almost tumbled over the railing.

And then the thing settled definitely on the ground, its rotors whirling, its engine roaring. The Chief glanced around, saw virtually every man in his crew rushing toward the craft. His voice erupted in a mighty bellow that drowned the roar of the engine.

"Keep away from that thing," he roared. "Do every damned

one of you want it to chop your heads off — not that they are any use to you." There were fearful adjectives. The men stopped still in their tracks, watching the craft. The Chief went toward it. The whirling of the rotors diminished, the roar of the engine subsided into a truculent sputter, died altogether. Nobody in the areaway moved. Doors on each side of the cockpit opened and two life-jacketed figures got down, a little stiffly.

From where he was watching, Jerry was unable to tell much about who they were . . . whether the man might be an admiral . . . or what he was. Then a look of grudging amazement flitted over his face. He moved over and stood beside Danny.

"That's Hank Grady, Danny," he said eagerly. "You remember him — Mrs. Grady's boy!"

"Looks like nothing can happen anywhere without some boy from the Woods having a hand in it, eh Jerry?"

"Reckon it's okay to go and look at it, Danny?"

"Wait. Let's see what happens. No hurry."

Hank Grady stood back, looked away from the Chief and toward the other figure moving to where the massive man was standing just out of reach of the tip of the rotors. Jerry saw the Chief's back stiffen, his arm flex and then his hand snap up to the visor of his cap.

That was rare enough, the sight of the Chief actually saluting somebody, but what happened next was even more astonishing to Jerry. Instead of returning the salute the man just held out his hand. Jerry strained his ears to hear what was being said between them, and he was sure that the man was saying, "I'm Stewart Ross, Chief — how are you?" The stiffness went out of the Chief's back and he brought his hand down. The Grady boy relaxed, too, and Jerry could hear him when he said, "Hi, Chief — how's things?"

"Just in time to eat with us, Mr. Ross," the Chief was saying. He ignored the helicopter. "You come and eat with us. This varmint you got with you here — his mammy must have dinner about ready up yonder in the Woods. Didn't he tell you he come from here?"

"Yes, of course," the Lieutenant said easily. "Would you like to go eat with your mother, Grady? Can you send him over, Chief?"

"Scarborough!" The Chief's voice reverberated around the Station, and the red-headed seaman astonished the rest of the Station crew by breaking into a loose-jointed lope toward the group under the helicopter's rotors.

"Yes, Sir," Scarborough said, skidding to a halt.

"Take Grady over to his mammy's," the Chief said briefly. "When you want him back, Lieutenant?"

"We're in no great hurry — say two hours if you can put up with us that long."

"Two hours, Scarborough. Go back and get him."

Judith Hale was aware of a feeling of mild incredulity at the easy, definitely urbane informality of the Chief when he brought the Lieutenant forward. He managed the introductions without any flaw that she could detect. He mentioned, with gestures that relieved any of them of the effort of formal hand-shaking, the names of others among the crew of the Station hovering nearby. The Lieutenant saluted Danny smartly and Danny as smartly returned it. The Sergeant saluted. Jerry acknowledged the introduction with level-eyed composure and backed away.

"Dinner's ready," the Chief said briefly. Nobody, Judith noticed, had come to tell him that dinner was ready but, she thought, here dinner would be ready when that massive man said it would be ready and not when somebody came to tell him that it was so. . . .

"If I could wash my hands, please," the Lieutenant said.

"Iowa!" The Chief's voice rose.

"Yes, Sir," the youth said, detaching himself from the group beginning to dissolve into the building.

"Take the Lieutenant to my quarters. Get out clean towels."

During the little wait in the big common room of the Station while Ross went to wash his hands, Jerry made his way to the Chief's side.

"I could have took Grady out to his mammy's," he said in a low aside.

"I need you here," Judith heard the Chief say. "Looks like they're gangin' up on us, and us rowboat navigators got to stick together."

Somewhere inside the Station a ship's bell sounded musically and the group began moving toward the mess. Judith found herself wondering, watching the Chief with mounting curiosity. Outwardly he was big and ungainly — uncouth, even, she thought. But, as she watched him, indeed from the moment she had seen him turn his back on her and move off in the opposite direction, there had been a growing feeling that every move he made, even the lifting of an eyebrow, had some planned purpose behind it.

Judith watched him as he went down the length of the mess to his place at the head of the long table. His face was bland, not quite smiling, and his eyes, under their heavy brows, were cool ... amused. She wondered a little uneasily what would happen now. Where would she — Judith Hale — be asked — or told — to sit? And Danny? Would she, the only woman, sit at the big man's right ... or would Danny, ranking, sit there? Stewart Ross came, trailed by a rather breathless Iowa.

"Sit anywhere you like — Miss Hale, here."

Judith saw that he was indicating the seat at his left and looking directly at her. She moved toward her place. She saw, too, that the big man was standing half between his own place and the place on his right, with a hand on the back of each chair.

"Mr. Ross, next to Miss Hale, if you like."

Danny, with a disappointed look, hesitated. The Chief looked at him and nodded at the second place on his right.

His glance continued around the table where the men were gathered, waiting.

"Jerry." The Chief's voice was curt. Judith looked on curiously. The Chief's glance seemed literally to take the boy by the shoulders and lead him from the door at the far end of the table. His hand fell away from the chair at his right and he stood behind his own place. Jerry's hands came up on the back of the chair at the Chief's right and he stood, waiting. He glanced soberly at the big man and looked down at his plate. The Chief bowed his head and rumbled through the traditional grace of men of the sea. He pulled back his chair, and every other chair at the table was pulled back.

Judith found herself continuing to observe the scene with a surprising detachment, as if she were watching some sort of play, the plot of which had not been — perhaps would never be for her — clearly indicated. Beside her the Lieutenant went about the business of eating with a cool, accustomed unconcern. . . . He doesn't see that he's sitting in the midst of a little drama of some sort and that he could be a part of it, Judith thought. She was sure that it was not an obscure drama . . . that it was she who might be too dense to fathom it. . . .

Across the table Jerry was helping himself with bland, unconcerned composure. Danny was a little flushed and, Judith thought, resentful about something. . . . Could it be that he had become suddenly rank-conscious? The girl hoped not. The boy they called Iowa was next to Danny, but he was almost forgetting to eat. He was watching the Lieutenant as if he were beholding, after long denial, some brightening hope, some admirable wonder now becoming tangible. She could feel the Chief's eyes, probing, searching, cool, sardonic. He had ignored Jerry since he sat down. . . .

"You ever fly one of them things out there, Danny?" the Chief asked suddenly.

"No, Sir — that's the first one I've ever seen."

"You were in heavy bombardment, weren't you, Major?" Ross asked.

"Yes, we were," Danny said. He glanced down the table toward the Sergeant.

Afterward the talk around the table became more general. Danny asked, hesitantly at first, about the basic engineering of the helicopter, how flying one differed from flying a fixed-wing aircraft. The Lieutenant, increasingly, took the lead in the talk. He was very eager, almost pleadingly enthusiastic, Judith thought. He spoke of the versatility of the thing, of how it could hover above a given point, of how it could fly backward, sideways, forward. . . .

"We're prejudiced, of course," Ross went on, "but I think that eventually the helicopter will be used for a good many types of rescue work, especially from shore stations like this."

Judith looked at the Chief. His face was blandly impassive. She saw Jerry look up at him directly, saw an eyebrow lifted in question — a gesture, she was sure, the boy had learned by association. But the boy said nothing. All down the table there was an inquiring, an expectant silence. Maybe the Lieutenant had touched a hidden spring somewhere, Judith thought. The Lieutenant laid down his knife and fork and pushed his empty plate away.

"I'd like to give you a little ride down to the Point and back and up around the Lighthouse, Chief," he said pleasantly. He looked at Danny. "And you, too, Major, if you'd like to see how it feels. They have dual controls. All our HO's right now are for instruction, primarily."

Danny waited for the Chief to speak before he answered Ross. He turned expectantly toward the head of the table, and when the Chief, smiling blandly, shook his head, Danny said that he would like very much to have the experience. The Chief pushed his chair away from the table and rose.

"We'll see how your gas holds out, Lieutenant," the Chief

said. "Or your endurance — we've got plenty of gas. There's a young'un sittin' next to Major Gray there that joined this outfit because he saw a picture of your buggy on a poster in front of a post office out yonder in some corn patch somewhere. If anybody's entitled to a ride, it's him. Take him first."

Ross looked across the table.

"Oh, yes, you're the man who showed me the Chief's quarters. Yes, of course, Chief."

"How'd you know that, Chief?" the boy blurted. Judith Hale saw the boy's face turn red with humiliation at his own effrontery. The Chief grinned down at him.

"Anybody else, Chief? Any others of your men?" Ross inquired. "How about —" He nodded at Jerry.

"Him and me are the last surfmen on this beach," the Chief said mildly. "Leastways, I aim to make a surfman out of him and I don't know whether I ought to let you corrupt him. Want to fly in that damned windmill, Jerry?"

"I wouldn't mind it," Jerry said, "but I ain't — give my time to Iowa there — or Judy." He blushed.

So that's how it is . . . the old surfman and the new gadgeteer, Judith reflected. . . . That's the little drama I've been feeling in these bones, is it? She smiled warmly across at Jerry, who regarded her with a not very well simulated disinterest. She wondered if she would be taking sides. The Lieutenant turned to her with smiling composure, his eyes questioning. She shook her head, smiling.

"Can you let me have a man, Chief, until Grady gets back?" the Lieutenant said.

The Chief nodded at the boy they called Iowa. "Just as well start on him, Mr. Ross. He's got a plumb virgin mind, and you won't have to unlearn him anything before you start teachin' him."

24

WHEN SEAMAN SCARBOROUGH CALLED FROM OUTSIDE THE kitchen door that the Chief said to tell Polly Gray that her folks would not be home for dinner, Augusta McGarrah, involved in the compounding of a certain sauce which, she maintained, complemented the taste of every species of fish, uttered a series of disjointed clucks, launching them upon the warm air of the kitchen with small jerkings of her head.

"Madam," Augusta said, "must all this —" she waved a comprehensive spoon — "go to waste?"

"Oh, it will keep until supper," Polly Gray said mildly, "and please don't call me 'Madam.' I'm — it just —" She stopped with a helpless little laugh.

"Oh, excuse me, Mad — I mean Mrs. Gray," Augusta stammered. "It's just that I'm used . . . ." Her voice ebbed away into silence.

The two women regarded each other with shy detachment. Neither had, until now, ever encountered one quite like the other. Augusta, habituated in the role of a paid servant — she had no illusions about her place in the Hale household — could not help looking upon Polly Gray with that degree of circumspection, of awe, which was the due of any woman who was mistress of her own house.

Moreover, this was the mother of the boyish Major Gray who was, in so far as Augusta's troubled judgment served her, the object of Judith's — she floundered for a suitable word when she came to think of that part of it. She wasn't sure now

whether Judith was in love with him, or whether this was another in her recurrent series of adventures, none of which,
to be sure, had ever taken just this turn before.

It did not occur to Augusta to evaluate Polly Gray on the
basis of the outward simplicity of her life, her house. She was
mistress of a house, this house — and she was the mother of
Major Gray. And she was the mother, also, of that alarming
young man who called her "Grandma" and who would not
wear shoes. . . .

Except when she went away, as on her trip to Norfolk with
Danny, Polly Gray had never in her life seen a hired servant.
Nowhere in the Woods nor along the Outer Banks was there
any such thing as a paid cook, or a maid. Women did their
own work, and if, sometimes, they were overwhelmed by it or
were sick, one or another of the neighboring women came and
helped. There was no thought of doing it for pay, for any
reward except the instinctive assurance that the helped would,
in turn and at need, help. . . .

And although she had never seen a woman curtsy in all her
life, Polly Gray had not been unaware of Augusta's somewhat
awkward flexing of her knees when Jerry took thought of the
fact that, until he noticed her, the poor woman was being
wholly ignored. The girl, Polly Gray thought, had done it out
of sheer habit, and there was no conscious lack of considera-
tion in her behavior. . . . It's just the way she was raised, Polly
Gray thought.

When Danny and the girl were gone, and when Jerry had
hurried the Sergeant through his breakfast and into the resplendent car, Polly Gray had invited Augusta to come and sit
in the kitchen while she cleared away the breakfast and washed
the dishes. The woman had come, too meekly, Polly Gray
thought, but with a little air of independence, as if she could,
if she were so minded, decline as a matter of right.

But Augusta came to the kitchen. After Polly Gray put away

the little that was left from breakfast, she began to pile the dishes in the sink. It was then that Augusta bestirred herself, insisting that she be allowed to wash the dishes; that she, at least, be allowed to dry them.

"You must be tired by now, Madam," she said primly. "Let me do it all."

Augusta dried the dishes, and afterward she followed Polly Gray to her room. She looked admiringly at its simple neatness. There were troops of questions that Augusta wanted to ask as she watched the Major's mother put the room to rights, but she held back before the barrier of her consciousness of her own station. She sat down, not very happily and a little lonely, while Polly Gray went to the other rooms; here, she felt, was no place for her. She had never in her life been in a room occupied by men . . . not since she was a girl in Ireland, anyhow. She thought wistfully of her brothers. . . .

Neither woman, even by intimation, alluded to either of the young people who were uppermost in their thoughts. Polly Gray put aside persistent questions about Judith that kept crowding, elbowing their way, into her thoughts; and, just as rigorously, Augusta silenced herself but wished that she might, somehow, get this placid, untroubled woman started talking about her son. She began with Jerry, hoping that from that start Madam would expand into talk about the older boy, the Major. But Polly Gray remained silent.

When she had finished with the two bedrooms, Polly Gray looked at the ship's clock above the mantel and said that it was time that she started to get dinner. She didn't know just when to expect them all back, but she always tried to have dinner ready when they came in.

"Would you like to sit here?" she said to Augusta. "You must be tired after your trip down the beach. It always wears me out."

"I'd like to come and help you, Madam," Augusta said with

a show of briskness. "I'm used to work, though it's been a long time since I've had a chance to do much in the kitchen."

Polly Gray found the presence of another woman in the kitchen a little disconcerting; she was used to her boys, and to other boys of the neighborhood. They prowled through the kitchen whenever it suited them, did errands for her, and either of her boys could produce a meal without undue confusion. She spoke mildly of these things but was careful to omit any word that would give this strange woman who called her "Madam" any feeling of being unwelcome.

"Sounds a little strange to me — men cooking," Augusta said with a touch of asperity.

"Somehow it doesn't to us down here," Polly Gray said. "I guess it must be because most of them have seafaring blood in them. Men cook when they're aboard ship and when they are at the Station. Jerry is almost as good a cook as I am, but I'm afraid he learned it out there and not from me."

By degrees Augusta put off the feeling that she was out of place and, when Polly Gray brought the fish for broiling, old memories were stirring in her, recollection of things she had, a long time ago, known how to cook. She was suddenly nostalgically hungry for a kind of sauce that once she had known how to make. But she was, none the less, surprised at herself when she suddenly suggested, almost pleadingly, that she make it for the fish.

Such things had little part in the culinary economy of the Woods, but Polly Gray did not hesitate. The woman called off the items that she would need: some flour, some milk. . . . Polly Gray followed the inventory and presently Augusta stood between the table and the range. Polly Gray watched her covertly, noted a certain hesitant unfamiliarity in Augusta's movements, but the brew in the saucepan did smell nice.

Scarborough departed and the two women ate alone when dinner was ready. Mostly they ate in silence, with Augusta clucking now and then and saying that it was too bad the others were missing so fine a lunch. They were washing the dishes again when Jerry let himself in at the back door without a sound.

"Hi, Mom — hi, Grandma," he said.

"Why, Jerry!" his mother exclaimed. "Have you had your dinner?"

Jerry nodded. "Just thought I'd stop and see how you were comin' along. Got to go up to the store and get Hank Grady. Scarborough brought him in, but he's hopin' he'll get a chance to fly in that damned thing they've got out there and he didn't want to leave."

"Jerry!" Polly Gray said. "You'll shock —" She stopped, looked helplessly around her, realizing for the first time that she did not know Augusta's name.

"Who — Grandma?" Jerry grinned.

"What damned thing are you talking about, young man?" Augusta put in briskly.

"Helicopter," Jerry said imperturbably but with a certain disdainful indifference. "They got the house," he added irrelevantly. "Guess they'll come over and stock up with whatever there is at the store if they ever get through with gapin' at that thing."

"Is Danny going to fly it, Jerry?" Polly Gray inquired.

"Fly in it, I guess — he don't know how to fly it."

"Aren't you going to, Jerry?"

"Naw," he replied indifferently. He was silent for a little, and then, "Mom, I guess you better get my other pants fixed. I got to go to school Monday."

Polly Gray looked at her son for an unbelieving happy moment, but before she could find the words she wanted, the boy had opened the door and was gone. From the back yard he called, "Mom, I reckon Hank'll want to stop and speak to you — be back by here in about a minute." They heard the jeep get under way along the road toward the store. Silence pervaded the kitchen when the noise of the jeep dwindled beyond the rise of the road.

"I wonder —" Polly Gray said, half aloud, forgetful of the other woman. Augusta said nothing, waiting. She hoped that here, at last, had come a break in the armor of Polly Gray's quiet, undemanding aloofness.

"Hasn't he been in school?" Augusta asked after a while. Polly Gray shook her head slowly.

"Not this year," she said.

"He hadn't finished, had he?"

"No, he would have been — he will be in the tenth grade."

But before Augusta could consolidate and exploit the small foothold she felt she had gained, Hank Grady gangled unannounced through the back door. He was older than Jerry, younger than Danny, tall and blond and awkward. He still blushed, Polly Gray reflected, every time he opened his mouth to speak.

"Hi, Miss Polly — howdy do, Ma'am," Hank Grady said, blushing. "Just stopped to say hello — Jerry's takin' me back to the Station. Got to go before the Lieutenant goes off and leaves me. Gosh, don't Jerry grow, Miss Polly! Soon be time for him to join up. Good-bye!"

And before Polly Gray could get in a word he gangled back out the kitchen door. The two women got a fleeting glimpse of his shoulders as they lurched past the window toward the road. Polly Gray got up with sudden energy and set about cleaning the kitchen. Augusta McGarrah felt, unaccountably, very lonely and very old. She wished Judith would come back. Hank Grady's voice was outside the kitchen door.

"Say, Miss Polly — you be on the lookout. I'll get the Lieutenant to come by here so's you can see it. We're goin' to show it to Mother, too."

He was gone again and presently the sound of the jeep departing Stationward drifted back to the kitchen. . . . Augusta

McGarrah, still unaccountably, felt older than ever. Nobody had ever called her from outside a kitchen door . . . not in a long time . . . and then she would not hear. She wished that Judith would come back. . . .

As before, Augusta dried the dishes, this time in almost complete silence, broken now and then by some idle or inconsequential remark by one or the other. When they were finished with the dishes Polly Gray said that maybe they ought to get out in the yard; it wouldn't do to disappoint Hank, since he was so eager for them to see whatever it was. She would get her mending, Jerry's pants, and they would sit in the chairs outside.

Polly Gray dropped her work bag in a chair and made the rounds of her flower beds before she came to join Augusta.

"You have a beautiful lawn," Augusta said. Polly Gray nodded absently and opened her sewing bag. Presently she looked up, listening to the sound of an engine, below, beyond the hills at the far side of the marsh. She stood up, shading her eyes against the sunlight. Augusta stirred in her chair, wondering whether she ought to stand up. She was comfortable where she was, but . . . . She stood up.

There had been talk enough about aircraft, about this strange and somehow revolutionary thing, since she and Danny had come from Norfolk and found the Sergeant there, but Polly Gray could not help an incredulous exclamation when the ungainly thing came grinding across the marsh toward her. She wondered uneasily if there could be something wrong with it. The helicopter came over the marsh, hovered almost over her head. The door was open, Hank Grady leaned far out, and she could hear his voice even above the roar of the engine when he called down an exultant greeting.

She thought of the day when Danny had come back in that monstrous thing that was so submissively obedient to his slender hands, and her mind ran ahead to the store where another mother, she knew, was waiting, pride and anxiety, with their lights and shadows, across her eyes. Polly Gray went back to her chair. The sun, now that the wind had dropped to a lazy whisper, was warm across the marsh. . . .

Judith's face was radiant when, a few minutes later, she almost skipped down from the car when Danny brought it to a halt beside the palm hedge. She came across the lawn toward the two women, and Augusta thought she had never seen the girl when she was so radiant, so outside herself. She was half laughing, half smiling, and a sapphire merriness danced in her eyes.

"It's been wonderful, Mrs. Gray!" she exclaimed. "We have a house and, Augusta, I just can't wait to see you in that little kitchen with a smudge of flour on the end of your nose! And a fire going in that fireplace — is there somewhere we can buy some wood, Danny?"

Danny, coming more slowly up the slope, smiled uncertainly. "I don't know where it can be bought, but some can be had."

Judith dropped into one of the chairs. Her smiling glance roved across the marsh before them and to the hills beyond it. The five houses were too far away, hidden by the intervening hills, to be seen from where they sat. She went on to describe the house more in detail to Augusta, left off with that to speculate about what they must get at the store before they could set up housekeeping.

"Jerry and the Sergeant drove up to unload our things. Is there a telephone, Danny? I must call Father and let him know where we are. And there are — Augusta, we've got to make lists and lists of things. You are always good at lists. Hadn't we better get along to the store and see what we can get?"

Augusta got up and said she would find a pencil in her bag. Polly Gray followed her into the house. The resplendent convertible came along the road and drew up behind Danny's sedan. Jerry and the Sergeant got out. After an almost curtly brief word, the Sergeant continued toward the house. Jerry dropped down on the grass nearby and looked around. Surfman was coming sedately down the hill toward his master.

"Where's the Chief, Jerry?" Judith inquired lightly. "I thought you were booked to drive him through the village."

Jerry's grin was absent-minded, as if he had only half heard the girl. He stroked the cat's back gently and explored Surfman's chin with a finger. The Station jeep drew up behind the convertible and stopped. Iowa waved an arm in greeting but made no move to get out.

"What does he want, I wonder," Danny asked.

"Sergeant," Jerry said briefly.

"What goes on here?" Danny demanded.

The Sergeant came down the steps. He had his bag in his hand. Jerry got up from the grass, took the bag, and went down toward the road. The Sergeant came across to where Danny and Judith were.

"I — the Chief thought I'd better come over to the Station for a day or two, Major," he said, hesitantly. Danny protested that it was unnecessary. The Sergeant's face became a dark, immobile mask. Presently he went down to the road and got into the jeep. Jerry came back and again dropped down on the grass, rolled over face downward. His chin rested in his cupped hands.

"Where did the Chief get this idea from, Jerry?" Danny's voice was impatient.

"Dunno," Jerry said, "but the Sergeant'll be around."

Danny lapsed into irritated silence. Presently Judith exclaimed, with mock seriousness, "Danny, it's just occurred to me!"

"What occurred to you, Judy?"

"That Chief of yours has not said word one to me. No, I'm wrong: he said — let me count — four words."

"Four? What were they?"

"It was while you were taking your flight in that windmill.

330 sand roots

He asked me, and I quote, 'Can you fry meat?' "

Jerry's laugh erupted and as quickly subsided. Danny turned toward him with a puzzled look. Jerry rolled over on his back, his head resting on his hands. His grin vaguely reminded Judith of a gargoyle . . . if gargoyles were ever young and disarmingly boyish.

"What did he mean, Jerry? You seem to be the almost sole interpreter of the Oracle of the Mountain around here."

Jerry's eyes hardened when he looked at the girl, but the smile around the corners of his mouth did not change.

"What do you mean — 'Oracle of the Mountain'?"

"Oh, nothing, Jerry." She remembered Danny's quick defensiveness when she had used a similar term earlier, and she wished that she had not, a second thoughtless time, offended further. "It's — it's just that everything seems to revolve around him somehow. But why did he want to know if I could fry meat?"

"Just a sayin' of Bill Henry's — or part of it," Jerry said.

"But what does it mean? It's too delphic for me."

"What's 'delphic'?" Jerry parried.

"Oh, Jerry," Judith said with a little pout, "don't be difficult. What's the rest of it?"

"Bill Henry says there's two places for a woman," Jerry said calmly. "One of 'em is in bed and the other is a-fryin' of meat."

For the second time that day Danny's voice flamed in anger when he exclaimed "Jerry!" The girl's face went scarlet. She tried to cover her confusion with a little laugh. It didn't come off very well. Jerry contemplated them both imperturbably, met Danny's angry eyes steadily.

"She asked me, didn't she?" he demanded bluntly.

When neither of them answered him the boy sat up, his back toward them. Without leverage from his hands he got to his feet. Without a backward glance he went down toward the road. Surfman sat up on his haunches, followed him, his tail erect as an exclamation point. Danny and Judith watched the boy go in silence, neither looking at the other. Judith wondered if he were going to get into her car and drive off.

Without glancing at the convertible, or at the modest sedan in front of it, Jerry passed between them as if neither existed. He crossed the road toward the marsh. Now and then they could see the white of his sailor's cap bobbing above the brown heads of the foxtails. They heard his full-lipped whistle ring out, the answering whicker of the brown horse. He did not glance toward the house when, loosely astride the horse, he reached forward with his toe and yanked at the rein, setting the horse on course toward the beach — and the Station. Surfman rode sedately on his shoulder.

25

NOVEMBER WENT OUT, RIDING ON THE SHOULDERS OF A TEMPES-
tuous northeaster. It fled before arrows of sleet and before the
hard, derisive laughter of the north wind that brought December. The wind roared under the eaves of the cottage on the
rim of the hill above the Point, and Judith Hale snuggled
deeper into the depths of the big chair drawn up before the
hearth, where a fire of driftwood lifted an answering crackle
into the chimney's throat.

Augusta, worn out by a day of diligent wrestling with a
somewhat temperamental oil stove but content with the small
triumphs that she had wrested from it, had long since re-
paired to the bedroom whose outer corner pointed directly
into the west. Now and then Judith, half dreaming before the
fire, was conscious of the woman's snores. . . . She must remember to chide her gently about it in the morning. . . . But
the supper Augusta had contrived was wonderful.

Judith's eyelids drooped as she watched the fire, and a sort of
exulting laziness enveloped her. The blazing wood beyond the
hearth sent out smells that were at once stimulating and relaxing. There were pungent smells of strange woods, dry and long-
seasoned by the salt spray that had drenched them on the
beach. There was the smell of burning oak. Now and then
there were spurts of blue flame when the fire touched some
chemical of the sea deep hidden in the driftwood.

Where the wood had come from was still something of a
mystery to the girl. When she and Augusta had returned to

the cottage with boxes of things they had been able to find at the store, a fire was beginning to blaze on the hearth; and neatly stacked outside the front door there was a pile of firewood. There was oak, some of it gnarled and twisted. It must have come from some tree remotely old, but it was dry, seasoned and, Judith saw, not newly cut. At the other end of the stack there was driftwood, some of it cut from huge timbers that had once, obviously, been timbers of a perished ship.

Across the level ground before the cottage there were the wide tracks of what must have been a heavy vehicle, a truck, but where it had come from was more than Judith knew. She remembered that there had been mention of buying firewood for the house and that Danny had said he supposed some could be had. But he had gone with them to the store, had driven back with them to the cottage. Danny had not stayed to supper. Augusta had urged him to, but with some reservations of mind: she was not in any measure confident of her capacity to cope with the oil stove and with things that came in cans. . . .

Mrs. Grady, Judith reflected, had been awfully sweet about their not having ration books. She said they could have anything they needed of what she had and they could bring her the points for it when they got them . . . of course they had ration books at home? Judith was not sure; she had never had to concern herself about such things. Augusta chirped that of course they had ration books, or if they didn't they could get them. Judith would telephone that Miss Simmons. . . .

But it was to the neatly-stacked firewood outside, and to the fire going on the hearth, that Judith's speculative, grateful thoughts returned. Could it be that Jerry had contrived it, she wondered. He had not returned to the Gray house before they left for the store, nor when they stopped there again on the way out to the cottage. Judith had not seen him since, astride that horse, he had disappeared into the tunnel through the yoepon.

The next morning was spent idling around the house, with little excursions into the kitchen, where Augusta, with a smudge of soot across a flushed cheek, was so preoccupied with the challenge of the stove that she had little to say. Now and then she looked at Judith pointedly, and the girl knew that Augusta wished she would go off somewhere and leave her alone to cope with problems that were her own. Her look implied that she had enough on her hands without Judith's complicating presence.

Judith pulled on a bright sweater and set off along the trail that wound through the young pines. The sky was overcast, and the vane at the top of the flag tower at the Station, she saw, yawed uncertainly, not able to make up its mind which way to point its long spear. Judith left the trail and set off across the grassy flat toward the dyke that obscured any direct view of the open sea. Serried ranks of sea oats, now losing the shining brightness of their seed-heads, waved beckoningly along the dyke.

Coming to the dyke some distance below the Lighthouse, she went along its crest until she came to the ruins of an earlier tower, where scattered blocks of granite continued their testimony against the angers of mankind. Danny — or was it Jerry? — had mentioned that the first lighthouse was battered down by cannon fire in 1862. She climbed over the big boulders and sat down near the top of the ruin.

Today the sea was a gray-blue. Off to her right she could discern the endless rolling swells moving in on the Cape, crashing against hidden shoals, sending up geysers of white spray. Some distance down the beach a truck was parked a little way up from the break of the surf. Beyond the surf the thin sunlight glinted on the blades of wet oars. Judith got down from her perch on the ruins, and when she reached the flat beach she turned south toward the Point.

As she drew near the parked truck, Judith became conscious of the towering figure standing at the top of the dyke. He was perhaps twenty feet above the level of the beach. His feet were spread apart, and his flattened palms rested against his hips. . . . The Chief himself, in person, she murmured half derisively. She wondered if she should change course so as to bring herself in range of him or turn about and retrace her steps up the beach. She chose the middle course and continued directly down the beach, walking just out of reach of the thrusting fingers of the surf that hissed along the sand.

When she came to the parked truck she stopped, watching in mild fascination as the surfboat jockeyed into position to make the run for the beach. Something of the crew's tensity communicated itself to her when the boat was poised for an instant on the crest of a wave beginning its ultimate roll landward. She saw the rowers poised, waiting. Involuntarily she held her breath when the boat came crashing on the beach, when the crew went over the side and took her gunwales in their hands. The boat rode in and the surf gurgled backward under its keel. The crew let out a collective sigh that was part relief at a thing accomplished, part momentary exhaustion.

"Good morning, boys — that was —" Judith stopped, uncertain of herself, wondering what she could say that would not betray her as an ignorant, gushing female.

The crewmen glanced impersonally at her, at one another, their eyes finally settling on the cockswain. It was he who returned her good morning. Judith glanced over her shoulder toward the figure towering above the dyke, wondering if he might have moved downward toward her, toward the men grouped around the boat. He had not moved in any single muscle, in so far as she could tell. She noticed, as her glance came back down the sand, the impression of the tires of the parked truck.

"It must be to some of you I'm due a lot of thanks for that wood," she said, with an effort at friendliness. None of the crew moved; none seemed even to have heard her. "It must have been," she went on a little desperately, "some of you —

the tire tracks at the house were just like that." She pointed to the tire tracks in the sand.

"Chief sent the truck up there with a load of stuff from his place up in the Woods. That's all we know about it, Ma'am," the cockswain said. His tone was impersonal, casually indifferent. He turned back to the boat. "Let's try her again, boys." The crew took hold. The boat pivoted on the center of its keel, swung around with its bow seaward. Judith walked on, crestfallen. The massive figure on the dyke had not moved.

They had not been, the girl reflected perplexedly . . . hostile, or even shy. Detached, she kept thinking. She looked again toward the Chief, immobile as a piece of bronze against the sky. The sea oats nodded their heads around him, almost as if they were worshiping him, she thought exasperatedly. She went on toward the Point, stopping now and then to examine a bit of wreckage, a piece of driftwood, a strangely shaped bottle, or a shell brought up from the deep.

"So this is the celebrated Cape Hatteras," she said aloud to herself when she stood on the blunt tip of the point of sand thrust out into the very ribs of the ocean. Once — years ago it seemed now: it was just before the beginning of the war — she had stood at the rail of a cruise ship that was taking her and her father, and of course Augusta, on a six weeks' journey to South America. She had told herself, while a young deck officer was telling her about himself, that one day she would stand on the Cape itself and look seaward. . . . There had been, always, a sort of inevitability about it.

"So this is the fabled Cape," she repeated to herself as she stood there, sighting along its blunt nose. She wondered if, from there, she could pick up the Lightship. She remembered that they had passed it, and the young deck officer had taken her to the chart room to point it out to her. He had pointed out all the local phenomena, the Gulf Stream especially, which he said came closer to the continental United States here than anywhere. He was a very precise and earnest young deck officer, and Judith wondered idly if he had survived the war. It had been years since she'd thought of him; he had asked her to think of him, sometimes. . . . She thought of Danny, wondering a little why he had not come over this morning.

When she thought of Danny a little frown drew lines between her eyebrows. She didn't want, just then, to think of Danny. She wanted to think of this adventure of standing on the Point of Cape Hatteras, as she had promised herself a long time ago. She would think about that; she would remember all the things the young deck officer had told her, about the Cape, about himself. Danny could wait. . . .

But, vexingly enough, Danny would not wait. He kept edging his way into her thoughts, and she wondered if it could be because he was, somehow, a part of it, of this Cape. The trouble is, her thoughts ran on, he is somehow a diluted essence of . . . of whatever it is about this place. But not like that towering, preposterous man back there on the dyke . . . or like that preposterous, equally improbable boy who had barged in upon her awareness like — like a friendly puppy. And just as unself-consciously had withdrawn himself when she had, unwittingly, hurt him.

"I just don't seem to be able to get the hang of the ground rules," Judith told herself, and she flushed at the realization that she was talking to herself like somebody in a house for the detention of the mildly mad. "And," she added, still audibly, "I wonder if Danny knows them, or has forgotten them and is not quite sure whether he wants to remember them or not. At any rate, there's some sort of fighting going on inside him — about something . . . and I'm sure it isn't me. . . ."

Judith contemplated the roiling waters beyond the Point with a little absent, half-rueful smile. . . . Danny was the same Danny she had known — and thought she was in love with; but somehow changed, somehow suspended between this little world that centered here and that other world of his, that world of wings and death — and a certain sort of glory, too.

But he belonged, really, in neither of them; and until he regained his bearings, in one or the other, Judith thought, how could she tell whether they . . . or how could he know for sure, either?

The girl was not startled, not more than mildly surprised, when Danny's voice, cheerful and a little relieved, came to her from the crest of the dune at her back. When she turned, he was coming down the little slope, precipitately. His cap came off and, when he turned to her after retrieving it, he carried it in his hand. The wind tumbled his bright hair over his forehead.

"Gosh, you're some explorer, Judy," he said. "Mr. Ragland told me he saw you coming down this way."

"So he's Mr. Ragland this morning," Judith said, her tone mildly provocative.

"That's what you call a warrant officer, and it sounds better than 'God of the Mountain.' " His face, momentarily serious, brightened. "Car's back over the dyke there — want to ride back to the cottage?"

"Must we go, Danny? I've adored walking on the beach and sitting here exploring."

"So you do your exploring sitting down, eh, Judy? Good way to do it."

She told him about the young deck officer and all that he had told her about the terrors of the deep off Diamond Shoals.

"Ever since that time I've wanted to see what the Cape looked like, and if there were people back of it. Curious people with a life of their own as strange and apart — maybe as savage — as this ocean."

"I guess you do find us strange all right," Danny said, "and maybe you'll think we're savages, too."

"Don't be childish, Danny."

"Want to go and explore some more? We can walk west along this way. That's where they find coral."

"There's no hurry, Danny — I like it here," she replied. "Where's Jerry, and how is he?"

"He's gone to school," Danny said. "Or that's where he left home for."

She sensed a reluctance on Danny's part to say anything more. He moved uncomfortably under the directness of her eyes. Judith looked at her watch.

"I think I'll walk back, Danny. It will be hours before Augusta has lunch ready. She was waging a hand-to-hand combat with the stove when I deserted. But won't you come over to dinner — supper we'll call it down here?"

"Gosh, there's no need for you to do all your walking in one day! Save some of it for tomorrow," Danny protested. But Judith, with a little show of stubbornness, insisted that she would walk back and that Danny should get along to his dinner.

"See you this evening about six — or any time you can come," she said. She turned away from the Cape, westward along the beach. Danny watched her go and then, rather drearily, went back up the dyke. He stood there for some time watching the girl's easy, confident strides taking her farther away from him. He went slowly back to where he had left the car parked.

Lunch, as Judith confronted it when she returned to the cottage, was a somewhat dubious affair, but there was an aura of confidence glowing in Augusta's face: she had made headway with the stove. She chirped like a sparrow when Judith told her that Major Gray would come to supper if she thought she could manage.

"Of course I can manage," Augusta chirped. "But what about the other one? Why didn't you ask him — the one that doesn't wear shoes and calls me 'Grandma'?"

"Oh, Jerry? I haven't seen him today."

After supper, which turned out even better than anybody

had hoped, Augusta made firm noises in the little kitchen, as if by sheer weight of determination she would intimidate the stove into obedience. When the last plate was back in the dish closet she refueled the tanks of the stove. Danny and Judith had pulled their chairs up before the hearth and neither seemed aware of her presence. She went to her own room, a small conspiratorial smile hovering about her thin lips. She came out again, crossed the room on tiptoe, and set a little stand between the two chairs. She laid an unopened pack of cigarettes on it, with matches and a huge clamshell for an ashtray. She went away without a word.

"If you just knew Augusta," Judith observed, "you'd know that's her most definite gesture of utter happiness and contentment with things as they are — or as they appear to be."

"She's pretty wonderful," Danny said.

Danny brought an oak log from the stack outside the door and laid it on the fire. Little ejaculatory spurts of flame welcomed it, fed themselves on it. The juniper-paneled room glowed with the warmth of the fire. Little shafts of glowing light from the flames played in the ruddy shadows of Judith's hair as she leaned lazily backward. Her wrists lay, inert, along the arms of the chair, and smoke from a loosely held cigarette spiraled upward.

Their talk was desultory, coming in little spurts of interest, feeding on some transient thought that touched the awareness of one or the other fleetingly. It ebbed away into pools of tranquil silence. There were things that Judith would have liked to talk about: things like Jerry, the Chief, the strange, apparently simple texture of life in the Woods and in the villages along the Outer Banks.

Very keenly she wished that they might talk about the towering figure that had, that morning, stood immobile at the top of the dyke. Ever since she had passed him there the feeling had been growing upon Judith that there was something symbolic in the thing that she had seen. It haunted her. It was as if he had stood there challenging the ocean to come, daring it to lay its hands upon any who ventured that way. It was, in a way, a grim picture, but heroic. Judith shivered slightly.

"Cold?" Danny's tone was solicitous. Judith shook her head, silent. Danny had half started from his chair as if to mend the fire.

Without looking directly at him Judith knew that when he settled back in his chair, Danny's hand, not quite relaxed along the arm of his chair, was closer to her own. She did not draw back her hand. She looked at it as if it might be detached from her, as if it might be another's hand. And she knew that after a little, when he had worked himself up a little more, his hand would touch hers. Hesitantly at first, then more confidently. She wondered how long it would take him to make up his mind to undertake the venture. Strange, how shy, how diffident he was . . . how like a little boy.

Judith knew when Danny lighted a cigarette with sudden energy that it was what the papers during the war called a covering movement. When his hand came back his fingers closed around hers with a convulsive little pressure. Judith did not encourage him with any responsive pressure of her own fingers, nor did she draw away her hand. She let it lie in his, warm, soft . . . friendly.

"I can't be that way about him after all," she mused to herself, "or I'd be all a-twitter at the first touch of his hand. But he is nice. . . ."

After a while Danny sent his cigarette in a shallow trajectory into the glowing fire. Little flames snapped at it hungrily, and for an instant the room was bright with its blaze. Then Danny took her hand in both his own, leaning over the arm of his chair. She could feel his eyes searching her face, eagerly, hungrily. One hand went gently, shyly, up her wrist. Judith let her fingers close lightly around one of his thumbs. She looked steadily into the glowing fire. Neither of them said anything. After a while she moved her wrist, looked at her watch. It was later than she had thought.

Danny came back the next day, and the next. Sometimes they walked on the beach, down to the Point; and sometimes, when the sun was warm, they sat in deck chairs outside the cottage door and looked out lazily across the flat toward the ocean. Sometimes they talked, animatedly or idly; and sometimes Danny held her hand. Sometimes they walked along the long rim of the ridge, past the Open Ponds where the eagles fished. Sometimes they sighted a deer as it flashed beyond a low hill. Once Judith knew that Danny had steeled himself for the venture of a kiss. . . . But not yet. Maybe never.

The days became a week. Judith had not seen Jerry since that day when he had gone down the hill and into the marsh to reappear a little while later astride his horse. Danny spoke little of him, when she asked, and then she did not ask again. On Saturday morning she walked alone along the beach, wondering if again she would catch sight of the towering lone figure looking down from the height of the dyke. The crew was at boat drill. Judith caught sight of the splotch of color among the shirts tossed on the sand, but she could not make out which was Jerry among the eight oarsmen offshore. . . . None of them glanced in her direction. She waited until the boat was almost back on the beach . . . but she could feel the grim thrust of the massive man's eyes between her shoulders. She moved away.

It was not wholly by accident one afternoon that Judith overtook Jerry as he walked homeward from school along the rutted road. She had been to the post office to get off the tardily written letters that her father had demanded when, finally, she telephoned him. She had stopped at the store with a list of things that Augusta needed in her adored kitchen. She had visited, and very pleasantly she realized afterward, with Mrs. Grady.

Children came trooping into the store and Judith knew that all of them must be, by now, on the way home from school. She said good-bye to Mrs. Grady, nodded casually to the girl that Mrs. Grady had introduced as Sally Tillett, and went out toward the car. Some of the children were looking at it in unabashed wonder, and when she got under the steering wheel she was sure some of them would ask her for a ride. She did not look directly at them, but she was far from admitting, or even consciously realizing, that she wanted no company.

Actually she was thinking about the strange way that girl had looked at her when Mrs. Grady introduced them. But for the look in her eyes, broodingly hostile but somehow half-ashamed, she would not have thought a second time about the girl beyond deciding with impatience that somebody ought to tell her a thing or two about how to use her make-up. . . . It shouldn't be done with a trowel. . . . The girl's mouth was a vivid slash that made Judith shudder inwardly with a feeling of revulsion.

Not until she topped the rise in the road did she glimpse Jerry. He was halfway down the slope, half hidden by the thick yoepon and myrtle, but she could see the tousled mop of his bright hair. He was bareheaded and Judith wondered what had become of the white sailor's cap. The sun caught the multihued plaid shirt across his shoulders. He was walking in the left rut of the road. His gait rolled slightly and Judith wondered if that was something that he had adopted from the Chief . . . or was it a part of his inheritance? She touched the horn button lightly.

"Give you a lift, Jerry?" she said when the car drew alongside him. She tried to make her voice sound casual, matter-of-fact, knowing the while that there was a nervous catch in her throat.

Jerry had stepped out of the rut, half turned to let the car pass. He had not looked around when he heard the horn, but now he looked at Judith calmly, with no light of recognition in his eyes. . . . As impersonal as those boys on the beach, Judith thought. Nor was there, she knew, anything of hostility in his glance. . . . It was just as if she were somebody he had never seen before.

"That's all right — I'll walk, thanks," Jerry said without any trace of feeling that Judith could detect. She knew that her face was reddening under his direct, impersonal glance. She avoided his eyes, her glance moving down to the thick book he carried negligently under his armpit. His hands were thrust deep down into his trouser pockets.

"Sorry, Jerry," Judith murmured. She let out the clutch and moved off down the slope. She glanced uneasily in the mirror at the top of the windshield: Jerry had resumed his walking. She looked intently into the glass, searching it, wondering if it must not conceal, somewhere, the boy's derisive, mocking smile.

When she came in sight of the Gray house she saw Danny. He was sitting on the front steps, idly. She wished she could hurry past, and she was about to go on as if she had not seen him. Danny got up, a pleased smile on his face. He called her name and started down the slope. She brought the car to a stop, waited. Her face was still flushed, troubled, when Danny came to the side of the car.

"What's the matter, Judy?" he demanded lightly. "You look like somebody'd pulled your nose or something."

"Jerry just refused to ride with me back there," she blurted and instantly wished that she could have the words back. Danny's face darkened.

"The unmannerly young whelp," he exploded.

"Don't, Danny — don't!" Judith's voice was low, troubled.

Danny leaned an elbow against the car and looked along the road. Jerry had come into sight, moving indolently, unconcernedly. Judith watched him in the mirror, wondering whether he would come down to the gate or cut across the yard through a gap in the hedge. He glanced casually in their direction, waved a casual hand at them, and went up the slope of the lawn. Surfman came down the slope to meet him, his tail stiffly erect.

Jerry picked up the cat in both hands, tossed him above his head, caught him nimbly and held him at arm's length. The wind was ruffling the boy's mop of bright hair. Judith could hear him as he greeted the cat, speaking to him as if he were a person. She was unable to distinguish the words at that distance. And then an irresponsible shift of the vagrant wind brought down a word. It was starkly, preposterously obscene but undeniably uttered in affection. It was as if the wind had taken the word in its fingers and tossed it in their faces. . . .

Danny's face went a dull red, the color of grim anger. His mouth set in a hard line and he turned toward the house irresolutely. Judith laid a gloved hand on his arm. The gesture seemed to crystallize Danny's purpose. He jerked away and started up the slope. Jerry's back was turned, his attention centered wholly in Surfman who, at that instant, was well above Jerry's head. Judith saw Danny's hand reach out and take hold of Jerry's shoulder roughly. Jerry spun around and Surfman plumped against the ground.

"Jerry!"

Danny's voice was choked with anger. He stood glaring at the boy. His hand, the left one, was still clutched in the folds of the bright shirt. Jerry started to grin but his face went suddenly immobile when he saw the look in Danny's eyes. Danny shook him roughly.

"Aw, Danny," Jerry said, moving his shoulder under Danny's grip.

Judith could not be sure, afterward, whether she screamed then: she hoped, without much confidence, that she did not. She saw Danny's hand, his right hand, come up, saw it flattened and ready. She heard it crack against Jerry's face. She saw the red flush start, and then the boy's face was deadly white, his eyes unbelieving, stricken. The boy stood still, as if life had suddenly gone out of him. Danny's left hand loosened on the boy's shoulder.

Not a single muscle anywhere in Jerry moved, save the muscles in his throat when he swallowed . . . hard. Judith was never quite able to believe what her eyes saw then. Without moving his eyes from their fixed intent upon Danny, Jerry, in an instant that was too brief for her eyes to measure, clenched his left hand, brought it upward against Danny's jaw. The arm came away, not dropping but moving, and hung, ready, at his side.

Danny reeled backward. His legs caught against the arm of one of the deck chairs and buckled. He sank down, slowly falling half across the chair. He tried to get up, shook his head jerkily. Then he went limp. Jerry stood, watching him until he went limp, for a moment longer. Judith wished that she could see his eyes . . . she was sure there was no hate in them, no anger. . . . Then he turned toward the house, picked up the cat, and went around toward the kitchen door. Judith sat numbly, unable to move. She slumped against the steering wheel. She closed her eyes and tears gnawed at their lids.

When she opened her eyes a moment later, Danny was sitting up, looking dazedly around him. One hand went to his jaw, exploring it. He looked muddily around, half rose from the chair, and slumped back in it. He put his face down into his hands, holding his head and swaying a little. After a while he opened his eyes and stood up. The convertible was gone.

26

WHEN THE WORLD AROUND HIM CEASED ITS DRUNKEN SPINNING,
Danny Gray sat down unsteadily in the deck chair against
which he had stumbled when he reeled backward from Jerry's
blow. He stared vacantly at the empty place where, a moment
ago — or could it have been hours ago, a lifetime ago? — the
convertible had been, where Judith Hale had been.

Although the world had ceased its drunken spinning, it was,
for Danny, a terribly desolate world, battered and blackened
like . . . . Danny thought of one of the places on the other side
of the earth, a place whose name he could not remember, but
there had not been much of it left after it had seemed to explode far beneath him, six miles beneath him, one morning
when the newly-risen sun was slanting across it. When he had
looked again the place was just not there. . . .

And now Judith was just not there. The green convertible
that had been there a moment ago — or a lifetime ago — was
gone, and as irretrievably as that place on the other side of
the earth. Danny had not seen her go, and he wondered, with
a little spurt of hope, if she could have gone before — before
anything happened. Maybe she had not seen him slap Jerry,
had not seen him reel backward. . . .

But no, she must have seen it. Danny remembered, now,
that her voice had come to him through the red mist that had
wrapped itself around him when he . . . . Danny closed his eyes,
tight, as if by that pretext he could shut out from his awareness
the ugly thing that, now, was beginning to come back with

stark, shaming reality. She must have seen it, every loathsome second of it. And now she was not there. . . .

Danny dragged his gaze away from the vacant place just beyond the palm hedge at the foot of the slope. He looked around slowly, his glance faltering unwillingly as it came around in an arc that would bring the house across his vision. Where was Jerry? Was he still standing there, up the slope behind him? And what would the boy's eyes say? What searing words would come out of his bewildered, unbelieving mouth? And had his mother seen . . . what had happened?

And if she had seen it, or if Jerry had told her, what would she think — but never say? Danny, eager to lay hold upon any straw to which he might cling in the desperation that settled deeper about him, knew that Jerry would not, now or ever, say anything to his mother or to any other soul, unless it would be the Chief. And Danny knew that, whatever things were in her thoughts, Polly Gray would not, now or ever, let any syllable cross the line of her lips. And that, when he had thought about it for a moment, would be the hardest thing to bear — harder, even, than the impact of that upswinging fist. . . .

After a while Danny glanced backward, up the slope and at the house, at each window of it and the door, wondering uneasily if his mother, or Jerry, might be looking out at him. The windows, the door, were vacant and there was no sign of Jerry anywhere. He listened. Now and then he could hear the sound of his mother's footsteps far back in the house where, he knew, she must be busy about supper. The thought of supper, of facing Jerry across the table, with their mother between them and from the chair that had been his father's — that he could not face, not now, not yet. . . .

Not until he had found something that he could say to Jerry could he face him. And what could he say? How could he tell him why he had behaved like that when he was not able even to begin to make it clear to himself? Now that his anger was gone he was, he thought perplexedly, not able to remember what it was that had kindled it. "Why did I slap him?" Danny muttered over and again to himself, and with each repetition the waters of humiliation rose about him.

Danny rubbed his chin ruefully. He found a tender area on the point of his jaw where Jerry's fist had caught him. "Gosh, that boy can hit," Danny murmured to himself, and with that thought there came a relaxing of the shamed tensity that goaded him. He even smiled a little when he considered the power of the slender, half-grown boy's fist.

"I got what was coming to me, I guess, but — but —" He almost wished that he had hit Jerry instead of slapping him. There's just something about slapping that can't ever be forgotten ... or forgiven. Danny remembered a teacher, a dreary, dehydrated spinster, who had, when he was very small, slapped him. ... He still hoped that she would stew in hell throughout eternity. ...

Jerry would probably let it go as if nothing had ever happened, say nothing; but Danny knew that, almost surely, he had killed something that could not ever be brought back to life. Jerry would go on as if nothing had happened, but he would be warily withdrawn, away from Danny and into himself. ...

Why had he done it? Why? — why? — why? Because he had said an obscene thing where Judith could hear it? Because he had, imaginably, been discourteous to her when he declined to ride with her? Because, the other afternoon, he had embarrassed her with his somehow jeering, but still innocently disingenuous bluntness? Or was it an accumulation of these things, of others like them? Or was it none of them?

Wearily Danny turned to the other horn of the dilemma. What would Judith, when he saw her again ... if he saw her again, say to him about slapping his brother? And no matter what she said, what would she think of him? Would what she said jibe with what she must be thinking? Would she be direct, and as blunt as Jerry could be? Or would she, without any word to him, just — just go back to where she came from and make an end of — of whatever it was, or had been, between them?

Or was there anything between them to put an end to? Of course she had come down here, with a frankness about her coming that had taken Danny completely off guard, off balance. Was she in love with him? Had she ever been in love with him? And if she had been, or might be, would she ever look at him again after she had seen him . . . like that?

Danny supposed wearily that she must be through with him, and he found himself suddenly dismayed by the realization. He knew, now that she was beyond his reach, that he wanted her — that he wanted her more than he had ever wanted . . . not like Sally Tillett that night, but . . . . . Well, it must be love, he thought helplessly.

"I don't guess I know what love is," he told himself audibly, "but this must be it." He remembered with what longing he had wanted just to touch her hand, to hold it, that night before the fire at the cottage. But now, of course, she would not see him again — ever. Nor would he, again, ever, touch her hand. . . .

A drop of rain flattened itself against the back of Danny's hand, lying inert along the arm of the deck chair. He glanced at the sky. Black, low-flying clouds were rolling unhurried from the direction of the Point. One of those squalls that are born with unpredictable suddenness in that triangle where the River in the Sea, the river that map-makers call the Gulf Stream, the North Ocean, and the South Ocean meet had made up and was rolling inland.

The drop of rain multiplied into a little flurry. Danny stood up and glanced uncertainly around at the house and down across the marsh. He saw that he had left the windows of the sedan open and, with a little sigh of relief that here was an excuse that would keep him, for the moment, away from the house, he went hurrying down the slope of the yard toward the car. He would close the windows before he went back to the house. By the time he reached the car, the rain was falling steadily. He got in and closed the windows. He lighted a cigarette, waiting until there was a lull in the downpour. He was without coat or cap.

Dusk thickened in the shadows of the live oaks and moved out into the road, slipping down across the marsh. Far off a wild goose honked, and above the marsh a disordered flight of geese circled and, with their wings upswept, settled down into the far edge of the lake of grass. There must be weather brewing, Danny thought, if these geese are coming in from the Sound for the night. He watched them dully through the rain-hazed window. The rain thickened.

Up the slope of the yard the newly-painted house became a white blur against the gathering dark. Danny could see the warm yellow light from the kitchen window slanting across the back yard. The front of the house was dark, its windows like black eyes looking down to the road. Danny felt a surge of uneasiness, as if he were being watched. It was raining too hard, now, to start up to the house. . . . After a while he leaned forward and turned the ignition key.

Just as well ride around a little before supper, Danny thought vaguely, and with a sudden access of relief he put the car into gear and went up the sloping road. He knew he was running away, postponing a dreadful moment when he would have to go back to the house and face Jerry . . . face Jerry's withdrawn, speculative — and inwardly contemptuous — smile and his mother's brooding but unquestioning eyes. He would see them when he came back. . . .

Beyond the slope of the rise, where he could look down upon the village hidden away in the Woods, the darkness was complete save for here and there a blurred light in one or another of the houses, where lamps were glowing. The Sound was a black pool that stretched westward into the blacker night. The car went smoothly, its tires silent in the soft, wet sand. Rain spattered against the windshield and against the windows. Lowering a window a little, Danny felt the air suddenly chill.

Danny drove down through the Woods, past the last house in the village, and through the dark, thick-growing pines that intervened before the sparser settlements were reached. Each of them was set around a little creek, estuaries of the larger Sound.... It was a relief to be alone, to be away from what he must face when he got back to the house. The effort needed to keep the car moving along the rutted road was, in itself, a relief from the tension gathering inside him. The car's flickering lights among the thick trees were somehow soothing.

Before he quite realized it, Danny was out of the Woods, past the last gnarled live oak that guards the westward entrance of the ten square miles of the forested area. Here the Sound and the ocean drew close together with scarcely a stone's throw of sand and naked dune separating them. The wind, with no tree to break its force, swirled the rain about the car, lashed now and then with a force that Danny could feel when the car swayed or answered the wheel sluggishly.

It was past suppertime now, Danny realized. He glanced at his watch. He told himself that he was not hungry anyway. He knew his mother wouldn't worry, that she wouldn't even wonder at his absence from supper.... Unless, of course, she had seen.... Danny put the thought out of his mind. He wondered whether it would be worth while to drive on to Hatteras village. He could see the glimmer of lights in some of the houses. He brought the car to a halt, irresolute. Presently he cut off the engine, flicked out the lights. It was comfortable, just sitting there, out of reach of — of things.

An hour passed without his being consciously aware of it until he looked at his watch again. Danny had lowered the window slightly and now and then the wind lashed his face with the sting of rain. He found it curiously soothing. In the dark, with the wind and the rain lashing against the car, he felt happily alone ... and secure against the distractions he had

left behind him . . . back there in the Woods. He was calm
now, as if the night and the wind and the rain wrapped him
away from vexation. He started the car.

When Danny turned the car around, the long finger of the
Light reached out to him across the Woods, flicked across the
rain-splashed windshield, moved along its unending sweep of
the horizon, measuring its beam on a ten-second interval . . .
six flashes to the minute, three hundred and sixty in the hour
. . . endlessly, through the night and until the sun was come
back out of the ocean. . . . He drove steadily toward the Light,
through the drenched, sleeping Woods. There were not many
lights in the houses now; even Mrs. Grady had put out the
lights in the store. There were no other cars along the road.

Danny came to the post office. Up the hill just beyond
and down the slope a little way would be the house . . . and
the thing that confronted him. He could not put off, now,
going back to the house, meeting Jerry face to face, meeting
his mother's brooding eyes — and, Danny realized, meeting
himself face to face. It was this latter thing that, now, dragged
at him. Danny thought that he might as well see if there was
any mail while he was here. It was not likely that Jerry had
been out in this weather.

By the glow of his headlights left burning Danny could see
that there was someone else who had come through the
mounting storm to see if there was any mail, a shadowy figure
at the other end of the flat panel into which the mailboxes
were set. Until she called his name Danny did not realize that
it was Sally Tillett. Her voice startled him when she spoke and
he drew back involuntarily toward the door. Since the night
he had carried her the memento he had brought from Tokyo,
Danny had scarcely seen the girl, and never alone. Once or
twice he had encountered her at the store, or along the road,
and had waved to her, or spoken casually.

Often — too often for his own comfort — she had been in
his mind, but Danny was somehow ashamed of the thoughts,

the impulses, that she prompted in him. Sometimes, when he thought of her, the marsh fire would surge through him and he would feel his face redden and his breath quicken in his throat until it seemed as if it would choke him. But when he saw her, something inside made him a little sick ... the way she smeared her mouth with that stuff, or the way she looked at him, from under lowered, darkened eyelids ... sideways. And when she spoke, her voice was husky, not like it was natural for girls in the Woods to speak. ...

But not now, not here in the gloom of the little space before the letter boxes. Her voice was clear, like it used to be, but with a note of sharpness in it. He could see the faint blur of her face above the dark of her coat and there were raindrops in her hair. She turned toward him from where she had been twirling the dials on one of the boxes. He wondered, uneasily, if she had been waiting for him.

"Danny!" Sally Tillett said again. Her voice was lower, almost whispering.

"Hi, Sally," Danny said. "What are you doing out a night like this?" His voice thinned out unsteadily.

The girl was silent for a little before she answered him. "I just came to see if there was any mail." Her voice was dull, listless. "There wasn't any," she added.

She took a step toward him, stopped. Danny could feel her eyes searching his face in the gloom. He shifted uneasily on his feet. He forgot that he had come to see if there was any mail for him, to see if there was anything that had come through about his assignment when his leave was up.

"Better let me take you home, Sally," Danny said after a pause. "It's raining like hell outside."

Sally Tillett appeared to ponder before she answered him.

"Would you mind, Danny?" she said after a while. Still her voice had nothing of — of that sultriness that had so amazed and discomfited him the night after he came back to the

Woods. She sounded like she used to sound when they were
— a long time ago.

Danny went ahead and opened the door of the car. The girl
ran down the steps and got in. She did not look at Danny
when he took a fold of her coat and thrust it inside before he
closed the door, nor when he opened the door on the other
side and got into the seat beside her. He put the car into gear,
backed it around and drove down the road through the
Woods.

By the glow of the hooded light on the instrument panel
Danny saw the girl's hands limply clasped in her lap, white
against the dark of her coat. He noticed that her fingernails
had lost the dark glitter of the polish she used. Her mouth —
she had left off the glaring lipstick. Danny remembered with
a twinge how Jerry had wiped the residue of that kiss away.
The dimples were not showing. One hand, the hand nearest
him, slid listlessly from her lap to the cushion beside her,
between them. . . .

Driving slowly with one hand, Danny let his other hand lie
on the cushion beside the girl's hand as he drove, let his hand
move, imperceptibly he thought, toward hers. Their hands
touched and Sally did not draw hers back. She made no response when Danny's closed over hers with a convulsive little
jerk. He pulled the hand toward him until it touched his thigh.
Still she seemed not to be conscious of it . . . even of his presence in the car. Danny glanced at her: she was staring through
the blurred windshield.

"Could we turn off here, Danny?" she said in a muffled
voice when they reached the side road that turned off toward
the little wharf where the fishermen serviced their boats, where
the mail boat used to come in. Danny glanced at her sharply,
disengaged his hand, and with both hands on the steering
wheel swung the car through the deep wet rut. He looked
straight ahead until they came to a little side road that swung

off to the left of the anchorage. He stopped the car, turned off the ignition and the lights.

"Is this where you wanted to go?"

Danny turned toward the girl in the dark. Outside, the wind rumbled among the trees back of them and slithered across the marsh at the edge of the Sound. The rain came down steadily. The girl sat silent, inert, beside him, and when Danny's hand explored the cushion between them, her hand was not there. He hesitated in momentary confusion, and then he felt her hand close over his own.

"Yes, this is where I wanted to come," she said quietly. "There is no other place, is there?"

Danny leaned toward her, clinging to her hand, with his other hand fumbling at her neck, and his fingers, hot and sweaty, sliding down her shoulder. He tried to draw her toward him, searching for her mouth with his. She pushed him away, gently.

"Not yet, Danny," she said.

Sally Tillett's voice was quiet, almost sad. Then she leaned against him, her head against his shoulder. Danny's arm went around her shoulders, drawing her toward him. Her hand went up to his throat, rested there for a little. His shirt was open at the throat, and Danny felt her fingers tugging gently at the second button, felt the button give and then her hand was against his breast. Danny felt a fleeting, irrelevant shame that she should know that he wore no undershirt. He held her other hand tightly, against his thigh.

"Danny," the girl murmured, her lips against his throat. Her hand across his naked breast pressed him closer to her. Danny knew that his breath was coming in loose gasps and that his hand, inside the collar of her coat, of her dress, was fumbling with foolish awkwardness. He laid his face against her damp hair and, releasing her hand, turned her face up to his. Her lips were cool against his own, clinging. She laid her head back against his shoulder with a sigh.

Danny held her tightly. After a while she stirred in his arms, drew away her hand from his breast. She sat up and without a word started to throw off her coat.

"It's too hot, Danny — and it may be in the way."

Danny wondered fleetingly at her studied composure. His own breath was panting and his pulse pounded in his ears. There was something calculated in her manner.

"Should we get in the back seat, Danny?"

"Sure," Danny said and he knew that his voice was traitorously insecure.

When they were on the back seat she asked him for a cigarette. He lighted it for her and the hands that held the match were unsteady. She seemed not to notice. She smoked, unhurriedly. Danny held her unoccupied hand in a tight grasp. He tried to draw her toward him, felt her body tense in resistance. After a while she lowered the window a little and dropped the cigarette into the rain.

"Are you surprised, Danny — shocked?" she said against his shoulder. Her hand was inside his shirt again. She had unfastened the third and fourth buttons. Her arm half encircled his body below the breast.

"No — no, of course not," Danny stammered.

"There had to be a first time for you, too, Danny," she murmured. And after a little she added, "And a last time for me."

"What do you mean, Sally?"

"Oh, nothing." The girl forced a little laugh. "This dress I've got on I made from that cloth — you brought me, Danny." She raised her head slightly and there was a note of irony, of bitterness in her voice. "It's buttoned down the front," she added. Danny felt his face burn and his fingers shook when he found the top button of the dress. The button came away. The pleated silk was soft under his fingers, her breasts cool.

The girl's fingers tugged at the buckle of his belt. Danny unbuttoned the dress to its hem, to the last button. The dress slid off her shoulders and he lifted her up. He threw the dress across the back of the seat in front of them and his arms crushed her to him. Her naked arms were around his shoulders and her lips were crushed against his in the dark.

After a while she put her hands on his shoulders and pushed him gently away. She reached for his shirt and found the cigarettes and the matches. She placed one between his lips and held the match for him. She leaned backward against the cushion. His arm was around her naked shoulders, his hand caressed her breasts.

"And now, Danny, you know." Her voice was low, a little sad, and dreamily content.

"Sally — you're — you —"

"I know what I am, Danny," Sally Tillett said slowly. "And now you know, among other things, what I am."

"Sally, you've got to listen to me!" Danny's voice was breathless, eager, pleading. He dropped his cigarette out the window and turned toward her. She pushed him away, gently, her hands lingering on his shoulders.

"No, Danny — not now. After a while, if you still want to." Her laugh began lightly, ended unsteadily, and she smoked in silence for a little. She put out her cigarette, leaned back, her hands clasped behind her neck.

"I am the first, Danny," she said presently.

"Well, what if you are? What of it?" Danny demanded.

"Nothing, Danny," Sally Tillett said evenly, but with a sort of wistfulness in her voice. "I guess I've always loved you, even when I was a little girl — only I didn't think about things like this . . . then."

"Talking can't change anything, Sally — let's skip it."

"No, Danny," Sally Tillett went on, "we can't skip things. I've tried. I don't know why things have turned out like they have. I don't blame anybody, not even myself. There were a lot — of them around after you left. You know how it's always been down there, in that house where I live. Well, it just happened. I guess I've been a slut."

Danny winced at the word. He tried to put his arms around her. He murmured protestingly.

"No, Danny — there's no use trying to fool myself. But I've always . . . when I'd let one or another of them have me, I'd be trying to make myself believe that it was you.

"It didn't work. The harder I tried to fool myself that way the more I would know that I'd never have you. Not all of you, anyway. I didn't know whether you even wanted me, like that. And now I know that I'm not worth having, except like this. That's all there is to it, Danny — you've let me have for a little while, this little while, something that I used to dream about. It's — well, I've had to rape you, Danny. And now I guess we'd as well put on our clothes and go home."

Danny put his arms around her and dragged her to him. He took her face in his hands, drawing her mouth toward his, and then he knew that her face was wet. He laid a finger across her eyes. He felt the tears seep through her lids.

"I — I'm sorry, Sally," Danny murmured, his voice choking. "Would you — will you marry me, Sally? Wouldn't that make everything all right? We could — you could go away with me. What happened while I was gone wouldn't matter."

"No, Danny, I couldn't do it. I couldn't let you do it. I'm not being what some of the boys I've let sleep with me call 'noble.' It just wouldn't work."

"But Sally!"

"No, Danny. I'd be bad for you, whether I went away with you or whether we stayed here. . . . Has Jerry talked to you about me?"

Danny was silent. The girl felt his hand relax its hold on her breasts, almost as if it had recoiled.

"So that's how it is, Danny." Her voice took on something of the stark artificiality that Danny remembered.

"Jerry despised me, not for what I am, but because he had some notion that I belonged to you; and that I was not, as these women in the Woods say, 'waiting for you.' I don't blame him, Danny. And, besides, there's this girl that's come to see you."

Sally Tillett reached out in the dark and without fumbling took hold of her dress where it lay across the back of the front seat and, with scarcely a motion, put it on. She buttoned it up, her fingers searching for a moment for the top button. She shook out her hair and reached for her coat.

His mind in a riot of confusion, Danny watched her dully. The girl took out a cigarette and by the flame of the match Danny realized, in sudden confused shame, that he was sitting there, next to naked, in the car with a girl who had all her clothes on. He felt Sally's cool smile flick his face. He fumbled into his clothes. He almost hated her.

She sure must have had a lot of practice putting on her clothes in the dark, Danny reflected bitterly. His confusion abated a little.

"Don't get out, Danny," Sally Tillett said casually when he brought the car to a halt before the house with the clematis sprawling across the front. The wind now tore at it and the rain beat dismally upon its limp leaves. Danny held the door, half opened, reaching across her. She laid a hand on his and looked into his face.

"You're not a virgin any more, Danny," she said, almost tenderly. "It has to happen to every man, sometime. You're nice and you're too good for me. Be a man, Danny, and make that girl — well, don't be a worse husband than she deserves."

"Aw, Sally, couldn't we — when can I —"

"You can't, Danny, if you were going to ask when we could have another round. I wanted you. I've had you. Now you are all hers."

"Don't say things —"

"We looked each other over up at the store," Sally went

on. "She didn't like me and I can't say that I'm so sold on her. But, when she smiled that superior smile of hers, Danny — well. . . . But Danny, don't you ever let anything come between you and Jerry again."

"How did you know, Sally?"

"I saw it, Danny," Sally Tillett said. "Or most of it. When she drove away from the store, I walked down that way, as far as the top of the hill. I could see. I saw — you and Jerry, and then she drove off. I was there in the shadow of that oak when you drove off. That's when I — laid my plans for — tonight. Good-bye, Danny."

Dazedly Danny watched the girl slip out of the car and run lightly through the rain and up the steps. He wondered if she would look around toward him when she opened the door, if he could see her face in the lamplight. The long finger of the Light flicked her shoulders as she went up the steps, and the raindrops glistened in her hair. The door closed behind her. She had not looked back.

27

AWAKENING TOWARD NOON, DANNY GRAY LAY FOR A WHILE with his arms crossed under his head, staring vacantly at the ceiling. The bed in the company room was unfamiliar, hard in comparison with the bed in the other room, the bed that he and Jerry had shared since Jerry was a little boy . . . the bed that his mother had bought for him when she had wanted, when his father had urged upon her, a blue silk dress.

This was the first time that Danny had ever slept in the company bed; and now, awakening in it brought back to him all the things that had happened yesterday, last night — things that had driven him, when he let himself into the house long past midnight, to hesitate before the closed door of the room that had been his since he could remember — his and Jerry's. And the door had been shut. Finally he had turned away from the door and gone into the other room. . . .

When he drove away from the house with the strange vine sprawling across its front, he went without any clear purpose. He knew he did not want, not yet, to go home. He drove aimlessly back up the road until he came to the turning where the road led down to the creek. Without conscious reason he turned, driving slowly through the pelting rain until he came to the place where the car had stood a little while ago. He stopped the engine and cut off the lights.

It was toward midnight, and the wind, veering, had begun to wane. It came now in fitful gusts; all passion was gone out of it. Danny lowered the window at his elbow and held out his hand. The rain, falling less steadily, was cool. He laid his head on the sill of the open window and let the rain fall upon his face. His face felt hot; he wondered if, somewhere, he had picked up some sort of fever. He closed his eyes, felt the raindrops pelting his eyelids gently. He rubbed the moisture away with his fingers, remembering that his fingers had been wet when they touched Sally's eyelids.

Why had she cried like that? And, Danny wondered, why did he feel, now, like he wanted, himself, to cry? And that, he told himself, was plain foolishness. What had he to cry about? He felt wonderful, and he wished that he had not let Sally go home, that he had her here with him right now. He would have his arms around her and his fingers would be tugging at the top button of her dress. And he would feel her slender cool hand inside his shirt and her lips against his throat, murmuring his name.

But something inside his throat hurt, almost choked him. And Danny wondered if he had caught a cold, being out in such weather, and if this was the beginning of a sore throat. But Danny knew that it was no physical malaise that made his throat hurt; he knew that something deep inside ached. He knew that he did not want to cry, but he knew that he was going to cry. He folded his arms on the sill of the open window, hid his face. He felt the wet of tears trickle around his arm; his shoulders shook.

After a while Danny's shoulders stopped their convulsive shaking. He began to feel ashamed of himself, ashamed that he, a major in the Army, a grown man, a man of — he put away the thought that began to form in his mind. He lifted his head and, clearing his eyes with the back of his hand, looked at the glowing dial of his watch. It was past midnight and he ought to be home. He would go home.

When he entered the house, Danny decided on the way home, he would go directly to his room — his and Jerry's room — and wake Jerry up and make things square with him. He would . . . well, he didn't know just what he would say — that would have to take care of itself. It *would* take care of itself. Jerry would understand what he wanted to say, even if he couldn't find the right words to say it.

But the door of the bedroom was shut. Danny could not remember that he had ever seen it so before, and in the moment of hesitation before the closed door another thought came to him. After he had squared things with Jerry, he would undress and get into bed and Jerry would be there, almost touching him when he lay down beside him. Jerry was an innocent child, even if his speech, too often, was soggy with obscenity and with stupendous blasphemy. They were words that had nothing to do with experience. Jerry was still, somehow, the little baby that he had, a long time ago, bathed.

He might even put his arm around my shoulder, like he used to do, Danny thought in a sudden uneasiness. . . . His arm would be . . . where hers was. Danny felt a sudden nausea simmering inside, deep down in his stomach; and he remembered the touch of Sally's hands on his naked breast, her lips against his throat. All of the things that had happened, down there beside the creek, came back to Danny and for a moment sent little shivers tingling along his arms, his legs, and spread out across his loins. He turned to the other bedroom. . . .

Danny's vacant gaze came down from the ceiling directly above his head. He looked around the room. His trousers were folded across the back of a chair, his shirt draped over them. He saw the buttons . . . the buttons with which Sally's fingers had toyed, loosening them. The shining belt buckle . . . all of the night came back to him. Danny went over it, detail by detail, and when he came to the last, when he knew that he had sat there almost stark naked in the presence of a woman clothed and calmly smoking, his face went a dull red.

Beyond the closed door of the room he heard his mother's quiet steps moving across the living room. He pulled the bedclothes up over his body and called out to her. She opened the door halfway, smiled calmly down at him. Danny felt his uneasiness stirring, and he wondered whether she would ask him where he had been so late at night, ask him why he had slept in the company room instead of his own bed. But Polly Gray had asked few questions in her life.

"I'll bring your bathrobe and slippers, Danny," she said mildly. She brought them, laying the robe across the foot of the bed and setting the slippers down where they would be within reach when he wanted them. She inquired if he had found the bed comfortable, was glad that he had slept in it. She did not mention the hour of his coming in.

"Where's Jerry?" Danny asked presently.

"He went to school," Polly Gray said. "I lighted the hot water heater if you want a bath while I'm fixing you some breakfast, but there's no hurry." She went out, closing the door behind her.

Danny went to the bathroom and shaved, scrubbed himself. He went to the other room and got fresh clothes and returned to the company room to dress. At breakfast his mother said that she had been thinking she would suggest that Danny take the other room, now that Jerry had grown to be such a big boy.

"He gets up so early, and he's always wondering if he might have waked you. He's at the awkward age," Polly Gray said.

"Maybe it would be better, Mama. Thanks a lot," Danny said uneasily, wondering how much his mother knew, wondering what she would think if she knew.

"If it wouldn't make too much work for you," he went on presently. "I guess I'll not be here so much longer — not for a while, anyway. I've got to get back and find out what they've got for me to do."

"I wish you didn't need to go back, Danny," Polly Gray said in her quiet way.

"My leave will soon be up, and — there's nothing for me to do here."

"How soon do you think you'll have to go, Danny?"

"Pretty soon, now. Maybe I ought to go along and kind of get my bearings."

"And leave Judith here?"

Danny's face flushed. "I don't guess she'd miss me — not now."

Polly Gray's meditative smile met his glance when he looked across the table at her. Danny did not want to talk about Judith, not now, or even to think about her.

"I guess I'll have to go on flying," Danny said, relieved at being able to shift the subject, to deflect it away from Judith. "It's the only trade I know, and I guess there won't be much demand for us now that they don't have anybody they want killed right away. I wish there was some way I could shift over to the Coast Guard and keep on in the air. What did you think of that helicopter the other day?"

Polly Gray said that it seemed like a wonderful thing from the one glimpse she had had of it when it came over. She added that Jerry had not seemed to think much of it, but then he was like Bill Henry — nothing would be of much use unless it had an oar. Across the table Danny watched her, listened with a feeling that he was not managing the talk very well. As soon as he got himself out of one untenable place he found himself in another: his leave expiring, seeing Judith again, and now Jerry. He finished his coffee and got up from the table.

Outside, the sky was overcast, gray, and the wind that came out of the northeast had an edge that cut naggingly. Danny said that he believed he would go out and stretch his legs, maybe walk over to the beach or down to the Station. He ought to see how the Sergeant was faring with the Chief since he moved out there.

Funny thing how that pair had taken to each other the past few days. He remembered his jesting proposal that he would stand them a mile apart and sit halfway between them and listen to them talk. Polly Gray smiled. She went with him as far as the front door and stood watching him as he swung off up the road toward the beach. Where the road began tunneling through the wall of yoepon he turned and looked back.

"Mama, tell Jerry the car keys are on the mantel in the living room if he wants to go anywhere when he comes from school," he called out.

Although it was past midday, the sky was unlighted by any glow of the sun beyond the low-hanging clouds. There was no wind, and the sea was leaden, listless. Long swells moved shoreward across its surface, spaced at unhurried, unpurposeful intervals. But they broke on the beach with a vengeful crack, sending long spurts of foaming water well up the beach. They looked, Danny thought as he watched them from the top of the dyke, like claws clutching at something.

Danny watched the sea absently for a while and then, yielding to a boyish impulse to see how far he could jump, catapulted himself in an arc toward the outer base of the dyke. He came down in a heap, loose sand flying over his uniform when his feet touched the earth. He got up, brushing off the sand from his shoulders, and was a little ashamed of himself for behaving like a child. He walked out on the beach and turned south, keeping well above the reach of the thrusting tide.

The beach was half obscured by a mist. The black-and-white spiraled striping of the Lighthouse a mile away was blurred and indistinct, and its crown, nearly two hundred feet above the tide, almost hidden in the thickening murk. He walked slowly, stopping now and then to pick up a curiously shaped shell, examine it abstractedly, and toss it toward the frothing surf. He waited until the object dropped into the water, and more than once he found himself just standing there, staring vacantly at the point where the shell had disappeared, where nothing was happening, perhaps had ever happened. Gulls crying their way through the mist looked at him with uncurious dispassion.

So engrossed was he with vacuity that he did not hear Judith Hale when she spoke to him. She had come out onto the beach along the trail that cut over the dyke at the Lighthouse. When she saw Danny standing there, face to the sea, submerged in his own thoughts — she could not know that he was not consciously thinking about anything — she hesitated, wondering for a moment whether she should turn back across the dyke without disturbing him.

I'll have to see him sometime, and it might as well be now, she decided. Their meeting again, after what had happened, might be easy, more simple if it happened on this neutral ground, unplanned, unforced. She went down the slope of the dyke, stopped a little way behind and to one side.

To the girl there was something forlorn about Danny as she looked at him standing there, not three paces from her, staring at nothing. His face was vacant, as his eyes must be, if she could see them. His shoulders drooped. She looked at the point of his chin, where Jerry's fist had cracked against it; she saw a faintly red splotch there. She wondered how badly it had hurt him, how deep and black some invisible wound might be.

"Well, Danny."

Judith tried to make her voice sound casual, detached, not unfriendly. She knew there was a telltale unsteadiness in it and she was glad when Danny did not hear her. She spoke again, this time more sure of herself.

Danny turned slowly toward her, unbelief in his eyes; not startled, but as if he were face to face with something that he had dreaded, that he would have avoided, but something that he knew, some time or other, he would have to face. Judith looked at him squarely and there was pity, compassion, in her eyes: compassion for one who, she knew, must be trying manfully to hide an inner turmoil, a thing compounded of shame, of bitter remorse, mixed with the dry, bitter ashes of dead anger. There was this in her eyes, and something more.

Danny's glance clung to hers for an instant and then he looked away, away at the leaden sea.

"Well, Judith," Danny said over his shoulder. His voice was lifeless, wearily resigned. Judith looked at him, unsmiling, but her eyes were tender. "Go ahead and say it, Judith — let's get it over with."

"Say what, Danny?"

"Say that I'm the yellowest heel you've ever seen in your life, and — you know what you want to say. Go on and say it."

Danny turned to face her squarely. His eyes smouldered and his face flamed. He seemed to have braced himself to hear what she was going to say to him. His hands clenched and his arms were crooked tensely. She could hear the hard, bitter ebbing and flowing of his breath.

"No, Danny," the girl said slowly. "You're not that."

"But — but you —"

Judith shook her head slowly. "No, Danny. Let's not talk about it — not just now."

"I'm leaving tomorrow."

Danny's voice exploded. It sounded almost like a swell smashing itself into foaming fragments on the beach. Judith looked at him calmly, her eyes questioning.

"Again, Danny — and so soon?"

"I've got to go sometime, and the sooner the better — now."

Judith's eyes were steadfast upon him, calm, questioning, troubled. After a while she spoke again.

"Couldn't we walk down to the Point, Danny? Don't say anything now. After a while, if you want to, we can talk, if there is anything that needs to be said."

"There's nothing to say, Judith. I'm just going away."

The girl turned toward the Point, and after a moment's indecision Danny followed her, walking apart. He looked doggedly away from her, outward across the leaden water. Judith walked with that effortless ease that was characteristic of her,

her long-limbed stride keeping pace with Danny's dogged plodding. Now and then he stole a glance in her direction; she was not looking at him but at a point somewhere ahead. He saw the mist forming little pearly beads in her ruddy hair. They walked in silence, past bits of wreckage that had once been ships, past the old, now disused station. They walked steadily, unhurried, apart; and each was somehow alone, aware of the wall that separated them. . . .

When they came to the rusting lifeboat, now half-buried in drifting sand but with the girdle of gaping holes still above the drift, Judith stopped.

"Let's catch our breath, Danny. I'm one of these weak-legged town women who can't take it except in carefully measured doses."

Judith sat down on the gunwale of the boat and took out a cigarette. Danny stood, looking down at her uncertainly. The girl lighted her cigarette. She looked up, smiling. Danny withdrew his glance, moved around the bow of the boat, and stood there out of the direct range of her eyes. His fingers drummed against the thin metal of the boat's hull.

"It just doesn't make much sense, does it, Danny?" she said after a space of silence. She did not look around at him.

"I guess it doesn't," Danny said dully, and when she did not continue, he said, doubtfully, "What do you mean, in particular?"

"Oh, everything," she told him. "You. Me. Us. Jerry. Mr. Ragland. Even Augusta is a little cockeyed since she's turned cook. Unless you come to supper and tell her she's the most wonderful cook that ever hit these Banks, she'll likely take to the roads — if there were any — hunting for somebody to feed. She's just about brought me down with gout."

"You don't want me coming to supper," Danny said gloomily.

"Why not, Danny?" She looked around at him with quiet challenge.

"Because —" Danny found himself unable to lay hand upon the words that he needed to continue.

Judith was thoughtful for a time before she resumed.

"I guess I've done a lot of thinking about you — since yesterday, Danny. It would hurt you if I told you what I felt — there at your house. But what I felt then doesn't satisfy me. There's something else, somewhere. I think there's a line for it in *Hamlet* — you'd never think that Augusta used to read me Shakespeare, and very dramatically, too, would you Danny?"

"Don't see why she shouldn't."

"Danny! Don't be like that! Sit down here and quit fidgeting. Augusta especially adores *Hamlet*, and she used to bear down when she came to that line — I don't know exactly where it is, but she'll tell us at supper — where Hamlet says, 'There was such a fighting in my heart I could not sleep.' I think that's the way it goes."

Danny had come around the bow of the boat and now he sat down on the gunwale, leaving space between them. He looked at her doubtfully, expecting her to continue. When she remained silent he demanded, "What's that got to do with me?"

"Nothing to *do* with you, Danny — it *is* you."

Danny stared at her, his eyes wide, troubled.

"It must sound kind of funny," Judith went on with a little self-conscious laugh. "But it is you, Danny. No, no, I don't mean about us. I don't think I even matter in it. But there's such a fighting in your heart about something that — that — well, it made that happen yesterday.

"I don't know what it is. It could be another girl. You see, I don't really know you very well. Not yet. But it could be something else. I think it is something else. I sensed it over there at the Station that day. Something about — oh, Danny, I don't know you at all, and your background here is too deep and too complex for me to even begin to understand it. . . . I don't want it to hurt, Danny, but when I saw you — slap Jerry yesterday I couldn't get rid of the feeling that actually you were slapping yourself. Were you?"

"I wish I had been," Danny said abjectly. Unconscious of the gesture, he touched the tender place at the point of his jaw. "You know, Judy," he went on impulsively, "I'm sort of proud of this sore spot on my chin — it hurts, but it doesn't hurt enough. Is that funny?"

"It isn't funny at all, Danny — it's nice. You're so young, Danny," she continued, "in a lot of ways. How old were you when you went away from here — the first time?"

"Eighteen, I guess — but it seems like a thousand years ago."

"Maybe it was," Judith said. "You left a boy here, not much older than Jerry, maybe not nearly as old. Isn't it wonderful how he's become a sort of extension of the personality of Mr. Ragland?"

"Some ways it is, maybe."

"But let's talk about you, Danny," Judith persisted. "You went off and left a little boy here. Maybe you left a lot else, too, Danny — all that this land of yours must mean to — how many generations is it?"

"I don't know how many. I'd have made the fifth in the Service if I'd stayed here and joined."

"Maybe that's where the trouble is, Danny. Have you thought about it at all?"

"I guess I've tried not to think about it." Danny was hesitant. "You know a lot of them said I was yellow, and worse, when I went off and joined the Army. Things were pretty bad out there —" and he waved an arm toward the dreary waste of the ocean — "and they'd got Daddy. I wanted to get away."

"And now you want to get away again. Do you really mean you're going away tomorrow?"

"Maybe not tomorrow — this week, anyhow."

"I'm sorry, Danny."

"Aren't — you'll be leaving too, won't you, Judy?"

Judith looked at him directly and then away, her glance moving in a slow arc, out to sea, along the Inner and the Outer Diamonds, and westward. Low on the horizon a thin line of light glowed; the clouds were beginning to lift. Wind stirred desultorily along the westerly reach of the sea; by evening the sky would be clear.

"No, Danny," Judith said after a while. Danny stared at her, puzzled, not quite believing. "Not now, Danny. I don't know why — I don't know how I'll explain it to Dad, if I have to. But I came down here to look for something that I felt — that I feel — must belong to me. I don't know how to say it, but there was something of here in you, Danny. I felt it.

"Now you are going away — part of you. But the other part of you — maybe it doesn't really exist — will stay here. It is something that can't be moved about. No, Danny, I'll not be going. Not now."

"What will you — what is there here for you to do, Judith?"

"That I don't know, not in words, Danny. But there is something here that I want — that I can feel. I've seen it in your mother's eyes, in Jerry's grin, even in the Chief's grim way of smiling. I saw it the other night when we were stuck and Mr. O'Neal came. I've glimpsed it sometimes in your eyes, Danny, and I think that's why I thought that I was in love with you."

"You're not in love with me. Not now — not after yesterday."

"Yesterday doesn't have anything to do with it, Danny. I could be, and I probably am in love with — silly phrase, isn't it? — part of you. With one part of you, but not both parts. There's that fighting in your heart, you know."

"But what can I —"

"I don't know, Danny."

"And you're going to stay on here after I'm gone?"

"Yes, Danny. There's something I think I need to do about myself, too, and I have a notion that here will be as good a place as I'll find to do it."

"What's that? What do you need to do about yourself?"

"I need to find out whether I'm a phony or not. I've got to find out what Jerry doesn't like about me, what the Chief sees wrong in me. Jerry is the other half of you, you know, Danny."

Danny became moodily silent, his face troubled, unhappy. He stared at the sea, across which the shadows of dusk were beginning to creep. The thin line of ruddy sky widened across the west.

"Is there another girl, Danny?" Judith asked, sitting suddenly upright on the gunwale of the boat, bracing her hands along it. Her long legs swung free.

"You mean — Sally Tillett?" Danny blurted, reddening.

"Is that her name?"

"Did Jerry tell —"

"Stop it, Danny. Nobody told me anything. It's just something that any woman would have known. There had to be a girl — here. You couldn't escape it."

Danny's glance was uneasy, almost furtively shifting, guilty. Judith smiled to herself.

"Is it serious, Danny?" she asked soberly. "Are you committed, and is this — my pursuing you — beginning to be bothersome?"

"No," Danny said hotly. He looked toward the Point, his face squarely away from the girl beside him. He wondered unhappily if she could see that even the back of his neck was red.

"What is she like, Danny?"

"She's just a girl, if it's Sally Tillett you mean. I guess you've seen her; she's always hanging around the store."

"You mean the girl with blonde hair and gray-blue eyes and two little dimples? Yes, I've seen her."

Danny was glumly silent. He continued to stare fixedly at the Point. Judith saw that the knuckles of his hand on the gunwale of the boat were white from the tensity of his grip.

"She could have been awfully sweet and pretty, Danny," Judith said softly. "Was she like — like this when you went away?"

"Skip it, Judith," Danny said shortly. He stood up. "It's — it's time we — you don't want me hanging around for supper, though."

"Don't be foolish, Danny. Of course we want you. Augusta will beam like — why, she'll be competition for the Light."

Augusta's thin face was flushed, smudged, and triumphant, signifying the contrivance of a miracle. She had found a fish suitable to her purpose, a challenging sort of fish that demanded imaginative and resourceful expedients. And although he was sure, when he trudged up the hill, walking in the rut across from Judith, that he had no appetite, Danny astonished himself and satisfied Augusta that here was a man who could eat, a man worth cooking for. She beamed upon Judith and Danny from the kitchen door, smiled a conspiratorial smile to herself, a smile so obviously conniving that she felt compelled, now and then, to duck out of sight, lest she be observed in her wickedness.

As they trudged the last mile homeward from the Point, the sky had cleared. After supper, so warm was the evening, Judith and Danny sat outside, ranging themselves on the bench that ran along the south wall of the cottage. The wind, soft and warm, came out of the west and stars blossomed in the purple field of the sky above them. Inside the house Augusta maintained a steady clattering of pans, indicating, the worthy woman hoped, that she was well out of ear range and, in addition, so busy with domestic pursuits that she had no time for other possible collateral interests.

Judith's hand lay on the bench, Danny could see by the glow of the lamp beyond the window above their shoulders. He started, boldly, to take it in his own, but the gesture wilted limply when he remembered . . . . His hand had . . . caressed Sally's breasts, had explored her thighs, had crushed her body against his own.

The recollection brought him nothing of joy, curiously, but a dismaying hesitancy about touching Judith's hand with his own. It was also that hand that had slapped Jerry. But he wanted to touch her. He thrust his hands deep into his pockets to keep them out of mischief, stretched out his legs before him. His shoulders drooped against the wall at his back and his chin was set hard against his breast. He was not happy.

Before them, under the starlight, the land rolled away toward the Point. Behind them the Light swung in its unending surveillance, its long, sweeping finger touching everything that lay before them, lightly, fleetingly. Out beyond the rim of the dyke that held back the sea the Lightship at the hidden point of the Outer Diamonds projected its answering beam.

Danny watched the two beams absently. Sometimes they met, interlocked for an instant. The Lightship was far off and its beam came on twenty-second intervals . . . every other time the beams came together. . . . The western sky had been stained with a warm apple green when they came outside, but presently it faded into a deep purple that was not quite black. Across the young pines the lights of the Station glowed in the dusk. The voice of the man on watch in the tower came across to them when he called to somebody on the ground seventy feet below him. The lights of an automobile flickered across the pines.

"You couldn't take it with you, Danny," Judith said.

"No; I guess you couldn't." Danny's tone was abstracted: Augusta's miracle-working with that fish had not been conducive to talk.

"Weren't you homesick for it when you were away from it?"

"I was. Lots of times."

"There's something here that I've never felt anywhere else," Judith went on. She seemed almost to be speaking to herself.

"I guess you must think that I'm an outlander steeped in a sort of synthetic enthusiasm not uncommon to tourists, but — but I can't look at all this impersonally. It isn't like a sky-scraper or anything like that. You look at those things and forget that you've seen them. But this thing here — it gets to be a part of you. Why is that, Danny?"

"I don't know, Judy," Danny said. He wished that she wouldn't talk, not just now — or at any time about that.

Judith's silence was questioning.

"You sound like Jerry, the way he's always running on about things. You know he calls that ocean out there an old harlot. Something he learned from the Chief."

"It must seem like a very real person to him, to them — these men who have known it — her — so long. And I guess she does behave like an ill-tempered shrew sometimes. Have you seen her like that, Danny?"

"You even call it a she, Judy." Danny laughed. "That's going native."

"I've been thinking I'd like to buy a piece of the earth down here and have a house on it, very like your mother's. Only with a big kitchen where Augusta could turn all her frustrations and repressions loose and chase them with what Mr. O'Neal calls a skillet."

" 'A-fryin' of meat,' " Danny quoted wryly.

"Maybe I'd learn to fry meat, too, Danny. I think I'd like to."

"Trouble with you is you don't have to. There'll always be somebody to do your frying for you. You're rich, aren't you?"

"I don't know — I've never thought about it, Danny. My grandmother left me — oh, I don't know how much."

"That's the trouble — one of them — between us, Judith."

"Why, Danny?"

"Well," Danny replied doubtfully, "if there was ever to be anything between us, all I've got is a major's wages and that wouldn't be anything to you."

"You've been going to the movies, Danny." Judith laughed.

Danny was about to answer but the noise of an automobile along the road at the bottom of the hill cut across his purpose. It was being driven at a surprising speed. He heard its springs whine when it bounced across a depression in the road and its engine race as if the rear wheels might be spinning in the air. It raced past, swept into the long curve toward the Station. Its taillight glowed in the dusk.

"One of these young bucks out of the Woods trying to show off to his girl," Danny said with mild disgust.

"He did seem pretty urgent," Judith observed. "I wonder if there's something wrong somewhere. He sounded like an ambulance, only there was no siren."

"No, I wouldn't think so," Danny said carelessly.

Before the car turned into the drive at the Station its horn sent a long, heralding blast before it. The sound broke the stillness of the dusk, shutting off for a moment the remote, interminable pounding of the surf against the beach. The car's brakes screamed and, so still was the night, they could hear its tires against the graveled driveway. The horn blasted the night again. They heard the Chief's mighty voice committing the driver to utter damnation for making so much fuss.

An interval of silence followed, but they could see that something must be afoot. Lights blinked on in the crew's quarters on the second floor. The Station became a blaze of light and after a little they heard the thudding rumble of a heavy motor being started. It sputtered in protest and then evened out in a smooth diapason. Another vehicle's exhaust began in a lesser key.

"They're starting up the duck. Must be some truck stuck out on the beach," Danny said idly.

"Sounds as if they've started everything they have in the house," Judith insisted. "Something must be happening somewhere."

"You ought to get the Chief to give you a ride in that duck

sometime," Danny put in without much interest. "It's the roughest thing with wheels on it."

Judith was silent. She sat, an elbow on her knee and her chin in her hand, looking speculatively across the dark toward the Station. The heavy exhaust that Danny identified as that of the amphibious vehicle, the duck, grew in volume, and in a moment they could see its lights moving. Instead of turning out toward the beach it continued toward the Lighthouse, taking the rougher, shorter road. Presently lesser vehicles came out into the road, four of them. Judith counted their lights. Across the dusk came the sound of a siren lightly, tentatively touched, as if the driver might be reassuring himself that it would work when needed.

"Is that an ambulance, Danny?"

"Sounds like it. Must be somebody sick or something up the beach."

The four lights came directly toward them into the wide curve skirting the foot of the hill. Judith watched them as they went, the awkward bulk of the small ambulance, the lean weapons-carrier, then a sedan and, at the end of the convoy, the jeep. The jeep's lights threw the sedan into bold relief for a moment.

"That looks like your car, doesn't it, Danny?"

"Could be. I've not had it long enough yet to know just what it does look like." With quick bitterness he added, "Now let's watch for the Chief — in his rowboat."

"That isn't like you, Danny," Judith said quietly and then, as if to herself, "but I wonder if it is, really."

"Aw, I didn't mean it, Judy — I was just trying to be funny."

"Not about that, Danny," Judith said seriously. She watched the lights disappear among the pines, saw in a moment their beams against the spiraled striping of the Lighthouse. Presently she said, "Could — shouldn't we go up that way and see if there's anything wrong — if there's anything we could do, Danny?"

"If you like," Danny said indifferently. "But what about Augusta? Take her with us?"

Augusta herself settled that point. She had no time, she said pointedly, nor the remotest inclination, to go gallivanting around at night; and, moreover, she had to mix that package of ready-to-rise rolls so they would be ready for breakfast; and as for staying there by herself, she found her own company by no means undesirable; and, besides, there was that little bride down in the last house — just moved in — and she might be lonesome, what with that man's stubbornness over yonder at that Station not letting that nice O'Neal boy come home nights.

Danny and Judith set off in the convertible, taking time before they got under way to lower the top and secure it. Augusta watched them from the doorway until the lights blinked past the turn in the road. Then she came down the steps and picked her way gingerly, flashlight in hand, toward the last cottage, where Mr. O'Neal's new daughter-in-law — not a day over eighteen — waited alone for the time when her young husband could come home on liberty.

By the car's lights, when they came to the Lighthouse, they could see that the convoy's tracks had turned toward the Woods, not continuing across the dyke and up the beach as Danny had supposed. The remote rumble of the duck's engine reached them and Danny said that it sounded as if it might be taking the hill down the road beyond his house. He seemed a little relieved at the thought that whatever it was that had precipitated this spurt of activity must have happened beyond that part of the Woods that concerned him immediately.

"Must be some boat in trouble out in the Sound," he said.

Judith drove smoothly, the heavy convertible taking the inequalities of the road evenly. She brought the car almost to a halt before the Gray house. The light in the living room was burning, but there was no other sign of life about the place. Danny could see, through the window, the chair in which his mother always sat. It was empty. Beyond, farther along the road, beyond the rise that divided the village, there were sounds of movement.

The shrill blast of the jeep's horn cut across the night. Judith, without a word, drove forward. At the top of the rise she stopped. Beyond the tops of the trees in the lower level of the village they could see lights moving in the creek, and the thrusting exhaust of a motorboat came to them. It went, at full throttle, along the channel toward open water.

"Whatever it is must have happened out in the Sound somewhere," Danny said.

Now they could see the running lights of the boat as it threaded its way along the channel. Judith wondered if, somewhere, she might hear presently the reverberations of the Chief's voice. Instead, she heard the renewed clamor of the duck's engine. It turned down the road toward the creek, its red and green running lights moving out in a straight course toward the open Sound.

"That's funny," Danny said, "taking that duck out in the Sound like that, if that's where they've started with it."

"Should we go down there, Danny? Or would we be in the way?"

"No, plenty of room; but — do you hear anything, Judy?"

"Hear what, Danny?"

"Thought I heard the engines of an airplane, but I guess I didn't. Nobody would be flying tonight — not down here, anyway."

The far-off beat of the engines became perceptible, momentarily louder, seemed to fade and then come again, nearer, louder. Far out in the Sound the hum of the boat's engine was becoming indistinct. Nearer by the duck labored forward, ponderous, slow, steady. Suddenly a flare's glow made a pin point of light on the dark Sound, grew, flamed against the night. The sound of engines above came now in a steady, mounting roar.

"Looks like they might be going to mark off a landing strip," Danny said, breathless. "Let's go down there and see if we can find out what's going on."

"Let's watch from here a little," Judith said quietly. "We can see from here."

By now the aircraft was above the flare the boat had set on the surface of the Sound, and suddenly the night became day with a light that had the blinding intensity of the sun. Judith glanced at Danny beside her in the seat. His face was white, set, bewildered. The fearful light swung lazily, back and forth like the pendulum of a clock, under the parachute that Judith could see above it. She saw the dark outlines of the plane as it cut through the light, its nose pointed down toward the now dying point of flame from the flare on the surface.

"Let's go, Judy!"

Judith put the car into gear and went slowly down the incline. There was nobody in sight, in the houses or along the road. Lights were burning in most of the houses as if their inmates had left hurriedly, without planning. They went past the store, came to the turning of the road where one prong of it went toward the creek and the little dock. There were figures of people, dimly lit, in the road. Some of them were gazing up and out above the Sound. Some of them, it seemed to Judith, had a dazed, stricken expression, as if their eyes had looked at something they could not comprehend.

Ahead the road forked again; one prong, the more used, bearing off to the dock, and the other, little used, off to the left and ending in the edge of the marsh. The road to the dock was dotted with people. There were a few vehicles: the jeep, the ambulance, Danny's car. Judith headed the convertible into the less-used road and stopped. Danny, as if oblivious of her presence, of her actual existence, got down and moved back to the other road. She heard his voice.

"What's the matter, Cedric? What's happened?"

Judith waited, wondering. Whoever it was Danny had addressed was silent. Judith could almost feel his reluctance to say anything, to speak. She wondered, in sudden panic, if something had happened to Jerry, or to Danny's mother. And then —

"It's Sally Tillett, Danny — tried to kill herself."

Another interval of silence, leaden, dead.

"How — how did she do it, Cedric? Tell me!"

"Carving knife."

"Is — is she dead?" Danny's voice was thin, wavering.

"Not when they left here with her. The Chief had her in a stretcher aboard the duck. Boat went out to light some flares so the plane could see where to land."

"How — who — where did they find her?"

"Happened at her house. Her mother must have found her. Somebody went after Miss Polly, and I guess she sent Jerry out to the Station. Didn't take 'em long to get here."

"Where is Jerry?"

"I think he went out on the boat."

"Was she — did they think she'd —"

"I don't know, Danny. I didn't get close to her. She looked pretty bloody from where I was — blood through the sheet they had over her."

"Was she — did she know anything?"

"She had her eyes shut when I saw her, but she didn't look too bad to me. It was a funny thing but I thought — you remember them dimples she had, Danny?"

Danny remembered the dimples. . . . Somewhere in the dark another voice, bitter, protesting, said if there had been a doctor on the Outer Banks they might have done something for her. Like it was, the voice went on, it would be an hour before they could get her anywhere and by that time she might not be living. Another voice, laying hold upon hope, said that there would be a doctor aboard the plane out there and maybe he could do something while they were flying to wherever they were taking her. . . .

Offshore the plane's engines rumbled against the silence that wrapped the Sound, and Judith could feel a quick, tense waiting grip the group in the dark around her. The engines roared, singly and then in unison under full throttle, idled into almost dead silence. Then came the deep-throated purposeful thunder of the exhaust. Their sound moved into the wind, and it seemed to fill the sky to the very brim, and the night trembled under the implacable rhythm of the propellers.

Breath came back into the lungs of the waiting group and Judith was sure she heard a long unconscious sigh of relief when they knew the plane was in the air. Voices, blurred and low-pitched, broke the stillness. Somebody said that he didn't know what people would do, in times like this, if it were not for airplanes. Somebody laughed softly.

"You ought to like 'em, Zane — you come mighty near bein' born in one of 'em when they hauled your mama out of here that time."

Far out over the Sound the climbing plane's lights blinked against the sky. The port wing light sagged and the starboard lifted; the plane was banking in a shallow turn. The lights swung around in a half circle, headed directly toward the little dock. Judith watched its course across the blackness, saw it veer slightly. Now she could hear another sound, the rumbling engine of the duck, the less strident exhaust of the rescue boat, coming nearer.

Again the soft darkness was shattered. Light seemed to explode in the wake of the plane when it let go another flare. It hung above the marsh, swinging under its parachute, descending slowly. For a moment the plane was starkly outlined in the incandescence. Judith could see the plodding duck coming toward the dock and the white hull of the rescue boat a little astern and to the starboard.

Some of the group around the girl went silently away, and when she glanced around she saw Sergeant Dragonnetti standing apart, alone. He was not looking up at the plane, nor at the two surface craft plodding across the water toward them. He stood as if he were made of stone. All life was gone out of his face; his eyes were dead in their sockets, frozen in a fixed, unseeing stare.

Jerry was standing beside him and Judith's breath caught in her throat when she saw his posture — feet bare and planted wide apart, palms flattened against his hips. His head was bare and his gaze was fixed on the rumbling duck. . . . Danny, she saw in the waning light of the flare, now dangling just above the outer rim of the marsh, was standing at the back of the convertible. He had laid an arm along the rim of the boot that held the top, buried his face in the crook of it. . . . The flare dropped into the water and dark came down again. In the instant of the light's dying Judith saw the white, immobile face of a woman, her eyes staring, seeing nothing.

Near the shore the rescue boat held its course toward the dock, following the channel, but the duck swung away directly toward the low shore, toward the little road that ended at the water's edge. Judith heard its gears grind when the power was shifted from the propeller to the wheels, heard the wheels when they took hold on the shallow bottom. It lumbered out of the water, dripping. Its lights cut a narrow path through the darkness along the little road. It halted just beyond the convertible.

The cover above the driver's compartment lifted and Judith saw the Chief's mighty shoulders rise slowly against the skyline. The driver's face was a blur beyond the misted windshield. The Chief swung his legs over the side and dropped, with amazing lightness it seemed to Judith, to the ground. He glanced backward along the hull of the vehicle, shrouded under its heavy canvas cover. He turned and moved forward, his glance searching.

Judith followed his glance, saw it come to the woman's white, still face, the staring, unseeing eyes. He moved forward again and Judith moved aside to let him pass. He seemed not to have seen her. When he came to the woman his great hand took hold of her arm. Judith heard his voice, marveling, as she heard it, at its soft gentleness.

"Too late, Mahala," he said. "We brought her back."

His head moved backward, indicating the dripping duck. He looked beyond the woman's shoulder and again Judith heard his voice.

"Polly," he said.

Judith saw a shadowy figure come closer to the woman, a strong hand reach out for her shoulder. The Chief turned away. He motioned with his hand to the driver of the duck and the lights clicked off, came on again dimly.

"Jerry."

The Chief's voice had not lifted in pitch nor expanded its volume. Judith saw the shadowy figure beside the Sergeant move. The boy said nothing. He stood, with his face up-turned, waiting.

"You got that car here? Go with your mammy."

Jerry half turned toward the Sergeant, looked back at the Chief. Judith saw the massive man's head nod slowly, a curious, comprehending smile curl around the corners of his mouth. When Jerry started toward the Sergeant his glance found Danny's face, white, stricken, in the half-light shed by the duck's dimmed headlights. He turned back to the Chief, his eyes questioning, pleading.

"Go on with your mammy, Jerry," the Chief said gently. "I'll look after him — if he needs it."

Jerry went back to the Sergeant. He took hold of his arm, and when the man seemed utterly unaware of the gentle pressure of the boy's hand, Jerry took hold with both hands. The Sergeant moved, as in sleep. The boy guided him around the back of the car to where Polly Gray's hands were gently insistent on the white-faced woman's shoulders.

"Okay, Mom. The car's right here."

"She — she doesn't seem to hear me, Jerry." Polly Gray's voice was grieved, troubled.

Judith was only half aware that the Chief had moved back to the duck. She heard his voice, crisp and commanding, and then the lights of the vehicle cut through the dark. The woman's face was again starkly etched against the darkness beyond. She saw Jerry blink his eyes against the intensity of the light, saw him look up at the Sergeant's rigid face. Polly Gray was a little in the background. Judith was not sure then — nor could she be afterward — that what happened was not part of some fantastic dream.

Life kindled in the man's eyes, flowed down across his face. His lips opened a little. Judith saw the tip of his tongue moisten them. His hands moved, as if without conscious volition. They took hold of the white-faced woman's shoulders. Judith heard his voice, unsteady for a syllable or two, and then stronger, gentle, compassionate.

"This is Jesse, Mother," she heard him say.

Somewhere in the little group Judith heard a strangled, unbelieving gasp. She saw Polly Gray's face recede, move out of the pool of light, saw Jerry touch the Sergeant's arm quickly. She heard his voice, as if from far off.

"You bring your mammy, Sergeant. Mom and me'll get the car started."

The white-faced woman turned slowly toward the uniformed figure that towered above her, lifted her head until her eyes met his. She made no sound. Judith saw the Sergeant's back turned and the two figures move slowly away. Judith heard the door of the car shut, heard its motor in labor along the rutted road, saw the dwindling red of its taillight. . . .

The Chief's voice at her shoulder brought Judith back to reality, broke the dead silence that held the group at the meeting of the two roads.

"You got your car here, Miss," the Chief said. "It's sort of got me blocked in here. You take Danny home. I got a few things to do here."

"Of course, Mr. Ragland. Yes, I'll take Danny home. We saw you from the cottage when you left the Station."

"Get him out of this," the Chief said, his voice low. "And if you was to have some coffee made by the time I get there, I'd like some."

28

AFTER THE NIGHT'S STORM, SUNLIGHT LAY WARM, ALMOST springlike, along the slope of the hill above the Point. The sky was a soft, misty blue, and no breath of wind stirred among the pines below the ridge, no blade of grass in the uneven plain that rolled away southward was stirring. The sun's light caught fleetingly the gaudy ruff of a cock pheasant above the pines and, higher, the Frisco Eagle — Judith had learned his name — patrolled the sky.

Last night the wind had howled across the Cape, roaring, snarling out of the northeast. The surf had battered the beach with the intensity of a barrage. Now and then the wind had taken hold upon the eaves of the cottage at the top of the hill and shaken the house as if driven by a personal wrath. Judith had heard Augusta, in the other room, stir uneasily in her bed. Gusts of sleet had rattled against the windows.

But the sun had come up out of a clear horizon, and now, after midday, Judith looked out upon a placid world from the deck chair outside the cottage door. There was no sound from anywhere except that, back in the kitchen, Augusta muttered darkly, though not without a measured satisfaction, against the perversities of an oil stove. That, and the dull, muted roar of the surf.

There was no wind, but the ocean continued in turmoil. At the Point Judith could see the waves when they leaped high into the air, white, iridescent in the sun. Farther out where, Judith knew from the chart pinned to the juniper paneling above the mantel, the warm river from the south flowed past the Outer Diamonds, clouds stood motionless in the still air.

It must have been quite a battle, Judith mused, last night. The Two Oceans that Jerry talked about casually must have met in head-on combat, the North Ocean coming down with all its turbulent strength to hurl itself at the warm South Ocean. For the moment, it would seem, the South Ocean had disarmed its enemy but, out beyond the Diamonds, the ancient battle must be continuing: cold water from the north battling it out with the warm water of that river, and the clouds were the smoke of battle.

But for the moment, for this little while, a soft truce of the winds brooded above the Cape. Judith stretched her slim legs luxuriously in the warming sun. The Frisco Eagle wheeled idly toward the Point, perhaps in search of a fish, perhaps just sunning himself. Sometimes, when the sea was like that, she would toss live fish on the beach. The water was too rough for fishing, even for an eagle. . . .

And in this windless, sunny day there would be poor hunting for those rather preposterous people in the next house. They had appeared two days ago, amazingly caparisoned in what, Judith supposed, must be some austere clerk's notion of what a gentleman, a solvent gentleman, should wear when in pursuit of wildfowl. Judith had first seen them when they were trudging up the hill from the car. They had loaded it so heavily that it refused to climb the hill.

They appeared to have also a complete arsenal. Judith wondered, with faint amusement, if they expected to encounter elephants and tigers as well as geese. The three of them made several trips between the car and the top of the hill, each time lugging bags, gun cases, and what obviously was a case of grog. Two of them were round-bellied and ruddy. The third was gaunt and dour. And they all wore outfits salvaged from the wardrobe of a musical comedy.

One of the men, one of the round ones, looked appraisingly

at Judith when he passed the first time, produced a furtive leer on the second trip, and addressed her as "Sister" on the third. Judith smiled with cool derision, and she knew the poor man's face was several shades redder. Since then none of them had appeared to be aware of her existence. They were out with the dawn and nothing was seen of them until they trudged back up the hill at dusk.

Somehow they didn't seem very happy — not nearly so happy as the young Coast Guardsman and his younger girl-bride who had taken the last and smallest of the houses. Once or twice Judith had picked them up on the way from the store. They were very young and very shy and very preoccupied with themselves. But they were friendly in their hesitant, blushing fashion.

Most of what Judith knew about them she had learned from Augusta, who had invaded their little house with a steaming, redolent platter of something she had contrived in the kitchen. Judith was relieved at the thought of having somebody to share with her the brunt of Augusta's miracle-making in the kitchen. She had turned into an amazing cook, and she was always hurt when Judith's appetite proved unequal to her prodigal productivity.

"Why don't you invite them over to dinner — supper I mean?" Judith proposed. "You could do wonders with those two pheasants I got yesterday."

The young people came, hesitant, shy, but with an elusive eagerness, too. Judith sensed that they wanted to look at her, especially the girl. They were curious about her and, on her own part, Judith found herself as curious about them. They were — and Judith disliked the word intensely — natives. . . . Except for Danny, they were the first guests she had had in the house.

Judith saw the girl's puzzled appraisal of the table when she came from Augusta's room, where she had left her coat. Judith saw her almost unconsciously counting the places and wondering why there were only three when there were four people in the house. Judith excused herself and went to the kitchen. Presently Augusta came in, attended by a nimbus of engaging smells, and without looking at Judith laid a fourth plate.

"Augusta is so wrapped up in her cooking that she forgets she has to eat, too," Judith said easily.

"She's sure a grand cook," the boy said with shy enthusiasm. He turned to the girl. "Ain't she, Leona?"

"She sure is, Junior."

"Junior?" Judith asked, smiling.

The girl colored. "That's what everybody calls him. His name is Bannister, after his father."

"It's an interesting name, but Junior's nice, too."

"That's an awfully pretty dress you've got on," the girl said, blushing at her own boldness.

"You're nice to say so," Judith replied. "I like it, too."

"It must be awfully expensive," the girl went on impulsively. "I'd like to have a dress like that, but me and Jun — me and Bannister are going to have a house of our own."

"That'll be wonderful — I'd like a house of my own down here," Judith said warmly.

Both of them looked at Judith a little incredulously, and then at each other. A little silence closed around them and Judith wondered unhappily if she had got off on the wrong tack again by being too enthusiastic. It was the girl who rallied, bringing the wavering talk back to an even keel.

"It's a nice place to live down here, even if it is pretty hard to get in and out most of the time and we have to do without a lot of things that we'd like to have." She glanced around the room. "You've made it nice in here — Junior and me wanted to fix up our little house some, but we're not going to be here very long. Junior's going to aircraft machinist's school."

Augusta appeared at the kitchen door.

"Young man," she said, fixing the boy with a determined

eye, "you look able-bodied — you come here and let's me and you get supper on the table."

Judith saw the girl's small, possessive alarm, a fleeting twinge of resentment at being left out of something that involved her husband, fling its small banners across her cheeks. The boy looked hesitantly at her and went off to the kitchen. The girl's mouth trembled. . . . Judith wondered why God had made the female of the species such a fool. . . . Bannister came back, awkwardly carrying the wide platter containing the two pheasants. He smiled self-consciously down at the girl.

Altogether the little venture into hospitality had passed off pleasantly enough, and before the dinner was through there had been, in the girl's manner, a certain almost patronizing self-assurance: she had her man. Judith smiled absently at the thought as she looked lazily out toward the Point and the battlement of clouds that hung above the horizon, swelling above the battle that seethed beneath them. . . .

Jerry's startling shirt appeared in the road below the hill. He did not glance directly upward, but when he came to the dividing of the road he turned up the hill toward Judith. She was aware of a suddenly quickened sense of anticipation as he trudged up the slope. It was the first time he had come to the house since she had been a tenant. Could it really be that long — or was it just yesterday? She wondered, not altogther idly, why his gun was not slung loosely under his arm. He must be coming with some specific purpose. . . .

"Hi," the boy said briefly when he was within range of her.

Judith wondered if she should get up to greet him, hesitated in indecision. It would not do to seem too eager before this strange child who was, in so many bewildering ways, mature and wise beyond his years. She decided to sit still. Her smile was cordial, welcoming. She leaned forward in the deck chair.

"Hello, Jerry," she said. "It's nice to see you. How have you been?"

"Okay," the boy said.

"Sit down, Jerry, won't you — the bench there. It's so nice and sunny outside, after the storm last night."

"Did blow a little," Jerry said. He settled himself on the bench. Judith watched him, her elbows on the arms of the chair and her fingers interlaced under her chin. The boy's eyes narrowed as his glance ranged around the horizon, coming back to the battlement of clouds in the southeast. "It's not over with yet," he continued, nodding at the clouds. "They'll bust loose after a while, maybe about night, and there'll be some more."

"How is your mother, Jerry?"

"She's okay. Mom and me want you, and Grandma in there, to come and take Christmas dinner at our house. We ain't got any turkey like maybe you're used to, but I got some geese and Mom's about the best goose cook there is."

"Jerry! How sweet of you both," Judith exclaimed, her face aglow.

"Bill Henry's comin' and that boy they call Iowa over there." Jerry nodded toward the Station. "He's a long ways from home, and I guess he's not so bad."

"I'd love to come, Jerry, but I don't know about Augusta." She paused, a playful light dancing in her eyes. "You know, I think this is supposed to be a secret, but I think Augusta has been hoping she could get rid of me somehow for Christmas dinner. Jerry, I think Augusta is by way of being in love."

"Damn!" Jerry said, "don't they ever get too old?"

"I'm afraid not, Jerry."

"Who's she after?"

"You know that young newly-wed couple down there — the boy's named Bannister. I don't know how she did it, though I guess there was no great secret about it, but she found out the boy's father is Mr. O'Neal — the one who helped us out when we got buried in the sand on the way down here."

"Oh, him," Jerry said. He grinned.

"At any rate Augusta's practically adopted them, and from the way she's been dropping hints I think she would like to have the bridal couple for Christmas and get the boy to bring his father."

"Don't see anything wrong with it — if she wants him. Ain't she never had her no man?"

"Of course not, Jerry."

"I thought I'd been seein' that old car he drives prowlin' up and down the beach. He was a good surfman in his day. I remember Daddy tellin' about the way he could handle a boat. He's got a medal and a good pension."

"He has beautiful eyes," Judith mused.

"Never noticed nothin' so pretty about 'em," Jerry observed, "but there's a lot of life left in him yet. Reckon she'll land him?"

"I really don't know, Jerry. I hadn't taken it very seriously, and maybe I've just let my imagination run away with me. But something has got into Augusta."

"Bet he'd have her out mendin' nets before the ink's dry on their — whatever they call that piece of paper that shows they're married."

"She'd love it."

"You mean bein' married, or mendin' nets?"

"Both, perhaps, Jerry."

Jerry grinned. He said nothing for a moment and then he turned to look Judith squarely in the eyes.

"You heard from Danny?"

"Yes, every day — or almost every day," she said slowly. The boy's sudden blunt shift of pace had caught her off balance.

"Mom had a letter from him today. Said he didn't know whether he'd be back for Christmas or not. Say, I got an extra goose I could give Grandma if you think she needs it to sort of bait Mr. Bannister with."

"She'd love it, Jerry! She's been grumbling at me because all I've been able to bring down is a couple of pheasants. We had them for supper when the bride and groom came over."

"She might need two — her feller is the damnedest eater on these Banks. Goin' to be good shootin' weather tomorrow. You want to go — Judy?"

"Jerry!" Judith cried with enthusiasm. "Of course I'd like to go. I — I've been hoping you would ask me, before the season closes."

"Women around here don't do much huntin' — not for geese anyway."

"Will they think I'm scandalous, Jerry?"

"Not you, I reckon. Can you get up before daylight?"

"Of course I can."

"Well, I'll holler for you, down there in the road. We might find one or two down around the Open Ponds if we get there before light."

"Couldn't I come for you, Jerry? It's a long walk. Or will you drive? Danny left the car here, didn't he?"

"I can walk," Jerry said, ignoring her question about Danny's car. Danny had left it, but for two weeks now, since the morning he had rolled it out of the shed to wash it, Jerry had not driven it. He had washed the outside, polished it. When he was sweeping the accumulated sand out of the inside he had seen something dully shining against the floor mat. He had picked it up in his fingers, turned it over, examining it. There was something elusively familiar about the button; he had seen the mate to it somewhere.

Then he had laid the thing on his flattened thumb and thumped it with his middle finger. It had sailed in a wide arc and been lost in the thick yoepon on the slope back of the house. He had remembered, then, where he had seen another, the others, like it, when he had glimpsed Sally Tillett, limp and bloody on the stretcher when they brought her back. He had put the car back in the shed. . . .

"May I drive you home, now, Jerry?"

"Naw, thanks just the same. I'm goin' over to the Station and see Bill Henry and the boys awhile — they'll take me home when they go to turn on the Light. I'll holler for you before daylight. Better wear some boots, if you got 'em."

Jerry went down the hill. Judith called after him, "Tell Mrs. Gray thanks awfully much, and I'll be happy to come."

The boy, half turning, lifted an arm in a brief, assenting gesture and went on toward the Station. The girl wondered what stubborn quirk in his mind kept him from using the car Danny had left when he went away. Had the break between them, if there had really been a break, not healed? Or was there some other reason hidden beyond her awareness of what went on beneath the placid surface there in the tranquillity of the Woods?

Augusta came along the grassy walk that connected the cottages. Judith supposed that she had been down to the last cottage visiting the young bride. She stopped, her eyes following the bright gleam of color that was Jerry's shirt, now almost to the Station.

"Did that young man have on his shoes?" Augusta's voice was severe.

"Since you mention it, I don't believe he did, Augusta," Judith replied. "But it's such a nice sunny afternoon he really doesn't need shoes."

Augusta clucked her disapproval and continued indoors. Judith returned to her meditative contemplation of the uneven rolling plain that ended at the Point, and to her preoccupation with the Woods. She relived that fantastic night, remembering the swirling kaleidoscope that had turned in the flaring light swinging like a pendulum under the parachute — its slow descending, like the falling of doom toward the dark surface of the Sound.

None of it had any substance of reality, and yet, it had all happened. She saw again Danny's white, stricken face, half hidden against his folded arms; the white, immobile face of the woman on the other side of the car; and the Sergeant, standing there like some fearsome image graven out of stone — and Jerry beside him, unconsciously falling into that posture that had, somehow, come to symbolize, in some nebulous sense, this whole fantastic region.

Judith knew now, when she thought back over the night, that there had been something calculated, and at the same time instinctive, in the Chief's studiedly casual behavior. She knew that if he had not sent her off with Danny, charged with the prosaic business of brewing a pot of coffee, she would have — well, she'd have started screaming hysterically, though she was not given to hysterics. But, on the other hand, she was not accustomed to stark melodramatics.

Danny seemed dazed when he got into the car beside her, not even aware that she was there. She called him softly after she got the engine started. He did not answer her, nor move. The Chief took him by the elbow and moved him, not relenting the pressure on Danny's arm until his hand moved away to close the door. She drove back to the Gray house. Danny got down and went ahead of her into the house. He slumped down in the chair next the hearth.

Judith spoke to him but he seemed not to hear her. She went, hesitant about entering another woman's kitchen, about making free with another's house, and clicked on the ceiling light above the range. She found the percolator, found matches, and lighted the stove. Presently the smell of coffee steadied her ... or perhaps it was the sense of being of some use, of finding something to do with her hands, that calmed her clashing nerves. When the coffee was ready, she poured a cup for Danny and another for herself and carried them into the living room.

Danny had not moved. He took the cup from her hands, his hands moving like the hands of an automaton. She sat down across the hearth from him, a little guiltily when she realized that she was sitting in Polly Gray's chair. She drank in scalding gulps. Across the hearth Danny stirred, lifted his cup thirstily to his lips, and drank. He drained it and set the cup back in the saucer balanced on his thigh. Presently he spoke, the words coming haltingly.

"Did — did it — did anything happen, Judy?"

"Yes, Danny — I'm afraid it happened."

Danny lapsed again into silence. His hands shook. Judith got up from Polly Gray's chair and crossed over to him. She took the cup and set it on the table beside him. She took out a cigarette and held the end of it to his lips, pressed gently, held a match for it. Danny inhaled deeply.

The wind was rising. The air had chilled. Judith lighted the fire that was laid, ready, on the hearth. She sat down, waiting. It was not long before the front door opened soundlessly. The Chief closed it behind him. He glanced at Danny. His face was impassive, but when his glance came around to Judith, light kindled in his eyes. Without a word she got up and went to the kitchen. She wondered if he would follow her into the kitchen. She waited expectantly for a moment before she poured coffee into the big, service-size cup. He was standing with his back to the fire when she came back to the living room. He took the cup without a word.

There was something quieting, reassuring, in his mere presence, Judith realized — not because of his massive physical strength, but because of something else, something that was not, in the jangled state of her thinking, easy to define. . . . She remembered him as he had looked that day, standing at the top of the dyke, looking down at the crew at boat drill and out across the water. . . . After he had drained the cup he handed it back to her and sat down in Polly Gray's chair.

"More, Chief?" Judith said. He nodded and Judith went to

the kitchen and brought it, with a second cup for Danny. Danny had scarcely stirred when the Chief came in. Now there was a feverish stain on his face and his eyes smouldered. His hands gripped the arms of the chair, tensely white at the knuckles.

When he had emptied the second cup, the Chief handed it back to Judith, shook his head when she asked if he wanted more. His gesture commanded Judith to sit down, and then he began, his voice even, casual. His words flowed on, like a slow, rising tide. He smoked with unhurried draughts on his cigarette. Now and again he glanced at Danny, and when he saw bewilderment, unbelief, in the boy's face, the pace of his words slowed.

"I've never blamed Mahala, in my own mind," he went on. "She was a pretty, high-strung girl when he brought her here to the Woods and left her. He belonged to the sea and she come to hate it because it took him away from her so much of the time. What she hated, she was afraid of, and you can't be afraid of that ocean out there. She's like a dog — a dog knows when you are afraid of him. But mostly she's like a woman.

"That Jerry — he knew it the first night the Sergeant was home. I knew him as soon as I got a good look at him. He had the markings of three or four generations I've known. But that damned boy wouldn't let on to me when I tried to find out if he knew anything. The Sergeant had his word he wouldn't say anything. Me and Jesse had it out, yonder at the Station the other day — first day you were at the Station, Miss. I tried to get him to go and see his mammy, and I tried to get him to talk to your mammy, Danny, but there's a stubborn streak in them Tilletts.

"Sally wasn't, inside, a bad girl. I've known that all the time, even when she was runnin' around these Woods with anything that had a pair of pants on it. She couldn't wait and maybe that was born in her. Her mammy's done a lot of waitin' all these years and she didn't like it. But anyhow she's got her a son in place of the daughter she ain't got now. Things just seem to sort of work themselves out if you give 'em enough time."

The Chief's voice trailed off. Judith went to the kitchen to make more coffee. When she returned with three cups on a tray, Danny had not moved. Jerry was sitting on the deerskin rug before the hearth. His chin rested in the cup of one hand. With the other hand he toyed absently with Surfman's ears. The Chief sat with his great legs stretched out toward the fire and his glance rested lazily on the back of Jerry's neck. Judith handed her cup to Jerry and went back to the kitchen for another for herself.

When she came back into the room, Jerry had drained his cup and set it on the floor beside him. He was leaning back, his shoulders against the Chief's knee. He was looking directly at Danny's face, but his brother seemed unaware of his scrutiny. Judith could not imagine what the boy must be thinking; his face was an impassive mask. He turned lazily, snuggling his shoulders against the Chief's knee, and sat staring at the fire. The Chief rested a massive hand on the boy's shoulder and a thick finger toyed absently with his ear.

Judith sat down. Danny seemed utterly rigid in his chair. At the other side of the hearth the Chief seemed asleep, except for the gentle moving of his finger against the boy's cheek. His eyes were hooded under their lids. Judith waited, unwilling herself to break the silence that held them, though there were questions that kept trooping up in her thoughts, little facets of the improbable thing that she had witnessed at such close range. After a while the Chief, without opening his eyes or stirring, spoke.

"Miss, go in there and see if this boy's bed is ready — he's sound asleep and damned if he ain't seen enough for one night without me wakin' him up for more."

Danny glanced around as Judith got up, but he did not stir.

She went, doubtfully, toward the room that she knew was Jerry's, searched for the light switch she knew must be somewhere on the wall beside the door. She clicked on the light. She went to the bed and turned back the covers, fluffed the pillows. When she glanced around the Chief was there, one arm under Jerry's shoulders and the other under his loosely limp knees. The boy's head rested against the Chief's shoulder.

Judith started to go past, back to the living room, but there was scarcely any space left between the bed and the dresser across from it against the wall. She stopped uncertainly. The Chief laid the boy on the bed, and she marveled at the gentleness of his hands when he loosened the shirt and slipped it off his shoulders and tossed it across the foot of the bed. He unfastened the belt and the faded dungarees came off. The Chief dropped them in a puddle at the foot of the bed and pulled the cover over the boy. Surfman hopped up on the bed and sat down beyond the sleeping boy's shoulder, watchful. The Chief went out and, following him, Judith clicked out the light and closed the door softly. Danny had not moved.

Judith drove back to the cottage at the top of the hill alone, but with the Chief's jeep following her. When she turned to climb the hill the jeep halted, waited until she reached the top of the hill and stopped the car in front of her house. When she clicked off her lights the jeep went on. . . . Danny had seemed not to hear her when she said good night to him. . . .

She had not seen Danny again. Next morning she drove through the Woods, slowed irresolutely before the Gray house, holding back against an impulse to stop. She drove past the house with the strange vine billowing across the front of it, but again she went on, not sure of herself or from what source these impulses to stop had come. There was no sign of life at the Gray house, and at the other house only two or three people seemed to be about. Judith did not know any of them.

Back at the store, with the help of Mrs. Grady, she placed a telephone call. Mrs. Grady's eyes widened as she listened.

The girl's voice, when she spoke to somebody at the other end, was crisp, commanding. "Of course it's difficult, Miss Simmons, but get it done. Tell Father I'm all right — and thanks a lot. How are you?" She clicked the receiver on the hook. That evening, toward dusk, the bus stopped at the Tillett house and put off a huge box. For once in her life Mrs. Grady let her own curiosity take her by the hand; she wanted to know what a blanket of gardenias would look like. . . .

"I'm so glad," Mrs. Grady told Judith a day or two afterward. "Without you, I'm afraid there wouldn't have been any flowers — they're so scarce down here this time of the year, and so hard to get from anywhere else."

"You're kind, Mrs. Grady," Judith said simply. "Will you tell the Sergeant, if you see him, that they were for him — and his mother."

Afterward, when she encountered him at the store, the Sergeant thanked her simply and without constraint. The taut lines were gone out of his face. His eyes were calm, remotely smiling. He was talking with Mrs. Grady when Judith came into the store, and Judith was sure that when Mrs. Grady turned quickly away it was to hide tears that were gathering in her eyes.

"I was just trying to persuade Mrs. Grady to cut my hair again. It's beginning to need it," the Sergeant was saying with an easy laugh.

"Jesse Tillett!" Mrs. Grady reproved him.

"I hope your mother is well, Sergeant," Judith put in.

"Very well, thank you, Miss Hale," the Sergeant answered. "I'm going to be stationed with the heavies out west when they get in from the Pacific, and I think I'll take Mother out there to live with me for a while. It's a nice post and I can get quarters. Change ought to be good for her."

"How wonderful, Sergeant," Judith said.

"But we're going to keep the house here — so we can come back to it if she gets tired of Army posts. I'm coming back when I retire. I'm going to try to get it painted before my leave is up."

It was this calm, almost stoic acceptance of things as they were that astonished Judith. She remembered the night beside the little creek . . . there had been no outcry. Among them all, she alone had shown any outward sign of inner turmoil. It was not, she knew, the stoicism of indifference, nor helpless resignation. It was a calm acceptance of life: its hazards, its joys, its griefs, and its bewilderments. There had been no wailing.

Only Danny, in so far as Judith could tell, had reacted in a way that was, at least partly, understandable. It seemed to her incredible that he could not have known, have guessed, the Sergeant's identity. If Danny had been observant or had possessed anything of what must be a native prescience, he would have divined it, she thought. That the Sergeant should have turned out to be the brother of the girl who . . . who had been Danny's girl . . . or might be still, in some fashion that Judith could not fathom . . . .

There must have been something between them, Judith mused, for Danny to feel that sense of shock — or was it desolation? — at her dying. There came again to Judith's mind the thing that Augusta used to read with such glib incomprehension: "such a fighting in my heart." Deep-hidden in Augusta there must be some warrior spark; she had rolled her tongue around the words, tasting them, savoring them. . . .

More than once during that long night, in which she did not sleep, she almost made up her mind to quit what, now, seemed a fool's errand, to go back home and forget the macabre night, to forget Danny, and to put behind her the quixotic impulse that had brought her to the Outer Banks. But could she forget Danny? Did she want to forget him?

Judith could not be sure that he had gone away until, three days after the burial of the girl, his first letter came. It was not a very coherent letter, and Judith read it with a wistful feeling that he should not have written it. It was crowded with disparagement of himself, beginning with that black month when his father lay dead on the sand and he had gone away, and coming down to that afternoon when he had slapped Jerry. . . . But there was no mention of the girl.

Nor was there any mention of the girl in the other letters that came. Sometimes they were brief, almost curt; sometimes they were long, rambling, not making much sense. Danny was, Judith was sure, tottering on the brink of utter despair. But she knew, too, that he would have to find his way out of the morass of conflicting emotions and loyalties. . . . Judith decided to wait.

"I guess I've sold my birthright for a little yellow leaf to wear on my shoulder," Danny wrote one day. "I've gone away —twice now. I guess, first and last, I've had a hand in killing more people than all my ancestors and their like have saved on the beach. My father was trying to save somebody when he died, but all I could think of was to go off and kill somebody else, maybe the ones who had killed him when he was trying to save somebody."

Judith took the letter out of the pocket of her green slacks and read it again. The light was beginning to fade out of the west, and the battlemented clouds along the southeast were mounting higher across the sky. She read slowly, stopping now and then to look out across the darkening water beyond the Point. The tops of the clouds were turning a glowing gold and the wind was stirring in their peaks. She could see them moving, swaying, caught between the wrestling winds. She put the letter back in her pocket, and when Augusta called her, she went inside where warm kitchen smells welcomed her.

29

SUCCULENT ODORS ISSUED FROM THE KITCHEN ATTENDED BY PURposeful sounds, and now and then, as Judith Hale got herself dressed, she could hear Augusta McGarrah's low and not wholly unmusical humming. Occasionally the woman was so forgetful of her own determined austerity that she emitted wisps of words that were, conceivably, some part of what must have been an Irish ballad which had to do with the more reputable aspects of love-making.

There's no doubt about it, Judith mused with a little smile tugging at the corners of her mouth: Augusta has become the object of a miracle — she's discovering spring for a second time and she's in love. Or maybe, Judith's thoughts ran on, it's the first spring she has ever had. Judith's smile was amused, tender — and a little sad. The sound of a dropped pan cut across her musing, and then there was silence in the kitchen.

Augusta's voice erupted and Judith was not quite able to believe her own ears. Augusta had said "damn!" with a considerable fervor. An interval of silence succeeded the expletive, and then there were a series of croakings, ending with yet another "damn." Then Augusta's dry laugh rattled out of the kitchen, coming at first in mildly hysterical overtones, and then more placidly. Judith came out of her room and went toward the kitchen.

"Augusta! You swore!"

"Well, did I now?" Augusta said calmly. "And what else

would a body do with an oven that's not big enough for two geese at one time? I ask you that?"

"Did it — make the oven bigger?" Judith was choked with laughter.

"Maybe it did and maybe it didn't," Augusta said, "but — how on earth did you manage to get the two biggest geese that ever came out of Canada or wherever it is they come from? Smaller ones would have done."

"I guess Jerry brought me luck," Judith replied. "Do you have to cook both? There'll only be four of you."

"It'll not be said of me that anybody who comes here to eat goes away hungry, especially on Christmas."

"I'm sure it'll be magnificent, Augusta, and I almost wish I were going to be here. Is there anything I can help you with before I go — set the table for you, maybe?"

"Not a thing, Miss," Augusta said primly. And then she added, her voice softening, "Junior's coming over after a while and fix some holly, and Leona said she knew where there is some galax."

"Junior?" Judith said, laughing, and Augusta turned back to the stove to hide the tide of crimson that slowly mounted her cheeks. "Well, I guess I'd as well be going along. Good luck, Augusta, and Merry Christmas."

"Same to you, Miss," Augusta said. As Judith went toward the front door Augusta called after her. "You sure you have your packages all done up? And you tell that young man Merry Christmas from me and to keep his shoes where he can get at 'em."

Judith took the three packages from the table beside the door and went outside. She dropped them on the cushion of the front seat of the car and stood for a moment looking down toward the Point. The sun was bright, but far out over the Diamonds fog lay low on the water. The air had a stillness that Judith had come to know as premonitory — this was the sort of day that could turn into almost anything. Already wisps of the fog had broken away and were climbing lazily above the Diamonds, drifting irresolutely.

The girl glanced along the road toward the Station. Even half a mile away, where he was turning into the road from the driveway, there could be no mistaking him: Chief Warrant Officer William Henry Ragland was afoot and, Judith could see, dressed up as she — and, had she known it, many beside her — had never seen him. He walked with an easy, rolling gait, his massive legs covering the road in an unhurried stride. Judith made no move to get into the car but stood, watching the Chief . . . waiting.

When he came to the foot of the hill the Chief turned upward toward the cottages, his even pace unbroken and not slowed by the steeply mounting road. His white-crowned cap was set at a somewhat rakish angle. The uniform, neatly creased, fitted him with the negligence of magnificence. . . . Some tailor outdid himself, Judith thought. . . . The shield of the Service gleamed above his cuff. There were ribbons above the left breast, a glowing cluster of them. Two of them were unfamiliar to her.

"Mornin', Miss," the Chief said casually as he came near. "Thought if you didn't mind I'd bum a ride over with you. They might need the jeep for somethin' while I'm gone, or they might have to come after me for somethin'."

"I'll be delighted to have you, Mr. Ragland." Judith managed a breathless little smile. "And anyhow, you'll be having that ride in this — this sex-wagon. My, but you're dressed up, Chief! You look wonderful."

"Christmas, ain't it? And excuse me for not sayin' it sooner, but — Merry Christmas."

"Thanks. The same to you, and many more, Mr. Ragland."

"I've had about my share already. This is my forty-second year in uniform, if I ain't got too old to count."

Judith slid under the steering wheel and tossed her parcels

into the rear seat, making room. The Chief got in, planted his huge feet flat on the floor. His knees came level with the instrument panel. Judith reached down at the end of the cushion and, pushing her heels against the floor, moved the seat backward. "I can still reach the wheel, Chief — and you'll have more room."

"I thank you kindly, Miss. There does seem to be more of these damned legs than there's any actual need of."

The Chief leaned backward against the cushions; his huge hands, enfolding three small bundles, lay loosely in his lap. Augusta's flushed face appeared at the door. The massive man looked up at her, and the impassive mask of his face broke in a slow smile.

"Goin' to get your hook into Bannister today, Ma'am?" he demanded blandly.

Augusta gave vent to a choked squawk and fled in confusion toward the kitchen.

"We better get gone from here, Miss, before I get my damned foot so deep down in my mouth that I won't be able to swallow a morsel of Polly Gray's vittles."

Judith started the car and swung around toward the road down the hill. The Chief rode in silence until they were past the Lighthouse. His eyes searched the eastern horizon appraisingly.

"Can't tell what the weather's likely to do when she starts off like this," he said. "She looks smooth and peaceable right now, but you can never trust her. Right now she's as calm as Polly Gray, but by moonrise she's liable to be actin' like Rufe Daniels' wife does most of the time — and it's a continuin' marvel to me how that man keeps her in throwin' dishes. It's sort of hard on him, the way they make these dishes: the thin ones that break easy against his head cost too damned much, and the cheap ones — well, I reckon he thinks sometimes his head'll come apart before the cup does." The Chief emitted an exaggerated, jocose sigh.

"Trouble with Rufe," he went on ruminatively, "is he's too damned nice. What he ought to have done was to get a slat out of the bed the first night he slept with her and left the print of it across her bottom. It would have saved a lot of dishes." He grinned with kindly malice. "A slat is somethin' like an oar," he went on. "There's times when they both come in handy, especially an oar when she —" he jerked his head, gesturing toward the surf rumbling beyond the dyke — "gets to behavin' bad.

"Of course Rufe's wife is a good woman — in a lot of ways," the Chief rumbled on. Judith wondered where this preoccupation with the vagaries of womankind, or of this woman she had never seen, would finally lead, but she was sure that the massive man was not talking idly.

"There ain't a woman in all these Woods that keeps a cleaner house than she does, even if she has to spend a lot of time goin' around pickin' up pieces of chinaware. She's a good neighbor, too, when she takes the notion, or she ain't too busy raisin' hell with Rufe. She's a religious woman, too, and as regular as August comes she gets religion all over again and gets up in church and tells how she's through raisin' hell with Rufe and with the help of her neighbors' prayers she don't aim to heave another dish at him. It don't do her no harm, but it ain't long before Rufe'll show up with a piece of stickin' plaster on his head.

"Rufe, he's a plumb smart fisherman, and I reckon he'd have been rich by now if he hadn't a-had to buy so many dishes for that damned woman of his to throw. And she'd have been lots happier if he'd spent more on bed slats and less on dishes. But the damnedest thing you've ever heard of is when she gets up in her church and starts a-prayin' over me. She thinks I'm a terrible wicked man. That woman you got back yonder, now — she's got the makin's of a dish-thrower in her: Bannister better keep an eye on her, especially the first day or two. Or nights, maybe."

Judith's laughter bubbled. The Chief fell silent as the car turned into the Woods and crossed the little bridge where, Judith always remembered when she rode over it, she had first encountered Jerry, the placid, mocking friendliness of his eyes, his smile that was, in so many ways, Danny's smile. But the weeks had subtly changed him. . . . The Chief's silence lengthened.

"Where's the boy they call Iowa?" Judith asked. "Jerry said he was coming to Christmas dinner, too."

"I guess he's already over there. He went off last night. Him and Jerry talk a lot — Iowa doin' his damnedest to convince Jerry that helicopters and such are goin' to be the thing from now on, and Jerry — well, as long as that boy lives there'll be a surfman on this beach, even if they have abolished the ratin' since the Coast Guard's been tryin' to act like it was a navy."

"Do you suppose there'd be a place for Danny, Chief, if something like that should happen — I mean, if the Service should become more — more mechanized?"

Big Bill Henry looked around at her, puzzled.

"I mean," Judith went on, confused by the directness of his glance, but determined, "I mean, could he shift over from the Air Force? You see, flying is all he knows — and I know that he wants to come home."

"How do you know it?"

"Why, why — he said so."

"When?"

"It's — his letters have been full of it."

"He can't row a boat," the big man said shortly.

"But Chief —"

"It takes an oar," the Chief said grimly.

Judith was relieved that they had come to the house and that the boy they called Iowa was scrambling up from one of the deck chairs on the lawn. He called out to Jerry, who answered him from within the house. He came out, and both youths came down the slope toward the car. The Chief had got down from the car and turned toward the house without a glance at Judith. He carried the three little parcels in a sort of basket he made of his fingers.

"You got a tree, Jerry?"

"Sure, we got a tree — Christmas, ain't it?"

"Put these things somewhere around it, and she's got some things there. See if she needs any help with 'em, Iowa."

The big man strode off toward the house, disappeared through the front door. Judith heard his booming greeting to Polly Gray, who came from the kitchen wiping her hands on her apron. Her welcome was placid, unhurried, warm. She took Judith to her room to leave her coat.

"We'll have dinner first and then we'll have the tree. Jerry insisted the dinner was the most important thing — the tree could wait."

There was no mention of Danny's absence during the dinner, nor afterward, when the dishes were washed, as they gathered around the tree in the living room. The Chief sat at one end of the extended table, Polly Gray at the other, with the two boys on her right. Judith had one side of the table to herself, her place set halfway. In the center of the white cloth a wreath of red-berried yoepon encircled a bowl of poinsettias.

"You wouldn't think them things would grow outdoors here this time of year, would you, Judy?" Jerry suggested after the Chief had rumbled through the grace.

"Oh, they didn't, Jerry!"

"Sure they did. And we had grapefruit for breakfast that growed right there in the back yard. Tree come up from seed Mom throwed out the back door a long time ago."

Judith exclaimed over the tenderness of the goose. Polly Gray carved it in long, thin slices, slices that seemed to Judith to melt in her mouth, and she wondered how well Augusta had made out with her two geese — and her three guests. There was wild rice, painstakingly gathered from the marsh, a growth now almost vanished before the devastation of wildfowl. There were vegetables, canned from Polly Gray's garden and, finally, there was potato pie.

At the head of the table the Chief ate with concentrated preoccupation, passing his plate back for a second helping, and even a third, of the goose. Jerry and Iowa seemed almost to outdo him in silence and in their devotion to their plates. Polly Gray ate sparingly, but her eyes were watchful of every plate at the table. Judith found herself just as quiet and as ready to pass her plate for more. . . . But none of them mentioned Danny. . . .

"Couldn't we wash the dishes — Iowa and Jerry and I? You must have been in the kitchen all day," Judith said to Polly Gray.

"Sure we can wash 'em," Jerry broke in. He looked doubtfully at Judith. "Maybe you'd better let me and Iowa wash 'em and you can wipe 'em — you ain't ever washed a dish with them hands, have you, Judy?"

"I'm learning — to fry meat, Jerry," Judith said evenly, her eyes smiling.

Jerry's face went scarlet, but his eyes held Judith's. He pushed his chair back from the table and stood up. "Let's get goin' — soon as I feed my cat. Then we'll go in yonder and see what Santa Claus fetched up. Mom, you and Bill Henry git."

When he had washed out the dish towels and was hanging them on the rack outside the kitchen door, Jerry observed casually, over his shoulder, "Danny missed a damned good dinner." He looked directly at Judith's surprised face when he came back into the kitchen. "Maybe him and you'll sit there next Christmas. Where you reckon you'll be, Iowa? Stompin' around in one of them damned cornfields?" He poked Iowa's middle. "Come on and let's make Bill Henry play like he was Old Buck."

"Old Buck?"

"Heck, yeah," Jerry said. "That's what they used to call Santa Claus down here, back when they had Christmas. They call it Old Christmas now. Had somethin' to do with changin' the calendar. Seems like after they started settlin' here people was so far from everywhere they didn't know for two or three hundred years that somebody had been monkeyin' with the calendar. Put on or took off twelve days, I forget which. Get Bill Henry to tell you — he remembers Old Christmas, and I reckon Mom does, too."

The six-foot tree, a cedar, decorated with tinsel and candles that, Judith knew, must have been stored thriftily away from year to year, stood in one corner of the room, the corner beyond the chair where Danny had sat that night.... With surprisingly mild protest Bill Henry acceded to Jerry's demand that he play Old Buck.

"Not that I'm goin' to get me a pair of cow horns and wear 'em," he grumbled. Judith was sure that, secretly, he was pleased. He sat down, cross-legged.... So that's where Jerry got that one, Judith thought.... Jerry sat down beside the tree, facing him, their knees almost touching. The others gathered around in a semicircle. The Chief took up a package from under the tree.

"This here one looks like it's meant for you, Polly," he said, holding it out to her. It was one of the packages that Judith had brought, and she was conscious of a little tremor of trepidation as she watched Polly Gray take the package, her fingers begin to tug at the knotted gay cord. Would they, all of them, think that she was overstepping the border, climbing the intangible barrier that separated her from them? Or was there any barrier, except of her own imagining?

Christmas shopping had been a not inconsiderable problem to Judith. Again Mrs. Grady had coached her in the procedures and expedients for coping with a single telephone line that served the Seven Villages, and again Miss Simmons had said it would be difficult. But the parcel had, in due time, arrived: a linen tablecloth with napkins for Polly Gray; two even more elaborately colored shirts for Jerry, with a muffler to match.

When it came to selecting something for the Chief, she had helplessly told Miss Simmons to get her father to pick out something for the biggest man he could imagine, but one shaped completely like a man. Seymour Hale had apparently passed the task to an establishment that prided itself upon solving the insoluble. But even now, when she watched the Chief's huge hands unwrapping his package, she was conscious of misgivings. He shook out the folds of a fabulous bathrobe, heavy, rustling silk, blue and lined with a lighter shade of the same color. Judith wondered if Jerry would laugh. Still, she was not surprised when he turned to her and said, almost inaudibly, "Gee, that's swell, Judy."

Iowa tore apart the slender envelope that had his name on it. "I'm sorry, Iowa," Judith said simply. "I'll have to get you to do your own shopping — I've just been sort of lost down here. You won't mind, will you?"

"Gee, thanks," the boy stammered. "Gosh — fifty dollars! That'll buy me a ticket home and back when I get my leave."

Judith breathed a sigh of relief when it was over, and then her throat filled when the Chief handed her a small, flat, and clumsily-wrapped package. She opened it, feeling Jerry's eyes searching her own and then looking away, quickly, self-consciously.

"There wasn't anything I could get around here that you'd have," he said, not looking at her. "That's — that's somethin' Danny give me before he left. I think he meant it for you. It's — it's from both of us."

Judith held the bit of delicately carved jade in her fingers. Her eyes were misty and she did not, for a moment, trust her voice; even her hand was unsteady when she reached out and laid it lightly on the boy's shoulder.

"He brung it from Japan — naw, it was China. They sent him over there for somethin' before he started home. He probably got it for a carton of cigarettes."

"It's perfect, Jerry," Judith said.

There were other things under the tree and the Chief grubbed among them with his massive hands. Polly Gray must, Judith thought, have been blessed with second sight on that trip to Norfolk when she had intuitively bought the oak leaves for Danny. Even Iowa had found a handkerchief at the store . . . but Judith could not know that it was one of a set that Mrs. Grady, with maternal prescience, had got for her own boy to give to some girl. The Chief sat moodily beside the tree.

"What's in them other bundles, Bill Henry?" Jerry prompted. The Chief emerged from his reverie. He took up one of the parcels, turned it loosely in his fingers. It was a little while before he spoke.

"I been goin' up to my house some, these last few nights, Polly," he said. He was almost shy, Judith thought. "Sort of kickin' around stuff up there. I don't go up there much, now; makes me feel old. But that's a good house. I had my boy in mind when I built it." The Chief reached out a massive hand and thrust his fingers into Jerry's thick loose hair. He turned him slowly about, until the boy faced away from him. The hand dropped to the boy's shoulder.

"I want you to have that house, Jerry," he said gruffly. "I want you to live in it, and I want you to have a whole houseful of babies. I want you to name one of 'em for me. I've put it down on a piece of paper. Mind now, it's a he-baby I want named for me."

"Okay, Bill Henry," Jerry said. His voice was quiet, steady, solemn.

"I got to rummagin' around up there last night, Polly," the Chief went on gruffly, "and I come across this thing here. You got the mate to it — remember? I thought maybe we ought to get them little pitchers together. Thought Dan might like it."

The Chief handed Polly Gray a square parcel. Her fingers trembled when she held out her hand to take it. It rested in her lap for a little and her eyes were remote, brooding . . .

remembering. Presently she began to undo the seaman's knot in the string that held the coarse paper around it. A little silver pitcher, intricately and delicately embossed, glistened against the dark texture of her dress.

"Thank you, Bill Henry," Polly Gray said softly.

"Where's the other one, Polly? You still got it?"

"I'll get it, if it's all right, Mom," Jerry said. His mother nodded. Presently the boy came back with another little pitcher in his hands, the duplicate of the other. Polly Gray set them in the palms of her hands and held them up. A wan shaft of sunlight from the window touched them. Judith's fascinated gaze could scarcely tear itself away from the two little pitchers. What significance, apart from their sheer, delicate beauty did these things hold? The Chief sensed her unspoken wonder.

"Her granddaddy and my daddy were together when that ship was wrecked," he said briefly. "Them pitchers were about all we were able to save — and we lost her granddaddy."

Judith thought, with detached amazement, of his use of the continuing pronoun. They were "we" down through the generations; and, although the massive man had not been born at the time, he still felt himself a part of whatever exploit gave these little symbols their worth. It was his heritage.

The little pitchers rested in Polly Gray's lap and her strong hands enfolded them. The Chief took up another of the parcels under the tree, held it over Jerry's shoulder and let it fall into the boy's lap. Jerry's fingers began tugging at the seaman's knots, folded back the paper. A leather case lay in his hands. He held it for a moment before his thumb found the hidden spring in the cover. It snapped open and Judith saw first, stamped on the white satin lining, the name of a fabulous jeweler. Inside glowed a wrist watch that, Judith knew, must have cost a surprising sum.

"I've been keepin' that for you, Jerry," the Chief said casually. "Feller I fished out of the water once sent it to me.

There's some readin' matter on the back of it, but there's room enough for your name down at the bottom, if they don't make it too big. The damned thing wouldn't go around my wrist anyhow, and I've never knowed I needed a watch. I can mostly tell the time without lookin' at any damned clock."

Without a word Jerry handed the watch back to the Chief, extended his left hand. The Chief took the watch and Jerry's arm turned, held still. The Chief unfastened the clasp of the heavy gold strap and snapped it into place. The two looked at each other, neither saying anything, until Jerry's hand dropped back. The Chief fumbled in his pocket, drew out an envelope, glared at Iowa.

"This here's for you," he said sternly.

Iowa took the envelope, opened it hesitantly. His eyes widened.

"Gosh — leave home for fifteen days!"

"You got one more," Jerry prompted when the excitement over Iowa's leave was subsiding. Without glancing down and without searching with his hands, the Chief took up the last of the packages under the tree. He did not look at it; his fingers began to undo the wrapping. A square, time-worn leather case lay across the palm of his hand. He opened it and his fingers caressed whatever was inside. He did not look at Judith, but the girl knew, when he began to speak without calling her name, that he was speaking to her.

"This here's not a present — not yet," he said, "but I hope it will be, girl. I reckon you'll think I'm a damned idiot, and maybe you're right. It was to have belonged to my boy, but she got him."

The big man fell silent and the lines about his mouth were hard, bitter and, when they relaxed, sad.

"He was on a cutter," he went on. "They sent him out when they began to get short of crews before we got in the fight. He was a good boatman."

Again he fell silent and only his fingers moved, softly, meditatively, across whatever it was that lay hidden inside the worn leather case. Judith glanced at Polly Gray, saw that her eyes were kindled with an unwonted light. Slowly the big hands moved, and through their fingers Judith caught sight of something that glittered, something that was bright with the yellow of gold, the blue of sapphire.

"When my granddaddy was young," the Chief went on, "he took a woman out of the water. She had this thing around her neck. They didn't get her husband — not alive. After she went home — her husband's grave is over yonder on the Point — she sent this thing to my granddaddy.

"There was a letter with it — it's inside here — that said it was his and for him to give it to the girl he married. He gave it to my grandmammy when he married her. She gave it to my daddy when he got ready to marry, and I gave it to my wife — my first one, that is. She died when my boy was a little feller. I never let any of my other wives see it."

Again an interval of silence fell. The Chief's eyes rested meditatively on Jerry's face. The boy returned his look, gravely silent.

"Since she got my boy," the big voice rumbled on presently, "I've intended for Danny to have it — he bein' the oldest. He's not here, not now. I'd sort of expected he'd be here. I'm leavin' it in your keep. If he comes back here and you marry him, it's yours."

Judith took the case, her face white, her eyes hidden below lashes that were wet. The thing lay in her hand, a gleaming blue star, encircled by a wreath of delicately chased leaves, the whole suspended on a golden chain.

"If it don't happen that way, give it to Polly there," the Chief said with sudden grim decision. "And you, Polly . . . ." The Chief stood up, his legs projecting the big body upward as if it had no weight of its own. Judith got slowly to her feet, facing him.

"None of that, woman," he said fiercely. "And if you try

kissin' me, dammit to hell, I'll take you across my knee and whale hell out of you! And I'll take that piece of junk and give it to the first . . . . Jerry, dammit! Ain't I goin' to get one damned thing out of you? Where's my Christmas present?"

"It's still there under the tree, you clumsy porpoise," Jerry said, "and you could have seen it if you hadn't been . . . . Here." Jerry reached far back under the tree and brought out a small parcel. "Thought you were tryin' to be cute or didn't even want anything."

Across the room's lesser confusion cut the sharp, stabbing sound of the jeep's siren. Judith, glancing out the window, saw Scarborough's ruddy head, saw him half tumble out of the vehicle. The sun's light had thinned and the sky beyond the marsh was darkening with rolling fog. Judith saw Jerry's shoulders flit past the window and in a moment she heard his voice, higher pitched than she was used to hearing it, insistent.

"Chief!" Jerry called again, but by then the big man was at the door, jamming his cap down on his head. He crossed the lawn, heading directly for the jeep, not waiting for the longer course down the walk. Then she heard him bellow: "Iowa!" The boy slid out of the room, tucking the two envelopes inside the top of his trousers.

Already the Chief was in the seat beside Scarborough. Jerry had disappeared into the interior. Judith saw Iowa go around to the back of the vehicle and climb through the open space where the plexiglass had been torn away. The vehicle turned crazily in the middle of the road, and with a screech went back in the direction from which it had come. Judith saw it duck into the tunnel through the yoepon.

"I wonder what's happened. They've gone off without a word to anybody," Judith said.

Judith turned to Polly Gray, who had moved over to the window. No sign of surprise showed in her face, in her eyes. She stood looking quietly out the window, in the direction in which the vehicle had gone. Fog was rolling across the marsh and the wind was stirring in the tops of the live oaks.

"Wouldn't you have thought they'd at least tell us what has happened?" Judith asked, her tone puzzled, tinged with impatience.

"No, Judith," Polly Gray's voice was quiet, even. "They never do — they never have. The sea has called them, I guess. That's something that all women — along these Banks — know. When the sea calls them, they go."

"When — when do you suppose we'll see them again?"

"That's something else we never let ourselves think about, Judith. They'll come back — when she's through with them. Sometimes, they don't come back."

"Oh, I'm sorry," Judith said.

"That's all right," Polly Gray said calmly. She was silent for a little. She had turned away from the window. "Wouldn't you like to turn on the radio and see if there's some Christmas music while I straighten up the house? There's always some litter about a party, isn't there?"

"Mayn't I help you, Mrs. Gray?"

"There's nothing, really, Judith. I guess we just get into the habit of straightening up. You get us some music and I'll sit down with you in just a little."

Judith turned to the radio and in a moment the room echoed to the sound of carols. It seemed somehow incongruous that the room should be filled with such music. It had been so lately crowded with the sudden portent of . . . evil. Far off, the muted, insistent surf beat against the shore, and it was as if the sea's voice mocked all people everywhere whose voices were lifted in the singing of carols. There was something of the sound of the sea's challenge in the very lifting of Jerry's voice.

And then the carols died and there was no sound left except the crackling inside the radio. The interval lengthened and then a voice said, "We interrupt this broadcast to bring you a bulletin that has just this moment come to us from Coast Guard Headquarters here. Six survivors of the crew of a Norwegian tanker have been picked up on a raft twenty miles northeast of Cape Hatteras. The tanker broke in half in a sudden storm off the Cape last night. One half of it is known to have sunk. No word has been received of the other half. Normally the vessel carried a crew of forty-two. A general alert has been sounded and surface craft have been dispatched to the scene. Those rescued are proceeding to New York aboard the merchantman that picked them up. The tanker's wireless was severed when she broke in two, and no distress call could be sent. Further bulletins will be put on the air as received. We now return you to our scheduled program of Christmas music."

30

"WERE YOU LISTENING, MRS. GRAY? CAN YOU IMAGINE THAT! Happening right here on our—on your very doorstep!" Judith's voice mirrored her excitement. Polly Gray came back into the room.

"Yes, I heard it, Judith," Polly Gray said calmly.

"Do you suppose that's the reason the Chief and the boys left here in such a hurry? Will they go out, do you think?"

Polly Gray shook her head slowly. "I don't know, Judith. We never know — until they come back."

"Couldn't we drive over to the beach — there's a radio in my car — and see what's happened? This is the most exciting thing that's ever happened in my whole life — I just can't bear it — and maybe there's something we could do to help."

"No, Judith," Polly Gray said with almost stoic calm. "I'll stay here. I'll be here when they come back. They might need me then — here."

A puzzled look came over the girl's face. She turned irresolutely from the radio, her fingers dropping away from the dial, which she had been turning aimlessly, shifting from one station to another. The room was filled with a disjointed, fragmentary caroling, with snatches of a great orchestra. The schooled, measured voice of an actor went through the cadences of the Dickens Christmas story.

"But I feel so helpless, so useless," Judith protested. "Just sitting here. Couldn't we make coffee for them, things like that, if they're going to be out there? It's cold and raw on the beach."

"They will manage for themselves," Polly Gray said calmly.

"But isn't there something we can do?" The girl's voice was impatient, rebellious.

"We can wait. That's the hardest thing that we women, here, have had to learn to do. But we've learned it, most of us. . . ."

"Oh, I'm sorry," Judith said, her voice scarcely a whisper.

"My mother waited and her mother before her — and I have waited," Polly Gray went on. "Sometimes I have thought that theirs is the easier thing to do, but I can not judge that."

The woman sat down, her hands with fingers interlaced lying in her lap. She seemed scarcely aware of the carols. Judith turned the dial back to the station from which the Beethoven Fifth, gathering its strength in mighty summation, would presently sweep to its mighty climax. . . . Far off the rhythmic beat of the tide became a dark tapestry of sound against which the violins sang. Outside the wind mounted. Somewhere a shutter rattled. Dusk gathered in the room.

"They think of the sea as a woman — that's how, you must have noticed, they speak of it." Polly Gray's voice was calm, meditative. "I think, oftentimes, that she must be as jealous of us as we are of her. And it wouldn't do for us to go out there — when she's having her way with them.

"And it may be that's why they don't want us out there," she went on. "They love the sea. They love us, too, but in the way that men love wives — not mistresses. I think, sometimes, Judith, they would be ashamed for us to see them with her. I'm afraid I must sound like a foolish, hysterical, neglected woman, but somehow you must understand — if you are going to marry Danny. Your heart will break, or his, if you don't. It has always been so."

The girl's lips were tremulous. "But — I don't know — whether I'm going to marry Danny. He's gone away."

"He will come back, to you and to her," Polly Gray said. Her voice was serene. Across the hearth the girl's face slowly sagged until it rested in her hands. Her shoulders shook. The woman heard a stifled sob.

The radio's voice cut across the stillness.

"Before we go on with our next broadcast," the voice said, "we bring you a bulletin concerning the ill-fated tanker that broke in half twenty miles northeast of Cape Hatteras. Six survivors of the crew of forty-two have been picked up by a passing freighter. Nothing is yet known of the fate of the other thirty-six. Sea, air, and shore stations of the Coast Guard have been alerted all along the Atlantic coast, and by daylight tomorrow morning a wide search of the sea frontier will be under way. Surface craft have been dispatched to the scene, and Army, Navy, and Coast Guard aircraft have been ordered to stand by.

"A brief message from the freighter aboard which the six men taken from a life raft are being treated for exposure states that they are in fair condition. Their names are not yet available. Weather as reported by the freighter earlier this afternoon is not favorable. We continue now with our regularly scheduled program. . . ."

Jerry let himself into the house from the back door without making any sound. The two women first learned of his presence when a light clicked on. Judith started up, as if involuntarily, and Polly Gray knew that the girl was about to begin with eager questioning. She laid a gentle hand on the girl's shoulder.

"Hi, Mom — hi, Judy," Jerry said casually. "Got to get my boots and take off this fancy gear." He disappeared into his room. Almost immediately he was back, in dungarees, his long rubber boots folded around his knees.

"Guess I'll wear this shirt, anyhow — might get cold out yonder after a while."

"Is everything all right, Jerry?" Judith's tone was anxious.

"Okay," the boy said briefly. He came around to the back of his mother's chair, stood beside her, across from Judith. He held out a limp wrist, encircled by the heavy strap of the watch. "Unhook that and keep it for me, will you, Mom — might get it wet. They say it's waterproof, but I don't believe it — not enough to take chances with it, anyhow."

Polly Gray loosened the strap and slipped the watch off over the boy's hand. She held it in her hands, examined it briefly before she looked up. Jerry was looking down at her, his eyes veiled, unsmiling.

"See you after a while, Mom," he said. "You, too, Judy."

With that he went out of the room, and in a moment the two women heard the sound of the jeep's engine, heard the gears complain as it got under way. The sound ebbed, was swallowed up by the far-off roar of the surf. Quiet came back into the room.

"So that's how it is," Judith said.

"That's how it is — that's how it has always been. And I suppose that's how it will always be, Judith."

As the night deepened, the wind rose and the beat of the surf mounted into an unending roar. Polly Gray went to the kitchen and made coffee. Judith lighted the fire, more for its cheerfulness than for its warmth. Polly Gray brought coffee and sandwiches, with slices of her Christmas fruitcake, and set them on a low table before the fire. The room was warm, placidly cheerful. Judith turned the volume of the radio down until it was a whisper, sure that her ear would tell her if there was any news from . . . out yonder.

Above the mantel the ship's clock measured the seconds, the minutes, an hour . . . another . . . and another. Daniel Gray had, long ago, muffled the bell hidden away inside the clock so that its ringing at half-hour intervals would not reverberate through the house. Across the hearth Polly Gray sat, mostly in a soft, unquestioning silence . . . waiting. She did not, ever, glance at the clock, Judith noticed ... she, whose waiting was not measured in the ticking of a clock.

But for the girl the clock's implacable ticking, the half-hour pealing of its muffled bell, the slow march of the hands across its face were the measure of time. She moved, restlessly, in her chair. The woman across the hearth seemed not to be aware of it. Finally, Judith stood up.

"I really ought to get over to the cottage and see how Augusta fares," she said. "You know, Mrs. Gray, this must be a great day in Augusta's life — she's in love."

Polly Gray showed no sign of surprise. A warm, half-amused little smile lifted the corners of her mouth. "Mr. O'Neal? Jerry told me. I hope she will make him happy."

"But will he make her happy?"

"If he's happy, that will be her happiness — if she's in love with him."

Judith flushed at the gentle rebuke.

"Won't you ride out with me, Mrs. Gray? I'll bring you back whenever you're ready to come."

"No, Judith, I'll stay here. Jerry might come in."

Lights were dim in the house when Judith drove up the hill, but in the last cottage along the row, where the young groom and his bride lived, the windows were bright with lighted lamps. Judith went into the living room of her cottage; there was no response when she called out to Augusta. She turned up the lamps, sat down before the unlighted hearth, and reached for a cigarette. Augusta had not neglected anything. She tossed the match from her cigarette neatly into the little nest of oiled paper. Flames kindled on the hearth.

Glancing around, Judith saw that the cottage was spotlessly clean, with no sign anywhere of recent feasting and merriment. She looked into the kitchen: every pot, every pan was in its place; the white enamel of the range was virginally clean. In her own room the covers on the bed were turned back.

That would be like Augusta, who never overlooked, nor missed, anything. . . . But the house was depressingly empty . . . lonely.

Then the door latch clicked. Augusta's face glowed contentedly when she bustled into the room.

"I was down at the other house," she reported calmly. "All the men are gone. I tried to get Leona to come on up here with me but she said she'd better stay where Junior left her. He might come in. The men, both of them, are gone — went off before dark. Some of 'em came after Junior, and Mr. O'Neal went, too. Reminded me of how they say an old fire horse is. I guess they're over yonder on that beach. I don't know what happened."

Judith told her the little she knew of what had happened. Augusta listened without comment. She went out and brought a fresh pack of cigarettes and laid it on the stand beside Judith's chair. She sat down, but Judith thought she had the air of a woman who had no purpose to remain stationary for any considerable time. After a while Judith said that she believed she'd drive back over through the Woods, since she was not sleepy. . . . Would Augusta like to go along?

"If you don't mind, Miss, I think I'll go back down there — that poor girl's all alone, and she wants to stay there in case Junior comes back."

"You're learning, Augusta — or maybe you've always known," Judith said. "I may stop in for a while with Mrs. Gray, but I'll be all right alone here, so don't worry about me."

When she came to the Lighthouse, Judith stopped the car and dimmed the lights. She left the radio on, turned down until it was a low murmur against the pounding of the sea just beyond the second dyke. Here a sharp-clawed wind tore at the tendrils of her hair under the knotted scarf. Overhead an occasional star could be seen through broken clouds that tumbled in disarray across the sky.

She got out and closed the door behind her. She walked

along the rutted, soft trail that climbed the dyke, dipped down into the hollow, and mounted the seaward rise. Sea oats rubbed their dry heads together with a staccato rustling. Beyond — below from where she stood — the sea writhed in torment and, with the wind, cried out against the frothing crests of long, rolling swells that came shoreward, spending their initial frenzy against the bar two hundred yards offshore and re-forming before they flung themselves on the beach at her feet. The tide was at flood.

Far down the beach to her right Judith's eyes caught the glimmer of lanterns. She strained her ears, wondering if she might hear the towering voice of the Chief above the sea's tumult. There was no sound except the dull, challenging roar of the surf's pounding. Two shadows, darker than the dark of the water beyond them, were outlined against the sea. The shadows moved, methodically plodding in vigil. Judith put by an impulse to call out to them, to run toward them with her questions. After a while she turned back to the car.

Without any definite purpose or objective Judith drove into the Woods. She would, she thought restlessly, go back to Mrs. Gray. The woman must be lonely there . . . waiting. But when she came to the house only the small light inside the living room door was burning: Polly Gray had, of course, gone to bed, the girl concluded. She drove on, down through the Woods, aimlessly, scarcely aware that she was driving. The radio hummed beneath the cowling, and the hands of the clock on the instrument panel marked midnight.

As she went along through the village Judith became aware that in every house, even at midnight, there was, burning low, a single light. In some of the houses there were other lights, as if people were still awake. But in most houses, a small single light, near the door. . . . The people of the village were waiting. . . . The women of the Woods were keeping their ancient, quiet vigil. . . .

Judith was only half listening when the cadence of the radio quickened, an aimless tune died in the middle of a bar, and a clipped, brisk voice came in its place. She reached for the dial in a little panic at the thought that she might have missed something. She let go the steering wheel. The car responded to her reflexes when she pressed the brakes. The radio's voice boomed across the silence of the Woods around her.

"From New York we bring you the latest bulletins from the Coast Guard Search and Rescue Force here. No further word has been received as to the fate of thirty-six members of the crew of the ill-fated Norwegian tanker, unaccounted for since their ship broke in half last night twenty miles northeast of Cape Hatteras.

"But with the coming of today's dawn a search will be under way above the lonely wastes of the Atlantic off the Carolina coast, with both air and surface craft taking part, weather permitting.

"From New York, within the next three hours, the first of the Search and Rescue aircraft will take off and proceed to a rendezvous off Cape Hatteras. By dawn it should be above that area known the world over as the Graveyard of the Atlantic. The big patrol plane, a Mariner, will be piloted by a native of the little-known village that lies hidden away in the woods back of the Cape.

"Major Daniel Gray, who was recently awarded signal honors when he returned from the wars in the Pacific, arrived in New York yesterday in the course of his efforts to obtain a transfer from the Army Air Forces to the Coast Guard, in which four generations of his family have seen service. He is being permitted to fly this mission only because of a shortage of personnel due to the holiday season. He volunteered to pilot the plane. . . ."

Judith watched the dawn come up like a flame beyond the Lighthouse, watched the pale flash of the Light on the wall at the foot of her bed give way before the spreading dawn. Clouds raced thinly across the sky before a waning wind that, when it came to the sea oats nodding outside the window, was listless, fitful. She had not slept; throughout the night she had lain . . . waiting.

Augusta had not come back to the cottage. Judith had left a lamp, turned low, against the window that looked out across the rolling pines toward the Point.

While she waited for the coffee to bubble in the percolator, Judith went outside to look toward the sweep of the sea. The thud of the surf against the beach was muted, as if the sea had wearied of the night's passion. The sun came up out of the low ridge of cloud that lay along the horizon, the ocean was the color of blood, and the white caps of the frothing waves were tipped with scarlet. . . .

Above the rumble of the surf came the measured, confident beat of propellers, far off to the north. When the Mariner came down over the Woods, the light made a whirling rainbow on each side of the plane's nose as the propellers caught and turned back the sun's ruddy glance. The big ship came steadily across the Woods, toward the Lighthouse and not higher than its crown. It's left wing dropped and the Mariner made a tight circle of the spiral-striped shaft, as if to get its bearings. It climbed toward the sun.

Judith went back into the cottage and poured coffee. By the time she had finished the second cup and come outside, the bastion of clouds along the east had vanished. The sky was clear and the wind came in gentle swells. Judith looked along the beach, her scrutiny moving from the Point northward, searching every object it encountered before moving on. Below the Lighthouse a thin gray smoke spiraled upward, as if someone had built a driftwood fire.

The girl went to the car and turned on the radio, setting the dial for a station that, she knew, would broadcast news events within a few minutes. When it came the news was perfunctory. There was, the report said, nothing new to be added to last night's story of the rescue of the six survivors. Search was under way, with aircraft and surface vessels from many points converging in the area to be searched, northeast of Cape Hatteras. They would fan out in a widening pattern until the entire area had been covered.

Augusta came along the crest of the ridge from the last cottage. She smiled a little guiltily, placatively, but at the same time Judith sensed an air of satisfaction . . . with herself. Something had happened to Augusta. . . .

"Heard any news, Miss?"

"Nothing much," Judith answered impassively.

"I thought I heard an airplane," Augusta said.

"One came over."

Augusta went into the cottage and Judith heard the preliminary rustling of pans, heard the door of the cabinet where she kept the coffee opened and closed. In the east the sun mounted, shook off its clinging cloak of mist. The Mariner was beyond hearing, beyond sight. Judith went into the house and closed the door of her room behind her. After a while, when Augusta called her to breakfast, all sign of the night's vigil, the hollowness of her cheeks, the wanness of her eyes, had vanished. After breakfast she went outside and settled herself in the sun . . . waiting.

Throughout the morning Judith sat in the sun, outwardly calm. She put away impulses that came to tug at her — an impulse to get up and turn on the radio, an impulse to get in the car and drive over to see Mrs. Gray, to see how she had fared through the night . . . and if she had news from anywhere. Perhaps she had not heard the radio when it announced Danny's coming — home. Judith put away that impulse and responded to another, more insistent, recurrent. She would not go down to the beach, or over to the Station, no matter how eager her thirst for some little drop of reassurance might become. . . . She would wait.

Now and then Augusta came to the door and peered down at her, and about midmorning the young bride came up from her cottage. She tarried outside with Judith for a little while. Judith found it difficult to find anything that seemed worth saying . . . anything that would not sound strained, forced, unreal. She wanted . . . to wait alone.

At the railing around the watchtower at the Station Judith could discern the figures of two men . . . a double watch. They leaned out over the railing, their gaze seaward. Now and then she could see the little jeep scuttling across the sand to the Station, and almost as soon as it had come it would dart away again and disappear beyond the dyke. She heard the solid roar of the duck's engine, and presently it lumbered out across the sand with the Station's big lifeboat lashed in its cradle. In its wake went the weapons-carrier with the smaller boat in tow.

By midmorning the sky seemed to vibrate with the far-off droning of engines but, strain her eyes as she might, Judith could not see any aircraft. There was no life along the road; no cars came, or went.

Judith got up from the deck chair and opened the door of the car. She slipped under the steering wheel and reached for the ignition switch. The starter took hold falteringly. . . . The battery needs some new life in it — using the radio too much, Judith thought. . . . She repressed an impulse to reach for the gear lever: she would let the engine run until the battery was strong enough to sustain the radio. She clicked on the radio, set the brake, and got out of the car, leaving the engine purring. She sat down . . . waiting. . . . Somewhere a baffled wife loosed her frustrations on behalf of the maker of some sort of washing powder. Judith shrugged it away. . . . The jeep raced crazily out of the driveway and cut directly across to the dyke.

Beneath the instrument panel's cowling the frustrated wife approached the day's climax of her misery. Her words were cut off as if a knife had sliced through them. There was a moment of silence and then a crisp, somewhat breathless, man's voice came. It was, for a sentence or two, not quite clear. Then it settled down, purposefully, confident.

"We clear all stations now to bring you what must be, we are sure, one of the most dramatic events in the history of broadcasting," the voice said. "This morning a member of our staff took off from New York aboard an Army bomber which had been ordered to participate in the search for missing members of the crew of a Norwegian tanker which broke in half off Cape Hatteras thirty-four hours ago.

"We have just received our first message from him, over the bomber's short-wave radio. The plane is now circling above a point off the North Carolina coast where a life raft has just been sighted with four men clinging to it. We take you now to the plane off Cape Hatteras."

The voice faded and another, far off, mechanical but clear enough, came.

"This is George DeVane speaking to you from the bombardier's compartment of a Flying Fortress over the Atlantic Ocean. I have not checked with the navigator to determine just where we are, but as I look off to the west I'm sure I can see faintly outlined against the horizon the shaft of what must be the Lighthouse at Cape Hatteras.

"We have just sighted a life raft. At this moment I am about one thousand feet above it and off a little to one side. Our pilot is giving plenty of room to a big Mariner circling below us. It was the crew of the Mariner that discovered the raft a few minutes ago. They passed the word along to us by radio and we have just arrived here. There are four men on the raft, which seems to be pretty heavily waterlogged. Two of the men have most of their bodies over the side and are clinging to ropes.

"From here it looks as if the raft were rolling pretty heavily, but the sea is reasonably calm. Our radio, a few minutes ago, sent out an alert to any ships that may be in this vicinity. The procedure is, as I understand it, that if the sea is too rough for an aircraft to risk landing, some passing surface craft will be diverted from its course to the scene. I have kept a sharp watch all day, and I have not seen a surface vessel since just south of Hampton Roads when we passed a Coast Guard cutter headed this way, about two hours ago.

"The Mariner is in a tight circle just above the raft now and we are coming down lower where I can get a better view. It looks from here as if the pilot of the Mariner, who is, I heard before I left New York, Major Daniel Gray, whose home is yonder in a village beyond that lighthouse — if it is a lighthouse that I can see — is trying to figure out the situation on the raft.

"From here I can see all four men now. One of them has waved his hand at the Mariner, but it looked like a mighty weak gesture to me. There is no response from the other three. One of them is lying face down with his feet trailing in the water. The Mariner has just dropped what looks like — I'll tell you in a minute — it is a life raft. The line from the life raft fell right square across the raft the men are on. One of the men, the one who waved his hand, has taken hold of the line, but it looks from here as if he is too weak to pull the raft toward him.

"Now the Mariner has come out of its tight circle and leveled off. He is climbing slightly and veering away from the raft below us. I can see the face of the man who reached for the line. It is turning as if his eyes are following the Mariner. I don't know what is going to happen — it looks from here as if it is all up to the pilot of that Mariner. There is not a ship in sight and it would take hours for one to reach here. From their looks the men down there on that raft would not last that long.

"The ship I am on is, of course, a land plane and there's nothing it can do. Two more bombers have arrived in the vicinity, incidentally, and are circling well above us, and I think I see a couple of PBY's coming over the horizon. There's not much they can do, either, though they are amphibians. The man who took hold of the line across that raft has just tried to pull himself aboard the life raft but right now he is lying still. Looks exhausted from here.

"That Mariner is going to risk a landing. He is taking a chance, that Mariner pilot. He has leveled off about a mile away and is headed into the little wind that shows from the smoke bomb he dropped. If he's as good as he looks from here and he's lucky he will set her down right at the raft. Now it looks as if that's what he's going to do. We have circled around right behind him and now he is right in front of my nose."

The voice ebbed into a silence that seemed eternity-long to Judith. She got up from the deck chair and started in a run toward the car. The voice came again, stronger.

"He made it! The sea is pretty rough but that Mariner is a big stout ship. It can take a good sea. The rear hatch is open now. I guess I should have said the after hatch. There is a man standing in the opening with an inflated yellow raft in his hands, ready to throw it overboard . . . no, he drops it over and another man holds it while the first gets aboard. They are on the windward side of the raft where the marooned men are and when he is cut loose — no, they're going to hold him with a line, paying it out as he drifts back to the men. The big plane's engines are turning over just fast enough to hold her into the wind.

"Now the raft has drifted down to the other raft, the one with the men on it and the man on the new raft — I hope I'm making this clear — is reaching out to take hold of it. He is bareheaded and he has a lot of bright blond hair. He's aboard now, lashing the little raft to the big one. Now he is taking hold of one of the men, a limp one, and rolling him on to the little raft. Now he has his hands on another. The raft looks full from here.

"He's back at the line now and it looks from here as if the

other raft, the one they dropped, is going to come in handy after all. It is alongside now and the third man is being rolled aboard it. The sea is a little rougher than it looked a while ago, but the blond boy is helping the fourth man into the second raft. He's in and the rafts are tied together, tandem fashion. The fellow cuts loose from the big, waterlogged raft. He waves to the men at the open hatch of the Mariner and they are beginning to haul on the line. It looks as if the blond boy is being left behind — no — he's overboard and clinging to the tail of the second raft. Not room enough for him aboard.

"Now the raft, the first one, is at the open hatch of the Mariner and they are lifting the men off it. Now the second raft is at the hatch and — wait a minute, somebody's got his hands under the blond boy's armpits. I'm not sure but I think he looked up here and waved at me. He's aboard now and the hatch is shut and all that's left to do now is to take the ship off, get back into the air and take these men to where they can get medical attention. They must need it. I'm not sure, but the ocean looks a lot rougher to me than it did fifteen or twenty minutes ago. The Mariner's engines are beginning to turn up and he's squared away for the take-off.

"She's under way now, but it's rough going — a big wave caught a wing tip but the other one came up just in time to shake off the full impact of it. She's gaining, but she's bouncing. Just now she looked as if she were clear but she smacked into the top of the next wave with a crack that I could almost hear. . . . She's off, but she sure staggered off, and from here it looks as if she's still groggy. Maybe it's because she hasn't got her flying speed — too early to say. From here it looks as if he had just wished her off the water. He's holding her down, just out of reach of the waves, nursing her along. Boy, that boy can fly. . . .

"We — the Flying Fortress I'm in — are alongside her right now, throttled back, and just above him. Gosh, it's that blond-headed boy that's flying her. He looks mighty grim from here.

I'm afraid now that he's in real trouble. One of his rudders looks bent out of line and the ship seems awfully sluggish to me. She's climbing a little, but mighty slowly. She's about a hundred feet up now, and that boy — it must be that Major Gray — is inching her around as if he might be heading for land.

"We are flying just about a hundred feet above him now. Just above us and back of us are two PBY's, with their yellow belly-bands that identify this new Search and Rescue outfit. The sea is really beginning to look rough and the air, too. This old crate is rolling as if she were headed through what the boys used to call flack — remember?

"Our radio operator has just scrouged in here beside me and he says the radio on the Mariner is out now. I've looked, and her aerial wires have broken loose at the tail where a wave cracked her. But she's steaming ahead, making about ninety knots, I'd guess. That's slow for a Mariner, just above her stalling speed, but at that rate it won't take many minutes to make landfall. I can see the Lighthouse from here now. It looks like a big stick of candy stuck in the yellow sand.

"Now I can make out some people on the beach a little below the Lighthouse. They've got a boat — no — two boats. The Mariner is losing a little of her altitude and there's some smoke coming from her starboard engine. But she's still plowing along. We've throttled back but now we have to pick up and climb and circle to keep our normal flying speed and still keep her in sight. The PBY's have moved in close on the Mariner's tail. Now I can see a little jeep from here, racing along the beach toward where the men with the boats are. Gosh, it looks as if they're ready to put a boat through that surf, and that, ladies and gentlemen, will be something. From here the surf looks pretty rough.

"From here it looks as if there is no choice for the Mariner. They're going to have to ditch her. Right now she is circling the Lighthouse in a wide, groggy turn, and she's trailing some black smoke from that engine. Now she is back over the water again. They've got that boat through the surf and it is bobbing like a cork. Maybe it would be nearer right to say that she's dancing like a ballerina. She's out beyond the second line of breakers now.

"The Mariner is coming down . . . lower . . . lower. She's just above the water now. The spray has hidden her . . . no, there she is, her wings just above the top of the water. The PBY's have come in low, just above her, and both of them have sent their yellow life rafts tumbling down, almost smack against the Mariner's wings. The waves are breaking over the wings and the lifeboat is coming up.

"There's a man at the stern of the lifeboat who looks like a giant from here. The hatch between the Mariner's wings is open and there is an arm reaching for one of the yellow inflated rafts. There are men on the yellow raft now and there's a line to the lifeboat. The giant at the stern is holding her steady.

"They are hauling now, and I believe the men they picked up a little while ago are all in the big lifeboat. As yet I have not seen the young pilot's blond head, but I'm sure he must be all right. There is a line from the ditched Mariner to the lifeboat now and there are the crew, in life belts, pulling them-selves along it toward the lifeboat. There's the blond head of Major Gray, last in the line. That makes nine altogether and I guess that's all.

"The four men on the raft are being lifted aboard the life-boat. The others in the water are climbing over the side. The crew of the lifeboat have their hands full. Now they are all aboard and that big fellow in the stern has swung her around toward the beach. If he brings her in he will be as good a skipper as the boy who took that Mariner off. . . . They are over the first line of breakers. The big man is steering with an oar and I can see his big shoulders heave. Hold it — something has happened down there. The lifeboat has sort of swerved off its — the big man has sort of sagged down in the boat and

I can see — I don't know what a shirt like that is doing in a lifeboat but from here it looks like Joseph's coat. Whoever is wearing it has moved back to the stern. He has taken the oar. He has swung the boat out of the trough that she fell off into when the big fellow dropped the oar. It — I can't see him now. The boat is poised now, right on top of a wave. The steering oar is deep down and holding her steady — there she goes — through the — I can't quite see her for the foam — there she is, her bow is well up on the beach and a lot of men are running toward her.

"The fellow with that shirt on has dropped the oar and is just standing there looking down at the big fellow who is lying terribly still in the bottom of the boat. There is a vehicle that looks like an ambulance coming up and they are lifting the shipwrecked men out of the boat.

"The waves are still washing about it. I'm sure the men around it are wet to their middles when a wave breaks but they have good solid ground under their feet. The big fellow is lying still and the blond pilot and the fellow with the shirt are bending over him. We are coming in low, now, and I'll give you my last glimpse in just a moment. . . . The men are all out of the boat now, except the big fellow. He is lying still and the fellow with the shirt is kneeling there, alone with him. We are climbing away, now, and I guess this ship will return to the search. That's all from me, ladies and gentlemen."

31

JUDITH WAITED. WHEN THE PLANES WERE GONE, AFTER SHE HAD
silenced the radio and stilled the purring of the engine, she sat
down again. She saw the jeep come slowly across the dyke,
saw the ambulance come in its wake. After a while the weapons-carrier came with its little boat and the lumbering behemoth with the lifeboat lashed in its cradle. They moved slowly,
as if weighted with a great weariness . . . or with weightier
grief. . . . The flag at the Station came slowly down to half
staff. . . .

None of them came along the road past the foot of the hill.
When they were at the Station they remained there. Judith
did not look toward the Lighthouse, nor at the dyke stretching
southward from it. Beyond it, hidden from her seeing, Danny
had come home. And the Chief had. . . . gone home. Augusta
had not listened to all that had come in the broadcast. Now
and then she had tiptoed silently to stand just inside the door,
where she could hear, but then had gone back to the kitchen
window, through which she could see the Lighthouse. . . .

When midday came Augusta came and stood beside Judith.
Once she started to reach out with her hand, to lay it in tenderness on Judith's shoulder. She drew back. Something of the
girl's aloneness communicated itself to her. She said, as gently
as she could, that lunch was ready and Judith must come and
eat something. The girl shook her head. Augusta went away
to the kitchen. After a while Judith went into the cottage, to
her room. She closed the door.

Augusta came out of the house and sat down. Through the long afternoon she sat still in her chair. The light waned. Along the road she saw the O'Neal boy coming toward the hill. He moved slowly, leadenly, with his head bowed. He did not glance toward Augusta when he went, by a shorter path, directly toward the house at the end of the row. Augusta went back to her kitchen and brewed coffee. She carried a cup in to Judith, hesitant before the shut door.

But when she opened it, without knocking, Judith was sitting on the side of the bed. If there had been tears, all sign of them was gone now. She was calm, a little pale, Augusta thought. But there was a new light in her eyes, a light that Augusta had never seen there . . . until now. . . . "She's a woman, now," Augusta said to herself, and she was suddenly very lonely.

Judith drank the coffee. She thanked Augusta absently, and the woman went away. Presently the girl pulled on a sweater and went outside. The sunset would be gray, tinged, lightened for a moment by a glowing gold that faded into a light green. . . . Jerry would say that there was going to be some weather tomorrow. . . .

In the dusk a figure moved along the road. From where she sat in the deck chair Judith could not be sure who it was, and when it came to the turning of the road at the bottom of the hill, her breath slowed, almost halted. The figure turned up the hill, and when it was halfway along the slope Judith saw that it was the boy they called Iowa. . . . He was hollow-eyed and the rims of his eyes were red.

"Good evening, Miss Judith — may I come up for a minute?"

"Of course, Iowa; I'm glad to see you — shall we go inside?"

"No, Miss Judith — I'll — I'll not bother you but just a minute. There's — I wonder if you'd mind if I was to ask you to do something for me?"

"Of course not, Iowa — anything."

The boy was hesitant, turned away, looking back at the Station.

"What is it, Iowa — sit down and tell me."

"That — that present you gave me yesterday . . . I wonder if you'd take it back and get something for me, Miss Judith."

"What could I get for you, Iowa?" Judith said gently.

"They said it was you that got the flowers for that — that girl that died. I wonder if you could get me some — for the Chief."

"Yes, Iowa, I'll get them."

"And if you could, would you tell 'em to put in a card — that says they're from me and Jerry."

The boy's voice broke and his shoulders shook. He buried his face in his hands, and Judith's hand stole gently across his shoulder.

"Don't try to tell me, Iowa — I heard it. But I thought you were going on leave — that was part of your Christmas present."

"No, Miss Judith, I'm not going. I've got to stay here with Jerry. I'm going over and stay my leave with him, if they'll let me."

"They'll let you, Iowa."

"Anyway, there's the funeral. I wish there was something I could — that somebody could do for Jerry."

"He must be terribly hurt, Iowa."

"I know he is, but he — he won't cry. I believe it would do him good if he was to cry. He just won't say anything to anybody. Not even to Danny."

"Is Danny — no, Iowa, I won't ask."

"Yes'm, he's all right. He got pretty wet, I guess. I don't guess there's a better flyer in the world than Major Gray.

"There was some that talked about burying the Chief there at Jerry's house," Iowa went on after a little, "but Jerry said they'd bury him up there at his place — that place the Chief was talking about yesterday."

"Where — did they take him, Iowa?"

"Nowhere yet, but they're going to move him over to the Grays' after a while and he'll be there until the funeral."

"I'll go over after supper and telephone about the flowers," Judith said presently. "Do you think it would be all right if I had some sent down — just for me?"

"Sure it would, Miss Judith. The Chief thought a lot of you, and you must know it. That thing he give you — seems like it was a thousand years ago, now, don't it?" The boy stirred. "I guess I better get back over to the Station, Miss Judith. See you tomorrow, I guess, and if you need anything, just get us word over to the Station."

Judith waited. The figure of the boy from afar off faded into the twilight. Lights came on at the Station below, and far out across the resting water, no longer troubled by any wind and forgetful of the day's anger, the Lightship blinked. The Light came on, its white finger searching, pointing, beckoning across the dusk.

Danny was halfway up the slope before Judith saw him, outlined in the glow when the Light's finger touched him, touched his face as he stood there, looking up at her. He came slowly toward her. The girl stood up, waiting. Danny's face was, when the Light touched it again, serene, with a peace, a contentment newly wrought. His smile was slow, warm, sure.

"I've come home, Judy . . . to you."

"I'm waiting, Danny. . . ."

THE END

In order to carry out arrangements made prior to Mr. Mac-Neill's death the rights to this book were given to St. Andrews Presbyterian College. The publisher wishes to express his appreciation to Mr. Dudley W. Bagley, Mr. MacNeill's administrator, to Mrs. Bagley, and to many of the staff, faculty, and trustees of St. Andrews for their interest and assistance while the book was being prepared, and particularly to H. Leon Gatlin III of the St. Andrews English department, who edited it.